TABLE OF CONTENTS

For more information, visit:
Website: www.michaelhooper.com.au
Facebook Page: www.facebook.com/michaelhoopertheark
Instagram Page: @michaelhoopertheark

Book design concepts by Michael Hooper
Book covers by Ashley Lee at The Design Blocks - thedesignblocks.com
Video by Violet Lee at The Design Blocks - thedesignblocks.com
Website by Raz Marcovich at Purplelink - purplelink.com.au

Paperback ISBN 978-0-6455690-0-1
ebook ISBN 978-0-6455690-1-8

ACKNOWLEDGEMENTS

DEDICATED TO

Georgie Hooper, the heart, spine and soul of my book of life.
Thank you to all my friends and family for the support
and help getting this book completed.

SPECIAL THANKS

Wayne Firns, Ashley Lee, Raz Marcovich, Violet Lee, Lorann Downer
without you I would never have had the courage
to move forward with this project.

CHAPTER 1

WHO'S SPYING ON WHOM

Hindu Kush Range Afghanistan

The bleats and screams echoed through the mountain range. A desperate flee for help. As another predator below looks up and watches the Golden Eagle soar off to its nest with the young goat in its talons. A strange feeling of loneliness hits him and a feeling of protection for his own kids and a longing to get home.

Captain Mike Madden (Sherlock) is the team leader of an Australian recon SAS team. Laying quietly in his observation position, the heat was getting to him, as he reached for his water bottle. With a mouthful of grit from sucking in the dust from a beard full of sand, he swirls a mouth full of water and spits out the water and grit, then takes another mouthful and swallows, easing the sting in his throat.

Grabbing his binoculars, he checks everyone is in position for their evac shortly. He checks the Taliban base they have been spying on for the past five days. All's quiet. The team has been recording information coming in and out of this desolate base. They are trying to prove that the intel they received of a new breakaway Taliban group forming was correct, and now the minutes are ticking down to extraction.

Sherlock's thoughts wandered about getting out of this heat and dust and shipping back home shortly. He quickly gave himself a mental bitch slap, 'shut up and focus. Think of home, and don't get home. Focus, focus.'
Sergeant Sebastian Morrison (2 Planks) broke his train of thought. Morrison, the second in command, repeated his ideas.

"10 minutes Sherlock. Can we go home early?"

"No," was the sharp reply.

"Can't wait to hit the waves 2 Planks; they were riding high the last time I checked," Corporal Deen Wellings (Quassy) added with excitement.

"Shut up and focus, you two," Corporal Katelyn Gouw (Steel) said. She had the lead in this mission and was only a couple of metres from the Taliban base. She is sitting in the enemy's pocket, without them suspecting. She had just recovered the microphones and surveillance cameras that recorded everything said and done in this camp. Mentally double checking to make sure nothing's been left behind to say the team was ever here. Laying in her Gilly suit, she listened intently to the conversation of two of the guards talking in the latrine. She needed the team's focus to watch her back. This was her first time on lead, and it was hard to keep her adrenaline in check. She was so close to the enemy; she knew which ones regularly bathed. This lot smelt like rabid goats.

"Steel, get ready to pullback in five, to stage one," Sherlock instructed.

"Copy," Steel replied.

Just as Sherlock was about to give the order to pull back, Quassy snapped over the comms. "Movement!"

"Confirm Steel," Sherlock requested, with a hackle rising on the back of his neck.

He knows there is no regular operation or patrol scheduled for this time of day.

"Approximately fifteen armed and organising."

"Fifteen confirmed," Quassy replied to Steel's count.

"Could be just a new patrol, Sherlock," 2 Planks stated, half convinced.

"Breaking into two groups," Quassy informed.

Tensions, and the hackles on the back of the SAS specialists' necks rise.

****

Mombasa East Africa

Above, calmly circling Mike Madden's team, a MALE (medium-altitude, long-endurance drone). The drone soared high, watching eagerly for the outcome of the ruckus below. Not flying any country markings. Only the operators know it's there.

"Father, I must protest again; this seems too extreme. You're putting these soldiers' lives in jeopardy."

"I know Ab, but I must know if they are the team; I think they are."

"You have been getting obsessive with them, a bit stalkerish, if you ask me."

"We have been planning the ARK for years, and we always knew when it was built, there were groups who would want to pull it down and us with it."

"But what makes you think this team would even want to leave the forces and join us?" Ab said.

"Because, like us, they believe in what they're doing. The SAS team fight for a chance for peace."

The pair went quiet and watched the proceeding below. Art Damani, CEO of AZTECK Industries, hates what he's doing. Nevertheless, he sent the information about the possibility of someone spying on this Taliban group.

'But it was for a good cause,' he thought.

****

Hindu Kush Range Afghanistan

The instincts that Sherlock was renowned for kicked into action. He relayed orders that were not challenged or even repeated, just done. "Steel, pullback fifteen behind my Ob spot. Smith (Corporal Zikmund Chvalat), contact base and change pickup to Delta LZ. 2 Planks, Quassy, Smith, form up. The Game is afoot." Without missing a beat, Sherlock directed his troops and received the answers he wanted to hear "copy, copy, copy, copy."

With regret, he knew what was coming, and with the call sign, 'the games afoot,' the team knew their jobs. They were to go into their backup phase of the operation, which was deception.

Quassy, the team sniper, moved swiftly from one ledge to another, trying to be careful not to stir up too much dust or mini rock slides on the shaley turf. He did not want to give away his position as he moved into his second position. "In position, move." He watches 2 Planks and Smith moving into their positions.

Their deceptive costumes flowed in the breeze as they also bounced from ledge to ledge. The Shalwar's and loose tunics hiding the bulletproof vests underneath. Smith and 2 Planks are wearing different headgear, one a turban and a Jinnah cap from the tribes of the Afghani Mountain people who are in conflict with the Taliban. Smith looked at 2 Planks beside him and gave him a thumbs up. He was ready.

"Team 2 ready, going into deception," 2 Planks said.

Steel wasted no time and moved through the thick undershrub to her designated position. As Steel made her way past Sherlock, she gave him a nod to confirm she was ready and focused on the task ahead.

Sherlock watched as one man shouted orders in Pakistani with a thick Russian accent. His men were breaking into groups, grabbing weapons and falling into position. Their leader wore no head-cover and had no Arabic features. Sherlock strained to listen to what he was yelling, but only could pick up a few words.

"They're on the move," Quassy said.

"Roger." Sherlock watched the teams leave the base perimeter.

Rough, unorganised, but agitated and fired up by the leader. This is a stark contrast to the sleepy five days of his team's mission. The team leader was at the back of one group shouting commands as the teams moved with pace into positions, straight at himself and Steel. 'Not good, not good at all.' Sherlock thought. The two teams started working a grid pattern, searching quickly.

Not to be outmanoeuvred, Sherlock made the call, "We'll go around the outside." 2 Planks could see that Sherlock and Steel were cut off from the team and were heading to the new LZ. So now he was in charge of completing the deception and getting to the Delta LZ on time.

Even though these times in a mission, where they had to use deception, are potentially dangerous, 2 Planks didn't mind a little 'in your face time.'

Giving the nod to Smith, he grabbed two of the six grenades he had lined up neatly in the dirt in front of him, like some OCD War machine. Pulling the two pins together, he quickly throws one in front and one in the back of the patrols to keep them pinned to one area. The commotion had the desired effect; soldiers were diving for the nearest rocks and keeping their heads down for cover.

Thunderous explosions and screams of injured soldiers rang through Smith's and 2 Planks ears. "The Taliban must die." 2 Planks screamed in Pakistani as he opened fire with his modified AK47 to capitalise on the sudden confusion.

Quassy opened fire with his LSR sniper rifle, keeping the heads down of the enemy troops.

"Leave our mountains," 2 Planks yelled.

"Your mother is a goat fucker," Smith yells in perfect Afghani, while 2 Planks looks at him, shaking his head. Smith could hear commands being yelled and ceased his random barrage of fire to listen and assess the situation further.

Smith saw 2 Planks reloading his weapon and didn't realise that stopping his barrage was what the Taliban commander was waiting for. He watched as the leader started yelling and directing his troops to outflank the aggressors from the ridge above.

As Smith watched their movements, a return volley of fire from two different areas concentrated on his position. Rocks and shale started flying up around him.

Finally, his brain convinced his muscles, 'to get the fuck down.' Zzzip, a supersonic bee, flew past his ear. Then another supersonic bee landed with a zzzip thump. It had happened in seconds; that's all it took; Smith hit the dirt, grabbing his shoulder.

"Mother fucker!" he yelled. "When did these fuckers learn how to shoot straight?" he shouted to 2 Planks.

"Where are you hit?" 2 Planks enquired while returning fire.

"A graze on the arm, nothing critical," he informed 2 Planks.

"Fucken hell," 2 Planks spat out.

"No, it's alright. 2 Planks, I'm fine," Smith assured him.

"No, it's not about you. You know Sherlock won't call it a successful mission if you've been hit."

"Oooh well, excuuuuse me for bleeding on your perfect mission, my arm's fine, thank you very fucking much for asking," sulked Smith.

"Shut up and start returning fire so we can get control again," yelled 2 Planks over the sound of heavy AK47 fire and some more of those supersonic bees.

"Anyway, I'll cover it up, and he'll never know."

"He'll know... He always knows," 2 Planks stated.

Sherlock and Steel were out of the kill zone. Sherlock from his position noticed the leader of the two groups screaming commands to his troops. By their immediate reactions, they feared him more than the hail of bullets raining down from the ridge above. Sherlock knew they could soon lose their advantage in the deception, so he puts through the call. "Quassy 1 o'clock. Cut the head off the snake." Within seconds, a shot rings out, and the Taliban leader drops to the ground.

Once again, thunderous explosions and the sounds of semi-automatic gunfire rang through the SAS teams' ears as they fought to get control of the situation by keeping the enemy squads pinned down. Sherlock and Steel, noticing the deception is working, started making their way past the Taliban encampment, heading to the Delta LZ fifteen kilometres away.

Quassy saw that the best time to head off was now. "Let's move."

Quassy covered 2 Planks and Smith from his perch. His team mates dropped back one at a time, covering each other and laying down continual fire to keep the enemy pinned. Once they reached the top of the ridge, the race was on.

"Ok, on me. Let's pick up the pace," 2 Planks commanded.

2 Planks set a cracking pace. The three soldiers reached a designated set view point where they could look back to see how close their pursuers were.

"Thank God we have a lazy bunch. Only 5 continued the chase and they're about ¾ km away. Let's get down to the fake base and continue the deception."

Quickly climbing down to the ridge, they make it to the fake camp site. 2 Planks looks around to see if everything is still in place, camp fire, empty food tins and meal scraps, a busted sandal, old worn blanket. There are two broken AK47s. To show the enemy they don't have the skills to maintain their weapons. 2 Planks nods.

"Ok, all set. Let's hit the track. 16 km to go."

2 Planks looks at his watch, and everything is within the time schedule, but there's no time to 'stop and shop'; they will get to the LZ just in time for the ride to the base, then off to some well-earned downtime. 'Time to surf,' 2 Planks thought, but then a bucket of ice water thoughts came crashing down, which he ended up repeating out loud. "Think of home, don't get home."

Quassy laughs, "you were thinking about surfing too, weren't you? It's amazing how Sherlocks' training sticks in your head."

"That's why we're still alive," Smith returned in a cold, sobering voice. "Focus, let's get home." That was the last word said between the group on the trek back, using hand signals to relay commands when traversing possible dangerous areas.

****

While reaching the top of a ridge that overlooked the enemy compound from the West, Sherlock retrieved his binoculars and looked back over the area where they had just ambushed the patrols. It looked like only four or five followed the deception team, but it was the eight that stayed and searched the areas where the team was set up. It troubled him, troubled him deeply.

****

Suddenly, the drone above slides off to the North, off to a rendezvous site almost 90 km away. Back at the drone command site, Art Damani sits back and smiles. He had faith in the team and excitedly couldn't wait to meet them.

****

Finally, Sherlock turned to Steel, gave a nod, and they continued on their path to the LZ. This is still a hostile territory, and there's still a long way to go.

There was a sense of relief when 2 Planks and the rest of the squad made it to the LZ with ten minutes to spare, covered in sweat and sucking in the big ones; they all looked exhausted. 2 Planks must have set a fast pace on their trek. Everyone knew the drill; they spread out to keep the LZ safe. The last few minutes seemed to last an eternity before they heard the whoof whoof whoof of the chopper.

The team loaded with the precision and speed of a formula one pit crew. Sherlock stepped last into the chopper, and it began its ascent, heading back to base. Sitting, not noticing anything passing by, Sherlock's thoughts kept rolling through his mind, trying to filter and analyse all he'd seen, but he always came up with the same answer.

"I know that look, Sherlock. What's wrong?" After forty-two missions, 2 Planks knew his friend well; something didn't sit right.

"We're all safe, we have the intel, the deception seemed to stick, a successful mission," 2 Planks summarised.

"The patrols," Mike said.

"Yeah, that was a bit of bad luck."

"2 Planks, they were searching... they were searching for us!" a chill ran up 2 Planks spine. The revelation was a bit too hard to swallow.

The ride back to base was quieter than usual, especially since they were heading on a much-deserved leave shortly. As Sherlock pondered the events and the unscheduled patrol, Smith had covered his wound with a jacket to hide it from Sherlock, and the others spoke quietly among themselves.

Exiting the chopper, Sherlock was the last to get off; as was his protocol, he would always be last and his team first; no one gets left behind.

Quassy threw his pack onto the lorry that takes their gear to their barracks. That thump, clunk sound of the kit hitting the floor of the lorry was a small but significant sound. The sound told him they were home safe, end mission.

Sherlock would give his report to his commander as the team stayed in formation outside base headquarters, waiting to be dismissed by Sherlock, their commander.

As the team walked quietly past the basketball courts and rec rooms, a familiar but unfriendly voice called out. "Well! If it isn't the Ghosties, having difficulty sifting through other people's garbage, boys?"

Sherlock turned and saw the unpleasant face that went with the irritating voice, Captain Garth Sipple, team leader for one of the other Australian SAS groups. Noted for his big mouth and tough talk. Captain Sipple had the highest kill ratio out of all the teams and the highest death ratio of members in his team (which he always seems to leave out during his rants). Nevertheless, he appears to be tolerated by the brass because of his father's high connections.

"Hard at it, I see. So did the brass finally put you on ice," Steel shot back.

"Quiet girl, the men are speaking; once you've finished cleaning your team's gear, you can head off to the mess and start preparing their dinner." Sherlock automatically shot out an arm to block Steel from jumping this idiot, holding her back and keeping her from biting out his jugular.

"Let it go," he whispered to Steel. "Let me handle this," Sherlock insisted. "Has it been a slow week, Garth? I haven't attended any funerals for your team, don't worry, I'm sure you'll catch up." Captain Sipple was enraged, throwing the basketball he was holding hard on the ground.

"Shut your mouth, Madden, take your little housemaid and piss off," Sipple snarled at Sherlock.

At the sound of "housemaid", it was on. Sherlock had to spin sideways to take the full force of Steel's body. She wanted to rip his throat out. It wouldn't be a bad idea. Sherlock knew Sipple would take it further and have her court marshalled for the assault... once he got out of the coma.

"Settle down, Steel, don't let him bait you." Steel's eyes raged with fire, despite that, Sipple didn't know when to keep his mouth shut; he stepped forward.

"Come on, let her loose, Madden. Let's see what the little girl has to say." Sipple stepped closer towards her. 2 Planks sees the step ahead as a threat, steps forward in front of Steel; he is 6'5" and pure muscle.

"Got something to say, Captain."

'Oh shit,' Sherlock thought, I can't hold two of them. 2 Planks would have no qualms with beating the living shit out of an officer if he was in the wrong. So, Sherlock had to pull rank to unravel this mess.

"Stand down! Both of you, don't get caught up in his dribble; he has to go play with his ball, so he can figure out a new way to kill off his team." That broke the ice and the tension. Steel and 2 Planks both started laughing, which they knew pissed Sipple off to no end from the points Sherlock scored.

"Just fuck off, the lot of you," Captain Sipple blurted out. Sherlock's team turned and went on their merry way, laughing out loud.

****

As the team reached the headquarters of the base command, 2 Planks brought the group to attention.

"At ease, team," Sherlock commanded, then he swiftly turned away and entered the offices.

Inside, Colonel Jim Briggs, Mike's commanding officer and General Thomas Blaine, Australian troop commanding officer. Sherlock saluted Briggs upon entering. The General had his back to Sherlock, so he held his salute for the General until it was returned. The General did that and quickly got straight down to business.

General Blaine straightens up, puffs out his chest, "Report Captain, was the mission successful?"

"I believe so, General," Sherlock responded.

"What's a, believe so? This is the army, son, the mission was a success, or it wasn't," the General bellowed.

"We encountered an unscheduled patrol as we were leaving, Sir," Sherlock informed the officers.

"Did the information get compromised?"

"No, Sir."

"Did you lose any of your team?"

"No, Sir."

"Then it was a success, Captain; it's that simple."

"Congratulations, Briggs; it's good to see one of your Captains knows how to keep his team alive," Blaine spouted.

"Thank you, Sir, permission to dismiss my team."

"Yes, yes, good work," Sherlock issued another salute to the officers, which was quickly returned. As Sherlock turned, he offered Colonel Briggs a head nod, pointing outside; he needed to talk to Briggs urgently.

As Sherlock left the office, the Colonel followed.

"ATTENTION!" 2 Planks commanded his team as the Colonel exited.

"At ease," Briggs said as he returned the team's salute.

"Team dismissed, hit the mess, showers, check and clean your gear, we will debrief at 1900 hours... Oh, and Smith get that arm seen too," Sherlock commanded.

"Team dismissed," 2 Planks issued the command and immediately looked at Smith with an 'I told you so' look. The team turned and headed for the mess. Most other teams hit the showers first, but 2 Plank's team always goes to the mess first because they know the Sergeant in charge always complains about the odour. He then issues a complaint to Sherlock, upon which Sherlock informs them to not do it again. Then the team does it again, and so goes on the mess joke.

Sherlock turned to Briggs. "It's about the unscheduled patrol."

"I thought it would be you were a little hesitant in there," Briggs enquired.

"Colonel, it was too coincidental. The change in attitude, urgency and the precise deployment of the troops to where my team was positioned. The base was sleepy, then it came alive. A 2-prong sweeping patrol, Steel and myself were cut off from the team, so I called in the ruse to help facilitate the team's extraction and changed the LZ and time," Sherlock explained.

"You know these things happen sometimes; you have plans for them," Briggs offered.

"Yeah, but you know I've been doing this a long time, Jim; I swear they were looking for us."

"But you feel the intel still has not been compromised?" Briggs enquired.

"Yes, I believe so."

"I'll get onto my man at ASIS (Australian Secret Intelligence Service) to see if there's been any chatter about the team; I don't think it could be from inside the base.

Very few people know what you do," Briggs informed Sherlock.

"I hope so, Colonel; I certainly hope so," Sherlock responded.

Sherlock digs into one of his pockets, pulls out an envelope, and hands it to the Colonel.

"What's this?" the Colonel enquires.

"It's an invitation to the boy's birthday party next month. I'll understand if you can't make it, but the boys wouldn't forgive me if I didn't invite you... No pressure." The Colonel started laughing.

"I will be home on leave too, so put me down to attend. I wouldn't like to disappoint the boys."

Don't worry about the other thing. I'll look into it." Briggs put his hand on Sherlock's shoulder; he might be Sherlock's commanding officer, but they were also friends. They had served together. He had put Sherlock's name forward for this position, and he was the godfather of Sherlock's eldest son; he was family.

Sherlock turned and headed to his digs; 'I'll shower first before I head to the mess to hear the complaints about my crew,' he thought.

CHAPTER 2

DAMANI MAKES HIS PITCH

Mogadishu, Somalia

The storm bay coloured BMW iX xDrive 50 dodged and weaved through the heavy traffic. There was no resemblance to any order in the traffic. Bicycles and scooters flew in and out of traffic in every direction, risking life and limb. Art Damani pushed a button to whine down the bulletproof window.

"Wow, look at the difference in architecture. Modern high-rises on one side and a 200-year-old Muslim Mosque on the other. It's like you cross the road into a different world." Art sat back, amazed.

The day was sunny and peaceful; one could easily forget that it could easily turn into a horror fest of gunfire and explosions in minutes, after all, this was Mogadishu. But today, it was sunny, and there was optimism in the air.

Aarth is an Indian-born tech billionaire tycoon who had made his first million selling internet porn. His parents were killed on a trade mission to North Korea when he was 15. At the ripe age of 45, he was one of the top five richest men in the world (the richest if people knew the whole story). Art accepted the sunny part of this day and kept his hopes high.

Fred Collier, Art's bodyguard, looked uneasy. Yesterday, in the briefing, Art had explained that they might all be killed tomorrow if things didn't go to plan. Terry Lamb, Art's driver, had commented casually, "Well, that will ruin my day. I've got a football game to watch tomorrow night."

Art had offered a business plan to the self-elected President and dictator of Somalia, General Hassan Abdullahi Abdi. Abdi was a brutal warlord who had taken control of the Somalian government in a coup over 10 years ago. Setting himself up as president. Running the government hadn't given him the worldwide legitimacy he thought he would receive. Known in the global press as the Mad King for his ruthless atrocities against neighbouring countries and his own people.

Art went through the plan in his head and what things President Abdi could throw at him and his responses.

"Five years," Art said to himself, but not realising he said it out loud. Fred turned and looked at him, but said nothing. Five years he had been planning this moment, this meeting. If he was successful, it could be a world change, if not just get him killed.

Art had taken many steps to ensure their safety. He had no army or police as his backup, just Fred, his security, Terry, his driver, a fantastic sales record, and a bucket load of money.

"Five years," he said again to no one.

As the car rolled up to the presidential office, the passers-by suspected nothing. They didn't know a deal could be struck to change their way of life for the better, and they didn't realise that the start of world peace could be a pen stroke away. No one suspected that there could be gunshots in minutes and Art's body could be thrown from a five-story window; life was full of possibilities.

Terry pulled up to a very modern, high-rise building. As Fred opened Art's door, Art gave him a stern look and said, "Stay frosty." hoping to get a little smirk on Fred's face. Nothing. 'The man was not alive, I'm sure of it.' Art thought.

As he turned around and looked up at the building, Art took three slow deep breaths, paused... and said to himself, "Go big or go home." As he walked through the front foyer, his footsteps roared with the sound of a giant coming; such was the confidence he exuded.

****

"Good morning, Mr Damani. The President is expecting you." The officer said as Art was ushered into the office of President Abdi. It was everything he expected it to be, and more. He had seen the pictures of the office and the president, but witnessing this giant of a man behind this desk and on his beautifully carved office throne chair was excessive, impressive, but excessive.

Art was trying to take it all in. It was obviously there for show, so he was trying to enjoy the show. The chair looked like a throne from a 1970s Tarzan movie. Hand carved timber, Rosewood he thought. There were the skins of lions and leopards draped off the sides and on top of the back of the seat sat a lion's head, obviously to portray that he was king and no one else.

President Abdi stood up, all 6'7 and one hundred and fifty kilos of him. He thrust out his hand in an excited greeting to Art; Art sensed he had something to offer.

"Mr. Damani, what a pleasure to meet you," the president chirped. "Please sit. I have been waiting for this meeting. To meet the man crazy enough to put such an outlandish, absurd proposal to the people of Somalia," he said, meaning himself.

"I read your proposal several times to fathom what I was reading. Finally, I just had to meet you out of curiosity to see how you thought you'd pull it off."

'This is the response I thought to get from the president, so no need to squirm in my seat just yet,' Art thought.

"Well, Mr. President, I'm not known for thinking small. Go big or go home," Art gave a little cosmetic laugh at the end.

"True, Mr. Damani, but there's big, and then there's way too much for you to carry. So let me see if I get your vision right before you tell me how you're going to get two counties that have been at war for decades to suddenly become friends and work together and share borders."

"Please go ahead, Mr. President; we need to make sure we understand each other," Art said politely.

"Okay, you would like to build a nature reserve on lands that cross Somalia and Ethiopia, to protect and repopulate endangered animals from all over the world, like a big zoo. But not just anywhere. YOU, want to build it in the Bale mountains, which I might add is a UN World Heritage-listed area. Good luck with getting permission from those tight arses." President Abdi gathered his thoughts. "You also want Somalia and Ethiopia to open their borders to work together in peace and harmony. Is this what you are proposing, Mr. Damani?" The cynical voice was what Art was waiting for.

"Well, that is a simplified version of my plan, but basically, yes. That is what I am working towards." War and fear kept this lunatic in power. The chess game had begun, and Art's internal clock gave him fifteen minutes to win the president over or be dragged out and shot.

"Mr. President, my ambition is to bring some of the world's leading scientists to your country and set up breeding programs to repopulate the animals of the world, especially those currently listed as about to go extinct, and thus bring billions of dollars of revenue and advances in medical research to your..."

The president abruptly barged into the conversation. "Yes, yes, wonderful for the animals and money and culture in Somalia. How did you think that dog of a president, Conde' and I would agree to such a ridiculous proposal?" Abdi said in a mocking tone.

Time for a change in tact; Art thought, "Mr. President, this is going ahead." Art said in a no wavering voice, "It's just a matter of whether you want to be a part of it. If so, what will it cost?"

Abdi yelled, as he hammered his enormous fist onto his desk. "You think you can buy me and buy my country; do you know who I am!?"

"I know exactly who you are," Art retorted in a calm but cold voice.

The following moves on the chessboard will result in a win or possibly death. The carrot or the stick? The carrot was Art's first choice; he hated the stick but was prepared to use it to get the game to checkmate.

"Mr. President, I don't want to buy your country or you. I want to give your country the funds, jobs, and future it deserves. Still, I need you, your influence, and control of your country. This is what your government is going to need for this transition. Somalia will only listen to you," Art nearly choked on the words. Still, he could easily replace him. He had three other presidential candidates in line waiting to be called up.

"This is what you have in your bank accounts right now... All of your bank accounts," The words took the President aback as Art opened his laptop and placed it on the desk facing the President. In front of him, the President saw five screens with all of his bank accounts, including the two overseas hidden ones that were supposed to be hidden. Nothing can't be found by Art or his company. That's part of being the giant of the world's tech industry. Art's company AZTECK, over the last 10 years, has led the world with its innovations. So, if the world uses it, Art has a back door into it. In this room alone, there are two microphones and two video cameras that have been here for six months undetected.

"$32.76 million is a nice effort for eleven years of... effort for your country, but... if you joined as a leader of change for your country, you and your family would never have to worry about money again. I would put you on ten million dollars a year for you to control your soldiers, weed out the troublemakers and retrain them into a well-financed peacekeeping force. You and your family could live in comfort and peace for the rest of your lives."

Art dropped the 'Peace' into his speech, knowing that his family lives in a soldier's compound, to protect them from reprisals for many of the President's crimes against his own people during his 11-year reign. The carrot was dangled now. It was time to see if it would be taken. It impressed President Abdi, the offer, but he kept his poker face to see what was available.

"I suppose the dog President has been offered the same deal?" Abdi calmly asked. "No, I haven't spoken to him yet; I came to you first because you and Somalia are more important," which technically was true. After all, all the first phase sites were in Somalia.

Abdi tried to play his hand and get control of the negotiation. "This all sounds impressive, if not totally unmanageable," Art sighed; he couldn't help it; he knew Abdi was pushing for more. There was more to be given, Aarth Damani was generous in the effort people put into their work, but Art needed Abdi to be submissive and work to support him, not always looking for his equal footing. 'Stick time,' he thought; this is where it could get ugly; even with the precautions he put in place, this monster, when angry, could still crush him with his bare hands.

"President Abdi, push button three."

Abdi looks at Art suspiciously and pushes button three. A look of instant shock and horror came across his face as he looked at the screen of at least twelve live video feeds of his family, his mother, wife, and four children. Horror soon turns to rage as Abdi slams both closed fists onto his desk, making a thunderous bang. Abdi springs up out of his seat, leaning over the computer.

"You dare threaten my family. I will destroy you and anyone who goes near my family," Abdi's eyes were filled with rage, teeth bared like a rabid bear.

"Push button four," Art said calmly and firmly. Without thinking, Abdi pushed button four. Instantly; the rabid bear's face was toned down by a slight confusion.

"What is this?" he demanded.

"The complete movements of you and your family for the last six months, plus every conversion with everyone you have spoken to," Art said.

Art's stomach tightened into a notch. Abdi quickly reaches for his desk's top draw, pulls out a Gold plated 45 magnum pistol, and points it straight at Art's head.

"I have had enough of this conversation; it was a poor decision to threaten my family, Mr. Billionaire; they will not find any sign of your body or your friends outside."

The click of the hammer hitting an empty chamber from his pistol sounded just as loud as a loaded chamber to Aarth Damani. But, to his credit, he kept his composer and didn't flinch. Even though he knew the pistol wasn't loaded, the entire event was extremely frightening. It was worth the $2000 he paid to one of Abdi's subordinates to empty Abdi's gun before the meeting. Well worth it indeed.

The shock and surprise on President Abdi's face was the opening Art needed to move into checkmate.

"Sit down, Mr. President; I told you this is happening, with or without you. What will it be, security for your family and your country or something else?"

The President slowly slid back into his seat as thoughts raced through his head. He glances over and notices his 2nd in charge standing by the door at attention, not flinching. He hadn't even seen him standing there this whole time, but he noticed him now.

"15 million, I want 15 million!" Abdi tried to have one final push for control, but the words choked as they came through his dry throat.

"15 million..." Art made a dramatic pause. "Done, Mr. President, push button five."

The President pushed the five on the keyboard and noticed his hands felt very heavy. Another look of surprise and shock came across his face as he looked at pictures of his eldest daughter in her school uniform talking to two other youths he did not know.

"What is this???" he inquired.

"These are the two street boys from a local gang that want your daughter to help them peddle their drugs through her school by using her family name and influence," Art hands over a manilla envelope to Abdi.

"These are the boy's details, names, addresses, and where the gang hangs out; consider it a gift. I want your family to live in safety."

Art rises to his feet, checkmate he thinks to himself. "Mr. President, I will be in touch with you shortly with the details of all our work in Somalia together. Take the rest of the day off and go give your family the good news." President Abdi rises, gathers some composer, and looks at the envelope.

"First, I have some work to do. Thank you, Mr. Damani; I look forward to working with you in the future." The men shook hands; Art then turned and walked to the door and down the hall into the elevator. As he walks to the foyer door, he struts with the form of a warrior, a giant slayer.

As he walks to the car, Fred Collier, his security guard, stands there with the door open, and Terry has the car running. Art stops in front of Fred and offers a smile.

"We are still alive, Mr. Damani, so I assume the meeting went well?" Fred inquires.

"We are alive; yes, it went perfectly," responded Art. As he nestles into his seat, Fred closes the door.

Terry speaks up, "To the airfield and home, boss?"

"Yes, Terry, home, but first we need to find a department store."

"A department store?" Terry enquires.

"Yes, I need to purchase some fresh undergarments."

Terry lets out a laugh. "Okay Boss, done."

CHAPTER 3

LET THE SHOW BEGIN

Aarth Damani looked out the large tinted glass wall across the river. The Blue Renaissance centre was a picture to behold. With its radiant ocean blue, the reflection copied onto the Detroit River, doubling the effect of its magnificence. It wasn't the only one with the colours on the night skyline showing off a patriotic array of red, white, and blue.

Art thought to himself that one penthouse room of a luxury hotel is the same as the next; it came down to service and scenery for him. Even though the views over Detroit were lovely, they weren't as spectacular as those in Switzerland or Australia, but it was nice here. Though the scenery wasn't ranked among the highest for Art, this was one of his favourite hotels. The Detroit Hilton had one of the best contingents of staff members he had encountered, with Lynton the Butler for the penthouse being the best staff member he had ever encountered.

Art turned and looked at the impressive work Lynton had done. He tastefully decorated the room in hot pink, Art's his favourite colour. Lynton had just enough of the colour in the room to make it feel homy without making it look like a 70's den of iniquity. Art walked to the table and beside the fresh bowl of fruit was a bowl of his favourite chocolate, chocolate covered Turkish Delights. Art unwraps a sweet and pops it in his mouth and heads to the refrigerator and finds Lynton doesn't miss a trick with a jug of freshly made iced coffee waiting there for him. As Art reaches for the jug, there's a knock at the door.

Lynton poked his head inside and said, "You have a visitor, Sir, Master Abayomi."

"Send him in Lynton, thank you," Art replied.

"Morning Father, any word yet?" Abayomi inquired. Abayomi Thoyana was Art's adopted son from a small village South of Bufila in central Toyo.

"Not as yet, but soon, very soon. Then the fun begins; Ab, you and I will be very busy for quite a long time. Have you heard from Lexi and Doby this morning?"

"Yes, they both reported this morning, rather excited by yesterday's inquiries from the expo. A 29% increase in inquiries with government and major corporations.

Father, how did you know that the government sector would turn up on a Saturday instead of coming during the week?" Ab questioned, puzzled.

"Well, the government delegations can say that they were busy doing their normal work during the week. But then travel in luxury, stay at the best hotels, eat lavishly, then claim it back off their respective departments as work-related on their days off. They then turn around and claim it off their personal tax at the end of the financial year. They all do it son, because their governments never close the loopholes."

Ab laughed hard. "Maybe I should try that."

"You have more money than you know how to spend," Art said with his phoney stern voice.

"Oh, I think I know how to spend it," Ab said confidently, smirking from ear to ear.

"I've told you; you can't buy Australia! Anyway, I have first dibs." The pair broke into simultaneous laughter, knowing they both liked Australia and its people. They have often dibbed up the Australian states as if they owned them, judging them on their food, scenery, and resources.

As the laughter subsided, Art pointed to the refrigerator and said, "There's a fresh jug of iced coffee there if you want some."

Just as Ab was about to reply, Art's phone blasted out its ringtone with the Queen song, "I want it all, and I want it now." Art took a deep breath and summoned his confidence and business voice. Ab called him the voice chameleon. He answered.

"Aarth Damani, yes. Hello, Mr. Tambuka," Art looked concerned and listened intently.

"Yes, yes, that is agreeable, and the committee has agreed to the announcement terms for tomorrow. Excellent, it will be a pleasure working with you, Mr. Tambuka. Yes, all's well; greetings to your family too; thank you and goodbye now."

Art's demeanour changed immediately; he went from the poker face, confident billionaire who negotiated billion-dollar deals every week to the excited carry-on of an 8-year-old on Christmas morning.

"They agreed, they agreed, yes! All steam ahead for plan A." Art was beaming. All the approvals for his world adventure have been granted. The phone call was from the chairman of the World Heritage Committee. The committee had voted on the proposal from AZTECK, Art's leading Tech company, for permission to build Art's dream vision on World Heritage land in Somalia, East Africa. The vote was unanimous. Even though Art suspected the approval for the grant would go through, he left nothing to chance. He had approached each committee member secretly to make his pitch because each had their own views on the proposal, especially since no other person, company, or country had been allowed to do it before.

"Congratulations, Father," Ab called out in a celebratory voice. "I am so happy for you."

Art suddenly dropped the rejoicing and walked to Ab.

"No, my son, this is a great day for all of us; you also have spent years planning and arranging this with me. We will make our mark in world history as New World innovators or abject failures!" With the words abject failures, Abs shoulders slumped. Art raised his hand and placed it on his sons' shoulders. "Don't worry, my son, I'm pretty sure it will be the first one!" Art burst out laughing. "Now go start the phone calls and tell the Inner Circle there is a meeting here tonight at 7.30. Once they have secured the closing of the expo site, now go." Art made a shooing gesture, and Ab briskly ventured off to spread the good news to the Inner Circle.

That night, everybody from the Inner Circle was there at the Detroit Hilton penthouse by seven, nobody wanted to be late. Truth be told, everybody was just as excited as Art; Ab now had increased responsibility; he was the person all the problems from other regions went to. Now he had his own division to control, but he was also the final link before things went to Art. At 23, it was a monumental undertaking to be the hub for this project. The finance alone was that of a small country, but he was up to the task; he had his father's support, which was all he needed.

Ab had a high intellect, but his organisational skills and his photogenic memory made him his own force to be reckoned with. Those skills came in handy when AZTECK was in negotiations with other corporations. Ab would stand behind his father at the negotiation table like a bodyguard/hitman; the pair had worked out a routine when the opposition was trying to push unfounded facts or figures in the battle. Ab had the permission to speak up and quote accurate statistics which could be verified instantly; for Art, it was like having his own supercomputer behind him. This ability of Abs gave Art the freedom but mainly the speed to negotiate at a pace that the others didn't have, leaving him to control the meetings.

Ab and Lynton finished their respective duties before everyone settled around the polished oak table. Trays of unique drinks and treats for the individual tastes of the Inner Circle.

Ab stepped back and had a look at the setup for the table, eight placings, each with a folder with the overall plan, plus their respective duties they were tasked with. Around the table was a setting for Art and Ab, always sitting side by side for a show of solidarity.

"Does it matter where each member sits? Any company affairs or romances that have to be catered for?" Lynton asked with a cheeky grin.

Ab laughed. "No, nothing... Not that I know of."

Later that evening, as they all made their way to their seats, the conversation was light, with some sharing business requests, some weekend leisure, and family time stories, and some just sharing their excitement about what they were about to hear. Of course, they all knew the plan's outlines already; some were more involved, but to listen to the boss say "it's all ago" was very exciting.

Art sat down last, straightened his folder, and spoke, "Let's change the world, my friends. As you have heard, we have received our last approval, which was from the World Heritage Committee, giving us the approval to build the ARK on Mount Bale." The room exploded in cheers and clapping. The excitement was electrifying. They all looked forward to their part in history.

Art waited for the clapping to subside. "Everybody has their plans and schedules, plus you have all the other members' schedules; you must understand any delays in your schedules will cause delays in other regions, which will cause delays in the project... I will not accept delays in this project." Art's voice had suddenly turned concrete. His resolve to get this project underway and completed on time was absolute.

"Ab will be in charge of local and international media to win the hearts and minds. Make no assumptions, people. We might be embarking on a monumental project for mankind with the ARK, but there will be many people, businesses, and governments trying to pull our work down because we are a private enterprise."

Art turns to his son. "Are you ready for this, my boy? You are going to be the face of the media for the ARK."

"Yes, Father, I am ready, but I have given some thought to the advertising face for the ARK," Ab paused. "How about instead of me, we use Samuel L. Jackson," Ab smirked. "Those Motherfuckers who think we aren't doing this for the benefit of all Motherfuckin mankind can stick it up to their Motherfuckin arses," Ab sprouted in his best Samuel L. Jackson impersonation; it wasn't terrific. Still, it was funny, and the Inner Circle burst out in applause and laughter.

"Ab, my boy, you could be onto something there," Art replied while catching his breath between the laughs.

"Tomorrow, we open up to the public with our announcement at the end of the expo. The press will be there, and the scholarship winners. We will open up about a lot of the tech we have been working on for the last five years. There will be nowhere to hide, and our competition will scurry to find out more about what else we've been hiding. There will be many people angry with us, dangerous people, especially in Somalia and Ethiopia; we will take their lively hoods away from them. They are going to challenge us, but they will fail."

Art closed his folder and paused a moment. "Is there anyone here who is not sure of their part or has issues they need to bring up now?" Everybody looked around the room, but nobody spoke; they all knew their parts and were prepared to administer them. "Good, my friends, then we will see you all at the big show and tell tomorrow. Thank you all for your excellent work so far."

The Inner Circle rose and made their way outside and back to their rooms. Except for Ab, who had one last thing to pass on to his father. "The boys have arrived and are ready, Father."

"Excellent, try to not kill anyone tomorrow, especially with all the press there... It would look bad," Art replied.

"I can't promise anything," Ab responded with a sly look. Then, finally, Ab walked off to head to his penthouse room next door. Art's final thought as he watched his son close the door was, 'Let the show begin!'

CHAPTER 4

MY HOME, MY CASTLE... SORT OF

Bryon Bay, New South Wales, Australia

Mike was breathing heavily and covered in sweat as he walked in the surf shin deep. He had just finished a 2-hour training session amongst the sand dunes along a secluded section of the Bryon Bay beach. He was doing his warm down session, shoes off and walking on the surf's edge, bringing his heart rate down. The gentle roll of the waves against his legs was a childhood obsession to calm himself down during stressful times.

"Good morning," Mike said as he greeted other locals who use this section of the beach. Families walked along the sand with children collecting seashells. Couples strolled along the golden stretch of beach, planning beautiful futures that included many days on this piece of paradise.

"Woo, good morning, Freckles," Mike said as he was greeted by one of his neighbour's dogs, who nearly knocked him off his feet.

"Morning Mike," came a voice from behind.

Mike turned and greeted his neighbour, a lovely blonde woman in her 50's.

"Morning Casey, are all Dalmatians this excitable?" Mike said as he wrestled with Freckles.

"Yes, pretty much. They love life but this one seems to have taken a shine to you," she said laughing.

"She always seems to be able to sneak up on me."

"Well, she's going into pup soon and it will be her last litter. It might be time to get your boys a companion."

"Could be Casey. I might hold you to that. Let me know when it's time. I'll get the boys to convince their mum."

"Coward," Casey said, laughing.

Mike laughed. "I pick the battles I can win."

"Come on Freckles, time to keep moving. We need to walk and Mike needs to go for a swim or shower."

Mike looked down and saw his clothes were drenched in sweat.

"That could be a good plan," Mike said, laughing.

As Mike watched Casey and Freckles walk off, his mood hit him again. Funny how it takes being knocked off your feet by an excited dog to help you forget everything. Mike didn't even know he was in a mood.

Pondering what needed to be done for the boy's party today, but trying to avoid that doubt that kept gnawing at the base of his skull, had missed something on his last mission?

In the two weeks since he has been home on leave, he had mowed the lawn four times, washed the car twice and the house once, not to mention the two-hour exercise sessions on the beach in the early hours of the morning. He couldn't sit still, the restlessness and the itch in the back of his skull. That unscheduled patrol was the question. But what was the answer? It's not as if he hadn't come across unscheduled patrols before, accidental discovery, or even team failure, so what bugged him about this one? He concluded that if he wrote down everything he remembered from that day, something may pop up.

It was his son's joint birthday party; even though they were born two weeks apart and in different years, Mike and Samantha often held joint parties for Oliver and Aidan to save family and friends from coming back-and-forth weeks apart. The boys didn't mind it; they were tight; they had the usual sibling rivalry stuff, but they shared a lot of interests, and their friends seemed to respect them for that.

Mike walked home and had a shower, then started setting up decorations and cleaning up the yard for the party this afternoon. Once he got it in his head to go to his study and jot down a few notes, he didn't notice the hours slip away, or Sam slip into the room behind him.

"Maldives!"

Mike jumped and nearly fell off his seat.

"Geez!" he yelled as he jumped.

"Startle you, did I?" Sam enquired slyly.

"No, I'm alright," Mike weakly replied.

Sam screws up her face. "Well, that's debatable."

Trying to change the point of attack, Mike enquired, "Maldives? You said the Maldives."

"Yes, the Maldives in February would be the best," Sam said.

Still not in the same game as Sam, Mike had to keep enquiring, "What about the Maldives in February?".

"For our holiday, our family holiday, to celebrate your retirement," Sam stated firmly.

"Retirement??? Who said I'm retiring???" Mike felt trapped; he knew he had stepped into one of Sam's verbal traps and couldn't think quick enough to get out. The shark was circling the poor little turtle, and the turtle had nowhere to turn to; all he could do was wait for the bite and hope it didn't hurt.

"YOU said!" Sam stated. "YOU, said to me eighteen years ago when we got married. The day I bring my work home is the day I retire! So, the Maldives in February, we can take the boys out for an extended school break."

The trap was sprung, and the shark had snapped its powerful jaws, 'killed by my own words,' thought the little turtle; he didn't stand a chance.

All Mike could get out was "I, ahh," and then the front doorbell rang, and Mike jumped out of his seat.

"I'll get it, dear, and I'll be back in just a moment." 'Saved by the bell,' Mike thought. I'm still in the shark's belly, though; this conversation isn't going to blow away too soon. As Mike ran down the hallway, he passed the boys going to the door. ZZooom. As their dad flew past, the boys thought, 'What the??' They both turned and looked down the hallway and saw their mum standing there. Arms crossed, standing in the doorway to dads' study, with the NUMBER 4 look on her face. The boys had come to number mums' facial expressions. She didn't need to say anything because she had a facial expression for it. So, now they knew why dad was running; everybody runs from NUMBER 4!

The boys turned to look at their father, who didn't have time to pull up on the lovely polished floor. The boys squinted, braced their bodies for the impact. THUMP, OOOOW as dad hit the door frame. The boys couldn't help but laugh; they knew it must have hurt, but they laughed.

Mike opened the door quickly to see Seb and Smith standing there, surprised.

"Did you just run into the door?" Seb asked.

"Ah yeah, newly polished floor, couldn't stop, sturdy door frame though," Mike hit the door frame to emphasise what he was saying.

"Ok, if you say so, Mike." Standing in the doorway facing his friends and teammates, he could see the change of expression on their faces, and then a sudden chill ran up his spine when from over his shoulder came a voice, "Hi Sebastian, Hi Zikmund," Samantha cheerfully greeted, but Mike could still hear the icicles hanging from each syllable of Samantha's words.

"Hi, Sam," they both greeted in unison.

"Everything ok, you two?" Seb enquired.

"Yeah, everything's gre..." but before he could finish his sentence, Samantha spoke over him.

"I caught him working!" Samantha stated.

"What? work work?" Seb enquired, with a shocked look on his face.

"At home?" Smith added, also stunned.

"Yes, at HOME, WORK WORK," Samantha stated again.

"You don't do that, Mike... EVER!" Seb cautioned.

"Never ever," Smith added. There was no rule that said you couldn't bring your work home, but you never did in this house with Samantha Madden as your commanding officer.

"Zikmund, here's a list of things we need for tonight's party. Could you please pick these up for me and take this one with you?" Samantha puts her hand on Mike's shoulder.

"And don't bring him back unless my husband comes back with him." Samantha had that ice chill in her voice again. "And make sure you all don't get arrested this time," she gives Seb a hard stare.

"I swear it wasn't our fault last time; they started it," Seb implored Samantha.

"I'll send the boys with you to chaperone. Boys, grab your hat and shoes, please."

"We'll bring Mike back, Samantha, and the groceries," Smith assured Sam.

"I know you will, Zikmund," she smiled. Smith liked Sam; she was the only one who bothered to use his real name.

"I will, too," Seb stated in a not-so-sure voice.

The boys came racing out past their dad and crash-tackled into Seb.

"Hi, Uncle Seb," the boys said in unison.

"Hell, Oli, we will have to start calling you Point Break soon if you get any bigger," Seb pointed out.

"Fresh air, saltwater, and roids. Sergeant 2 Planks is what good soldiers need."

Oliver offers a salute; Seb returns the salute, then shrinks to the stare Samantha was giving him.

"Kids these days, where do they get this stuff... Television pfft," Seb states with a shrug.

"Hmmm," Samantha returns.

The boys offer Smith his usual greeting, "Hi Smithy," with a few fist pump bombs.

"Ok, boys, off you go, have a good time." Samantha hugs them, and the boys start for the car.

As they all turned for the car, Seb said to Aidan, "How're your grades going, Adi?"

Aidan replied, "Excellent, Sargant Sir, better than Oliver's. I'm Officer material!"

"Why would you want to be like those wan..." Seb looks over his shoulder and sees Samantha is still in earshot and staring at him; he decides to use a different word, "people."

"Cause dads one, Uncle Seb," Aidan stated, "Good answer, my boy, good answer."

The shopping centre was crazy today, with shoppers snatching up bargains for Mother's Day, which was coming soon. The team's battle plan was to get some drinks, sit down, and work out where to find the items Samantha needs. As Smith laid everyone's glasses on the table, Mike says to the boys, "Don't tell your mother we had these, or she'll crucify me for filling you up before the party." The boys only offered some mumbled assurances, as they had already started on their jumbo thick shakes.

Mike was staring at his thick shake as if it wasn't there.

"Well, what was all that about this morning?" Seb asked.

"Just a misunderstanding, no biggy," Mike said, nonchalant about it.

"It didn't look like a misunderstanding; Sam looked like she knew exactly! What she was going to kill you for," Seb stated.

"Dad got a number 4," Little Aidan said to the table, nodding his assurance of what he saw.

"Shit!" Seb lowered his voice, realising that it came out louder than what he had proposed, "Geez, a 4! No wonder you were running when you hit the door," Seb said, understanding the situation now.

But the person who didn't understand was Smithy; his head was going from side to side, trying to figure it out. Until it got the better of him.

"What's a number 4???" Then, almost instantly, with the precision of an elite ice-skating duo, Oli and Aidan turned to Smithy and pulled a number 4 on him simultaneously.

"Geez," said Smith.

"Never get that woman angry enough to do a number 4 on you," Seb stated.

"What were you working on that was so important?" Seb asked.

Mike put his head down and started sucking on his straw.

"Oh My God! You're still obsessing over that patrol."

"They were looking for us Seb."

"Maybe, and if they were, we handled it," Seb assured him.

"What if there's more?"

Oliver pushed into the conversation. "The 3 P's. Plan, Practice, perseverance."

Everybody fell silent and stared at Oliver. Oliver returned their stares, confused.

"What? That's what you're always telling Aidan and I. Plan and train. You know you might have a leak. Plan and train for it. It's a no brainer."

"That's my Point Break. Sargant material he is. Logical, precise and doesn't moan and bitch," Seb said, giving Oliver a high-five.

"Unless he has to clean his room," Mike added. Everyone fell silent... Then burst out laughing.

"Ok, I can't argue with my own logic thrown back at me. Let's get this gear for your mum and get this party jumpin," Mike said while trying to dance in his seat.

"Nobody says that anymore, Dad. And don't dance, it's embarrassing," Aidan said, taking a break from his Thick Shake.

"Ouch."

Later that day, everything was running like a well-oiled machine, which is how Samantha likes it. Sam was cleaning the kitchen and could see through the window that the men were hanging up the last of the decorations, and the boys were cleaning up inside the house while she prepared the last of the food for the barbeque.

Then, finally, Sam saw the boys head out into the backyard to see their father, probably to bug him again about when they would be allowed to build the remote-control planes Seb and Zikmund had bought them for their birthdays. Plus, all the extras their father had bought for them as well.

'I wonder what they heard that I'm not supposed to know,' she thought to herself. 'The boys will make great hostage negotiators one day.'

Sam checked out her kitchen window, and the party set up had turned into a backyard game of Rugby League. Aidan was complaining to an imaginary referee appealing for a penalty for a high tackle, and Seb was standing there pleading to the same imaginary referee that the tackle wasn't high. Aidan got his penalty. While arguing about the penalty between these hardened, killer Special Forces, Aidan ran away and scored. Winning the game for his team.

"Come on, let's go start the barbeque; the quests will arrive soon! Smith, no petrol this time," Mike said.

"The boys liked it last time," Smith added. They laughed and headed over to get ready for the party.

The boys and their friends were having a great time by the amount of screaming in the last hour. Mike was talking to some of his neighbours when he heard another car pull up in front of the house. Everyone was here that was coming, except the Colonel.

Two large boxes walked around the corner of the house with two legs, two arms, but no body or head.

"This is as heavy as it looks," a voice cried out. The Colonel was attached to two huge boxes. Mike and Samantha raced over to lend a hand.

"My god Jim! what did you buy them?" Samantha queried after feeling the size and weight of the boxes.

"Oh my God, you bought them their own mortars, cool!" Mike yelled in a joking sense of excitement.

"No, but something just as cool," Jim replied. As Samantha was heading to the table to put the presents down, Oliver flew around the corner and nearly took out Jim, his mother, and the gifts in a major collision. He pulled up just in time. One look at the presents his mum and dad were holding and said, "Holy shit," with a pure joy that only children can produce on birthdays and Christmas. Oliver turned around, knowing he had just sworn in front of his mother, "Sorry, Mum."

"You're forgiven this time cause it's your birthday," Samantha assured him. Oliver turned and saw Colonel Briggs.

"Uncle Jim" Oliver raced over to the Colonel, stopped in front of him, gave him a proper salute, stood there holding the salute, waiting, waiting! Finally, Colonel Briggs snapped to attention, returned the salute, then Oliver crashed tackled him with a giant bear hug.

"How's my favourite Godson," Jim enquired.

"Awesome, but my team still hasn't found Aiden; sneaky little Yoda is shooting us, but we can't pick where he's shooting from, and I'm the only one on my team left; I've got to find him."

With that, Oliver races off to try to find his sneaky little brother's hiding spot.

As Mike watches his son race off on the hunt, he notices something out of the corner of his eye on the roof; he could barely see it because of the spotlights hung up around the yard for the party. Mike nudges Jim and points to the roof; Jim squints and holds his hand beside his eye to get a better look.

"You're kidding!" Jim inquired, amazed.

"Nope, that's him," Mike replied. Both men stood dumbfounded, watching this tiny figure crawl around slowly over the roof under a thermal blanket. You could barely make him out; no wonder his brother couldn't find him.

"You have a natural sniper in the family," Briggs says.

"Not if his mother sees him up there," Mike replied, laughing.

"You got a moment to talk?" Jim asked.

"Work?" Mike enquired.

"Yes, best we take it inside, as I'm on probation with Sam for working at home."

The men walked into Mike's study.

"What's up?" Mike asked.

Jim handed him an envelope. "Orders and I did some digging on your patrol problem on your last mission. They were looking for your team... Sort of?" Jim informed him.

"I knew it! What do you mean, sort of?" Mike was confused; he felt like the General, 'you either are or you aren't, son,' he thought.

"I got onto my contacts in ASIS (Australian Secret Intelligence Service), who got onto the yanks, who got onto a double agent in the area, etc. But, he said, he got the info from local sources in the area. So yes, they were looking for you, but the kicker is, they were searching for Afghani Mountain men coming from the northeast. So that's your cover story! no mention of Australian Special Forces."

Mike pondered a second on what Jim had said. "It makes no sense; the mountain men scenario is a tactical cover for us; no one knows that, just you and our team."

"Exactly, I reviewed your debrief, and I assess that you must have been spotted in your gear by a Russian or Pakistani drone, and they passed it on to Taliban contacts. It's the only thing that makes any sense," Jim offered.

"Yeah, maybe!" Mike wasn't sold on the assessment, but it was feasible. Mike holds up the envelope Jim gave him.

"Where are we off to now?"

"Back to Afghanistan, chasing up more of the things you got on your last mission," Jim said.

So, on that, the men went outside and joined the party. The night was a hit for all, with great food and friends. The boys had a great time, especially opening the presents. Samantha was very proud of the boys they raised. When they opened Uncle Jim's gifts, all the boy's friends couldn't contain themselves; it wasn't a mortar. He had bought the boys a remote-control model tank each, made from light steel, which they could build with their dad over the rest of his leave.

CHAPTER 5

THE WORLD MEETS THOR & LOKI

Kylie Lannister looked out the window of the MMM 104 FM chopper.

"That's going to piss a lot of people off today, Romano," the traffic reporter told the pilot.

"You're on in 30 seconds, Kylie," the voice said through his headphones.

"Good morning, Rosie. We have an urgent traffic update. The media build up at the Detroit Auditorium is causing major traffic problems. At the moment in its only one lane access through Clinton Drive. So, commuters, I'd suggest skipping the downtown area this morning if possible. There's going to be a lot of people late for work this morning."

"Thanks Kyle, it seems the AZTECK announcement today is causing some interest. I'm switching over to Jennifer Hidey now, our eyes and ears on the ground. Jenny, what's with the media frenzy?"

"Good morning, Rosie, Kylie's right. The media turnout is enormous. It is the same kind of turnout for a presidential visit or major rock group. The word on the street is that the announcement by Azteck today is going to be world changing, but AZTECK officials are being tight-lipped. I interviewed a few AZTECK staff from the expo that just closed. The staff said that the secrecy around the announcement is so tight that only the heads of AZTECK know what the announcement is. So, there's electricity in the air. I know this reporter can't wait to find out. On another note, Rosie, call me crazy, but I swear I heard a roar of what sounded like a lion coming from the back of one of the AZTECK trucks this morning."

Rosie laughed. "Well, maybe AZTECK is going into the circus business. There you have it, listeners. Jenny, our eyes and ears on the street, says there's big things coming in the announcements today. Stay tuned, this is Rosie Samson coming to you from MMM 104 FM Detroit's rocking music station.

9.45am, and to say the auditorium was buzzing was an understatement. The electricity in the room was like a rock concert just before the main act came out. There were over three hundred candidates for the AZTECK scholarships with family and friends, around one hundred staff members from AZTECK who stayed after the expo's closing to see the big announcement; not all staff members knew of the new plans. Art and the inner Circle kept tight-lipped to keep this story from leaking out and spoiling their thunder.

Also, there were over one hundred tv crew, staff, and reporters in the room, a good turnout thanks to Ab. As the head of public relations for the project, Ab had his finger on the pulse and, in his short years in training, had made it his goal to figure out exactly how the media works. Ab found out that it's much like the halls of the Whitehouse. The offices of the media can open to the sound of coins jingling.

Ab had greased the palms of three major social butterflies of the media world, telling them that the AZTECK announcement at the end of the expo was big, world-changing, so they spread the word through their friends and contacts in the media, who told their contacts, etc., etc., etc.

"This is going to be big; they're not announcing some new toaster oven or mobile phone, you have to be there, or you'll miss out," that was THE WORD, and it spread and was eaten up by the press. So, Ab thought how cheap it was to buy them, an exclusive each for three reporters; they would be the first to spread the word.
The production manager turned to Art and Ab, "Five minutes Mr. Damani."

Art gave the nod and turned to Ab. "Ready to change the world, son,"

"Yep," Ab hesitated.

"Nervous??" Art inquired, concerned for his son, who is about to take on the world at the age of 23.

"Yep!" Ab blurted out.

"You're not going to be sick, are you?" Art enquired, worried.

"Yep," Ab said, looking squeamish.

"Seriously!"

"No," Ab replied with a smirk.

"You can be a little shit sometimes, you know that," Art replied, feeling he just stepped right into that one.

Abs's grin got more prominent, "Let's go change the world, Father!"

The auditorium quieted down when the lights dimmed, and a whole new atmosphere engulfed the room. The lights on the stage lit up, and a spotlight hit the side stage as Ab walked out to a massive round of applause and a few wolf whistles. He had friends in the audience that he had made while training at AZTECK. The applause gave Ab a considerable buzz, and the wolf whistles made him blush; he took to the mic like he was born on a stage, and this was just another day at the office.

"Hello, thank you, everyone, especially the ones that wolf-whistled." Ab put his fingers to his ears, making the 'call me' sign, which sent the crowd into laughter.

"My name is Abayomi Thoyana. I am CEO of AZTECK's new African Division, in charge of public relations. I would like to welcome you all here, to our media friends (who would stab you in the back at a moment's notice to get a scoop), AZTECK staff (more cheers and wolf whistles from the rowdy group). Last but certainly not least, the recipients of this year's AZTECK scholarships and their family and friends.

Tonight, we will announce the opening of a new project in Africa that will be world-changing, bold, and brilliant, linking new technology with mother Earth and starting up a new era of peace and cooperation. Planting a flower of world hope in one of mother nature's most beautiful gardens.

But… even though I am your PR man, I think it is best to come from the man that had the dream and has now made it happen. So, let's give an enormous Detroit round of applause to the CEO, founder, dreamer of AZTECK international, My Father, Aarth Damani." The crowd went wild. The rock star had arrived at a standing ovation from the staff and recipients of scholarships from AZTECK… and the media clapped.

Art strode into the light from the side stage, waving to the crowd and taking control of the mic, as Ab stepped to the side. "Thank you, thank you, it's nice to be greeted with such kind words, especially when you didn't have to pay someone to say them." The crowd burst into laughter.

"Thank you to my son; you are just as much a part of this dream as I."

"50/50?" Ab enquired while leaning into the mic to be heard.

"Don't push your luck," Art snapped back to the roar of more laughter.

"Ab is right tonight; you will hear the outline of a new world-changing measure. It is too elaborate to explain in one night, too far-reaching to comprehend in one night; actually, the more you run it through your mind, the more questions and the more far-reaching you will see it go… So let me introduce you to THE ARK… Stage one!"

Art had swung his arm to point to the middle of nowhere. Centre Stage, a miraculously 3d schematic began slowly twirling in mid-air. One could see the outlines of Ethiopia and Somalia marked on the presentation with the contours of mountains and plains accordingly. The crowd issued a collective "Awww" as if Art had presented 'Behold FIRE'.

He continued, "In the region of the Bale Mountain, on World Heritage land, a world-leading research park stage 1, will be built to safely breed, protect and house in natural environments endangered animals from around the world. Stage 1 will start with the most seriously endangered." The crowd was already on the edge of their seats, including the media.

The press was trying to comprehend 'how he got this approved'.

#1/ It is being built on World Heritage land (how the hell did he pull that off?).

#2/ He's building this zoo in the middle of two nations that have been at war for decades (how the hell did he pull that off, and how long did he really think it will last before the missiles are firing over his petting zoo?). The media were a cynical lot but a necessary evil.

Art continued after a brief pause to let it sink in. "There will be an 8-stage plan but an infinite opening for future expansion. I know what some of you are thinking... lovely idea, but you're building it in the middle of a war zone. As of today, a peace accord has been signed between President Husain Abdullah Abdi of Somalia and President Abiy Akufo-Conde' of Ethiopia".

The crowd was all a buzz; the media was all over themselves, trying to grab their phones to ring editors and producers to get them live feeds and more tv crews here, immediately! This was news, not just because of the peace accord (which will be mentioned over and over in the coming month, that the UN couldn't even pull off). Also, the fact it is being built on World Heritage land. It's nice he's protecting animals; the media perspective is 'what sells.' Art raised his hands to quieten the room and continued.

"A lot to swallow? Then it's best to hear it from the gentleman themselves." Art once again pointed to nowhere land on stage, and once again the miraculous appears, the 3d presentation disappears, and a screen drops from the stage ceiling on cue. Two faces appeared on the screen. A live feed from both nations, the Presidents of Somalia and Ethiopia.

A sudden change sweeps across the crowd. The booing started because these two Presidents are not new to bad press. Reported repeatedly for atrocities against each other and their own people. Calls of "dictator" and "murderer" were shouted from the crowd. Then, finally, Art steps up to the mic and raises his hands.

"Please, please, respect! We all have opinions on current events worldwide. So, I ask you to hear these gentlemen out. Take what they say into account concerning what they're offering Africa and the World. Please continue, President Abdi," Abdi read off a prepared speech (written by Ab) announcing the peace accord. He rattles of the plans of a unified system to help the ARK, the promise that it offers the people of their two nations and Africa in general, and finishing with the announcement that they will be holding media releases to announce the new developments in both their countries.

While the speech was being read, Ab was running it word for word in his mind. Ab kept listening to President Abdi's breathing, waiting for the first sign he would add something of his own to the speech. But, unlike his father, he wasn't a total optimist; this guy is a dictator responsible for thousands of deaths in his own country and, God knows how many in Ethiopia, so Ab put on a 2-minute delay in the speech so he could pull the plug at any time.

Then, with the slow intake of breath, he's preparing to say something else; Ab's finger lightly rested on the disconnect button. He wasn't in a hurry, as he wanted to hear what he was going to say and still had time to cut him off.

"I would like to add something also, Mr. Damani, if I may," Ab's finger tensed, ready to pounce. "I would like to say that as of tomorrow, I will put to the Somalian parliament that I will step aside to hold democratic elections. In two years, after the competition of stage 2 of the ARK" Abs finger relaxed, he will let this one go through. It was not new to Art and Ab, as it was part of the agreement, but to the press hearing it, it will drive them into a frenzy, and it did! From the initial booing from the crowd when he first appeared on the screen, he was now seeing and hearing thunderous applause and a standing ovation.

On the screen, President Abdi's shoulders go back, and his chest puffs out with pride as if he had made all this happen. Art stood there happy for the Presidents to receive their applause; Ab, on the other hand, thought he would 'lose his breakfast' while they had their moment. Ab knew Abdi couldn't be trusted; it would only be 18 months before they found out.

After the address by President Abdi, Art thanked both Presidents and wished them all the best, and said that he was looking forward to working with them. Then, the screen turned off and disappeared back into the ceiling.

Art looked at the crowd and said, "You have heard some incredible news today, but, as the tv salesman always says, Wait, there's more." Art had the crowd enthralled now; what else could there be?

Art continued, "As you know, AZTECK is the world leader in electronics, biotech, and more, so we pooled our collective knowledge and resources to help protect the ARK. But, as we all know, poaching is rife in Africa, so these animals will need around the clock protection and surveillance."

Art sucked in a big breath; he had been looking forward to this part of the display… "It gives me great pleasure to introduce the prototypes of our protection and surveillance team of the ARK." Art once again waved his magic arm, and the large double doors to the opposite end of the auditorium swung open, and four figures were bathed in the spotlights in the entrance, not moving, just standing there. Then, after their slight pause, the figures stepped into the room, only a few steps. The room was filled with awe; voices could be heard, "What the!" "Damn, they're huge!"

At the top of the steps were two security guards holding large leashes and on the end of the leashes were two massive predators, a Bengal tiger, and a black leopard or black panther. Art continued, "Their names are Thor and Loki" Art gave the security guards a nod, and they quickly bent down to unclip the leashes from the cats' collars. Things went a little frenzied at that stage, especially among people sitting closest to the main entrance. Both cats let out a roar, a deep primal growl that didn't do much to calm this crowd.

"Please don't be alarmed; my boys will not hurt you."

The cats started making their way down the aisle, moving slowly, sleekly with the grace of Lords of the Jungle. Occasionally turning sideways to look at the people seated, they headed towards the stage.

"Thor and Loki are the first two prototypes of our bio-engineered technological animal range. Both have the exact attributes physically of their living counterparts, but they don't sleep, don't eat, and never forget, all our animal guards in the reserve are equipped with the latest surveillance equipment. Basically, Thor and Loki are large robotic cats. They will look, act, smell, and be programmed to act accordingly around their live counterparts as instructed by the leading animal specialists in the world."

The guests sitting closest to the aisle were visibly shaking. The cats had made their way halfway down the walkway.

"THOR, LOKI sit!" Straight away; both cats respond to Art's command.

There will be an army of robotic animals protecting the endangered animals; no one will get near them without us knowing, and mark my words, they will protect the animals to the death.

In a change of tone, Art continued. "If anyone had noticed, my son Ab is sitting behind a laptop, at the edge of the stage. He is commanding the boys. We have biometrically linked these 2 to me as protectors. Which means they are connected to me verbally, and by my smell and sight, boys come!"

Art commanded, and both cats sprang to life, ran down the last of the steps, and leapt onto the stage. Both circled Art and eventually sat a couple of paces behind him on either side, watching. The crowd loved the display and the natural grace of the animals, finding it hard to believe they weren't real.

"The ARK will be protected by animals such as these, including eagles and other bird life especially designed for surveillance. It will also be protected with the longest fence since the Great Wall of China," Art shares a giggle with the crowd. "Equipped with the latest high tech and a joint special police force from Somalian and Ethiopia's military. So, poaching will not be a problem; these sentinels will never be distracted." The crowd let out a roar of laughter and giggles; Art could see that they were looking behind him at the boys and knew Ab was up to something.

"Let me guess?" Art enquired from the crowd. "Loki is licking his genitalia." Art slowly looked over at Ab, sitting behind the laptop. He was laughing with the crowd. Then, Art swiftly turns back to the group, "I might have an opening for a new CEO in Africa; soon." Immediately, Loki sits up perfectly straight and military, which brings another round of laughter and applause.

"There will be later stages that will allow access for the public to enter and see the animals. Also, there are so many more online live feeds to keep up with our progress. We will have media releases and blogs on our web pages to answer any questions. Peace in Africa and a rejuvenation of the earth's animal resources is what we aim to achieve."

Art turns and takes a quick peek at Thor and Loki, then turns back to the mic with a smile. "Well, I suppose we must get onto the important part of the evening, the reason most of you are here… the AZTECK scholarships," cheers and more whistles from the excited recipients.

"This year, I apologise for the cryptic response. This year you all received the 'you were successful' response to applications,' but nothing else except an invitation and free pass to the expo and today. There were a record-breaking 326 successful applications, the highest ever given out by AZTECK," more whistles and cheers. "Congratulations to you all. There will be desks in the foyer for you to line up and collect an envelope. In these envelopes, there are instructions for further incentives for you." There was a collective shock through the crowd, and an electric fever pitch could be felt as the recipients waited on every word Art was saying.

"Besides your scholarship, AZTECK has released another 100 million dollars to the scholarship fund." Woos, gasps, and the nervous chatter was fever pitch now.

"In the envelope, there are offers to fund your research. Instant job offers to join AZTECK and finish your studies while working with us. In addition, some of you have been offered funding and training, working in the ARK." The crowd erupted; the recipients and families clapped and cheered this giant of a man and his generous company.

Art let the cheering go on, then addressed the crowd again. "Once again, congratulations to our hard-working scholarship entries, and thank you very much to our media friends. I hope we didn't give you too much to write about; Ab will address you shortly to tell you about the times for the press releases. Again, thank you all, especially my staff from the expo who hung around today," more cheers and wolf whistles from the crowd.

People started making their way to the foyer to collect their envelopes and read them to their excited friends and relatives. Then, the media began packing up and moving towards the side of the stage, waiting to hear from Ab.

As Art was about to cross the stage, he noticed a small crowd was gathering at the front of the stage, hoping to attract Art's attention; Art was never one to walk away when requested to speak, especially by future staff members. His staff loved their boss, a hard taskmaster, but cared for his team and gave them a great work environment.

As Art approached the front of the stage, one young lady called out, "Mr. Damani, may we meet Thor and Loki?" "But of course. Ab, can you switch the boys over to me, please?"

"Yes, Father." As Ab replied, he was sitting down behind the computer again; after hitting a few keys, he nodded to his father that the boys were under his control.

Art issued a command, "Come boys," it was said in a gentle but firm voice, to which the big cats responded immediately. "Move to the front of the stage and lay down." The cats did precisely as requested and immediately were inundated with pats and strokes of their fur.

One person caught Art's eye; she was in the second row, trying to push past the crowd to get a stroke of the boys. Art was good with faces; she was Ms. Rosi Jensen from Colorado. Art remembered her from her work and her portfolio from the scholarship application. As the young lady squirreled her way to the front of the line, Art addressed her, "Hello, Ms. Jensen, good to see you here." Rosi froze and slowly looked up, mouth open, with that 'the rockstar knows my name look.'

"Hello, Mr. Damani, how did you know who I was?" she inquired.

"I've been following your work and am very impressed with it," Art said. Suddenly, everyone stopped what they were doing and looked at Rosi, wanting to see who this rockstar/tech god was impressed with.

Rosi felt everyone's eyes on her but got out a "Thank you, Mr. Damani. I have a quick question about Loki. His fur feels real, but there is a certain shimmer to the ends. Are they made from optic cables?"

"Very impressive, Ms. Rosi," Art replied.

Once again, everyone stopped and turned to look at Rosi; with that, 'the rockstar/tech god called you by your first name look.'

Art answered by saying, "Maybe I could answer that better if you take up your offer to come work with us" Rosi kept stroking the side of Loki before the penny dropped.

"Offer, what offer???" Rosi turned, shocked.

"You obviously haven't collected your envelope yet; I'll say no more. I wouldn't like to spoil the surprise," Art sheepishly replied.

Rosi let out a high-pitched squeal and did what her own personnel Happy Dance. "Yes! Yes!" Rosi let go with a fist pump, but as she turned, she did something that had Ab and Art talking about for hours that night. She ran her fingers through the fur on Loki's head, between his ears. There was nothing unusual about that, except that Loki must have gotten a whiff of her pheromones. Instantly, Loki started brushing up against her arm and purring like some giant kitten.

Art was instantly gobsmacked; he turned towards Ab; Ab was crossing the stage; he had noticed it too; their eyes met. They gave each other a nod and a look of, 'we will talk about this later.' Loki differed from Thor; Loki was equipped with a prototype hormone sensor. He was being trialled to detect people's moods and their actions, according to those relating to the smells. Loki was training for aggressive behaviour in animals and people. As part of the program, he also had a range of other emotions he had to work on yet, but there was the proof. 'It does work,' Art reflected.

Art stood up from his crouched position and spoke to the small group at the stage, "You will have to excuse us now; AZTECK waits for no one, even me; I will say goodbye and thanks for coming today." Art turned to the boys and commanded, "Follow." Then he and the boys walked off the stage.

As he was about to leave the scene, he could hear Ms. Rosi Jensen screaming, "Mum, Mum!" as she ran up the stairs to the front foyer. Art exited the stage with a grin on his face.

****

That evening, over dinner in Art's penthouse room, Art and Ab discussed the exciting developments of Loki's behaviour with Ms. Jensen.

"So you're saying that Loki started behaving like that after Rosi's arm brushed across his face?"

"Yes," Art replied excitedly. "It was like he smelt something from her pheromones, marking her as a friend, just like he does for me," Art continued.

"That's incredible. That is exactly like we programmed Loki to do… but there are also concerns," Ab replied.

"Such as?" Art felt a mood changer coming; but he knew what the problems were, but he wanted to see if his son could make all the connections.

"One, he was in Father mode, which does have that protection for you and people around you. But to go into a Baby Kitten mode, to someone else, is not what we thought the reaction would be."

"And 2?" Art enquired.

"Well… that process had been switched off on his program till it was worked on more."

Bingo! Art thought he had put it all together.

"Well, we will have to put Loki back in straight away, we need that looked into, and we will need more safety protocols to freeze him in case he goes out of his programming by himself again. The last thing we need is an AI Armageddon."

Art started laughing, and Ab joined in.

"I don't think we are anywhere near that yet," Ab insisted.

"All good; anything else to report, Mr. HUB Master?" Art enquired

"One minor issue in America, I'm waiting for a response to my directive, so I won't bore you with any details yet; other than that, all is in their parameters of production; Africa is actually ahead of schedule two weeks."

"Brilliant, just brilliant. My son is very proud of you; you are doing an excellent job. I'm so proud; I will shout for dinner tonight."

Ab laughed. "Very funny, the dinner is always booked to your room."

"Well, tonight, I… sort of changed it to yours," Art put on a sheepish grin and laughed.

****

WHILE BACK IN AUSTRALIA

Samantha went into the lounge room to check the boy's cleaning effort before the party started. She grabbed the tv remote to switch it off; just before she hit the button, "This is Tori Speakman. We will shortly be crossing live to Detroit USA for the of the announcement of the signing of the Peace accord between Somalia and Ethiopia and the Billionaire who made it happen."

Samantha was stunned, her finger frozen over the remote. Sam knew Mike, and the team had done many missions into this region and said it was like hell on Earth. But, frozen as Samantha was, her vocal cords worked just fine. She let out an ear-piercing, "MIIIIIKE!".

The three Special Forces men came bursting in from the backyard, nearly smashing through the plate glass doors. Trying to get inside the house simultaneously to rescue Samantha from whatever made her scream like that. Home invaders, a snake, or maybe a giant rat was in the house, as many possibilities ran through Mike's mind and the relevant action required to save the day in seconds. As they reached Samantha in the lounge room, she stood there, pointing to the TV.

At first, the men checked the room and surrounding area for trouble, not seeing anything; they focused on what Sam was pointing at, the TV.

"What? Is there an end-of-year sale on?" Zikmund said with a cheeky, wise-ass tone.

"No, that!" Sam replied, pointing at the TV with the remote firmly in hand. The men stood there and listened for ten minutes as they crossed to a live feed in Detroit about a peace accord between two nations that have hated each other for centuries.

Quietly taking it in, that a billionaire negotiated it with two robot cats and wants to build a zoo there, what? At the end of the broadcast, Samantha turned off the tv, Zikmund was the first to say anything.

"Great! We won't need to go into that shit hole again."

"How the hell did he pull that off? The UN couldn't get them to budge in the last ten years," Mike asked, confused.

It was Seb's question that made them all feel uneasy.

"How the hell did we not hear anything about this going down?"

"Good point," Mike replies. "The Colonel said he was coming to the party tonight; he might have some answers," he also added.

"I know this is important to you guys, but don't bog down the party with work talk tonight; it's the boy's night," Samantha asked them.

"We won't spoil tonight," Smith assured her.

"Thanks, Zikmund." Samantha leaned over and kissed him on the cheek. The 10-year Special Forces soldier went as red as a tomato, blushing; it looked like his head might catch on fire.

"How come I never get kisses on the cheek for being good," Seb sulkily protests.

"Because Zikmund never gets my husband arrested when he goes out!" Samantha said with a grin, knowing Seb hated to be reminded.

"Aw, come on, it wasn't my fault; they started it," Seb protested.

"Don't worry, Seb, I'll get over it…one day," Samantha cheekily added.

CHAPTER 6

ARK HUB

The breeze carried the scent of pyracantha and Jasmine trees as it wafted across this small mount. Bee-eater birds hovered around the trees, picking off the abundant fruit. The Greenwood shrew scampers around the base of the trees, picking up the leftovers that the Bee Eaters have discarded. This was a time for work and getting the family fed for all the native animals in Bale Mountain this time of year... BUT, twenty metres below this little marsupial, another busy bee works hard at it.

Doby Heinlinker sat at his terminal and marvelled at his good fortune. He was sitting in the HUB, the central core of the ARK. Basically, the brain of the ARK, the HUB, was a room the size of half a floor of a high-rise building. There were three terminals in front of the screen, one for himself, his tech partner, Lexi Eldridge, and Abayomi Thoyana, the son of billionaire Aarth Damani. Ab was the second in charge of the company and the central hub contact for all divisions worldwide.

"I should rewrite the program on these video screens," Doby said as he sat by himself in the HUB. "What's the point of having 12 large video screens and not one of them playing cartoons?"

Doby pushed his wheeled console chair along the perfectly smooth floor; he slid across to the conference table with his feet in the air. He sat on the other side, looking at the 12 screens all at once.

"Sometimes, you just have to get a look at the big picture. Everything is in order, with no faults. Perfect!"

The HUB was filled with every kind of communication imaginable. Mr. Damani was big into leaving nothing to chance. He said he never wants "The ARK" to become some series of documentaries about robotic animals that took over Africa.

Just as Doby was marvelling at the computer perfection, the phone rang and he nearly lost control of his seat, grabbing onto the table to prevent from falling on his ass. He scurried to the phone.

"Hello HUB, Doby speaking. Good morning, Doctor McTagash. How can I help you?"

"Morning Doby. I have a request. I have just been going over the night's footage of the new gazelle herd. I feel they may not be settling in as quickly as I had hoped. I need more surveillance of the herd to pick out if there is a leader in the group that might affect the whole herd. Can you arrange that for me, please?"

"Certainly Doc, I'll send 2 eagles over to record their movements. What is it they are doing? I watched the footage and didn't notice anything."

"They're running."

"Ahh, aren't gazelle supposed to run?"

"Yes, but not that much. I think there might be a herd leader with anxiety and he's running the herd ragged."

"Oh, ok I'll get right on it, Doc."

"Thanks Doby."

As Doby hung up, he pushed his chair across to his console. He straightened his Avengers T-shirt, tapped the head of his lucky Spiderman bobblehead on his desk.

"Captain Doby to the rescue of the gazelles," he yelled. Then quickly looked to make sure no one heard him. His fingers flashed over the keys and signalled two eagle monitors that were in non-priority areas. He hit enter on his keyboard.

"Done. Gazelles saved."

'Life is good,' he thought.

Doby lived his whole life in front of a computer screen, writing programs from a young age, and breezed through college and University with ease… except for the constant teasing that all nerds and fat boys get at school, but it paid off. Doby received a job offer from Mr. Damani and worked for Art for seven years. With pride is now the head Controller/Programmer of the ARK.

****

The door banged open to the HUB to wake Doby from his daydream.

"Morning, Asslicker!" a voice booms through the opened door.

"It's Heinlinker, NOT, Asslicker Lexi. Why do you have to be so crass every morning?" Doby protested.

"I don't know, Asslicker. It's probably because I wake up horny every morning," Lexi informs him with a cheerful note.

"See what I mean? I don't need to know that," Doby said, embarrassed.

"Oh, come on, Doby, my love, don't tell me you don't wake up with a little woody in the morning."

"What? NO!" Doby protested.

"I'm sorry, Doby. I didn't mean to embarrass you; let me give you a big hug to make up." Lexi moves over to Doby on his office chair, gives his head a big hug and a kiss on his forehead. Doby's face is smothered in Lexi's breasts, and Lexi knows it. The low-cut tops she wears always show off her ample 14DD breasts.

"Oh, come on, stop it," Doby protested; even though he liked her perfume, she always smelt like some kind of flower. Doby pushed her back.

"You shouldn't do that; Mr. Damani wouldn't like it," Doby informed while glowing bright red from embarrassment.

"I've never done it to Art. Do you think I should?" Lexi teased.

"No! Not if you want to keep your job."

"Maybe I'll get a promotion," Lexi pondered jokingly.

"I'm sorry, Doby. I did bring you a gift though." Lexi darted back outside the door and grabbed a couple of items off a table in the next room.

"Ta-Da! Your breakfast, my King!" Lexi bowed with her hands out.

"Your favourite, crusty bagel with cream cheese and salmon and one jumbo strawberry milkshake," Doby felt embarrassed again and started blushing.

"Thank you, Lexi. It was very nice of you."

"No sweat for my favourite man." Doby grabbed the food and took a deep breath of the warm bagel.

"Mmmm, almost worth getting your boobs rubbed in my face for," Doby says.

"Are you saying your bagel is nicer than my breasts?" Lexi challenged.

Now Doby is no man of the world, but he was smart enough to know that there was no safe answer to this question, so he grabs his milkshake, starts sucking, and turns to his console.

Lexi, a stunning, fashionable Goth, wears all black clothes, black lipstick, a black bra with a torn blacktop to show off her ample cleavage. Although, since being recruited or snatched by Mr. Damani. Lexi now has enough money to buy all the designer clothes she likes. She hasn't changed her style, but all her outfits are from the world's top designers.

Lexi Eldridge considered herself, like Doby, a lucky person. She was approached by an unknown person four years ago to arrange a meeting with someone who had important information about her future wellbeing. Cryptic, to say the least. Lexi worked in the protest group Anonymous as a hacker, a secretive group of world hackers trying to even the playing field against governments and corporations for the average person.

So, many governments were actively chasing their members, so going to a secret meeting with an unknown person while you're in hiding around the world is not usually a brilliant plan of action. But, finally, the intrigue of it all got the better of her; she agreed to meet and went along that evening at 10 o'clock to meet this cryptic person.

Planton Avenue was nowhere in the world of nowhere, more like an alley than an avenue, dark, creepy, rat-infested from all the unregistered food joints on the street, plus it looked like a great place to get rolled or jabbed or even both. As she was waiting in this alley, behind a pizza joint in Chicago East, she felt vulnerable and stupid for coming; at any moment, FBI cars could come and block off each entrance, and an entire world of hurt would start. She decided that she wasn't going to stay and went to turn to leave when a figure appeared at one end of the alleyway and walked towards her. As the person got closer, she could make out this person was wearing a cap and hoody, like some kind of rapper.

"Who are you?" Lexi called out to the figure, no answer.

"What do you want? I have a gun," Lexi challenged. Of course, she didn't have a gun, but she thought it was a dumb move not to bring one.

"I know you don't, Ms. Eldridge. You are perfectly safe with me."

'I know that voice,' Lexi thought, but from where?

"Let me introduce myself, Lexi." the mysterious figure pulled back the hood of his jumper, and his hat fell off on the ground; the whole image of some tough gangster was lost, as Lexi stifled a giggle.

Art bent down to pick up his cap. "My name is Art Damani."

"You! You're the head of AZTECK industries," Lexi said, astonished.

"That is correct."

"What do you want with me, and what's with the whole hoods and dark alley shit?" Lexi challenged.

"My apologies for the theatrics; even though I have blocked all video surveillance for two blocks, you're too toxic to be around at the moment."

"Me, why am I toxic?" Lexi queried.

"Because of the group you're associated with, Anonymous."

"Hahaha, the hacker group, you think I'm with those losers? You have the wrong lady, chum!" Lexi almost pulled off the greatest bluff. She was very convincing, but Art Damani already had all the answers, so he pretended he didn't hear her protest of innocence.

"Lexi, I arranged for us to meet so I could offer you some information I came across."

"What information could you have that could help me, the winning lotto numbers?" Art continued again, pretending he hadn't heard her little outburst.

"Someone in your organisation has sold you out… to the FBI; he planted info in your flat, on hidden drives." Art handed her a file with photo evidence; Lexi reluctantly accepted the folder.

She felt cold and terrified. She opened it slowly and flicked through the first few pics. Lexi's mood suddenly changed.

"That prick!" the pictures showed her latest ex talking to the FBI in her flat.

"I'll kill him!" Lexi was boiling over for the moment, forgetting her fear.

"I apologise; my plan was to steal the evidence from your flat before they raided it. But for once, the cybercrime units got off their butts and were efficient. There is also this." Art handed her a micro-recorder and earpiece. Lexi quickly grabbed the earpiece, put it in her ear, and hit play; she listened for a couple of minutes as her ex gave the FBI information about her but not the rest of the group. Finally, Lexi pulled out the earpiece and handed the recorder back to Art.

"Why are you doing this for me? What do you want out of it?" Lexi enquired, feeling drained.

"I have a proposition to offer you. I estimate the FBI will dig up everything they can find on you and make their initial arrest tomorrow, so we don't have long. First, I want you to know I have no interest in Anonymous, just you! I want you to come work for me. I will get you out of the country tonight and have the papers drawn up by a lawyer for you to move your mother to a nursing home of your choice. Yes, I know about your mum. She will be safe, well cared for, and out of the FBI's reach. I will destroy all the evidence the FBI has on you, including the tapes, and give you a fresh start back on the streets again, or I destroy the tapes and files, you come to work for me, earning more money than you have seen. You are safe, your mum is safe, and life goes on; what do you think?"

Lexi looked him over. "All this is based on the premise that you can get into the FBI headquarters and computers,"

"Correct," Art answered.

"Buddy, Anonymous hasn't been able to do that yet," Lexi challenged.

"I don't make offers I can't keep; I will do you a deal. I will hide you tonight, then in the morning, we will get your mum, and the pair of you will be out of the country within hours. Then, if I can't pull off what I have said with your files, I will pay for you and your mum to go to any country in the world with 100 thousand dollars to start a new life together. Do we have a deal, Lexi?"

"Yes, we have a deal!" Lexi offered her hand. She had no choice but to accept his offer, or her life was about to go down the toilet and her mum, too.

****

Lexi's daydream was broken when the office door was opened. Doby and Lexi are greeted with a joyous, I am happy every morning smile and acknowledgment from their boss, Art Damani.

"Good morning to you both; how's my favourite pair this wonderful morning?" Art lifted his head and took a big whiff of the air.

"Oh my God, crusty bagel with salmon and cream cheese… smells so good," Art said, euphoric.

"I thought you were allergic to seafood, Art?" Lexi quizzed.

"I am, dear girl, but I love its smell. I hoed into a delightful piece of fish from Australia, but the damn thing always thing tried to kill me… it's was very rude," Art let out a weird cackle.

"What excitement do you have to report this morning?" Art questioned.

"I am happy to report we are three weeks ahead of schedule on an overall front," Doby informed. "We had an issue with inferior cabling that is being built into the fencing matrix; I have sent a memo to Ab. The Doc rang this morning, and I helped her save the gazelles. No biggy," Doby said in a suave voice.

"Thank you, Doby, and what of our wall Lexi." Art turned to Lexi; Art was, in fact, talking about their complex computer firewall that would stop any outside hacking into the ARK.

"My part is done; it's in Doby's hand now to turn it into 0 and 1s," Lexi said proudly.

"I used every bit of technology AZTECK has. The spiral wall protection runs on mathematical algorithms like a Rubik's cube. Remember Art, nothing is impenetrable, given time. So, we set up the old shell game. Once anyone got halfway through the spiral wall, it would be detected and traced and we would let them in to a false site, which would kick them out again."

"So, we let them in and then cheat… I love it!" Art yelled.

"How long before you can run the test drive, Doby?" Art enquired.

"Three days," Doby said.

"Put aside all your other work and hand over what you can to Lexi and have it up and running in two; our schedule has been moved up…!"

Before Art could inform Lexi and Doby of what was behind the schedule change, he heard footsteps coming down the hallway, the footsteps of Ab. Although Art was sensitive to his environment and the people around him, anyone could tell these were the stomps of an unhappy camper. Of course, Art already knew what Ab wasn't happy about, as he had sent a memo to him and the head of the African Division about the reason for the schedule change.

Three steps before the door to the HUB, Ab started his complaints, "No, no, no, no way are we doing this!"

Lexi and Doby were taken aback by Abs' manor. It's not that they haven't seen Art and Ab argue before. On one occasion, they exited the elevator on the hub floor arguing, walked through the HUB, and down towards the computer terminals arguing without missing a beat. But whatever it was, Ab was definitely not a fan.

"Father, are you mad? we can't do this!" Art looked at Ab and tipped his head towards Lexi. Ab turned and had clearly forgotten they weren't alone.

"My apologies, Lexi and Doby; how are you both this morning?" Ab enquired.

"A lot better than you, so it seems, Ab," Lexi said, a little bemused; Lexi didn't fluster easily.

"Yes, I am sorry, this memo, this…!" Ab paused and looked at Lexi and Doby, "He hasn't told you yet, has he?" Ab enquired.

"No, I was waiting till you got here before I informed them," Art informed them.

Ab took the opportunity to get in first.

"Father wants to invite the President to be the first to try our game hunting reserve."

"What, the President of Somalia???" Doby enquired astonished.

"The President of the United States!" Ab stated emphatically.

"WHAT? Well, that isn't happening," Lexi added.

"See, Father, I'm not the only one against it."

"No, that's not what I mean. Art can invite whomever he wants to the reserve. But the protocols involved in moving the President of the United States of America out of the USA are huge. To come to a war-torn area of Africa where they hate Americans, they won't let him come. Sorry, Art," Lexi informed them all.

"Well, it won't matter then, so there's no need to worry."

Ab turned and looked at his father. "Oh my God, you've already sent him an invitation, haven't you?"

"It should be at the Whitehouse in two days, but you have all stated it won't happen, so there is nothing to worry about…"

CHAPTER 7

THE INVITATION

"Calli, get this out straight away."

"Yes, Sir."

"Coming through."

"Whoa, watch where you're going."

"Has anyone seen the Chief of Staff? He's not in his office."

"I think he's with the President."

On its best days, it's like a beehive; everyone is busy, everyone knows their job, and even though there are so many people around, everyone just flows around each other, and no traffic is halted.

That is the view of one of the female executives from the White House West wing media section.

Then there are days like this morning when the lift opens, and you see a Monster truck revving up to make a run for the Oval office. To get in the way was to be run over and destroyed. This morning the Monster truck was the head of the CIA, Director Damian Spelling.

As he exited the elevator, he had a fixed look in his eyes, 'Dare to get in my way' and lookout.

"Make way! Yes, good morning, don't know, don't care!"

Spelling stomped his way down the hallways. He had staffers diving for cover; one poor young intern came in contact with him as he came out of an office, papers went flying everywhere. Spelling stopped briefly, looked at the intern, snorted, stepped on the documents, and continued. The intern stood there waiting for an apology that wasn't coming.

As Spelling reached the Oval office door, a Secret Service officer stepped toward him and politely informed him,

"The President is with the Chief of Staff, Sir."

"They will want to hear what I have to say, son."

He brushes past the Secret Service officer and barges through the door. The officer follows just in case the President wants him removed. Of course, the officer hoped he got the chance to remove him; he never liked Spelling, always walking around like he was more important than the President. Spelling started his rant once he had entered the room.

"No Way, No Way, are we going to accept this invitation!" Spelling bellowed.

The Secret Service officer leaned around Director Spelling and looked at the President.

"Sir?" he enquired with a head tilt towards Spelling.

"It's fine, Thomas; Mr. Spelling obviously has something important to say," the President informed him. On that, the officer turned and went back to his post.

"Damian, I don't know if I will ever get used to you getting a copy of my mail at the same time as I get it?" the President enquired.

"We can't accept this invitation. To go to Somalia, to hunt robots; that's insane!" Spelling said in a 'You know I'm right,' voice.

"Actually, it sounds like fun. Did you get an invitation too? You said we???" the President said in a tone-it-down voice. This President, for all the press natter about being too nice, that wasn't the case behind the Oval Office doors he wouldn't be spoken down to. That would be disrespecting the job and the office. He had the patience and the fortitude of Washington and the charisma of JFK, which made him the most popular President since JFK. He encouraged reasonable discussions among political parties to sort out issues that actually helped the American people, all of the American people. James Edwin 3rd seemed the complete package in his first term in office.

"You know what I mean, James."

The President tilted his head down and looked over his glasses at the Director of the CIA.

"Sorry, Mr. President," Spelling corrected himself.

"I don't know, going to a robotic hunting reserve sounds like fun and politically correct. The world hates game hunters. So, building a robotic one caters for the professionals to test their skills and bring in money to help the endangered animals. I think Mr. Damani sounds quite switched on."

"How are things in Somalia since Mr. Damani and his ARK moved in?" The President inquired of the CIA chief.

"At this point, stable."

"And what of their relationship with Ethiopia?"

"Stable, at this point," the chief responded.

"What did you find out about how Mr. Damani got these 2 countries to sign a peace agreement?"

But, then, feeling inadequate, Spelling had to admit.

"Nothing, as far as we have been able to confirm; there is evidence he only met them face-to-face once."

"Once, how is that possible? The United States and UN have been trying for fifteen years, and now things are stable."

The Chief of Staff finally entered the conversation. "In eight months, their economy has thrived. AZTECK has invested a lot of money into the country, unemployment is down. There are new hospitals and Red Cross centres. They're protected by the same people that stole their relief and drove them out of the country."

"How long before we could arrange to go if we intended to do it?" The President asked his Chief of Staff.

"At least six months to be able to put everything in place, Mr. President."

"I really think America needs to be a part of this before someone else steps in," the President said.

"Both of you, look into what needs to be done to accept his invitation. Damian, start digging around on what you can find out about Mr. Damani and his ARK, but I want this done stealthily. I know the risks of going there, so let's go in and out before anyone knows I've been. Linwood, organise a Trade delegation to look into lifting restrictions of dealing with Somalia, but don't tell them when we're going. Draw up a plan; we will organise a meeting in two weeks to discuss it and any problems."

"Yes, Mr. President," The Chief of Staff agreed.

"This is madness, but yes, Mr. President." On that, the two men turned and left the office.

The President turns slowly and looks at his head of the Secret Service, Chad Langdon, who was quietly standing in the corner, taking it all in.

"Do you like to hunt Chad?" the President asks him.

"It's been a while, Sir, but I hope it is only robot animals we have to deal with."

"Me to Chad, me too."

CHAPTER 8

ART & HIS MORNING WALK

As fresh a morning air as Art had ever smelt, a light breeze blew the fragrance of Jasmine into the air. The view was spectacular from the air pad at the top of ARK mountain. Sweeping plains with contrasting rocky mounts and thick jungle outcrops. This area had it all. Art liked to start his morning walks from here; the view and fresh air cleared his mind in some kind of funky African Zen thing.

"Good morning, Art," came a chirpy response from behind.

"Whoa!" Art, startled, nearly made him jump over the safety rail of the Air pad.

"Gee, sorry. I didn't mean to scare you," Lexi said apologetically.

"No, it's fine Ms Lexi. I was worlds away trying to process everything."

"I come here for the same thing. You must have a lot to process, trying to run all this and all your other businesses worldwide."

"I have a lot of good people working with me, who know what decisions to make for me."

"So, what are you processing this morning?" Lexi asked.

"Oh, the fact I haven't heard from the President yet. The fact the animals are arriving every day now and all the enclosures aren't ready yet. Why, Tyson needs to test his robots in the food hall, scaring Mrs Sanders and which path to walk down this morning to go meet Ab."

"Hmm, a lot to think about. Let me help you. With the President, no news is good news. With the animals, you have already set up extensive areas for them to roam in till their homes are ready. The staff love Tyson's robots and they are on social media daily helping with free publicity, it's only catering that are so uptight about the robots, but look who you hired to run catering. And the path to meet Ab, the path of less resistance, is the best one to take," Lexi said with a giggle.

Art laughed heartily. "Is your mind always this relaxed, Miss Lexi?"

"Yes, after morning coffee." They both chuckled.

"Well, I'm off to meet Ab and our new animals. You have a fantastic morning, Miss Lexi, and thanks for the advice. I might have to turn you into our personal therapist for the ARK."

"No thanks, too many crazy people in the anthill."

"Hahaha, on that I'm off. Come Thor, Loki, come."

The cats sprang into action and set up a pace 2 steps behind Art. Using their built-in scanners, they can detect everything around Art long before he can see it.

'Strange' Lexi thought to herself. She noticed while talking to Art that Thor the tiger sat motionless and dutiful waiting on a command from Art while they were speaking, but Loki the Panther was looking around, taking everything in... observing... watching... learning. 'Strange indeed'.

****

Art kept a steady pace to get some kind of exercise; there hasn't been a lot of me-time or family time since the ARK got underway; he made a mental note to arrange a day out with Ab. Art was rounding a bend when Loki bounced a few steps ahead as his sensors picked up someone ahead.

Art looked up from Loki to see Tyson Lumming, head of the bio-engineering section, doing some stretches.

"Good morning, Tyson. How is the world's best bioengineer this morning? Enjoying some morning exercise?"

"Yes, couldn't miss it; what a beautiful day outside," Tyson said.

"Magnificent, good to be alive day... Well, all those days are. What horrifying creatures are you unleashing on poor Mrs Sanders from catering today?" Art laughed.

"Nothing, I have to lie low for a while," Tyson said.

"Lie low, why?" Art asked, confused.

"You haven't heard? In that case, I am extremely sorry and I will pay for any broken plates and items."

"Why!" now Art was worried.

"I unleashed one of the new animals into the food hall and tested him by taking him off my control and letting him process everything naturally." Tyson said as if it was nothing.

"What animal did you release?"

"A baboon," Tyson said in a low soft voice.

"Oh my God, what happened?"

"Well, everything started fine, a lot of cute monkey things, until he met Mrs Sanders. Once the yelling started, the baboon got scared then, defensive, then territorial. It ended in a gladiatorial fight with the baboon throwing crockery and Mrs Sanders fighting with a bin lid and mop."

Art stood there shocked; mouth wide open. "Who won?"

"The baboon didn't stand a chance. I recalled the baboon to my lab and Mrs Sanders was yelling up at me in Swedish. I don't know Swedish, but I don't think the words weren't very ladylike."

A moment passed in silence between them before Art spoke again.

"Are you still having issues with the eagles?" Art enquired.

"Yes, fitting all the tech in is the problem."

"Why not make it bigger? I don't think anyone would object to a bigger Eagle."

"But that brings in a whole new set of issues, more power needed to fly, bigger motor, etc. I will get there, morning walk, some coffee, and an excellent breakfast, and inspiration will miraculously arrive," Tyson laughed.

"Well, we are so lucky to have you here, Tyson; all this is possible because of your excellent work. Well, I'll be off, have to keep moving before my body cools down... Not that it's warmed up yet," Art started laughing at his own humour. Tyson really liked Art, what he was doing here and how he has supported his work.

A sudden wave of guilt came across him as he thought about how he had been spying on him for the last 18 months for the CIA. He hasn't had much to report. His work keeps him busy, and he's not part of the Inner Circle, so his communications haven't had much to offer, apart from what's generally happening at the ARK.

****

Art continued on his morning stroll with Thor and Loki in tow. Finally, he heads to the bottom, to where a significant service road that can handle cars, trucks, and heavy movers. He marvels at the quality of the landscaping around. It looks like someone just carved a route through the jungle without disturbing anything, which is good, he thought, as that was part of his promise to the UN world heritage committee, that everything evolves with the natural surroundings. He turns and looks back at Mount ARK, 'My God,' he thinks; it really looks like a mountain or a massive hill.

Beep! Beep! An ARK lorry came driving up with Ab at the wheel.

"Morning, Father. Did you have a pleasant morning stroll?"

"Stroll! I'll have you know I pumped some hard steps down that mountain."

Ab looked at his father, pulling a 'who are you kidding face', "Really."

Art flexed a few muscles and did some stretching movements.

"Yes, I'm all stretched and ready to help the workers."

"Father, get in the car before you hurt yourself."

As they were about to take off, another lorry drove past and beeped, and the driver waved to Art and Ab. He has some new releases of robotic animals on the back ready for patrol, two small lynx cats, four eagles, and one nasty looking Baboon; Art thinks if they look like the real thing, I better stay away from that enclosure; once again, he wonders if that's the baboon that lost the fight to Mrs Sanders.

****

Ab drove them both to compound 4, where the new arrivals stay for a week while they have veterinary checks and get used to their new surroundings. As Ab drove to the gate, one of the wranglers held the gate open while they went through. Two trucks were waiting to be unloaded, a semi-trailer and a smaller truck. The smaller truck seemed to be shaking a lot.

Art and Ab got out of the lorry and walked over to the semi, backing up to the unloading ramp.

A very robust fellow with an Australian accent and wearing a slouch hat came around the back of the semi. "Hey you, little fella, think you can manage to pull the gate open," he said to Art.

Art runs to the gate, excited to help. "Yes, I'm sure I can manage a gate."

"And you, sonny, we don't have spectators here; this is a working area. Grab the door handle on your side and open it when I say. Oh, and try not to break a nail. Ab says nothing as he heads to the back of the semi.

Just then, one of the wranglers comes up beside the Australian.

"Boss, you shouldn't talk to them like that; don't you know who they are?"

"Don't care; if they're here, they have to work the same as the rest of us."

"But they're..."

The gruff Aussie cut the wrangler off mid-sentence. "Said, I don't care."

The semi backed up slowly. "Now! Open the doors." Ab and the Aussie pulled the doors open just in time as the semi backed up to the dock. Banging on the side of the truck, he tries to persuade the animals to come out, but no, they won't.

"Guess I'll have to go in and move their arses," the Aussie says to Ab. The Aussie climbs to the top of the semi; he pulls back a tarp near the front of the truck. Before he hopes inside, Ab calls out to him. "What's inside?"

The Aussie smiles and says, "Six elephants."

"Elephants! You can't go inside a confined space with wild elephants!" Ab said.

"That's what the loonies who run this joint pay me for; it's in my job description. Hope they have a good staff hospital plan." And with that, the Aussie drops inside.

"Yah, yah, come on, move your fat asses." Seconds later, inside, there was whistling and clapping as six elephants exited the truck, heading down the ramp into the enclosure. Three female African Bush elephants and 3 baby elephants. Straight away, they head to a man-made watering hole.

As the semi pulls away from the ramp, Ab sees the Aussie standing in the back of the truck, smiling. He jumps down as members of his team close the semi doors.

Ab and Art walk over; he warmly sticks out his hand to greet them.

"Ab, Art. What brings the big knobs down here today?"

"We just wanted to see the new arrivals and tell you in person what else we have purchased from other countries," Art said excitedly.

"Geez, it must be exciting to come all the way down here to tell me."

Art puffed out his chest and announced, "Baboons."

The look on the Chief wrangler's face dropped as if his worst fears had come to life. Dan Hooper was as rough and rugged as any outdoorsman. Been a country boy, hunter, and wildlife wrangler all his life. But apes, he can't stand.

Dan had a shocked look on his face. "Baboons! There is a reason God is making those things extinct. They're nothing but trouble and respect nothing or nobody. And you're bringing them here?"

"Yes, sixty of them and their King, so it seems. It was a package deal. I had to take the lot."

"I suppose we're building a giant cage to keep them contained?"

Art was confused now; he thought the news would please Dan. 'Maybe that's why the Kenyan wildlife park was so keen to get rid of them.' Art thought.

"No, but they have their own area," Art replied.

"Unless it's totally closed in, they will make the whole park their territory. Then, one morning, you'll wake up, and a damn baboon will be in bed beside you. They have no boundaries, Art. You'll have to talk it over with Dr. Sarah." Dan looked over at the gate and saw someone coming into the enclosure. "Speak of the devil, and she shall appear."

Doctor Sarah McTagash, the chief Veterinarian surgeon at the park, approached the group. "Morning, animal lovers and ape haters," she said with a huge smirk on her face.

"I see you've heard," Dan said.

"Yes, I got the email this morning and thought I should give you a heads up, but it seems like Art and Ab have beat me to it. I thought you might be a little... tense this morning if you had heard. So, I thought I'd come down for a little chat."

Dan put on an exasperated face. "He's bringing in 600 baboons, Sarah."

"No, only 60, well 61 with the King," Art confirmed.

"A King, for Christ's sake, haven't any of you ever watched Planet of the Apes?" Ab started laughing, but Dan didn't see the humour. "I think that movie was based on chimpanzees and gorillas, Dan," Ab said.

"Apes an Ape," Dan said.

Art didn't want Dan stressing over the baboons, "Dan, whatever you need to contain them, you'll get so long as Dr. Sarah approves it. But I have to ask Dan, why do you hate baboons so much?"

"Ten years ago, I tracked and captured animals in Angola for wildlife research. We had twenty of the little bastards trapped in a net, and they were putting up a hell of a ruckus. Some escaped as we were pulling them out from underneath the net. We were all covered, face masks, thick gloves, and heavy full-frontal aprons to stop them clawing us, but one got around behind me..." Dan stopped his story, but he had Art and Ab transfixed on an outcome.

"Oh my God, Dan, what happened???" Art said.

"He bit me on my arse... He bit me on my arse and laughed at me. So, I threw off my helmet and chased him one hundred meters into the woods. He ran back to his family. There were over a hundred of them!" Dan stopped again for a dramatical pause.

Ab couldn't stand it any longer.

"What were they doing, Dan???"

"They were all laughing at me."

CHAPTER 9

COMMITTED

The mini sand tornado spun with ferocity as it captured the empty fuel canisters and rags, spinning them to the top of the funnel and discarding them with little regard. The air was dry and hot; the horizon covered in a heat mirage effect all too familiar in deserts. Unfortunately, the early morning heat and dust storms didn't slow everyone down today.

Shindand base, the allied headquarters in southern Afghanistan, is electrified as usual this morning; before a mission. Everybody had a purpose, and if you didn't, stay out of the way.

The special briefing last night has Capt. Sipple's team going on point with two new members in his team. Serious discussions had delayed the briefing, as Cpt Mike Madden argued that heading in on point on the mission with two new members was risky and that his team should take the lead. Mike saw it as being responsible. Capt. Sipple took it as if he wanted to hog his squad's limelight; Sipple was an idiot. Still, General Thomas Blaine, Commander of the Australian forces in Afghanistan, ruled in Capt. Sipple's favour after accepting his reassurances that his team would function perfectly.

The briefing was always the height of professionalism, unless Capt. Sipple was involved. Sipple was always willing to throw in cowboy comments about how 'His boys' would ride in and save the day while other commanders were working out every corner they would need to turn and any resistance.

****

The airmen gave the signal. All clear for take-off as Captain madden watched from the edge of the platform. Wind blowing sand in his face as he watched the Alfa team leave. He checked his watch, 3am everything is on schedule. He turns and heads to the hangar to check his team is prepped and prepared for backup just in case anything goes wrong with the Alfa team.

"Ok, going over it again. The target is a small compound outside of Mirdawud. The area has four buildings on corners of a block with an open courtyard in the centre. The mission is a search and kill, with an open order to look for intel and possibly a prisoner. Intel from local and international agencies has six men from the resurgent Taliban breakaway group meeting to quickly plan attacks on soft targets. Intel suggests no military backup nearby, so the chance of detection or being overrun before evac is slim. The only significant variable is that the buildings were right beside a major highway, leading to quick reinforcements or local pumped-up troublemakers. So, a low-key predawn in and out is the best option to avoid these factors, but we know low-key is not Capt. Sipple's MO. So, we're on call, you've prepped and stay in this hangar until I advise otherwise. 2 Planks and I will be in the operations room watching everything go down. Copy."

"Copy," the team replied.

****

As Sipple's team landed and moved into formation for the one-kilometre hike to the compound.

Sipple's team moved through the outside East yard and into the central compound. Quickly two men moved into the shadows to watch the doorway to the first building and the other buildings for movement. The four other members moved into the first building; each building had two floors, with the top floor having a balcony. Capt. Sipple gave the hand signal for the soldiers to break into pairs and search each room. Less than a minute later, both teams met at the stairs, signalling that no one was found. Capt. Sipple gave the signal to move up the stairs and split again to search the top floors. Mike and Seb watched intently on the screens, which showed the helmet cams of each of the soldiers. They watched as the soldiers emerged, each team giving signals that the first building was clear and to head outside to regroup.

So far, so good, with the team not detected. Once again, the soldiers peeled off to watch the entrance of the next building and the compound. The team worked their way through the second building with the same result. Capt. Sipple let out a few choice words over the comms at his frustration.

Mike and Seb had a heightened sense of agitation. "Where's the weapons? NO bomb-making equipment, NO signs of anybody preparing for anything! Bad intel? Have we missed something?" 2 Planks asked.

The team moved into their positions and entered the third building. As two of the group split off to the left, Capt. Sipple and another turned right. Within seconds, things erupt on the screens back at the base as they watch both teams simultaneously come across sleeping men on the floors of the rooms. The soldiers on the left moved quickly, pouncing on the man, pinning his arms and gagging his mouth. Out of his reach was an AK47. He attempted to reach the weapon, but it was useless as the soldier pulled his arms behind his back and zip-tied them. Even with the gag, the tied man was still making a racket, "Bag him," one soldier commanded; the soldier quickly pulled out a black hood and placed it over the man's head. The commander of the second team suddenly heard silenced gunshots in the next room. One soldier pulled the hooded man to his feet.

Capt. Sipple didn't see the sleeping man on the floor when he entered, but he saw the AK47 leaning against the wall. As the other soldier checked the corners, Sipple moved into the room. Suddenly, muffled shuffles and voices are heard in the adjoining room; Capt. Sipple froze to see if it sounded like it was under control. The sounds could be heard in this room, but wouldn't be heard outside.

Sipple saw movement in the dark corner of the room; a man was sleeping in the dark corner under a dark grey blanket. The noises from the room next door were enough to stir the man from his sleep, and as a reflex action, he reached out for his AK47. Capt. Sipple's moved swiftly and jumped on top of the waking man to secure his arm from reaching the rifle. The man woke quickly with the force of someone jumping on him. Having his armed pinned, he immediately went into a survival mode 'fight or flight. 'Fight' was his answer. The man squirmed and bucked, trying to break free. Capt. Sipple used all his strength to hold the man in check; it was like riding a mechanical bull, but sober.

The captain's grip was loosened while the man was trying to buck free. He immediately signalled to the other teammate to end it; seconds later, two silenced shots rang out in the room as the man fell limp in Sipple's arms. Pushing the man off of him and getting back to his feet, Capt. Sipple grabbed the rifle, removed the clip, and emptied the chamber; he threw the gun onto the bed and moved outside.

The men dragged their prisoner outside and left him in the care of one sentry. He then turned and saw Capt. Sipple behind him.

"One down, no munitions," he informed the Capt.

"One down, same," Sipple replied. "One building left, at least four still missing, be on guard," he added.

The team entered the last building, heightened nerves and reflexes, as there was only one building left to search and still four men missing and bomb-making equipment and munitions to be found. The ground floor revealed nothing, and the team gathered ready at the base of the steps. Mike and Seb were on edge, too, knowing there was only one floor left to search.

The team stood at the doors of the last two rooms on the top floor. Capt. Sipple gave the order to enter. The teams entered with speed and purpose, guns up ready, safety's off, fingers on the triggers. As they entered, the pointsman moved into the centre of the rooms, sweeping the corners in front of them, the second man sweeping the corners behind.

"Clear, clear" were the calls from both rooms.

"Fuck!" screamed Capt. Sipple into his mic. "Fucking intel." He gathered his men at the top of the stairs and signalled to the compound.

Colonel Briggs sat quietly watching and listening in the communication's corner room; he moved to the mics and picked one up.

"Recheck each room, look for hidden rooms and hatches," he instructed.

"I know the fucking routine, Madden; I don't need you to fucking tell me my job," Capt. Sipple returned.

"This is Colonel Briggs... And keep comm chatter down," Briggs instructed.

"Yes, Sir, on to it," Capt. Sipple replied, muttering fuck fuck fuck under his voice.

The team went back and swept the last building they entered. Nothing! They next entered the building, where they shot the man and grabbed the prisoner. The upper level provided nothing, but the room with the prisoner did.

Upon checking, they found a hatch in the corner under a rug. 'A hatch that led underground, great,' Capt. Sipple thought. 'Advancing down ladders into a room, one at a time quietly, without getting shot, great fun, not,' he sighed.

The team gathered at the hatch; they knew the routine. One man lifted the catch, two men with night vision covered the hole, and one man covered the doorway. The men got in their positions; as Private Jack Newell bent over to open the hatch, gunfire erupts from below, smashing through the hatch and hitting Newell in the arm.Private Newell scrambled back and crashed against a wall. Two of the team returned fire through the hatch. The room was alive as the gunfire erupted and Sipple's men returned fire. Capt. Mike Madden also flew into action; he immediately got on the mic and ordered his men and the chopper pilots to prep to move.

"A bit early to jump yet, isn't it?" Colonel Briggs asked Mike.

"I don't believe so, Sir; they shot first, which means they knew our team was up there, which means they had time to call for more men," he told the Colonel.

"A good assumption, Mike. Sergeant, go prep the men for departure; Mike, you stay here for now and see how this unfolds."

"Yes, Sir," Seb replied and left the comm room to join his men.

After the men had returned fire into the hatch, Capt. Sipple grabbed a flash-bang grenade off his vest, pulled the release, and dropped it down the hole.

"Fire in the hole," Sipple yelled as he turned his back. Automatically, the men turned their backs and covered their ears. Then, WHOOM, a loud bang and a flash of blinding white light filled the room below. No sooner had the light receded, that Capt. Sipple advanced down the ladder sideways one-handed with his automatic rifle in the other hand, ready to shoot; when he was halfway down the ladder, he jumped off, landing on his feet in a shooting position. A quick appraisal of the room saw there was nobody else in the room except the man who fired through the hatch, and at the moment, he was lying dead on the floor, having coped three rounds to his chest with the return fire from Sipple's men.

"Clear," he called, and another of his team dropped through the hatch beside him. The room was about half the size of the space above; it was a guardroom for another room they imagined was on the other side of the heavy door, on one wall.

Wanting to quickly keep pressing the advantage, Capt. Sipple had to wait till Private Newell had his arm patched up so they could continue. Then, after Newell was bandaged, he aimed to guard the door as the other member took a position at the top of the hatch.

Capt. Sipple grabbed another flash-bang grenade off his vest and showed it to his Sergeant, who nodded that he knew what was going on. Unfortunately, a momentary lapse and a precautionary call came too late as the Sergeant opened the door enough to loft the grenade inside. A barrage of bullets hit the door, one nearly taking Sipple's nose off, leaving a nick off the top, a calling card to remind him how close he was. Capt. Sipple threw the grenade into the centre of the room and quickly retracted his arm before he got hit like Private Newell.

As the Sergeant was closing the door, something happened, a soldier's premonition maybe, but both men caught each other's eyes as they both remembered what they were chasing, bomb makers! He heard the door latch click as if in slow-motion, just before he heard the first explosion and felt the pressure from behind the door. The door then smashed into him and sent him flying across the room. Capt. Sipple, whose quick reflexes and the fact that the walls to the rooms were cut from rock, avoided most of the blast but was hit with flying shrapnel from munitions and exploding furniture. The team member at the top of the ladder was lucky to avoid injury as he had his back turned as the pressure of the explosions and flying debris flew up through the hatchway, pushing him to the ground, filling the room with dust and smoke.

****

"GO GO GO," Colonel Briggs said as he pushed Mike towards the doorway.

"DELTA TEAM EXTRACTION 1, this is Colonel Briggs; prepare for extraction of the Alfa team. Capt. Madden is on his way to the tarmac."

Within a minute, Mike was with his team and on his way to extract Capt. Sipple. Little did he know the explosion didn't go unnoticed.

****

Capt. Sipple's ears were ringing as one of his team was helping him to his feet. Both men went to the pile of debris, frantically clearing it to find their comrade. As they cleared the rubbish, they came across a bloodied arm sticking out from under the door that blew off its hinges. Hoping to find his Sergeant attached to this arm, the two men lifted the heavy door to see the Sergeant coughing and spluttering from the dust and debris.

"You ok," Sipple asked his Sergeant.

"Aagh shit! I can't feel my arm, and my shoulder doesn't want to move either. Capt. Sipple checked the arm and shoulder and, finding it wasn't life-threatening, helped the man to his feet.

"We need to extract fast; that may have attracted some attention."

"Ya think!" his teammate replied.

"Are you ok to go?" Sipple asked his Sergeant.

"Yeah, let's get out of here. Get me to the ladder."

"My comms down; what's happening with extraction?" Sipple asked.

"Extraction team and ride are on their way." The team member offered the captain his comm set.

As the men struggled up the ladder, things were hotting up outside. An old four-wheel-drive was being watched by the colonel and the compound lookout. It stopped up the road about 300 metres with its lights on after driving past, when the explosion went off below. Three men were seen exiting the vehicle and retrieving what looked like rifles from the back of the 4x4. They appraised Mike of the situation from the comm centre. The men re-entered their truck and slowly drove back down the road towards the compound.

"Incoming hostiles, one vehicle, possibly three shooters," the lookout informed the team. The men quickly scurried outside and set up positions.

"Let them come into the compound and check it out; take them out on my call," instructed Capt. Sipple. "Extraction team, how long to extraction?" Capt. Sipple asked.

"Five minutes, Alpha team," was the reply. "Roger," Sipple replied.

The car with the inquisitive armed men pulled up; they turned off the engine and exited the vehicle, making their way to the lights at the front of the truck. Slowly they walked towards the building, guns raised, looking around for signs of life and the cause of the explosion. One man was three paces in front of the others and was about to enter the compound.

The SAS lookout had taken his eyes off the prisoner, who was listening intently to the chatter on his captor's comm; he could speak enough English to understand someone was coming and 'that' someone was armed and weren't friends of these soldiers. At that moment, the prisoner jumped to his feet and ran, yelling in Arabic. He ran past his captor and was only barely able to make out anything in the dark with this hood over his head, crashed and fell over some metal garbage bins, making a considerable racket and alerting the men coming into the compound.

The noise scared the incoming men half to death, making them open fire with bursts from AK47s and SSKs. The first man unleashed a blast towards the noise of crashing bins and muffled yelling. Cutting the prisoner in half, killing him instantly. Simultaneously, the other men opened fire, spraying bullets everywhere. The SAS guarding the prisoner fired and took the closest man out in the commotion. The other two intruders, one peeled to his left and hid around the corner of the nearest building, and one made a beeline for the vehicle for cover. As he reached the car, thinking he had made it, a burst of fire rang out and hit him between the shoulder blades, killing him instantly. Another of the SAS was moving to a better position when the third intruder turned the corner, firing in his general direction. He was caught in the open with an advancing enemy, with nothing to do but shoot back now. As he beaded in on the enemy and was about to fire, a round caught him in his shoulder, throwing him back. His reflexes made him pull the trigger in response, hitting the enemy with bullets to his leg and hip. Before the man could even fall to the ground, Capt. Sipple entered the compound's centre and started advancing toward him and the fallen team member.

As the man looked up, three rounds caught him around his heart, freezing his mind for just a moment to play the last thought that he would ever have. 'Why did we stop?'

"ALPHA, three vehicles heading in, southbound, approx. Time, 4 minutes." Came over the comms. Just as Capt. Sipple received the message, he could hear the incoming extraction choppers; 'this is going to get very ugly shortly,' he thought.

"Alpha extraction, Delta team, high probability of hot LZ, suggest north-side extraction," Capt. Sipple commanded.

"Copy," Mike responded. Capt. Sipple instructed the injured men to make their way to the north-side of the compound. After heavy arguments that they could still fight, they did as commanded.

"Vehicles have slowed their approach, assume they are working out how best to attack, expect them to flank," Col Briggs informed.

"Copy," Sipple replied.

Capt. Sipple could see movement out of the corner of his eyes; Madden's team was here. He felt a hand on his back, "Captain, your rides here. Take your men and extract; we'll cover your exit," Capt. Madden informed him.

"Roger," and he spun around and signalled his other two men to get on the chopper.

Delta was briefed on the chopper, on what Mike wanted from them, especially since the information came through of the three vehicles coming in. As the helicopter landed, the team hit the ground running. Quassy was heading to a southern building on the second-floor balcony with his SR98. 2 Planks and Steel hit the entranceways into the compound with anti-personnel mines and tripwire flash-bangs. The object was not to stand and fight; it was to delay, so the teams could extract safely. Smith was helping the injured Alpha team members into the chopper.

As Capt. Sipple made it to the chopper with the last of his men; Smith gave him a nod and left to join his team.

****

Smith ran to Sherlock, placed his hand on Sherlock's shoulder, and gave him a nod sideways to say, 'Time to go.' Sherlock twirled his hand in the air to signal back to the chopper. 2 Planks, Steel, and Smith spun and headed towards the helicopter. Sherlock knew Quassy couldn't see him from his perch, so he ran up the steps to get him out.

Quassy watched the three vehicles intently through his scope; they had their windows down and were shouting instructions to each other. 'Buy some comms, you cheap bastards,' Quassy said to himself.

He heard someone coming up the stairs, and seconds later, Sherlock appeared around the corner.

"Time to go, buddy," Sherlock informed him.

Quassy replied, "I'm not going these guys are just splitting up now and will hit from all sides. I can slow them down, take out two of the drivers for the team to get away safely."

"I'm not leaving you here?" Sherlock stated.

"I'm not staying either; meet me two clicks North of here for pickup. You know it will be easier for one person to sneak away in the commotion, now GO, before it's too late."

"Two clicks, we'll be there," Sherlock said; it was true, and he knew Quassy wouldn't have suggested it if he didn't think it would work. So, Sherlock patted Quassy on the shoulder twice and left.

As he made it back to the chopper, the rest of the team was already inside. "I'm staying with Quassy to slow them down; move two clicks North and pick us up there, GO!" After his instructions, Sherlock turned and headed back to Quassy when he heard a shot ring out. Quassy, they're heading in, he thought. As he sprinted back, he heard the chopper behind him take off.

Quassy saw the three vehicles move apart and start to head in. He gauged their speed, and he had to get two shots off at the three drivers, 'no time for three shots,' he thought. He had a look without the scope and saw which were travelling fastest, centre and East, so exit to the southeast. He looked back through his scope and prepared his first shot, shot and left, shot and left, he kept repeating. If he timed his shot right, he wouldn't have to move his rifle much for the second shot.

"Come on, come on," Quassy fired his first shot; he hit the driver centre mass and adjusted to the left. As the second driver came silhouetted by the morning sun rising from the East, he fired his second shot, hit! He immediately swung to the right to check the third vehicle, but it was about to go behind the highway side building. As he was about to turn back to the centre vehicle, he heard an explosion. It sounded like a rifle grenade, and before he could think who it was? A familiar burst of gunfire from a familiar weapon, the Austeyr F90G. Sherlock, he didn't leave!

Job at hand, Quassy swung back to the centre vehicle; three men exited the car and headed towards the back for cover. Quassy put two rounds in the back of one man and one leg shot in a second; he fired a few shots into the car to pin the remaining man.

As Quassy swung to the car on the left, he heard a gun battle erupt to his right, another rifle grenade, and half a clip from a semi-auto; he's trying to pin them. As the left vehicle came into view, he could see three men behind the car and one slumped over the steering wheel. One man poked his head from around the corner of the back of the vehicle, "Bad move, Chucky," Quassy said as he fired and took the man down with a headshot. This fired up the other men; a barrage of random shooting went all over the place.

'They obviously haven't spotted me yet,' Quassy thought. The thought was short-lived as the men from the centre car knew precisely where he was, and a barrage of fire riddled the concrete wall behind him and showered him with cement pieces. A poorly thrown grenade failed to find its mark and exploded on the ground beside the building. 'Return fire, smoke grenade, get the fuck out,' good plan, Quassy thought. As the men in the centre car stopped to reload, Quassy emptied his rifle into the back of the car and threw a smoke grenade to cover his retreat.

Sherlock heard and saw the smoke grenade go off and knew Quassy would be falling back, so he did the same by emptying his magazine into the car, throwing the smoke grenade, and getting the hell out of here. 'We need a head start and a clear run for a hundred metres to dump these bastards,' he thought. Sherlock turned and ran to the centre compound and found Quassy guarding his retreat.

"Had enough fun?" Sherlock asks; Quassy laughs, "Yeah, if being showered by concrete while bullets rain around you is fun, I needed to stretch my legs, anyway."

"Two clicks, then home, let's go," Sherlock says on the run.

The plan was, or what they hoped would happen, to hold them back, then retreat. Then, the enemy would converge on them from the compound's South, East, and West entrances. That's why the entrances were rigged by 2 Planks and Steel. That was in a perfect world; unfortunately, this was Afghanistan. So, the West and East men decided to go around the outside and come in from the North entrance, which was precisely where Sherlock and Quassy planned to exit.

As the men from the Northern car entered the compound, they triggered the traps set by the Delta team. An explosion with an ear-piercing ring, the white phosphorus glow of the flash-bang, and the skin-piercing shrapnel of the personnel mine caused screams of pain and confusion, which Sherlock and Quassy didn't know gave them a twenty-metre head start as they sprinted out of the compound. Unbeknown to them, the enemy was surrounding them from both sides.

Sherlock could see a rise in the ground ahead, a ridge maybe that would give them cover from the men chasing them. He estimated they were twenty metres out of the compound and a hundred metres from the bank. 'A piece of piss to a trained digger,' he thought. That's when he saw them; they both saw them.

The pace picked up, as they didn't know they had been spotted yet. 90, 80 metres, they heard the yells, followed by the gunfire. Quassy turned long enough to see three on his side and two on Sherlocks. The gunfire was wild at first, spraying all around them, then they started to take their time and zero in. 60 metres! The shots began zipping past their ears like wild, angry bees. The sand was kicked up around their feet. No hits so far,30 metres!

That's when it happened. Like something out of a mummy movie, the sand ahead rose, and creatures not born of this Earth, 'Emerged.'

The sound of return fire was a breath of fresh air. As in front of them, three soldiers exited the sand and started firing back at the Afghani rebels. The rebels in the open were only interested in shooting the retreating soldiers. Still, the precision shooting and rifle grenades cut the trapped rebels down swiftly as Sherlock and Quassy jumped over the sand ridge, hitting the ground hard. The sand mummies started shaking off the sand after they were sure no one else was following. Puffing; Quassy got up and put an arm out to Steel; she grabbed his arm back as a sign of thank you. Sherlock brushed the sand from himself and stared at 2 Planks.

"30 metres! you waited till 30 metres to open fire!" Sherlock firmly stated.

2 Planks put his hand on Sherlock's shoulder.

"Sorry Boss, we were taking bets; we wanted to see if you could make the 100 metres... You failed," 2 Planks replied, laughing. The group was laughing. Sherlock looked back at the compound and ahead in the direction of the extraction chopper.

"About one thousand, eight hundred and eighty metres to go, a good morning for a jog." Sherlock turned and started jogging North, trailed by his team.

CHAPTER 10

ART & THE SPY

As Art Damani made his way through the levels of the ARK this morning, he was decidedly more chipper than usual, if that was even possible.

"Good morning, Mr Rumbard, how's is your swing improving? Have you got rid of that slice yet? Nancy, good morning, something smells delicious. Mrs Dunich, is Mr Snuffles, recovering from his operation."

He made his way up to level three because he had a purpose this morning. He had a request to make of Tyson Lumming, the ARK's Bioengineer. Art knocks on the door, showing respect for Tyson's work space.

"Good morning, Tyson. May I have a word if you're not too busy?" Art said from the doorway.

"Never too busy to talk to the person who signs my pay cheque. Please come in, Mr. Damani." Art enters the room; he loves visiting Tyson. He has the most exciting job and makes Art the most exciting toys in his spare time.

"I've told you to call me Art, haven't I?"

"Yes, but old habits are hard to shake, but I'll try to remember."

"So, how is the eagle problem going?"

"Glad you asked Mr. Dar... Art," Tyson recanted. "I solved the issue of weight and getting all the tech in. I scanned the AZTECK inventory and found a product I could adapt; I came up with another idea but didn't know if it was possible till here." Tyson handed him a thin plastic film.

"This is from our phone technology!" Art stated.

"And here," Tyson handed him another piece.

"A feather?"

"Yep, a feather for the eagle made from the phone cover plastic with solar panel tech embedded in it. Now the wings of the eagles are solar panels, getting rid of the solar strip making the bird lighter, and as a bonus, we can do this to all the bird range, making them all lighter and capable of collecting 65% more power!" Tyson stood there proud of this achievement; it was a significant breakthrough for all the animals.

"AB-SO-LUT-ELY BRILLIANT! You are a genuine genius, Tyson Lumming; congratulations," Art started shaking Tyson's hand and patting him on the back.

"Now I have some wonderful and important news. Now, this is a high-security issue, and technically, you shouldn't be told; it's only for the Inner Circle, but it affects you as well, so I will inform you too. Keep this to yourself. In about 6 months we are getting a special visitor, he is coming to try out our hunting safari and will be given a tour of the ARK, so, if possible, I would like to know if all my toys would be ready by then."

"Six months? Well, I guess it's possible. I would have to share out some of the work in the division, but yes, it is possible."

"That would be fabulous, Tyson," Art said joyfully.

"Well, don't keep me in suspense; who is coming???" Tyson asked excitedly.

"The President of the United States," Tyson's face went blank.

"What?"

"That's right, I invited the President of the United States, and he has accepted. We are just not sure of the date yet," Art said.

"Wow! Like Wow! And he's coming to look at our work; that's exciting" Tyson was still trying to grasp this development and keep up with the conversation.

"So, you would like your toys finished within 6 months? Yeah, I suppose it's possible; we will get it done if the other sections do some of the easier constructions. Here, let me show you how far we've got with this one." Tyson turned around and headed to the back of the room, where there was a workbench and a portable table. Tyson moved to the side of the workbench and grabbed a large white tarp. "Get a load of this!" Tyson pulled the tarp, which fell to the ground.

"Oh my God! Whoa!" was Art's immediate reaction.

Standing in front of him was a 7-foot reconstruction of a 50's version of Frankenstein's Monster; this life-sized robot was even scarier than the movie creations, as he hadn't had his plastic skin put on yet, showing all his inner workings.

"What do you think, Art?"

Art immediately recognised the use of his Christian name and hoped it was the start of a closer relationship with Tyson.

"It's fantastic! Very scary without the skin though, not suitable for junior staff or roaming the food mall" they both laughed, Tyson more so. Because he plans to send Franky down to the food mall to see Mrs. Sanders when she starts early one morning.

"I can't show you any movements as Franky isn't powered up at the moment, but check this out; the reason we built Franky was to perfect size to weight ratios for making large robotic animals and perfecting their walk; well, we did it. Now, look at his inner skin. That's the new Kevlar weaving I have been working on. It's not totally bullet-proofed, but it performs 40% better than standard bulletproof vests. It's close to marketing soon after we run more tests."

Art stood there with his mouth open, genuinely amazed. "There's another Billion-dollar market worldwide," Art said.

"Franky goes down to coverings tomorrow, then diagnostics to have his programs installed and tested, so say a week for his maiden adventure."

"That's great; we will have some fun things to show the President when he comes," Art said joyfully.

"Just don't get them shot! I've heard those Secret Service guys are trigger happy," Tyson warned.

"I will look after our toys."

By toys, Art meant robotic monsters. Art loves the old Hollywood horror movies and has requested Tyson build five of them. Frankenstein's Monster, The Mummy, the Creature from the Black Lagoon, the Werewolf, and Christopher Lee's version of Dracula. Art patted Tyson on the back.

"Brilliant, my boy." Tyson had another bout of guilt. He regretted what he was doing to this man who was doing so much for him.

"Just doing my best, Art, just doing my best."

"You're doing fabulous; this reserve wouldn't be open if it wasn't for you, Tyson."

Another guilt punch to the gut. Tyson was glad he didn't have anything real to report, as he had no access to anything apart from his work and AZTECK standard industry items. Art turned in the doorway as he was leaving.

"I bet this will be a trip the President will never forget!"

CHAPTER 11

THE OVAL OFFICE & THE SATELLITE PHOTOS

Even though the bullet-proof glass windows didn't open, the room felt airy and well-lit. The new light beige rug and mahogany table matched with eloquent splendour with past Presidents' ancestral portraits. The room seemed deftly quiet, although you could hear the buzz of the beehive outside.

The Oval Office of the President of the United States was as majestic as it has ever been. Still, all this was missed by Damien Spelling, the head of the CIA. Spelling was sitting anxiously in the White House Oval Office, waiting to meet with the President and chief of Staff. Spelling sat there and watched, but tried not to listen to the President while he was on the phone. He was still running through his head about how he was going to explain the information he has on AZTECK and Mr. Damani. Spelling was nervously shuffling papers back and forth in his folder, which the President noticed while on his call.

'That's not like him,' the President thought, 'he is probably the coldest person I have ever met; he wouldn't have to think twice about bombing a childcare centre just to kill one terrorist.' Spelling was one of the old administration's staff inherited when he won office. Just then, the side door opened, and the Chief of Staff came in, nodded to the President, and went and sat down across from Spelling. They exchanged somewhat cordial greetings, neither liking the other, but they had to work together. The President said his goodbyes, hung up the phone, and went and sat next to the Chief of Staff.

"Good morning, Damien; how are you today?"

"Fine, Mr. President, doing well."

"Great to hear; I've been looking forward to seeing what you have for me today" the President gestured towards the folder, which had been shuffled more times than a pack of cards in a 24-hour Gin Rummy game.

"Well, first off, Mr. President, we haven't found anything in his business dealings or personal life of Mr. Damani and AZTECK that we didn't already know. Adopted his son from Western Africa. Parents were killed in North Korea on a trade delegation. Made his money in the porn industry and then made his millions on mobile phone tech. There was an FBI file on him and a link to the group ANONYMOUS."

"What came of that?" The President asked.

"Nothing, the lead went nowhere, and some files of evidence went missing," the CIA chief informed.

"As for Mr. Damani in Africa, we believe he only had one face-to-face meeting with the Presidents of Somalia and Ethiopia, but I am told President Abdi reports to Mr. Damani regularly now."

"Reports to Mr. Damani? A President, what on earth does Damani have over Abdi?"

"There was an incident with his daughter and some drug dealers at the local school. He then started enforcing his new drug laws. Since then, there have been ten state executions and over 100 drug dealers imprisoned," Spelling informed them.

"There is now a joint Somali and Ethiopian police force patrolling the boundaries of the reserve and AZTECK farms in surrounding towns. I reissued a spy satellite to go over the reserve to see what was happening! This is the image," Spelling hands a couple of photos to the President.

"My God, he's done all that in 18 months?" The President looks at the before and after photos, going back and forth, trying to pick the differences.

"And this mountain? It's not in the before picture?"

"That's his headquarters, Mr. President," Spelling informs the President.

"He built a mountain! And that's his headquarters? How much money does this guy have?" the President asked rhetorically.

"Well, actually, it's growing, Mr. President; his stocks have been going up since he announced the peace deal and the ARK; it has hit a note with the public, especially the younger generation," the Chief of Staff informed them.

"That's why I think this government needs to be a part of things there. On another note, word has come back from Mr. Damani that President Abdi isn't happy with all the air support with my movements. He has also asked that support aircraft stay in international airspace. He has agreed to a low-key approach and approved all special forces teams to accompany me. I will travel in our C-141 Starlifter cargo plane with the Presidential car; I know, I know, don't start at me. It's his country, and he calls the shots." Director Spelling sat there staring at the president in disbelief.

"Ok, what else do you have, Damien?" The Director of the CIA hesitated to give the President the other photos. The President noticed the change in the Director and his hesitation.

"What is it? What else do you have?" The President inquired.

"Well, the second time around for the satellite, this came up when we enlarged the photo," Spelling handed the President the photo.

"Oh my God!" The President started laughing. The picture was of the helicopter landing pad on top of ARK mountain. Art Damani was flipping a bird up into the sky in the photo. Somehow, he knew the satellite was spying on the ARK.

"How did he know?" the President asked.

"We are not sure, Mr. President; we believe somehow, he is tracking our satellites!"

"This was the next pass." The Director reluctantly handed over a photo. Here again was an enlargement of a picture of the same landing pad, but this time Mr. Damani was alone on the helicopter pad; he seemed to be 'Mooning' the spying satellite.

"Oh, my goodness, he definitely doesn't like you spying on him, does he?" The President offered.

"It gets worse!" He handed the President another photo.

"What the..." the President was stunned "... Is that?"

"Yep, almost all of his staff." In the photo were over 100 people mooning the American satellite. As the President hands the image to the Chief of Staff, he can't restrain himself from letting out a little laugh.

"Well, he certainly has staff loyalty," the Chief of Staff offered jokingly.

"You said almost all his staff, Damien. Do you know how many staff are in the mountain?"

"He has 136. Seventy-four working at any one time during their shifts... roughly... I have a man inside. He informed us that there was a $5000 bonus for all non-essential staff who took part in the photo."

"So, does your man know how they know about the satellite?"

"Ahh, no, he is not high up enough in the food chain. They have a section that they call the HUB, which runs everything and where the brain trust and top people meet Mr. President."

"It gets worse, Mr. President. Knowing that he knows we are spying on him, I repositioned a different satellite to go in at a different time, different latitude... This is what we got." Spelling handed over another photo to the President.

"What???" The President leaned over and snatched a picture out of the Chief of Staff's hands; he kept looking from one photo to the next.

"How is this possible?" The President was staring at a photo of the ARK, well he would have been, but this time, it was gone, not just pixelated to cover the area from view, but actually gone, as if it wasn't there... ever. Instead, there was just a landscaped area of the natural mountainside.

"How?" Was the only word the President could get out.

"We don't know at this stage. We are looking at it from all angles. Maybe he hacked our satellite. We just don't know! What makes it worse is I asked our defence team if we could target the area now with a missile. They said no! to the computer, this image is real!"

"Oh my God," the Chief of Staff murmured in a small voice, looking at the photos again. "And this is the place you want to go hunting???" He challenged the President.

"Oh, I'm going; we need to be friends with this man and his tech, not his enemy."

"Linwood, send the date through and start communication with Mr. Damani, and send through all our requests that will need to happen for me to go. Also, let me know what he says to do about President Abdi. It's still his country, and we are just visitors."

"Yes, Mr. President, at once," the Chief of Staff assured the President.

"Damien, keep surveillance on Somalia and its borders, but back off on spying on his mountain; it obviously pisses him off. Linwood will keep you informed of the dates and proceedings for the trip. Seems like I'm going hunting! Do you hunt Damien?"

"Yes, Mr. President, I do; I have my prey in mind." With that, the head of the CIA's face turned back into the sneaky evil look the President usually has to deal with.

"Don't piss him off before we get there, Director. We don't want to turn this trip into a shit show."

"Yes, Mr. President. If you'll excuse me, I have work to prepare."

"Yes, certainly, Damien. Thanks for your work so far, and let me know if your team comes up with any more breakthroughs." The Director turned and headed out of the Oval Office with a nod.

****

Spelling headed towards the elevators; he had given the President all the photos of the satellite surveillance... All but one. The last one. The Director had issued orders to do one more pass to confirm the results of the missing mountain. What he got was not expected and not appreciated by Spelling. In this photo, Mr. Damani was standing in a field, the same landscape as the last photo with the missing mountain. Flowing grass and wildflowers on the hillside, and he was holding a sign up. Spelling asked to have the image enlarged. On the sign, it read...

"Don't forget Kylie's birthday... again," and in smaller print was *"she wants a ring"*.

"Who is Kylie?" The young technician asked the Director.

"No idea, young lady, no idea. Print off one copy of the photo and delete the image."

"Yes, Sir," the technician responded.

Damien Spelling knew exactly who Kylie was! Kylie was his wife, and yes, it was her birthday, and yes, again, he had forgotten her birthday last year. Is this prick spying on me? The irony was lost on Spelling, but the fury wasn't, 'I will get you, you little prick, I will tear your fucking mountain down around your ears,' he thought. He took the afternoon off to get his wife a birthday present. He almost forgot again. This thought infuriated him even more, so he headed home to speak to his daughter to see if her mum was really after a ring... She was!

HELL HAS NO FURY LIKE A CIA DIRECTOR SCORNED!

CHAPTER 12

THE TERRORISTS

The howling wind blew up the sand in a tempest as the caravan of eight camels fought against the storm; the herder was trying to make it to the depot before the storm got any worse. The new hastily built buildings stood in direct contrast to the others in town, which looked desperately in need of care; their bright new colours reflected the region's traditional colours. Hotel, stock/department store, and even several cafes and eateries lined the main street of Marsabit, in the Northern part of Kenya. It has become a thriving town due to increased work at the AZTECK ARK or the surrounding factories and farms started up by AZTECK. Business was good, and life was improving for now. Even though the ARK was in neighbouring Somalia, other African countries in the vicinity also saw the benefit of increased trade as more transient workers were making their way to Somalia.

Three men of Asian appearance sat at a corner table at a popular eatery/coffee shop. These three weren't here for the food or coffee. Instead, they sat there watching all the exits and people in the room. After five minutes, when they seemed happy with their surroundings, one man spoke.

"We have been commissioned. We have five months and two weeks to prepare. We are targeting someone who will be at one of the reserves at the ARK. You need to recruit as soon as possible to get them into the country without notice, and they will need to find work here to stay under the radar. All munitions will have to be acquired locally to avoid detection, and you will need to find your own 2nds as we will split up on this mission. The intel, contacts, and plan will be sent to you through the normal channels. Only yourself and your 2nds are to know the target and plan."

"Who is the target?" one man asked in a Korean accent while his eyes surveyed the room and its people.

"We will get five times our normal fee because we may have to disappear permanently afterward."

"Who is the target???" the third man impatiently asked. Then, finally, the first man pushed a folder across the table with one piece of paper inside. The man's shock was instantaneous; it was the seal of the President of the United States.

"What the fuck!" said the second man, totally surprised. The third man spoke more calmly.

"This is too big; why would we need the kind of heat this will bring?"

"I was chosen, and I choose you two. We have worked together many times, and I trust we will do our jobs accordingly, so the plan doesn't fail," the 1st man assured him.

"Look over your part of the plan. We will get together in one week to discuss what we each need," The first man said. He looked over and saw that the third man still had reservations.

"Look over it tonight and let me know in 24 hours if you're in," said the 1st man,

"It seems a big ask. Everyone will look for us," the third man reiterated.

"Yes, I understand the risk for you," the first man stated.

"Ok, settled. One more round of drinks to celebrate our fortune and piece of history. I will pay since I dragged you both into this," the first man said cheerfully.

"And so you should," the second man spoke up. The first man rises to go to the counter and order the celebratory drinks. As he does, the third man rises and heads to the bathroom. Minutes later, the men downed their drinks after making a wish for good fortune. Anyone seeing these men in conversation would have noticed little, and only one thing would have stood out to a professional. They never spoke each other's names in public, no Christian name, no surname, or even nickname; that was their training, and their training was everything.

As the men exited the eatery, the 1st man, who was calling the shots, said to the second.

"Do you have time for me to show you something for the mission?"

"Yes, of course," the second man replied.

"Read the mission and get back to me soon with your decision," the first man said to the third; the man nodded and left to head to his apartment.

After walking 100 metres down the road, the second man turns to his leader and asks, "What is it you wanted to show me?"

"This," the first man pulls a disposable rubber glove out of his pocket with a small vial wrapped inside; the container was empty; he threw it in the bin.

"There are no maybes or out of this mission." The second looks at his leader and nods in understanding.

The first man hands a key to the second, "Go clean his room tonight."

That evening in the emergency ward of the Marsabit General hospital, a local training intern, at the start of his night shift, declares a John Doe dead at 6.32pm due to a heart attack.

CHAPTER 13

NEW MAN & INVITATION

The morning was a clang and clatter of pots and pans. The air was filled with the delicious aroma of cooked bacon, eggs, coffee, and waffles. The men raced around like busy worker ants getting their choirs done, but the atmosphere was light with the chitter-chatter of social networking continuing as they scampered around. Tuesday morning, breakfast at the base was always the best. Apart from the usual army grits, the head of the kitchen, Sergeant Wilbur Stoken, would come in early and pitch in with the cooking, making an extra treat to add to the menu and the delight of the troops.

Stoken, commonly known as "GRUBS," was known for dishing out his meals on a Tuesday and thanking everyone for their service. Grubs was a unique person whose appearance gained him his nickname. One time, not bothering to shave after doing an all-nighter for an officer's function, he cooked all morning for the enlisted men and women for their Tuesday treat. Not bothering or even having time to change, he served out pancakes to the waiting hordes with a face full of stubble, thanking them for their service. There were no complaints about his cooking, though, regularly surprising the servicemen and women with Eggs benedict, Flap Jacks, and today's special waffles.

****

Seb was just dressing after having showered. He went for a morning run with Deen, Smith, and Katelyn. Mike declined the offer to join them, as he had been requested to attend a meeting with his Commander, Colonel Jim Briggs, at 0700. Seb told the others he would meet them at the mess and save him a seat.

Tuesday was their morning to gather as a team with Mike. Usually, eating together was typically impossible because of their particular skill sets. Deen Wellings, the team's sniper, code-named Quassy after the hunchback of Notre Dame. He was up early twice a week to fly out with other snipers in the corps to a particular spot someone found that offered various challenges in distances, wind directions, and temperatures that affect their shots. Teaming up together to discuss different scenarios and results.

Katelyn (Steel) and Zikmund (Smith), both trained medics, donate two half days (when available) to the base hospital emergency ward for added skills training and to "Give Back" to their comrades. Many resident doctors commented on their skill levels and told them there was a job waiting for them if they ever wanted to give up the field. Captain Mike Madden turned up at his commander's office 10 minutes early and knocked on the door.

"Come in," the voice of the commander rang out. Mike entered the office.

"Mike come in, please sit." Mike was known as the team physic, a great reader of people, with an eye for details which got him the code name, Sherlock.

"Can I get you a coffee?"

"No, thank you, Sir," Mike replied. The hackles stood up on Mike's neck, 'offering a coffee,' Mike thought, 'this can't be good.'

"Well, how have things been going? It's been a while since the incident of the extra patrol looking for you. We got no results from our false missions to check for leaks, and do you feel we have done enough to combat it?"

"Yes, there have been no unscheduled patrols, but we have also been doing extra training and preparations for this, just in case it happens again. As much as one can prepare for that."

"Yes, I am sure you have been. I have seen your changes and, like you have said, as much as you can, especially with the limited tech you use," the Colonel offered.

"We use what we know and have," Mike said.

"That's why I appropriated more funds for the team and have ordered new upgrades and equipment, also, the latest tech that should help you work from a safer distance than what you are working now."

"That is great that you are thinking of the team's wellbeing, but we are quite safe and trained for what we do now. Anyway, with all this new tech, we would have to retrain the team and field test it before we could safely deploy." Mike informed the Colonel.

"Glad you brought that up, Mike; I have the answer to that, too."

Mike felt his stomach sink. So, this is what this is all about. The Colonel grabbed a folder on the side of his desk and placed it in the middle. Mike knew from the folder it was a personnel file.

"No thanks, Colonel, I have enough members in my team as it is," Mike stated.

"Mike, he is just what you need; he is a tech genius extremely high IQ."

"Colonel, we are Special Forces; we have no room for an egghead on the team; he would be a liability to the mission and all of us."

"He has passed all the training to qualify for the specials. He has a high rating in rifles to qualify for a gunner, specialises in communications. Also, it has come from up above, so we both have no choice but to accept."

"Oh, just great," Mike moaned. He leaned over and grabbed the file off the Colonel's desk and opened it.

"Oh, hell no, how old is he, 16???" Mike was wrecked.

"He's 24."

"Colonel, he doesn't look like he has started shaving yet."

"Then issue him a fake beard; what part of IT CAME FROM HIGHER UP, don't you get Mike?"

Mike sighed.

"When does he get here?" Mike asked.

"You won't get him for two weeks until he gets back," The Colonel's voice trailed down when he said 'gets back'; Mike didn't miss that.

"Gets back from where?" Mike questioned the Colonel.

"They requested him to take psych leave for a month," the Colonel reluctantly offered.

"Psych, leave! You're kidding me; you want me to take on someone with mental issues? Is this some kind of joke, Colonel? You know I wouldn't jeopardise the team like that" Mike let out another enormous sigh.

"What do you mean 'requested' to take? They don't usually request; you get sent on psych leave," Mike enquired.

"Well, technically, they couldn't prove he did anything wrong. They believe it was him but couldn't prove anything, so they requested leave from him," the Colonel said.

"Did What?? what was he supposed to have done?"

"He... blew up a toilet," the Colonel added.

"A toilet???" Mike said, confused.

"Yes... While a mess Sergeant was sitting on it," Mike laughed for the first time.

The Colonel added, "The story goes, a mess Sergeant made cracks about how young he looked. Joked about giving him a junior size meal and embarrassed him in front of his peers. He was supposed to have been heard threatening the Sergeant. Two days later, the toilet exploded with the Sergeant on it."

The Colonel opened the report and read, "Multiple lacerations to the testicles and porcelain shrapnel to the buttocks." The Colonel put down the file.

"Why didn't they charge him?" Mike asked.

"Because they couldn't prove it was him, the device was made from household items easily found on the base; the MPs couldn't trace anything back to him."

"So, how did he get fingered for it?" Mike asked.

"Seems like it happened on another base that the lad was based at. He was brought in for questioning and psych eval and asked to go on leave because of the lack of empathy for a fellow comrade. Did I mention he is an overachiever with explosives training?" the Colonel added.

Mike grabbed the file off the desk. "We'll see if he pans out," Mike informed the Colonel.

"He will be back in time."

"Back in time for what?" The hairs on the back of Mike's neck raised again; this morning's surprises weren't over yet.

"We have a cakewalk for you and your team," the Colonel said.

"There's no such thing," Mike added.

"You and the team are headed to Africa on a special assignment; you are going on a PR and training trip to the AZTECK ARK as ambassadors for Australia."

"Oh, this day just keeps on giving," Mike said, disgruntled.

"It came from the top, and I have been told they requested your team personally."

"How is that possible? No one is supposed to know who we are?" Mike said, alarmed.

"Yes, I was thinking the same thing but haven't been able to find anything out; maybe you can ask him when you get there."

"Ask who?"

"Mr. Damani, he was the one who asked for you." Both men fell silent.

The Colonel handed Mike another folder. "Australia is looking at a major trade deal with AZTECK, and your team is going there to test some of the gear and help prepare the joint Somalia/Ethiopian forces to protect the ARK."

"Colonel, you want us to go out on a PR mission with everything that's going on?"

"I agree, but it's out of our hands. As a sweetener for your team, it will accrue all the points required for your next leave, so it's a cushy job. Go test some gear, give the locals some pointers, get looked after by a billionaire, and go home to your loved ones. Plus, you will be able to road test the new guy to see if he fits; it's a win-win."

"For whom?" Mike added.

"You go in three weeks," the Colonel informed Mike.

The rest of the meeting contained an exchange of pleasantries, how the family was going, etc. This weighed down on Mike, the new guy, a different mission, everything out of his comfort zone. Finally, Mike left the office and checked the time, still in time for the team breakfast. 'I want doubles this morning,' he thought as he walked off to the mess, heavy in thought.

****

As Mike entered the mess, he checked around for his team; he spotted them sitting at a table, all dressed in their uniforms. Ready for battle, always prepared; each member had their rifle leaning against their leg, not to show off. It was just part of their training, to always be ready. Weapons in a mess weren't allowed, but they gave special dispensation to Special Forces teams.

Mike walked up to the start of the queue; he took a deep breath; waffles, yum. As the line moved along, Mike came face-to-face with the Sergeant in charge of the mess, GRUBS. As the Sergeant placed the two waffles on the captain's plate, he offered his usual Tuesday greeting. "Thank you for your service." Mike reacted; he didn't know what made him do what he did. If you had asked him later on why he did it. He probably would have said it was because of the sincerity in the Sergeant's voice. After the words came from the chef's mouth, "Thank you for your service."

"No, thank you, Sergeant," Mike saluted him; Mike held the salute for the Sergeant to return it. The Sergeant quickly brushed his hand on his apron, stood to attention, and returned the salute. The other enlisted men in the queue and the men serving breakfast noticed what happened and quickly stood to attention and saluted. This doesn't usually happen and promptly became a Mexican wave event. Seb reacted first because he was watching Mike as he came in. Seb quickly jumped to his feet at attention and saluted, even without knowing what was happening. The rest of the team quickly jumped to attention and saluted. The enlisted men and two officers in the mess, not knowing what happened, jumped to attention and saluted. The mess

Sergeant saw what happened and had a massive swell of pride and patriotism, 'this is family,' he thought.

Katelyn looked over at Deen during the salute. He was standing at attention with a large piece of waffle sticking out of his mouth. Katelyn shook her head; Deen reacted by loosening the bite on the waffle and letting it roll down the front of his uniform and onto the table; Katelyn rolled her eyes in disgust. Finally, Mike ended the salute, and the Mexican wave unravelled itself again. Everyone sat down. Murmured voices could be heard.

"What was that all about?" Finally, Mike got to the table and was greeted warmly by the team.

"What was that all about?" Seb said, enquiring about the salute.

"I don't think he realises how much his Tuesday specials do for morale, for the teams," Mike said.

"Well, he does now," Seb replied, laughing.

They all started chatting about the news from home. Seb informed Deen that the waves on the West Coast around Perth were perfect at the moment. They joked about hijacking one helicopter and some extra fuel cans and heading to Perth; Mike informed them, "not until after today's weapons training." Mike then told them after weapons training this morning that he was giving them a free day until a mission meeting at 1900 hours.

"Seb, you don't get a free day. Meet me at my quarters after weapons training; we have things to sort out." Seb looked at the files Mike brought in and looked back up at Mike.

"That bad?" Seb enquired.

"You have no idea," Mike replied; both men left it at that and went back to their waffles.

CHAPTER 14

PASS OUT THE INVITATIONS

The smell of freshly roasted coffee filled the air as Art Damani filled the stainless-steel pot. Lexi and Doby were chatting away in the next room as their fingers flew over their keyboards, not distracting them in the least. Doby's Hi-Vis Marvel shirt contrasts with Lexi's all-black Addams family look.

"How did the meeting go with President Abdi?" Macca asked Art.

"Fantastic, he's all on board and excited about the prospect of having a meeting with the American President."

"But?" Macca probed, since the look on Art's face didn't match the words coming out of his mouth.

"No, everything went great. Abdi said he was looking forward to the Americans lifting trade embargos and more money coming into the country. He also said his trade adviser would contact us shortly to arrange for the delegates to meet. He was happy to join the President and us for a formal dinner ball, so, yes, everything went extremely well," Art finished.

"But," Macca pushed.

"You've known me a long time Macca?" Art asked.

"Yes, I have," Macca replied.

"And you know I have a knack for sensing things and people."

"Yes, guilty on all counts," Macca offered.

"Well... I swear he already knew he was coming; we have no evidence to say otherwise, but I swear he knew." The look on his friend's face troubled him. He had a sense for things, and it sounded like it went exceptionally well... Too well, perhaps.

"Well, the management heads of the World Widlife Fund and World Animal Protection groups are in your office waiting," Macca advised Art.

"Fantastic, I have been waiting for this day for a long time. Doby would compare it to the forming of the Marvel Avengers or the Beatles. A lot of hope for the future if we gel together," Art said excitedly. Then he turned and quickly shot off down the hallway to his office.

Art burst into his office like a whirlwind, apologising for keeping them waiting, shaking hands and introducing himself.

Mr Carter Robins CEO of WWF and Mr Steve McInnes were both shocked and pleased with the excited and friendly greeting from Art Damani, both not knowing what to really expect from the meeting.

"Let me start by saying I'm a huge fan of both your organisations and so is my son Ab, who apologises for not being able to attend this meeting."

"Well, thank you Mr Damani, I'm sure Mr Robins and myself would like to say we appreciate what you're doing here at the Ark," McInnes says.

"Yes, actually we are both surprised at the invitation for the meeting and being able to stay a few days to look around," Mr Robins says.

"My pleasure, gentlemen. I have a proposal for you both and it wouldn't hold much clout if I didn't give you a chance to look around at what we're doing. I'll rush right in, I'm not one for small talk at business meetings, and this is a business meeting. I would like both your organization to join the Ark. You, will need to supply four of your best and brightest to live here with there families here at the Ark. Ab and myself are the new boys on the block and your organisations have been doing this work for decades. Thus, we need your expertise to join with our researchers, scientists and games crews to pool our knowledge to know where and how to best service the needs of the animal population. As we speak, four jaguars are being unloaded into their early stay pens, where they will be monitored 24/7, till they're released into their new homes. Now, some minor details. The four staff will be housed and wages paid for by AZTECK, so they will be off your budgets. You will retain your names and normal operations but I will double your normal budget. So, basically you go ahead as normal but with more money to fight the good fight. I know you both have your workers around the world campaigning governments and private owners to release captive animals. From now on, the ARK will do your heavy hitting. We will set up coups to overthrow governments or have men to pop around and 'make them an offer they can't refuse'."

Both the wildlife CEO's faces were blank, did they just hear Damani say he would assassinate people to recue animals?

"Guys, I'm just kidding. Everything's legit," Art said, looking at the faces of the two CEO's.

"So, you have a few days to look around. I'm guessing you will have a ton of questions. Write them all down before you leave and I will have answers for you by the time you land back home. Do you have any questions?" Art asked.

"Yes, just one for now Mr Damani. Why, did you build the ARK?" Mr Robins asked.

"Why? Because I can and someone should." Art said with great pride in his ARK.

****

ONE WEEK AGO

In a dark back alleyway in Marsabit, two figures stood in shadows, barely visible. Both figures were male and extremely well built; military by stance; rigid and unmoving.

Across the laneway, a lone figure emerges from the dark and walks two steps toward the men.

"Raise your hands," one soldier instructed him as the other searched him for weapons.

"Clear," the soldier called over his shoulder as a huge, imposing figure walked from the shadows behind. As he stepped forward, a moment of moonlight hit the face of President Hussain Abdullahi Abdi.

"Tell your Master the terms are agreeable."

"I have no Master," the voice returned strongly.

"Anyone with money is your Master. But I must admit I am surprised you came alone; if I wanted to, I could have taken the infamous Water-Tiger down," President Abdi raised his hand, and four red laser pointers, the kind used on rifles, came on pointed at the Water-Tiger.

"Not very cautious of you, Tiger. Lucky we are on the same side," President Abdi said.

"Are we on the same side, Abdi? Just because you are paying for this mission... doesn't mean we are friends. I will get the job done, and you will get your country back," the Water Tiger spat back.

The President baulked at the insult, not to use his title and the tone in which he spoke. As the President took one step forward, the four laser pointers turned their sites on the President, "What???" startled, the guards drew their sidearms and pointed them at the Water-Tiger.

"As you said, Mr. President, lucky we are on the same side." A moment later, the laser pointers were pointing at the ground in front of the President.

"I will pass on your message to my contacts, stick exactly to the time schedule, and you will get your country back with all its new riches... If you don't, I will collect my payment from you personally!" The Water Tiger stepped backward until he disappeared into the shadows.

The soldiers looked at each other as one said, "Creepy little fucker." They both laughed, and a voice rang out down the laneway.

"I heard that!" The soldiers looked around and couldn't make out where it came from. Finally, the soldier who had spoken got a whack over the back of his head by the President.

"Idiot, go find our men," the President said, annoyed, but a warm glow flourished inside, getting my country back, yes!

****

The terrorists stayed in the shadows for 15 minutes while the soldiers bumbled around in the dark, picking up their unconscious team.

"I noticed you didn't tell him about the Australian SAS team being there," Water Tigers second said.

"It is not his concern; we have to deal with them. The less he knows, the better; he can't open his fat mouth if he doesn't know about them," Water Tiger replied.

"And the Australians, Tiger?"

"I will get on the channel tonight and see what is available; we will need an extra team. We have the element of surprise, and there are only six of them and they are Australians; how hard can they be?" So, the pair drifted back into the shadow and joined their team.

'Time is getting closer, and things are changing daily; we will earn every cent this mission,' Water-Tiger thought. He had to choose his men carefully, as there could be no leaks with this target, or we might find ourselves targets before we even pull the trigger. So, all facets of the plan have come together. He believes General Abdi will do his part, but he didn't trust him, 'so Abdi may have to be a free hit before he retires but not till Abdi pays him,' he thought, 'no loose ends.' General Abdi will get his country back, so he must play his part.

CHAPTER 15

THE CRASH & BURN

A single light illuminated the office, giving it an eerily quiet ambience. Lexi and Doby had finished for the night, and the night cleaning staff had already come through. Of course, Art would tell no one this, but late at night, when everything has been shut down apart from night staff, as you look over the rails from the higher levels, the ARK feels like a tomb of some alien god. He walks into his office and Ab is waiting there for him.

"Father, it seems we missed something exciting the other morning," Ab said.

"Really, what? Do tell."

"Remember when we went and helped Dan Hooper with the Elephants?"

"Yes, that was very exciting."

"Well, the small truck that was rocking all the time, that was Buttercup, the female Rhino. Dan said she gave them a hell of a time.

"But not as much as 600 baboons trying to start the next planet of the apes," Art joked.

Ab laughed, "Poor Dan, but I must admit. I wouldn't like to be bitten on the arse by a laughing baboon."

"And what happened with Dan and his baboon issues?"

"I believe Dan and Dr. Sarah are still in negotiations. Dan wants automated machine gun turrets, and Dr. Sarah wants a low voltage electric shock fence."

It was Art's turn to laugh heartily, "That Dan, he's a card. I saw the trucks yesterday. Were those the gazelles?"

"Yes, Father."

"Fantastic. We need to confirm with Royland the horticultural specialist about the koala grounds as well."

"What did you decide you wanted to do about our other find? We can't just ignore that someone was planning a murder and not do anything."

"Just hand the information to the police as per usual."

"But shouldn't we do more surveillance to get more information about it for the police?" Ab insisted.

"No! We aren't the police; we have spoken about this. It is not our job to police the world, hand over the information anonymously, and let the police chase it up."

"It seems a waste when we have all this technology," Ab stated, dejected.

"If we did this, became the world's police, we would have to choose a side," Art stated.

"Be on the side of what's right," Ab said.

"If life was only that simple, my boy. What is right depends on who's side of the line you're standing on," Art took some deep breaths and centred himself.

"Ok, and what is the news on whoever is trying to hack and crash our West Coast American site?"

"It is as you thought, Father, ILLUMIUN CORP. We tracked the hackers' funds back to them. I believe it is over the Lanthanum mine in Taiwan. They increased the prices to everyone else it sells to except us, and Illumiun is their second-biggest buyer after us. How do you want me to respond, Father?"

"Hand it over to our Americas branch. Your work here at the moment is too important."

"How would you like me to inform them?" Ab asked in a very businesslike voice, trying to conceal his displeasure at how his last conversation ended with his father.

"A crash and burn! Wait till it is their pay period, add two zeros to the workers' pay, and take two off the executives' pay. Then, crash all files with the word Lanthanum, so they know who did this."

"And the hackers?" Ab asked.

"Pin it all on them and hand it over to the FBI cyber-crimes unit."

"This will take time, Father."

"That is fine, my son. It will give you more time to complete your mission."

"My mission? what mission?" Ab asked, surprised.

"I want you to buy the Lanthanum," Art informed him.

"You want me to buy the mine! But, Father, that will be expensive, and there will be obstacles from the Taiwanese government." Ab stated, shocked at such a bold move.

"No, son, I want you to buy the corporation that controls the mine and two other rare mineral mines." Ab stood there looking at his father, shocked; his brain was spinning; he knew instantly, processing it all, that this was an enormous task, with things just getting started at the ARK. Art broke Abs' train of thought.

"Your mission. I want you to front seat this takeover. Pick your team where you need them from. You know how we work and how we process a sale. This is your first big purchase, and I believe you're ready. If at any time you need advice, you know where I live. No time frame, just get it done. If being the HUB gets in your way at any time, pass the info through to me, and I'll take up the slack. Now go, no training wheels this time; you can do it."

Art faked sob into a tissue, "Oh, my baby boy is all grown up now." Art made a loud fake, blowing his nose into the tissue.

"FRMMMM, go now, fly and be free," Art waves his tissue at his son.

"You had to make it weird, didn't you?" Ab stated.

Ab turned and went to walk out the door; he stopped in the doorway and turned to Art.

"Thank you, Father," the pair smiled at each other, and with that, Ab left the room. Walking down the hallway, Ab's brain was telling him, 'Too much to compute, need energy!' With that, Ab went down to the late-night food stand and got himself a milkshake and a tray of mixed cake treats; he needed sugar and time to process this all.

CHAPTER 16

TERRORISTS IN THE COUNTRY

The back alleys of the southern province of Marsabit were dead quiet, a stark contrast to the hustle-bustle of day trade. It was mainly a business/market area with few residential dwellings. A lone figure stands in the shadows, waiting, listening intently for any sounds that were out of place. 'It's better to be safe than dead,' he thought; he finally moved down the alleyway to the address a few doors down; he slipped down a side alley and moved up to the back entrance of the dwelling.

The creaks of the ancient wooden steps seemed to echo for eternity, 'so much for stealth,' he thought. He uses a coded set of knocks, then the door opens, and he is greeted and asked to come inside. The man that greets him ushers him to a seat at the dining room table. Nothing is said. The host places a small mobile phone on the table and says nothing; he knows this procedure; it is common practice in this group. He is waiting for his spotter to call in that all is clear and safe to proceed with the meeting.

A couple of minutes later, the phone beeps with a text, and the number '1' comes on-screen as the 'all clear' signal. The guest waits for his host and commander to open the conversation, but the host keeps looking at the phone. Moments later, the phone beeps again, and a two came up on the screen, and then again, a three on screen. 'Three spotters, they are taking many precautions this time,' the guest thought. The host pushes the phone aside and speaks, "It is good to see you; I hope you are well."

"Yes, I have been blessed," the guest replied; the last check or call sign was the answer, "blessed" is the password. It was a signal that the guest had not been compromised outside by any enemy. All of Water Tiger's 2nds were on Interpol's most-wanted list, so every precaution was vital. The host was none other than North Korean People's Army special operations Ji-tae Jin, known worldwide as the Water-Tiger. Number 1 on Interpol's most-wanted list, responsible for a dozen bombings worldwide and suspected of releasing a deadly virus in Seoul four years ago.

"How are preparations going?" Ji-tae asked.

"Very good. All is as it should be. My men are in-country and working, avoiding detection. My armaments are coming across the southern border tomorrow. I have memorised the timetable and scouted our entry; I feel, though, that there is a chance none of my team and myself will collect our pay. Going up against two American Special Forces teams and Somalian regulars will be a gigantic task."

"You will have the firepower and element of surprise," Ji-tae informed him.

"With all due respect, I don't think the American Special Forces will be napping when their President is around, but we are ready and prepared to do our part. I must ask, though. I have been researching the ARK; the whole reserve is one big surveillance area; even with my teams' distractions, how do the other teams get to the President without detection?" the guest asked.

The guest is Chao Zhang, a mercenary trained by Ji-tae seven years ago. He had done a ten-year stint in China's people's liberation army before stepping out, or disappearing would be a better term, to look for a more profitable way to work with his skills.

"Yours is not the only distraction, plus we are getting a man on the inside that is taking down the surveillance; all is prepared. We should be on top of the Secret Service before they know what's hits them. Is your exit strategy sound?"

"Yes, it is," Chao responded.

"Just in case the heavens don't smile upon you that evening. Is there someone, family perhaps, that you would like your fee to be sent?" Ji-tae asked.

"No, but there are quite a few women who would like to get their hands on it, though," the men laughed, which was good to break the tension.

"If we survive this mission, we will probably need to go into hiding for good." As the laughter subsided, Ji -tae spoke again, "Well, you know the procedures: maintain cover, check your link for instructions; we will go dark on the day and only break it if the mission is to be aborted. Otherwise, once we are inside, you know the planned frequency channel for the mission. May the heavens smile on your team," Ji-tae said, "And with you too."

The men shook hands, and Ji-tae sent a text. Moments later, three responses came back: C, C, C. All is clear. Ji-tae opened the back door, and Chao left, watching every shadow as he walked back to his accommodation.

CHAPTER 17

OYSTERS & PASSION

Once again, the smells of the hub were filled with fresh coffee, salmon bagels, and bacon burgers as Lexi punched away quietly on the keys. Doby had worked quietly for hours, passing only the required conversation to get their work done. It was Friday, time to party tonight, well for Lexi anyway. Lexi and Doby are very organised. They have a set amount of work that they want to get through for the day, and with-it being Friday, neither wanted to do any extra hours tonight.

"Do you like oysters?" Doby asked.

Lexi was surprised by the break in the silence and her concentration.

"Sorry, what?" Lexi replied.

"Do you like oysters?" Doby repeated.

"Oysters, yes, I love them," Lexi said. She waited for Doby to continue the conversation, but he fell silent. Minutes passed, and it got the better of her.

"Why did you want to know if I like oysters?" She quizzed Doby.

"Oh, I heard in the food hall this morning that some of the staff are taking the bus to a new oyster bar near the coast tonight," Doby replied nonchalantly.

He continued, "I was thinking of going; I thought you might like to come too."

"Are you asking me on a date, Asslicker?" she said excitedly.

"No, I was just thought you might want to come... And it's Heinlinker, not Asslicker," he said, frustrated.

"Then I don't want to go!" Lexi stated in a loud, disappointed voice.

"Why not???"

"Aren't I worth taking on a date?"

"Of course, you are," Doby said, confused.

"So, you just don't like me, then?" she teased.

"Of course, I do."

"So, then you don't find me attractive," Lexi kept teasing.

"Of course, you are" Doby felt he was trapped in one of Lexi's spinning firewalls.

"Do you think I'm hot?

"Yes!"

"And you want to take me on a date?"

"Yes." Lexi let him off the hook.

"Was that so hard?"

"You make everything hard," Doby said; before he realised the sexual innuendo in the comment, Lexi didn't miss a beat.

"Do I make you hard, Doby? Ahhh, that's so sweet that you find me hot... Do I make you hard every day?" she teased.

"Oh my God, please stop. My head is spinning; what just happened?" Doby asked, confused.

"You asked me on a date tonight, and I give you regular boners," Lexi stated.

"Ahhh," Doby's head slumped and hit his keyboard, "Ouch," he said in a small voice. Lexi sat there looking at him with a Cheshire Cat grin.

****

Doby came to Lexi's apartment 15 minutes early, just in case she was running late; he hadn't had much experience in dating, but he had heard all the stories of women running late, still putting on their makeup, or not being able to pick the right shoes to wear. He knocked on the door.

"Come in, Doby; it's open," Lexi said in an inviting voice. As Doby entered the apartment, Lexi had her back to him as she grabbed a small clutch purse from the dining table. Doby was stunned. He always knew Lexi was beautiful, but this vision in front of him was breathtaking. Lexi was in a skin-tight black mini dress, with bright red sequin shoes with red laces that wrapped around her long, succulent legs. Her clutch purse was the same sequent red as her shoes. She had her hair down, flowing down her back.

As much as Doby thought this view was beautiful, Lexi turned to face him, and his jaw literally dropped. He stood there, mouth open, without saying a word. Lexi was usually in her all-black attire, including black lipstick and eyeshade. But tonight, she was working an all-natural look, lite blush, lipstick only one shade darker than her natural lips, and a pastel lilac eyeshade. Doby was mesmerised.

"Is there something wrong? Is it too much?" Lexi said, confused, looking at her outfit, wondering why Doby was staring and not saying anything? Then, finally, Doby spoke in a soft, gentle voice, "You're beautiful." Lexi blushed, blushing to a point she could feel the heat in her cheeks. It wasn't the words Doby said; it was the sincerity in his voice that made her blush and feel very special. It's been a long while since she had heard those words.

"Thank you," she said as she kissed Doby on the cheek, which made him blush.

"Do I make you hard?" she asked him.

"You just had to make it weird," Doby replied, smiling, but the answer was 'YES!' he thought.

"Come on, Asslicker, I'm hungry, and we don't want to miss the tank," she walked behind Doby and closed the door behind her.

The TANK was a modified transport coach. It has all the luxury of soft bucket seats, an in-house movie screen, bullet-proof windows, reinforced steel plate sides, and comes with its own soldiers. Two AZTECK armed security guards. Mr. Damani takes no chances with his staff; he knows what country he's in.

The ride in was a blur to Lexi and Doby as they constantly chatted about small talk things. Finally, the tank arrived at the COASTER OF COASTS oyster bar. As Lexi and Doby exited the tank, they heard the cheers, clapping, and out-of-tune notes of someone signing. The Coaster of Coasts was an Oyster bar and karaoke club, which neither of them minded at all.

Doby paid the cashier for his and Lexi's entrance and dinner. As they were ushered to their table beside a side wall, Lexi was taking in the ambience of it all. The club had a Beatnik style, with late sixties décor and moody lighting. The stage had those sixties psychedelic pattern artwork. The only thing that didn't fit was the music, with people trying to belt out 70's, 80's pop, and country sounds.

Doby sat and contemplated undoing his belt as he felt his stomach was going to explode. He had eaten too much. The seafood, meats and desserts were all fresh and there was ampul variety.

Lexi and Doby's night flew past. With a few drinks, good laughs, and an array of over-the-top singing, made it magical for both.

****

The singing continued in the Tank on the way home from the production department. Lexi and Doby sat on the back seat in the corner, neither saying much in case they said something that would ruin this special evening. Halfway home, Lexi made her move; as Doby seemed to be shy, she suddenly put her hand between Doby's legs and grabbed his penis tightly, "Hey," Doby says in sudden shock. Lexi looks into Doby's eyes, "I want you to take me to your place tonight... Or am I going to strip off your clothes and fuck you right on this seat, in front of everyone?"

Doby stared at her. "You wouldn't!" but he could see in her eyes, yes, she would. Doby felt excited and terrified at the same time.

"Ok, ok, I'll take you to my place," Doby agreed.

"Pussy, I thought you might like to do me now," she giggled.

"Not in front of everyone and have them staring at you naked," Doby protested

"Aww, my knight in shining armour, very chivalrous," Lexi teased,

"Can you let go of my dick now, please?" Doby asked, looking at her hand in his groin.

"Not a chance, buddy; I'm hanging around, just in case this sucker changes his mind," Lexi teased.

"Have you got a pair of rolled-up socks down there to impress me?"

"No! And don't make it weird."

"Damn, then you and I will have a long night, my friend. Let's see if we can put those oysters to good use," Lexi said. She leaned onto Doby, and he put his arm around her. Lexi felt a buzz all over her, a feeling she hadn't had for a very long time, a feeling all was good in her life. Doby was feeling euphoric, in a dream state; his penis was being grabbed by this beautiful woman who threatened him with sex; this doesn't happen in his life. He decides to just go with the flow and see what happens. The rest of the ride home was quiet, with the pair cuddling in the back seat, Lexi holding tightly on to her prize. She fights back the temptation to unzip his pants and take a peek.

****

They quickly made their way to Doby's room, almost sprinting, as if time was of the essence and they would turn into pumpkins soon. Doby kept fumbling with the keys to the front door, and Lexi, in her impatience, just wanted to kick the fucker in. As Doby opened the door, the pair almost fell through into Doby's lounge room. It was a frenzied atmosphere as both virtually ripped each other's clothes off, not wanting to waste a second.

Finally, Lexi yanks Doby's Marvel boxer shorts down and finally sees what she had been waiting for.

"My God, you're a HORSE Asslicker," Lexi stated.

"Woo." The shock and suddenness of what Lexi did next made Doby step back a couple of paces. His feet were still tangled up in his boxers and trousers. He stumbled back, landing on his arse, hitting the floor with a thump. Lexi started ripping off his pants and boxers.

"Do you want to go to the bedroom?" Doby asked.

"No, here's just fine!" As she climbed on top of Doby. Sitting on him almost naked, except for a red G-string, Doby thought that he had never seen a woman so beautiful. Lexi was in hyper-drive now; her sexual urges were usually hard to contain as she had a high sex drive. However, with the increased workload of moving to a new country, her sex life had to take a back seat. So, for Lexi, there wasn't a microsecond to wait, and all the shackles were off.

She grabbed her G-string on the side and reefed it off, snapping the side string. Then she placed herself over Doby and passionately threw herself into the moment. The pair were enfolded in each other the rest of the night and early into the morning in a loving embrace, only stopping to catch their breath before continuing in a haze of sexual ecstasy.

They had only slept for a couple of hours as the night's entertainment went till 5am. Lexi got up to shower. Doby joined her and left a shirt and boxer shorts for her outside in the bathroom. Lexi looked at herself in the mirror, dressed in Doby's Spiderman tank top and Spiderman boxer shorts. It gave her a warm feeling, a feeling of being wanted.

Lexi was in the kitchen making coffee, thinking about last night, the great food, the way the production crew wouldn't stop singing on the bus. She was stirring her coffee for the fiftieth time when Doby came out and sat on the other side of the kitchen bar. Lexi brought the coffees around to the table.

"Are you alright?" Doby asked.

"Yes, you just ruined me for any other man," she said jokingly.

"Yeah, right," Doby said, not convinced.

"I was going to go downstairs to order some breakfast," Doby said.

"Why don't you just order it by phone and have it delivered?"

"I would, but I want to try something in the Hub, so I'll have yours delivered."

"You want to work?" Lexi asked, surprised.

"Yes, I had some ideas come to me last night" before he could finish his sentence, Lexi cut in.

"You were pounding me last night and thinking of work???" she said, shocked. Trying to find the words to defend himself, he said, "It must have been all the blood rushing to my head."

"That is not the head the blood was rushing to." She looked down at his penis to make the point.

Lexi smiled and said, "Order me double for breakfast; I'm starving. Is it alright for me to stay here for a while? I don't want anyone seeing me walking around in your boxers and top?"

Doby let out a big laugh, "Of course." He went to the bedroom to get changed.

Lexi scolded herself for being a pig and overeating. As she finished her breakfast. She took a tour of Doby's abode. The walls and shelves were filled with superhero items and stuff from movies, props, etc. A closer inspection of one framed picture on the wall, she read the engraved tag at the bottom of the frame, *Original film from Marvel animated movie 1992. This was a piece of the actual movie film the artists drew on; wow.* Looking again at the other pictures and pieces of movie props, they were all original pieces. "Doby is a collector. Cool," she said out loud.

Walking through the apartment, she came across Doby's office, or gaming room was more like it; he had a state-of-the-art setup with multiple screens around his custom-made desk for panoramic viewing. Within the middle of the desk was Doby's laptop. Lexi decided to have a little fun and see if she could crack Doby's passcode. She said to herself, 'I won't look at what's on his laptop, just see if I can crack his password, maybe leave a note on the screen thanking him for a great night. She turned the laptop on, and the password line came up on the screen; she clicked on the password section and started typing, "Marvel, that would be my first guess," she said aloud. But, as she looked up at the screen, no word came up with her tying. 'Strange,' she thought. Lexi checked to see if she had appropriately clicked on the password section, and she had. She sat for a moment, wondering why she couldn't enter the password section. Then, looking at the screen again, she noticed a little glowing spinning ball in the top left-hand corner. Going against her better judgment, she clicked on it. The screen came to life and what came up on the screen terrified her! It was HER Sphere, HER firewall.

Feeling confused, she went through thoughts about why Doby would need such a firewall on a personal computer. Tiny fingers of mistrust ran up her neck, trying to weave into her mind. All the years of suspicion Art Damani had instilled in her about the company secrets, and everybody wants to pull us down. We need the Sphere to protect us, were interlacing into her thoughts. With a significant mind flush, she pushed them back. No! This is Doby; he's a straight shooter. He probably has it on his computer because he was perhaps working late on it before we ran it on the mainframe. Yes, that's it, of course it is. Having successfully pushed back the distrustful thoughts... For now, she continued to hack in and this time leaving a note 'thanking him for last night and telling him to stop pinching her shit!'

She got out of the computer chair and went to the dining room and her purse. Finally, she reached her purse and grabbed her phone out of it, hobbling back to the computer, walking deliberately bowlegged; she reached the seat and slowly lowered herself down. She went to her phone, where she kept a copy of the algorithm that is the password of the Sphere. As she read the files, she typed in the sequence.

"There," she said and hit enter. She sat back and watched as the worm rolled and travelled into the Sphere, 'six levels,' she thought, in the first section of the Sphere. Surely, he hasn't put the entire sphere on his laptop; that would be overkill. She watched the worm through levels 1, 2, 3, 4, 5, and 6. Then the mid-level of the Sphere came up.

"What???" she said out loud. 'Doby has the whole Sphere on his laptop,' she thought; Why? She watched the mid-Sphere section come up, and her worm started squirming, spinning, nowhere to go, and so did the tentacles of mistrust squirm and spin up the back of her neck. It was only seconds before her brain snapped to attention. The worm was spinning and not entering the Sphere. It was only another second before she realised he had changed the algorithm; she couldn't get in; why? She turned off the computer and closed the door and walked out of the room. She walked to the dinner table, grabbed her purse, dress, and shoes, and left the apartment to head back to her living quarters.

****

Later, Lexi decided to unwind and headed to the poolside lounge to relax and listen to music. Lexi didn't even notice she was swinging her feet side to side, keeping to the beat of one song she and Doby had sung together at the karaoke bar the night before. Her mind seemed to try to unwind, but unfortunately, for every bad thought about why Doby had the Sphere on his laptop and a different password, she could come up with a logical answer on Doby's behalf... So it was a draw. Nevertheless, the music continued pumping through her ears, and Lexi was oblivious to what song was even playing.

Lexi woke with a start and realised she must have nodded off; she checked her watch and realised she had slept for over 2 hours on the lounge. Deciding to be proactive, she got off the lounge and headed to the food mall, got some lunch and coffee, and headed up to her apartment to do some washing.

As Lexi reached her room, she noticed a large manilla envelope on the floor in front of her door. She looked over the envelope; there was nothing written on either side. She opened the envelope as 'it must be for her as it's in front of her door' she thought.

Lexi tore open one end of the envelope and looked inside. To her surprise, it was her phone. 'My phone? I must have dropped it, and someone has returned it', she thought. Then, thinking back to where she last remembered having it, a chill went up to her spin. 'In Doby's office,' I must have left it there. Looking inside the envelope again, she sees a small piece of paper folded in half; she reaches in and grabs it. On the piece of paper was a brief message.

"I believe this is yours; the algorithm was an old one." He knew! Doby knew she had been on his computer and tried to hack in. A wave of shame and regret washed over her; she reread the note, blunt and straight to the point; he was pissed.

What to do! Apologise, I suppose, maybe just be honest and tell him you were going to leave a note for him, 'Then why not just write a note, Ahhh fuck!' she thought, I had just spoiled a lovely evening, he won't trust me now. My God, WE WORK TOGETHER! My God, we FUCKED and WORK TOGETHER; AHHHH, it keeps getting worse. She went inside her apartment and flopped on her lounge, feeling miserable; her favourite coffee tastes bitter now. She thought, 'do I ring him or face him?' either way made her feel like shit, 'serve yourself right, you're a dumb bitch' she thought.

****

Doby made his way to the delivery dock after receiving a call from the storeman, saying that a crate had arrived and that it was enormous. Doby was excited; he had been waiting for this delivery for some time, a new edition to his collection. During a charity auction, Doby had outbid hundreds of people online for the original Thor Hammer from the set of the first Avengers movie. Mounted in a glass case and polished timber frame. He had paid a small fortune, but it was well worth the cost, especially since the money was for charity. Doby reached the docks and was surprised at the size of the case. He knew it would probably be big, but not this big. There will have to be some reshuffling of his display to be done. He was pushing a trolley with his prize on it to the elevator, filled with excitement that a child has on Christmas day. He had almost forgotten his displeasure that Lexi had tried to hack his computer. What was she thinking? It pissed him off to no end, but he believed Lexi isn't the kind of person with malicious intent... Even though she used to work with the notorious ANNONYMOUS hackers. I will catch up with her later to talk to her.

Doby started unwrapping the crate, ripping off the protective cardboard with excitement. Once open, there was a manilla envelope inside, which he thought must be a delivery docket and proof of purchase for the hammer. Casually throwing the envelope onto the table, Doby looks at his latest acquisition. It was magnificent, a lot bigger than he thought. It would take a bit of effort to wave it around. Chris Hemsworth didn't have any trouble, but then Chris Hemsworth is ripped, not CGI ripped, but really ripped. Doby sits at the table and ogles at his prize, looking at it with the same awe as if it was the real Thor's hammer. Doby was pleased with himself and had those same thoughts he had recently of life being good since he joined AZTECK.

Casually reaching over to the manilla envelope, he opens it to look at the dockets. An icy wave came over him as he looked at a photo inside. He felt so cold, numb, and instantly ill to his stomach. There was a note inside with the pictures. His hands were shaking violently. He didn't realise that his heart rate was soaring, and he was going into shock. Moments later, he was violently ill in his bathroom, bringing up his breakfast and lunch. As he leaned over his toilet, trying to steady himself with a hand on the wall, he noticed that he had brought the photos into the bathroom; they were partly spread out on the floor. He was looking at pictures of his mother tied up on a chair, gaged. Beside her were two pairs of hands, one pair holding a Baltimore newspaper showing the date, and the other pair had one on his mother's shoulder, with the other a large knife to her neck. He started spinning and dry retching. He once again put a hand out to steady himself, pushing himself up; his legs felt like they were made of rubber, with no bones at all. He wiped his mouth on a towel and staggered to a dining room chair. The house swayed, and he felt like he was in a dream. He grabbed the piece of paper and reread the note.

Doby Heinlinker, as you can see, we have your mother. Her safety is now in your hands. You will follow our instructions exactly, and you will have your mother back unharmed. She has not seen our identities, so we are not worried about releasing her once you have done what is required of you. We know WHO you are, and as you can see from receiving this letter, we know WHERE you are. ON the 23rd of August at 6.15 pm, you will initiate a collapse of the ARK fence security, Animal security protocol, and telecommunications.

That is all that is required of you, and your mother will be released. Take heed of what I say next and know what I say is true.

If you contact the police or authorities, your mother will die violently.

We know Aztecks' capabilities; if they start searching for your mother or us, she will die painfully.

If you fail in your task and the systems are not taken down on time or at all, she will die painfully.

If you do as is required, we will release her unharmed.

I will keep her safe till then.

Get to work.

Doby's chest tightened as he looked at the photos again. It was increasingly harder to breathe. The last of the images was a photo of his mother's medication; there was no doubt it was her. Again, he found it hard to breathe. He began to panic; he needed air; he needed to be outside. Doby jumped out of his seat and ran to the elevator, hitting the button repeatedly as if it would make the elevator come faster. Luckily, there was no one else here, as the look on his face and the colour of his skin would have alarmed them.

He found a secluded area and paced back and forth, back and forth. "This makes no sense," he said aloud to himself. "Why my mother, she has nothing to do with the ARK? Take down the security, why?" The pacing continued and only wound Doby's stress further. "The date, why then, there's nothing special..." Then the penny dropped.

"Oh NO, they're after the President!"

Doby paced the grounds. Having thrown off the initial horror of it all, he had to come up with an answer. Playing it repeatedly in his head, save his mother or save the President. As the balance tipped towards his mother, the consequences of what he will do scared him. Involved with murdering a President, life imprisonment, execution? There was no real question about it. He was saving his mother, and that was it. But, how to do it? Anything he does, Lexi would find and correct. How to do it?

****

Lexi went to see Doby and apologise face-to-face; it was the only way to maintain their friendship and working environment. So, she headed down to see him at his apartment. Lexi felt so nervous, vulnerable, and sincerely sorry; she meant no disrespect. Lexi knocked on the door. She waited, still no answer. She could leave, but what if Doby is home and knows it's me and is ignoring me? She softly speaks to the door, "Doby, are you home?" No reply.

****

Doby heads back to his room and start working on ideas to do what these people want. Determined now, he will save his mother; he will sort this out. Walking briskly, every second counts. He rides up the elevator, focused, smelly; what was that smell? He looked down at his shirt and saw vomit stains down his shirt. A shower, some coffee, and food, and I will fix this.

****

Lexi continued talking to the door, apologising and explaining why she had done this, how she had such a wonderful time last night. Then please speak to me! No response. Maybe he's out avoiding this confrontation. She decides he's not home and will catch up with him later.

****

Doby rounds the corner to his apartment and digs the keys out of his pocket. Hurrying to get inside, He doesn't want to be seen like this. Once inside, he throws the keys on the table and heads straight to the shower. Turning it on strips down quickly, and hops in. It's too hot, but he doesn't care or notice. He thinks he hears a knock on the door. 'Who could that be? They know WHO I am, WHERE I am, have they infiltrated the ARK? are they watching me?' fingers of paranoia grip him, 'leave me alone, I will do what you want, just leave me alone,' he dips his head under the shower to drown off the noises.

CHAPTER 18

WATER TIGER IS READY

"On our right are the rhino plain lands, and the mountainous rocky outcrop is the baboon sanctuary. Not even the Rhinos go in there; they know better." The tour guide says with a laugh. As the four-wheel-drive bus bounced around the track, showing off the outer region of the ARK.

This local tribesman approached Art with an idea of starting a tourist drive around the ARK to help him employ himself and feed his family. Art was so impressed with the man's drive that he bought the appropriate vehicle and leased it for a small fee. With the expansion of the ARK, eventually, areas will become open to the public on which the tribesman could expand his business.

The tour guide was very entertaining and full of local knowledge, having been born and raised here. The tourists didn't mind the dusty trail, and it seemed to bring alive the entire atmosphere of life in Africa. The bus rattles around the boundary fence of the ARK, excited visitors snapping photos of animals in the distance, "Are those REAL animals or robots?" one excited child sitting behind him yelled out to the guide.

"We don't know, they all look the same, and the ARK staff say no one is supposed to know," the guide replied.

'The animals and security will be down, but we still have to deal with the real animals,' Water-Tiger thought. 'More munitions. We can't stray from our time schedule, definitely more munitions.'

As the bus took a detour around the private airstrip, Water-Tiger imagined the attack on President's cargo plane, then the insurgence of his team at the edge of this section of fencing. If required, we will help the other team overwhelm the Special Forces guarding the plane and the support helicopters. We cannot have Special Forces behind us as when we go for the Eagle.

'Finally, the last area where the poachers we contracted will break through the fencing and entry, drawing the ARK Security forces in. With the town riots planned, there should be enough to distract local police and army regs. All timed to perfection and an exit strategy just in case something goes south. Like Heinlinker, I have put everything into play. So far, there has been no attempt to find or rescue Heinlinker's mother, so I assume he is playing his part. A lot of moving parts and a lot of trust from new partners. Two things he didn't like were trust and new partners. If I get betrayed, I will be back for them.' he thought.

****

Back at his apartment as he pondered over the maps and schedules, 'there was a lot to like and dislike about this mission. Five times their regular payment, the fact they may have to retire and go into hiding for the rest of their lives. I have money invested; it may be time to disappear. Identities won't be a problem with the multiple lives I have set up worldwide in safe places. I have no family, so he has nothing to leave behind. The work is where the problem could lie; can he walk away from the work? It's been my whole life since I was a soldier in the North Korean army, then the Korean people's army special operations force to hire gun; it's been everything to me.

He allows himself a thought which is unwise in his line of work, Target, Kill, Paid. That's how in-depth of what is required, but the thought lingers 'Why? Why now? Easy mark, away from home, hostile country, but relations between the US and his homeland are no worse off than ever were. Is it this President, the new JFK they call him?' Too many thoughts might be due for retirement if I start asking WHY?

CHAPTER 19

THE BREAKTHROUGH

The smell of sweat and coffee permeated the air in Doby's apartment. Clothes hurled everywhere, no washing done for weeks, dishes and takeaway containers with half-eaten meals thrown around the kitchen. Even the carpet had a path worn on it from weeks of constant pacing through the night. Doby worked day and night for weeks. He was trying to perfect something that would pull the required sections down that he could plant in the system. Installed and unnoticed and on time for his mother's sake. He had prepared to go to jail as well. So, he began moving funds into his mother's account, knowing they couldn't touch it, and also opened a Swiss account in his mother's name.

Doby had feigned illness to work from his apartment, but he was running out of excuses to not make it look suspicious. Having to attend work and act happy, knowing that people will probably die for his mother to live. He knew the system; he helped to build it, but he wasn't the only one who worked on the system. Ab and Lexi had been bombarding him with, 'are you alright?' for weeks. He has been trying to avoid eye contact with Lexi. Which is really weird after what they went through together after their date.

'System, system, systems, he knew he needed a code worm, one long enough to cause havoc and bring the required systems down, but not all systems. He was told by the note to bring communication and security down, that's all, and in a show of backbone, that's all he will bring down.

He was running out of time, a week left, and not enough time to think of the answer and get it done. Time was running out on his mother; time was not his friend... Time. Need time... time! That's it! Time was the answer.' The penny had dropped.

"Lexi's Sphere is on a time spiral, rotating different algorithms that mesh with the same sequences. If I change the algorithm, so nothing changes and gets noticed. If I add some extra code to each algorithm, random hidden nothings, then when all the codes met at a certain spiral, BAM, the comms and security are affected. Yes, yes, yes, it could be done. I will need to time it perfectly," he said to himself.

"I'll save you, Mum," he said out loud. "Coffee, coffee, I will need lots of coffee. It's going to be a long night," he spoke out loud to an empty room. As if all his sensors came back to life at once. He sniffed his armpits and reeled back from the stench.

"Maybe a shower while the coffee is brewing," his stomach growled, "and something to eat," he said again.

Doby had lost seven kilos since he received the letter three weeks ago. Stress, working long hours, more stress had contributed. The weight loss hadn't gone unnoticed by Lexi; he looked gaunt and pale. She had brought it up to Ab and Art a few times about Doby's health; they assured her he was fine after speaking with him.

"Just stomach bugs and lack of appetite, that's all, Art; everything will correct itself soon but thank you for the concern; I appreciate you guys looking out for me," he responded. Art, a great reader of people, he felt something was off, but everything he said rang true; he would make sure he popped into the HUB more often to keep an eye on things. He had noticed a different dynamic in the HUB with Doby's typical laid-back attitude missing, but then he has been sick. Lexi was worried and on edge; her co-worker was ill, and she was concerned about him. Has he missed something?

More visits to the HUB are definitely on the cards.

CHAPTER 20

THE PRESIDENT HEADS TO AFRICA

"Geez! Excited much," Ab said to Tyson.

"The rumours have been circling for days that a big event and someone important was coming," Tyson replied.

The auditorium was like an ant nest; all the worker ants were here, speculating on what was about to be announced.

"A ball, I heard," one lady said.

"No, it's someone important, probably President Abdi," another lady added.

"It can't be Abdi," one man stated.

"Why not?"

"You said it was someone important," the man replied, to which the group started laughing.

The room was abuzz with chatter. You couldn't hear a thing over the ramble... until the Queen bant stepped into the room.

Physical attributes have no bearing on the stature of someone. However, with respect to the small physic of Aarth Damani, he had the stature of a giant and the utmost care from his staff. As he walked into the auditorium, the crowd went quiet, and those who kept talking were given the evil eye by the masses.

"Good morning, everyone. Thank you for turning up. If you hadn't, you would have been fired," Art's jest bringing a round of applause and laughter. "The rumours are true; an important visitor is coming soon. Their identity will be not be disclosed until the last minute. Yes, we will be having a ball and trade talks over a week. I will talk to each department head about the requirements needed over this week. This meeting is an apology, a pre-apology of sorts. There will be a lot of minor disruptions and inconveniences during their stay, so I apologise now for these things. Let me say that this will be the first major event and phase for the ARK to be recognised worldwide. I am already proud of the work done so far by you all and know that you will make me proud through the future visit."

"Catering managers, I would like you to submit menus tomorrow and we will select the food from to be served. I know this is short notice, but the event was of significant importance. Decorators will be in through the week to work in the ballroom. Also, all ARK staff have will go through security checks and will have to wear a security tag till the end of the visit."

Art and Macca that afternoon had a trial run on the animated hunting safari that AZTECK had built for hunters to test their skills. ½ hr, and both men were exhausted, chased around by a panther and rhino. The all-clear was given, with no faults or glitches detected. Like in a computer game, the animals could not harm the hunter. Once they were in a kill zone on their prey, the animal would stop, and the vest the hunter was wearing would light up or send an electric shock, depending on how tough you set the hunt requirements. Nobody has tried 'higher settings and electric shocks' since the testing stage, because there were some unfortunate bladder control issues had to be addressed. Of course, the animals didn't have all the benefits. If they were shot with the laser rifles, where they were hit, they would lose the use of that limb or body function till the animal conceded and the hunter won.

Everything was rolling into place through the week, with Game warden Hooper overseeing the arrival of wildebeest, lions, and giraffes. He was in deep consultation with Dr. Sarah over the final touches to a panda and Bengal Tiger area. It was a fascinating time as the Ark animals arrived in trucks two by two.

****

In the HUB, things seem to get back to normal. Doby was working back in the HUB and seemed to be getting back to his old self, except for the weight loss, Lexi thought. She still wasn't game enough to bring up what happened after their date, the sex, or that she betrayed his trust. But at least they were talking again, even if it was only a civil chat about work.

Doby was happier since he came up with a way to bring the system down, but he wasn't stupid. He knew they might still kill his mum anyway, but he was prepared to find them and chase them worldwide to make them pay if need be. So, he did his part; he came up with a way to bring down just those two systems and no others; he wasn't bringing the whole ARK down.

****

Art was awoken by a security guard at 5.20 the following day; it seemed there was a problem with Mrs. Sanders. She fainted outside the giant walk-in freezer, and the night shift nurse was brought in to attend.

Art quickly threw on some clothes and joined the officer. As they headed down the elevator to the food mall, he thought, 'not today, not today.' The Secret Service was flying in today to oversee the arrival of the President, and we can't have anything go wrong in front of them. They entered the expansive kitchen and saw the nurse with Mrs. Sanders sitting up on a gurney; thank God she was alright, but she looked very shaken.

Art knelt down beside her. "Mrs. Sanders, dear, are you alright?" Art asked, concerned. Mrs. Sanders tried to speak but couldn't get any coherent words out, just mumbles and a syllable now and then, but there was anger in those eyes.

'Oh my God,' Art thought, 'have I worked her so hard that she has had a mental breakdown.' Art put his hand on her shoulder and on the shoulder of the nurse.

"Please take gentle care of her," Art said, concerned.

Mrs. Sanders tried again to put some words together, but her shock, or whatever, was still stopping that. Art thought he heard one word during her mumbles, but he felt he must have misheard it; he thought she said "kill." Art thought. He stood up and headed to the Security guard.

"Do we know what happened?" Art enquired.

"Oh yeah, it's in there," said the Security guard, tilting his head to the large walk-in freezer.

"What's in there?" Art asked.

"Have a look, Sir," the guard gestured.

Art opened the freezer door slowly, expecting to see something horrible, a giant dead rat, or something that would have his presidential trip cancelled. Instead, as he looked inside, all seemed normal. He could see about two metres into the freezer, and the rest was covered in a fog or mist, which is the air circulating to keep everything at the right temperature. But, again, all was normal, boxes stacked on either side with use-by dates stapled to the outside of containers.

Art stepped a few more steps into the freezer. Then, WHOOSH, the mist was parted by something moving fast in front of him. Art was startled and, to add to the effect of absolute terror, was a six-foot man walking out of the mist towards him; it wasn't any man; it was Christopher Lee's Count Dracula! the Count stepped towards Art, raising his arms and cape.

"I want to suck your blood," he snarled and showed his fanged teeth. Even though Art knew what this was, his brain hadn't registered it yet; all it registered was 'get the fuck out of here.' Art overbalanced, stepped backward, and fell on his arse. Later, he would tell people that the freezing cold on his ass woke him up and realised what he was seeing. It was Count Dracula was one of Art's toys. Tyson Lumming had placed it in the freezer, and as usual, Tyson had picked on poor Mrs. Sanders to show how brilliant a job he had done.

After the rap on the knuckles for scaring Mrs. Sanders half to death, Art made Tyson apologise. Art gave her a couple of days off with full pay, courtesy of Tyson Lumming's paycheck. Then secretly congratulated Tyson on an excellent job of getting the toys completed before the arrival of the President. But, of course, Tyson wasn't finished with his testing just yet. Frankenstein was cleaning the toilets in the morning. There were just as many screams in the male toilets as in the females. Wolfman doing dishes in the kitchen. Thank God Mrs. Sanders wasn't back yet. The Mummy walks security at night with Thor and Loki. Then last, the Creature from the Black Lagoon sunning beside the pool. The staff were actually getting used to them and continued snapping selfies with them for social media.

The Secret Service agents weren't so receptive to the oversized Monster figures, so Tyson had to convince them they were only big robotic toys that could only do what they were told to do. Move an arm, sit down, wave, etc. So basically, Tyson didn't lie; he just didn't tell them they could do over 1000 things.

One service agent, a young officer named "Agent Hobbs," seemed to take his job a little too seriously. Continually complained to the head agent that they should contain the monsters in a room or shut down during the President's visit; this pissed Tyson off immensely. So, Tyson set the Monster team's visuals to facial recognition in a mischievous state of mind for payback. The agents didn't know about it, and every time 'Agent Hobbs' walked past, their eyes would follow him, creeping him out.

****

Things weren't going any smoother in Washington as the heads met to discuss any last-minute chatter about the President's trip to the ARK.

"It's still a dangerous move, Mr. President. There's chatter out there that something is moving," Damien Spelling, head of the CIA, said.

"What specifics do you have, Damien?" the President asked.

"Nothing specific, just a lot of extra chatter going on in the circles."

"I must agree with Damien, this time, Mr. President. It seems a risk to leave the country for such a trip," Secretary of State Vincent Pinto agreed.

"I disagree wholeheartedly. Peace between two warring African nations, both nations' economies, tripled in 18 months. We need to be seen to be a part of this, even if it's just supporting trade," the President insisted, "I have been told by our national trade minister that he has been approached by AZTECK to expand in the United States. No, this trip must continue. Linwood, how is everything with the Secret Service at the ARK?"

"All is secured, Mr. President. All requirements have been met, and the Delta team security will touch down two hours before you as required; it comes down to you to say yay or nay, basically Sir."

"That's a yay unless someone has something specific to say, nay?" the President looks around the room; no one has anything to offer.

"Ok, let's get this show on the road. Nothing is set in cement; we will pull the plug if something comes up 'that's verified.' Otherwise, I'll start packing. Thank you, gentlemen, that will be all. Linwood, can you stay back? I have some things that need doing for the trip." On that, the men picked up their folders and made their way out of the Oval office.

"Linwood, is everything ready? We won't get another shot at this."

"Yes, Mr. President, everything is as we arranged," the Chief of Staff assured him.

"So, you think this is a good idea then?" the President asked; the change in the expression of the Chief of Staff made the President think otherwise.

"Speak, Linwood, you know I like your honest opinion," the President pushed.

"An American President heading to a country that only 18 months ago hated Americans, that have been at war for 50 years... until 18 months ago. Going to a robotic safari in the middle of the wilderness in a country run by a vicious dictator...until 18 months ago... What could possibly go wrong?" The Chief of Staff looked at the President blankly.

"Geez, Linwood, you know how to kill the mood... Lighten up! We have set everything up to be secure. I want you to go over everything with Chad and make sure he gets everything he wants for his team on this trip."

"Yes, Mr President."

****

The final 2 days passed quickly for the President and his delegation. All was a bustle at the ARK for the Secret Service as the Special Forces arrived to give the all-clear for the President's plane to land. Even though Commander Chad Langdon had studied the maps of the ARK'S areas carefully. He was still overwhelmed by the sheer magnitude of the area's circumference. The only fact that bugged him was the seven minutes by copter from the airfield to where the President was hunting. Landing anywhere near the safari site for the Delta team would leave them in unprotected areas.

****

The welcoming band was doing last-minute tune-ups on the tarmac at the ARK. Honing their skills before getting to play the Star-Spangled Banner for the American President. The welcoming delegation arrived at the airfield in time to have their security tags checked before entering the restricted space. African Clan elders were invited to give a blessing to the group and their mission. To represent AZTECK were Art, Ab, and Macca, Ab, who just flew back in time as the Mineral Conglomerate held him up with a stalling of the takeover bid in Taiwan. At the edge of the tarmac were twenty security team members. They were put together comprising Somalian and Ethiopian military. Shining like new toy soldiers off an assembly line, the men looked impressive and had been drilled accordingly by their Commander, Major Tamoa Acondia, formally of the Ethiopian National Special Forces.

Art, Ab, and Macca arrived five minutes before the landing. The Special Forces teams moved into specific areas to cover the aircraft, as did the Secret Service team on the ground. The landing was smooth, and as the jet taxied into position. There was a height of excitement in the air and not just from Art Damani. To have the President of the United States here at the ARK was a massive deal for the staff, who spent the week scrubbing every inch of their work areas to make them sparkle.

On the other hand, Ab was still not impressed; he still believed inviting such a figurehead to the ARK was inviting trouble. Tyson Lumming was also not impressed with the interruptions to his work schedule and spent the week upgrading new systems into the Monster brigade. The Secret Service and other staff members of the ARK see the monsters as Art's toys. That they may be, but Tyson sees them for what they really are, and so does Art. The first step in perfecting human movement in robotics. Each of the monsters is a test pattern for further studies to perfect a life-like robot and, therefore, have an insight into how to mesh robotics and human limb replacement.

The Secret Service lined the bottom of the plane's stairway leading to Art and his welcoming crew of African Clan elders. The door opened, and on cue, the band started playing Star-Spangled Banner, and exceptionally well, Art thought. The President did the usual, standing on top of the stairs and waving to the crowd, posing for the press gallery that followed him everywhere. The press invited on the brief tour were told they were not to speak of the trip until the President was on his way home, thus avoiding any trouble in the country.

The President was met by the Clan Elders and given a welcoming blessing and local flowered wreath. He thanked them all for their welcome into their beautiful country. He then moved on to Art. Art was like a school kid meeting his favourite rock star, shaking the President's hand vigorously.

"Welcome, Mr. President; it is such an honour to have you here," Art said.

"No, Mr. Damani, the pleasure is all mine. I am a huge fan of what you're doing here."

"Well, thank you, Mr. President; I can't wait to show you around. May I have the absolute honour of introducing my son Ab Thoyana," Art stepped aside to allow the two to meet.

"Another honour. I am a big fan of yours, Mr. Thoyana, 24 and 2nd CEO of one of the largest companies in the world. You are an inspirational figure to the youth of today."

"Well, thank you, Mr. President; maybe we will get time to speak of youth affairs in the United States while you are here," Ab pressed.

"Abayomi, I really hope we do; I would love to have your thoughts," the President responded.

The President was introduced to Macca Salisbury, CEO of AZTECK African Division, and then taken for a security guard tour.

"Very impressive for a private security, Mr. Damani."

"They are all ex-soldiers from Somalian forces and Ethiopian regulars, Mr. President." The President walked along the line till he came to their Commander, Major Tamoa Acondia. The Major was clearly at least 7 or 8 inches taller than the tallest soldier in the line.

"This is Major Tamoa Acondia, the Security commander," Art introduced. The President put out his hand to shake with the Major.

"God Lord Major, are you 7 feet?"

"With thick socks, Mr. President," the Major responded.

The President laughed, "I bet you don't get too many men arguing with your orders," the President jokingly added, "They only do it once. My mother is bigger than me, and we don't argue with her either," all the men laughed.

"Well, Major, you are to be commended; your men are a tribute to your work."

"Thank you, Mr. President," Major Acondia returned.

"I do have a question, Major, if I may?"

"Please go ahead, Mr. President," The Major said.

"After all these years of fighting between Somalia and Ethiopia, is it difficult to keep together a joint force?" the President asked.

The Major maintained his military stance, firm and proud. Everyone on my team came to us; they all believed in peace and stability. Plus, I have no trouble maintaining stability in my team... My team loves me."

The President and Art burst out laughing. "I'm glad of that because I'd hate to be on your bad side," The President said.

The President and his entourage made their way to a line-up of vehicles. They were all open seated, except two brought in to drive the President around. At the last moment, the President requested to be seated in an open car to better view the park. This sent the Secret Service into a meltdown. To keep all parties happy, one bullet-proof vehicle drove behind the President's car and one in front, just in case for a quick rescue. Also, on the other side of the security fence, two vehicles ran parallel to the President, one on the other side of the wall and one ten metres in, looking for anyone in the area.

"Mr. Damani, this fence is impressive. The cost for just the fencing alone would have been staggering."

"Well, I got it at cost price, as I own the companies that make it, and it's a good tax write-off since we are a Non-Profit Park."

The President let out a huge laugh. "Good one. I'll have to remember that next time I push the house for funding."

The tour continued on, with the conversation between Art and the President ranging between the animals viewed and which ones were robots. Also, about the remarkable reconstruction of the animals' natural habitats. To a bit of a dip in the trade talk questions how the USA may help with trade.

"It's easy to forget that you're a private business and not a small nation on its own, Mr. Damani."

"Yes, I sometimes forget that we are guests in this country. Even though we strive to help build up these great nations, we are still their guests.

Just then, the driver in front hit the brakes. A call came through from the front car, "should we stop and offer assistance, Mr. President?"

"Assistance with what?" the President asked.

Just then, three figures ran out in the open. The man in the front was wearing a slouch hat. Charging after them was a huge rhino, who seemed to be mad at them. Art started laughing, "that's Dan, our game warden, and the delightful lady chasing him is Buttercup; she's such a friendly rhino."

"She doesn't look friendly," The President said.

"Dan's probably just playing with her. He's Australian."

The President looked at Art in disbelief. "Ok, if you say so. You can move on; officer Mr. Damani says it's fine."

Dan Hooper, the ARK's Game warden, watched as the motorcade moved on and disappeared in the thick foliage.

"Typical. Bloody bosses never want to get their hands dirty." Dan looked down from the tree; he and his staff climbed. "Aw, come on, Buttercup, give us a break, will ya!"

Up ahead, we are coming up to the Vet hospital where the new arrivals are quarantined and nurtured to better health before releasing them into a new habitat." The vehicles rolled up in their convoy line as the Secret Service exited first to take their positions before the President could exit; Art looked around at all the fuss and leaned over towards the President.

"Do you ever tire of all this fuss?"

"Every single day," the President gives Art a smile.

"We are ready for you, Mr. President," the Secret Service officer said.

After being introduced to the hospital staff, Art turns to the President.

"You'll have to excuse the absence of our chief veterinarian today, Mr. President; she was called out to the new tiger's compound on an urgent visit. One of our surveillance animals picked up, acute anxiety and breathing irregularities in one of our new releases."

"Your surveillance animals have the technology for body scans; that's amazing."

"Not all animals can do it; some are just spy cams and heat signature adapted, so we move animals into the areas, if need be, to do body scans. In this case, there is always a body scan substitute in the area of new releases. It can be a terrifying ordeal after spending your life on a chain, so we monitor them."

"How do you get a hold of the animals in the first place?" the President inquired.

"Some are well known through zoos and public shows throughout the world. Some are reported weekly now by animal liberation groups. So, some we buy, some we trade with our robotic animals and some we... acquire," the President looked at Art after his last comment.

"I'm not ready for sainthood yet, Mr. President," Art offered him a wry smile.

"This is truly amazing what you have done here, truly amazing."

The President finished his tour and was ushered inside for lunch at the food mall. Once again, the President and his entourage were blown away by the sheer magnitude of everything. The ARK Mountain looks like a small mountain or large hill. But inside, a complex beehive of levels seems to go on and on. The food mall was a winner with everyone, given 45 minutes for a break for lunch. Some were stumped on what to eat, as the choices seemed endless. The lunchtime entertainment had the President in awe; the Monster squad put a show on.

The thought of being served by a robotic Count Dracula with the exact facial features of Christopher Lee was astounding. At the same time, Frankenstein, the Wolfman, and the Creature from the Black Lagoon sang songs with The Mummy, adding in the well-timed uuurg, which was priceless.

As the President marvelled over the Monster Squad, he started asking questions about them.

"Mr. President, as much as I would like to take credit for these works of art, let me introduce you to the genius behind them. Tyson comes over here," Art started waving his arm for Tyson to come over and join the conversation.

"Mr. President, I'd like to introduce you to Tyson Lumming, our head of Bio-engineering and Biomechanics," the President stuck out his hand for a hearty shake, as was his way.

"Mr. President, it is an honour." Tyson watched the President's facial expression, and there was no recognition from the President that he knew who Tyson was or that he was working for the CIA.

'How could the President not know, he thought, am I that deep undercover?'

"Mr. Lumming, the pleasure is all mine," he greeted warmly.

"I am just blown away by your mastery of these robots; each is amazing in its own way."

"Yes, they are precisely that, Mr. President; each is its own unique test model for robotics, even though the choice of characters was Mr. Damani's. Each is a test subject for a specific type of advancement testing.

"Amazing, what kind of test was each made for," the President asked eagerly.

"Well, I made the Creature from the Black Lagoon for water sealing under pressure. Frankenstein was to get height and strength with balance correct. The amazing thing about Franky was when we first tested him after all the calculations were correct, he actually walked like Frankenstein's Monster, so Mary Shelley got it right. Dracula was facial recognition and speech, no blood-sucking."

The President had a good laugh. "Thank God for that; I will sleep better tonight."

"The Mummy was fireproofing, and computer analysis, and last but not least, was the Wolfman. He was the actual work, human muscle movement. We have been working on copying our work from animals to human movement; it's a lot more complex."

"Human cloning?" the President was taken aback a little.

"No, Mr. President, we're are not cloning humans; we are copying them. We hope one day to have artificial limbs available with binary infusions. To have limbs that can move exactly like real ones for people who have lost theirs. If we can get it right, they will function straight from the cerebral cortex, making them react exactly like a real one."

"Oh my God, that would be amazing; think of the trauma it would reduce if people knew they could get a new limb just like the one they lost."

"Exactly, Mr. President, exactly. Even though the park was designed with the protection of robotic animals, they are just a chance for us to perfect the science, to market for Azteck."

"Mr. President, please excuse the Monster squad and myself; they run on battery power and are due for their dinner; it's been a pleasure, Mr. President." Tyson finished and moved up his sleeve; on his wrist was like a mini-computer screen wrapped around his forearm. Then, with the touch of a few keys, the Monster squad stopped what they were doing and made their way back to their coffins or recharging stations.

"Well, Mr. President, I believe your Secret Service men wish to show you to your quarters; you must be exhausted from your flight and day touring."

"On the contrary, Mr. Damani, it's been an amazing day, so much wonder to take in. The ARK is truly a work of genius and a great footnote for mankind to follow." The President stood up and shook Art's hand.

"Good evening; I will see you in the morning," the President said.

"Enjoy your quarters, Mr. President," Art offered. Art had thoroughly enjoyed his day with the President. He was charming, intelligent, observant, and a skilled conversationalist... but... Art was disappointed in one way. He didn't ask the one question he thought he would... That one question!

CHAPTER 21

EASY GIG

Clang, clang, clang! The sound of the clock's old-fashioned alarm woke the President. 'No wonder nobody slept in, in the '70s,' he thought. To get up himself to his own alarm was a rare pleasure, instead of attendants coming in early to get him started for the day. He quickly hit the shower, and while soaking in the abundant water pressure, the President went through his own mental training by remembering ten new things he learned yesterday once he arrived at the ARK. Also, going through his schedule for the day, which he always memorises the night before.

"Human robotics," he said aloud in the shower, "Oh my God, fantastic, scary tech though, in the wrong hands."

Dressed and focused, the President always has things to do and worlds to conquer. He couldn't remember having such a good night's sleep in years. His lush apartment was as good, if not better, than any presidential suite he had ever stayed in. The President grabbed an orange off the table and started peeling it. Mr. Damani had done his research well, with a bowl of his favourite sweets and fruits in the room. He grabbed the folder of 'other worldly events' left for him to look over by his attendant. There was still a mountain of rubber stamping and situations to look over. Another shooting in the South, riots, and retaliation. 'If I do anything in my term as President, I have to come up with some way of working these situations out to the benefit of both sides,' he thought.

****

Fifty km away, six SAS soldiers exit the American Army transport at the local airport in Lugh Ganana. It's never the most pleasant of rides, but the men and women of this team never complain; they have had a lot worse. They transported their gear by a luggage train to the waiting troop transport provided by the ARK.

As the troop transport was being loaded with their gear, the newest member of the team, Corporal Thomas Ash, was getting a grip on the large crate he had brought with him, loaded with new advanced recon gear to be field-tested for the team. 2 Planks walks up behind him.

"You need a hand with that kid?" he asks.

"Ah, yes, it's a little on the heavy side. You know I'm not a kid?"

"Yeh, I know! And if you ever blow up a dunny while I'm on it... Sleep with one eye open for the rest of your life," 2 Planks informs him.

With Sherlock in the front, 2 Planks noticed the mood was quiet and nobody was talking with the new guy there. He noticed that the new boy kept his head down and was staring at the crate he bought with him.

"You know, kid, you're part of the team now; you don't have to carry anything alone. Just ask, and any of us will help, as will you if any of us need help. That's what this squad is about, your part of our family now," 2 Planks said genuinely.

"Thanks," Thomas replied.

"Why the big crate? You know you can't take that into the field with you?" asked 2 Planks.

"It's my mission from Colonel Briggs," Thomas replied.

"First day on the job, and he gets a personal mission from the boss. How come I never get a personal mission?" Smith chimed in, sounding irritated.

"You have a daily mission, that's why, to be fucking annoying, now shut up and let him finish," 2 Planks responded.

"He wants me to upgrade all our field gear, sound, and sight with a high-tech analyse grid. To see better, hear better, break down less, repair easier was my mission," Thomas told them.

"Holy shit, are you some kind of tech genius, Thomas?" Steel asked.

"Yes, actually, I have a knack for being able to pull tech apart and make it better."

"No shit," Quassy said.

"It's funny that we are going to AZTECK; they approached me when I was in UNI and offered me a scholarship worth a fair bit of money," Thomas said.

"And you turned it down?" asked Steel, amazed.

"Yeah, I joined the forces instead," Thomas replied.

"Are you some kind of glory hound, looking for some action?" asked 2 Planks, concerned.

"No, not at all, my brothers in the service, in the Navy," said Thomas.

"Oh, a fish," said Smith.

"No, more like a Squid; he's a Navy diver," Thomas said proudly.

"Well, he must have balls; that's one job I wouldn't want, a really tough job to do. I'd rather be shot at and have Smith jabbering in my ear all day," said 2 Planks. The team broke out in laughter, except Smith, but they needed it to break the ice.

"Once I finish the upgrade, you will see and hear better. Supposed to be safer," said Thomas.

"Where's the fun in that?" asked Smith.

"No more hanging out in latrines; I can handle that," said Steel.

Thomas looked stunned, "we hang out in latrines?"

"Yep, where the mic meets the shit, literally," said 2 Planks.

Thomas was really stunned now, sitting there with a blank look.

"I'll give you till we leave this place, and if you haven't fixed a better sound device to get us out of the latrines... You're on permanent shit duty. Let's see how much of a genius you are now, the clocks ticking," Steel challenged Thomas.

The rest of the trip was a lot lighter on the way in; they felt they had started breaking the new boy in. But, while in the front, Sherlock was brooding or slightly confused about why they were here, why a private company invitation, how did they even know who we were?

As the truck carrying the Australian SAS team approached the front gates of the ARK, they all stood up to get a look. The entrance to the park certainly lived up to its name. The front was a giant timber ark that you drove through to get into the park. On the other side of the ARK, you were met by security gates and officers to show the correct entry papers. 2 Planks also noticed that the fences looked sturdy.

"Jurassic Park, isn't that what it looks like to you guys?" Smith said.

'Yes, that's exactly what it looks like. Concrete barrier bases with steel fencing and wire panels. Just like Jurassic Park,' 2 Planks thought.

"Geez, they don't build robot dinosaurs, do they? I didn't bring a big enough gun," said Quassy jokingly. At that joke, they sat down again. Then, they travelled through the inside of the ARK entrance to get to the security gates.

"Geez, this is creepy. What's with all the glass panels?" Smith said.

"We're being scanned, a lot of tech for a zoo, don't you think?"

"Maybe they're not convinced the ceasefire will hold," 2 Planks responded.

Art was waiting to greet the SAS soldiers at the barracks near the airport. As the truck stopped, Sherlock stepped out, and immediately a gentleman he recognised as Mr. Art Damani came racing over to meet him.

"Captain Madden, so very pleased to meet you; I hope the trip wasn't too arduous?" Art greeted.

"No, not at all. In our line of work, we are not used to comfort anyway," Sherlock replied.

"So, so true, that's why it must be a big relief when you are back home with family," Art said.

"Yes, indeed it is," Sherlock replied.

Sherlock introduced the team before they clambered into a lorry that the Security men used to get around the park in. The vehicles were slow; as the tour progressed, they came to the barracks in the park where the team would stay for the week.

"I choose this area for you to train in. It has a vast array of different landscapes and an area of 34,000 acres to play in, not that you'll be playing," Art said.

It was perfect for the new electronic gear trials that Corporal Thomas would be testing.

"How is this fencing a deterrent for poachers? It's not as robust as the fencing on the entry?" Mike asked.

"Yes, you're right, a matter of future expansion. I suppose the fencing around here doesn't have the strength as the front, but it has the technology. Each panel is its own grid. You can't cut into it or bypass it, like old security. We know of breaches within seconds; we know what it is from the animal surveillance. The security here is armed well enough for poachers, and we have the numbers with the animal security, tigers; lions; rhinos, and soon an elephant. They're all around here." Art waved his hands in the air.

"Cool." Thomas had been listening in on the conversation and was indeed impressed.

"You would have found out firsthand if you had taken up my offer 5 years ago, young man," Art said to Thomas.

"Yes, just because I missed out on you the first time doesn't mean I give up; I keep an eye on future prospects," Art told Thomas.

"Wow, I'm a prospect," Thomas said to Sherlock.

"Kid, I'd shoot you for desertion before that happens," Sherlock told him.

Thomas sat back with a smile, mumbling, 'I'm a prospect' under his voice.

****

The tour inside was just as fascinating as it was outside. The great work at the hospital was nearly as impressive as the pool and food mall. Well, to Smith and 2 Planks, anyway. The team was in awe of the entire complex, thinking it was some kind of Disneyland. But nothing compared to Tyson Lumming and the Monster squad, though, especially for Smith. He was a big fan of the early horror movies.

"Have you finished with the selfies, Smith? Can we go now, before he asks to marry one of them?" Steel joked.

"Don't be stupid, Steel; they are all males," Smith joked.

"Nothing would drag him away from his blow-up collection anyway," Quassy chimed in; they all started laughing.

"Oh, hardy, ha-ha," Smith said sulkily. Then they all thanked Tyson for the display and headed to the HUB.

****

First, the HUB was explained by Ab, who demonstrated the surveillance capabilities at their fingertips.

"Lexi, I love your fashion sense. Your outfit is amazing," Smith said.

"I don't think it's her outfit you're interested in and stop drooling on the ladies' hand. She may want to use it again," Steel chimed in.

"Very funny, don't listen to them Lexi, they're jealous of anyone with style."

Sherlock noticed things quickly, and he thought Doby had a nervous twitch to him; he put it down to the fact that with two people running all this hardware, the job must come with a lot of pressure.

"Hey, Kid, we should have just hired these guys to upgrade our gear. Is yours as good as this?" Steel teased.

Ab looked at Thomas and said, "What do they mean?"

"My first day in the team, and my job is to bring them out of the dark ages with new tech," laughed back Thomas.

"Good one, Kid, now you're getting the hang of it," 2 Planks praised Thomas. Smith listened to Ab and Thomas speak about the team's gear and what they should use. His head turned from side to side with his mouth open, like the clowns from a carnival.

"What did they just say?" Smith asked.

"They're speaking nerd, don't try to understand them; their brains are wired differently," Lexi said.

Then everyone had a laugh again, except Doby.

The team was driven back to their barracks to set up and go through their gear.

The barracks were spacious, with a presentation room for meetings and classes. Bunking was a standard issue with two showers and toilets, with trunks at the end of the bunks for personal gear. Quassy had his usual bitch: they never made the trunks big enough for his guitar. Gear stashed, there was a small kitchen for them to prepare lunch, even though no one was starving because they wanted to feed their faces on free food and drinks tonight at the ball, except 2 Planks. He was always hungry.

Thomas impressed Sherlock with how quickly he got set up to maintain his gear. Thomas had set up on a table behind Steel. On the other side of Steel was Quassy. Thomas was working away constructively, oblivious to what was happening around him. At one point, Thomas stood up straight to stretch his back; he casually looked over towards Steel; she was bent over her table working on her kit. She had the ass of a supermodel. Not wanting to think of a teammate in that way, but her butt was only a few feet away, and it was beautifully shaped; it was hard to miss. Quassy noticed Thomas had recognised Steel's butt, as they all had, and remarked on it. Quassy threw a small screwdriver onto Steels' table to get her attention. Steel looked up, and Quassy made a head jerk towards Thomas with a smirk on his face.

Steel knew; it was on! "I can feel you looking at my ass! Are you looking at my arse, Kid?" Steel said sternly without turning. Kid didn't know how she knew, and felt ashamed for looking now and scared as well.

"No, I wasn't looking at it," Kid pleaded.

"Oh, you weren't, so my arse isn't good enough for you to look at! Is that what you're saying? Steel spun to look at Kid, who looked like a trapped bunny in a snare.

"Yes, yes, it is; it's a great arse." As soon as the words left Thomas's mouth, he regretted them.

"Oh, so my arse is great! I suppose you'd like to grab my arse!" Steel stomped over beside Kid; he felt trapped. All this talk about her arse affected parts of his anatomy, and he was terrified she would notice it.

"No, no, I don't want to grab it," he protested.

"OH, so my arse is great, but not good enough for you. That's what you're saying!" Yes, it is, but! But!" Kid didn't feel he could say anything right without offending Steel even more.

"Ok, then my arse is great and good enough for you to grab... Well, go ahead."

"Go ahead???" Kid said, confused.

"Grab my arse." Steel was beside him and turned her body, so her arse was beside Kid.

"Grab my arse, boy!" Steel barked at him, out of the pure terror of this woman, grabbed her ass cheeks with both hands.

"You will not get laid if that's the best you can grab a woman's arse!" Steel informed him. Thomas gave them a gentle squeeze.

"Do I make you hard, soldier? Don't you lie to me!" Before Kid could bite his tongue, before it had a chance to say anything, it wagged.

"Yes," came spiralling out. 'I'm dead,' Kid thought. Steel spun around and quickly grabbed him by his erection, but she had pulled a knife from somewhere even more rapidly and held it up against the bulge in his trousers.

"DON'T YOU EVER LET ME CATCH YOU CHECKING OUT MY ARSE AGAIN, OR YOU WILL NEVER GET TO PLAY WITH THIS AGAIN," Steel gave his dick a tug.

"Got it!"

"Yes, yes, I got it."

Steel let go of him and spun around to walk back to her table. Kid couldn't see that she had a grin from ear to ear; this was a routine she had pulled many times before.

Thomas could feel the sweat running down his back; it felt like a river. As he stood there with his head down, not daring to look up in case she was watching him, he turned to his side, away from Steel, and noticed everyone was watching and smiling. They had set him up good. He fell for it, hook, line and sinker.

Wanting not to look like a total baby after his performance, he said, "Steel!" She spun around with that same menacing face she just had on.

"What is it?" she snarled.

"Since I squeezed your arse, and you grabbed my dick... Does that mean we're engaged???" Steel couldn't handle it; none of them could. Finally, they all burst out laughing hysterically.

"Great comeback, Kid!" 2 Planks yelled.

2 Planks turned to Sherlock. "I think I'm going to like this kid."

"Steel?" Thomas asked; Steel was still trying to catch her breath from the laughter.

"Yes, Thomas?"

"Would you do me the honour of sitting beside me tonight at dinner?" he asked.

"Thomas, I'd love to," Steel replied.

"Aww, come on!" Smith protested, "You didn't let me take you to dinner after you pulled that stunt on me."

"Yeah, but you were creepy," Steel joked, bringing another round of laughter.

The maintenance finished, Sherlock thought there was not enough time to do a drill, so he gave them the time to relax before dinner tonight; the news went down famously, as all free time does.

Free time meant different things to different people. As 2 Planks curled up in a foetal position napping, Smith and Steel were getting dirty, trying to perfect a move where they could change a magazine in their rifle while rolling on the ground. Thomas set up a table with measuring scales to weigh the team's gear; he tried to add new tech for them but kept to the same weight range they usually carry. Sherlock flipped through maps and folders he brought, working out what drills they would perform while here. While all this action and non-action went on, Quassy sang and strummed away on his guitar, playing a John Denver tune.

CHAPTER 22

DINNER WITH A JACKAL

"This just seems wrong," Mike said to Seb.

The pair were standing in the office of the barracks at the ARK training site. Through the window, you could see the jungle outside, a thick, lush pasture of low shrubs, and behind that, a dense forest cluster of trees so thick that a couple of metres in, it seems to turn into impenetrable darkness.

"What seems wrong?" Seb enquired.

"Getting all dressed up in an army barracks in the middle of a jungle."

"Well, we will just add it to all the other weird shit we've done with this team. Just another day at the office," Seb said, laughing.

The team was prepared for the ARK's special dinner for the President. Mike and Seb were going with the tie and dinner jacket look, Smith and Dean opting for the open shirt and sports coat look, but no one was prepared for the Katelyn and Thomas dinner look. Katelyn was dressed in an ankle-length turquoise dress that shimmered like fish scales. No matter which way she turned, she glistened radiantly. The dress was skin-tight and clung to every curve of her body. She wore her hair up in a Japanese bun with Jade chopsticks poking through her hair and turquoise high heel shoes. She looked amazing, and she walked with such eloquence in her high heels.

Thomas, on the other hand, had a style all his own. He wore an open hot pink shirt with tight black leather trousers. A 3/4 length black leather jacket that looked really expensive, with black and white wing-tipped shoes.

"Damn, Thomas has got style, Mike. He makes me feel old," Seb said.

Mike laughed, but he agreed Thomas has style.

As they were waiting to be picked up, Smith walked up behind Thomas.

"Hey Thomas, I'll give you 50 bucks to swap seats with me," he whispered; Thomas turned around, "I wouldn't do it for a 1000."

Steel overheard the conversation and turned around and gave Thomas a kiss on the cheek.

"Thomas, you look hot tonight," she added, just to piss Smith off some more.

The transport dropped the team off at the food mall, making their way to the elevators. There was a gate for security to check all guests before entering. The elevator was run by a Secret Service agent. There were two agents on each floor and eight in the banquet room that were visible.

All were part of the deal struck by the White House to allow the President to attend. Even the security team for the Somalian President Abdi had to disarm, which surprisingly the President agreed to with no fuss. The banquet hall was decorated amazingly with natural flora from the region and African cultural gear from Somali Clans. The colours were radiant, and the displays were erected tastefully, with a natural balance.

Once the team was inside, they wasted no time heading to the bar with free drinks, the calling for the night. They were all professionals and didn't need to be reminded that they had training tomorrow to keep a limit to the number of drinks taken through the night, except Smith, he had to be reminded.

Mike ordered a drink and decided to find the host and thank him for the invitation. He saw Art talking with both Presidents and a Secret Service agent; at first, he thought he would wait and catch up with him later, then thought what the hell and marched over to butt into the conversation.

"Good evening, Mr. Damani," Mike greeted Art.

Art turned quickly and greeted him warmly, "Mike, glad you're here; I want to introduce you to some people, Captain Mike Madden; I'd like you to meet President Abdi and President Edwin, oh and the head of the President's Secret Service Chad Langdon."

Mike greeted the two Presidents warmly, shaking their hands, then he went to shake Chad Langdon's hand, and they both hesitated before shaking just enough that Art noticed they knew each other.

"Do you two know each other?" Art asked curiously.

"Yes, we met during allied war games in Australia around eight years ago," Mike offered.

"You were in the service then, Chad," Art queried.

"Yes, I was a captain in the Special Forces, on an opposing team from Mr. Madden." Sensing some hostility, Art couldn't help himself. He wanted to know more, and so did the Presidents.

"Who won?" each asked both the men.

"We did," Mike offered.

"Because you cheated," Chad quickly threw in.

"Oh," Art said, astonished.

To quickly rectify the situation, Mike offered, "We took advantage of an unwritten loophole in the rules." Art was inquisitive now.

"You took your team dangerously through a Naval Live-Fire range!" Chad said angrily.

"And outflanked the captain's team, took the flag, and didn't lose a man," Mike quickly added.

"Dangerous, with no regard for his team," Chad kept pushing that point.

"It's not dangerous if you buy the firing times and co-ordinance off a naval officer for two cases of beer and a bottle of Johnny Walker Black Label," Sherlock finished. The Presidents and Art laughed heartily till they noticed Chad wasn't amused by the situation.

"Like I said, you cheated," Chad offered.

"It caused some feathers to be ruffled, but the head overseers of the war games still gave us the win, and they were American officers," Mike said, as he wasn't going to back down.

A woman with a stylish business suit appeared and leaned over to whisper into Art's ear and then left swiftly. "Gentlemen, I must break this conversation; They have informed me they wish to start our dinner; please take your seats." All the men broke off to find their seats. As President Edwin was walking to his seat, he turned to his head of the Secret Service.

"Well, that was awkward," he said.

"Not at all, Sir, water under the bridge," the head of Security said.

"Didn't seem that way; looked like the war games were still continuing."

"Not for me, Sir, past tense, moved on." The President looked at him with a 'who are you kidding' look, on which the Security Chief just shrugged.

Katelyn waved to Mike to tell him where they were seated. Thomas sat next to Katelyn, and Smith sat across from them and threw daggers at Thomas all night.

Seb watched as trolley after trolley left the kitchen area and the aroma of so many different dishes swept the room.

"Stop drooling on the linen, these tablecloths probably cost more than a month of your salary," Mike joked to Seb.

"Do we get paid for what we do? I thought that was just appearance money."

The conversation was light around the table, except for Katelyn and Thomas, who played up the whole 'date thing' to piss Smith off. Sharing each other's meals, "Oh dear, you must try this." "Oh this dish is divine just like you." Thomas brought her glasses of champagne and giggled and laughed throughout dinner. At one stage, Seb thought he might have to pour the jug of water over Smith to cool him down or throw it on the two feral cats parading on the other side of the table.

After dinner, the team broke up and mingled, even the two lovebirds. They finished their show-and-dance, and it was time to move on. Katelyn found herself alone checking out one of the fabulous African exhibits when a voice came from behind.

"Hi," she turned to find Lexi standing behind her.

"Hi to you too, Lexi; enjoy your dinner?"

"Yes, I had this fabulous oyster dish, but now, thinking about it, I shouldn't have. The last time I had oysters, it didn't go down well," Lexi said.

"Were you ill after it?" Katelyn enquired.

"No, it ended in a 12-hour Love and Lust session."

"And that's a bad thing?" Katelyn sounded amazed.

"Well, I did something silly, and now the person has me back on a friend without benefits."

"Yes, that would suck," Katelyn agreed.

"But, enough of my sad love life, the night's still young, but girl, you have to lend me that dress someday, or I'll be forced to rip it off you!" Lexi said, playful.

"Now there's a thought. I might just be forced to say no!" Katelyn teased.

"My God, Katelyn, you didn't have the oysters too?" At that remark, the girls laughed vigorously.

"Well, I suppose I should keep mingling to keep Art happy. Don't get my dress dirty," Lexi teased.

Lexi went to turn when Katelyn spoke, "Our dress and I will be around all night."

"I noticed you didn't say no yet?" Lexi queried.

"Never say never," Katelyn said with a wry smile on her face. Lexi blew Katelyn a kiss and walked off to do her entertaining.

Deen and Smith were chatting to a couple of young African women from the Trade delegation, enthralling them with their encounters as Special Forces operatives. They didn't seem to mind breaking protocol by saying what they did, because they weren't even sure the young women understood a word they were saying. Seb had joined Katelyn at the African exhibits. Thomas was chatting with Ab about technical nerd stuff.

As Mike finished a conversation with a lady from the African trade delegation, he turned and walked straight into a conversation between President Edwin and President Abdi.

"Captain Madden, just the man, to lend an impartial ear," President Edwin said.

"I'm not sure about that. I'm a soldier, not a politician," Mike said, trying to stay out of their conversation.

"President Abdi says that war is as inevitable as a sunrise, and I disagree, believing that the sunrise should bring hope and a way to stop the wars," President Edwin made his case.

"Well, it's easy for me. I'm sent to fight. I don't get an opinion on who to fight. I fight my enemy," Mike responded.

"And who is your enemy, Captain Madden?" President Abdi asked.

"That's easy, Mr. President, the people, shooting at me... And the people who sent the people to shoot at me." President had a laugh at this, but President Abdi didn't see the humour.

"To answer your question," Mike said, "You are both right. Looking through history, it is showered with wars and conquest, still to this day, more wars and conquests. So, are humans going to really change? Then, look at the ARK and the wonderful effect it's had on this nation and Ethiopia; you were fighting not so long ago. Everybody puts the praise on Mr. Damani for what he has done for this country, but to me, President Abdi should be praised, he allowed it to happen, he nourished that seed of hope in the new day."

All the men were silent; Chad Langdon, head of the President's Secret Service, said 'kiss arse' under his breath.

"I didn't know you were a philosopher, Captain Madden?" President Edwin asked.

"I never said I wasn't; I had just never been asked my opinion before. Could you excuse me, gentlemen? I think some of my team need to be reminded that we have training tomorrow. Excuse me," as Mike walked off, President Abdi said, "Yes, thank you, Captain, for your insight," at which Chad Langdon was saying under his breath.

'Oh please!' Mike couldn't get away quick enough. He didn't need to remind his team they were professionals, but he didn't want to get into a political debate with a madman.

Mike needed some air after that last conversation, so he went for a walk outside the banquet room. He walked down the hallway and came to the balcony looking into the centre of the ARK. Amazed at how all this fits inside a hill, impressive. He heard footsteps coming down the hallway behind him, and he knew that his moment of peace would be short-lived. He prayed it wasn't Abdi wanting more praise; he could only say so much without losing his dinner.

"I'm very sorry, I couldn't get there in time to save you," said a quiet voice behind him, the voice of Art Damani.

Mike turned to greet his host. "I saw you get trapped by those two, the optimist and the destroyer of worlds," Art and Mike laughed.

"I'd love to know how you got him to agree to all this," Mike waved his hand towards the ARK behind him.

"I bought him!" Art replied quickly. Sherlock was an expert judge of character and truthfulness, and he believed he was talking to the real Art Damani.

"I didn't think you could buy power, people?" Mike asked.

"Once he steps down and holds an election, I will give him a token job as a delegate for the Somalian people and AZTECK. He and his family will want for nothing," Art informed Mike.

"Do you trust him?"

"Not as far as I could throw him, which is not far; the man is enormous!" Art said

"That's why your front gate is battle proof, strong enough to stop trucks coming in from the front and concrete placements for soldiers to fight behind."

"You're very observant, Mike," Art replied.

"But I don't get the outer fences; they would be more vulnerable."

"Yes, but no one could get through without us knowing, plus I have other cards in play. I hope one of them will succeed and the park can expand as planned. I'll keep my eye on Abdi; many people are fortunate with the country's turnaround. They wouldn't be happy if he stirred up things; let's hope he takes up my offer. He is supposed to announce the election shortly, fingers crossed."

"More like rifles loaded," Mike added.

Mike turned to look over the balcony again, and the men went silent for a moment.

Art spoke first. "You have two questions; you would like to know, don't you?"

"Well, yes, actually!" Mike realised Art was like him and could read people's body language, but knowing he had two questions that were just freaky, he thought.

"Two why's. Why are you here, and why is this here?" Mike waved his hand around again.

"Well, I'll answer the second one first because I have been waiting for someone to actually ask that question. Most think, crazy billionaire, wanted something to do, ah, let's build an ARK."

"Yeah, pretty much," Mike said.

"But there's more, isn't there?"

"Yes, crazy, but more like a Trillionaire, if only they knew. You have lots of billionaires doing different things around the world. Look at Musky trying to fly to Mars and colonise for the people of the Earth. You know. Good on him. I hope he succeeds and runs the planet on solar power and charges everyone entry. I haven't given up on Earth just yet, I haven't the power or the money to save every country, NATO and the UN have stuck their noses into a lot of places, but they haven't offered people a choice to change or a viable way to do it. So, I thought, what if I could get two countries to stop fighting, and fix their economy so that the people had a chance to really live. No famine, no wars, and as a side bonus we save endangered animal species and trying to repopulate the planet. Now, say that happened, my guess is others would want to join, and bingo look who sends a trade delegation. I can do this!" Art finished; they both fell silent again.

Mike spoke first this time, "So prove things can be healed and show countries it's doable, that's why," Sherlock said, then he continued.

"But you're also a realist, and you know people are going to try to tear you down."

"Exactly," Art answered.

"The first genuine test is Abdi. If he sticks to his word, then if people see the American President on board and then, and then..." Art continued.

"This is a great idea and seems to have gotten a grip, but why are we here now?"

"Well, that was just a case of timing. After your last mission in Afghanistan, nearly went south," Art stated.

"Yes, and that's another thing; how do you know who we are, and how do you know about our classified missions?" Mike stated.

"Well, that kind of answers the first question, Mike. AZTECK is a lot more... ahead in tech than people know. We haven't released tech because we don't think the world is ready for it. If the CIA, Mossad, or the Kremlin knew what we could do, they'd want it and try to find a way to take it. The bottom line is that a lot of technology comes from different companies, spyware, listening devices, bugs for snooping, etc. People don't know that I own most of that tech through the years. The companies are owned by different people... But they're not, so for years everyone's using our tech, and we developed it, so we know how to hijack it, and when someone comes up with something new, I employ them, buy it or find someone else to sell it to me."

"Holy shit!" Mike said, astonished.

"Exactly, it's a tremendous burden to bear, especially when my son keeps pushing for us to set up some secret world police to do right for the world," Art said, exasperated.

"Doing the right thing depends on what side of the fence you sit on," Mike added.

"Exactly what I said to him, Mike. We have the technology to spy on anyone, anywhere. I came across you guys several years ago when you were here in Somalia. I was checking everyone's backgrounds and connections with the people we would deal with here in Somalia. When we came across a transmission between your team and your base. We watched all local military transmissions, and nobody had a clue your team was in their pocket. Impressive. So, I started looking into your team and became a fan of your work. You guys have primitive tech, but can still get most of the information you need."

"Most?" Queried Mike.

"Well, you guys can't be everywhere like I can," Art added.

"So, you see, Mike, I can't be the world's police. We hand it over to the authorities anonymously if we come across something important. This tech level in the hands of a superpower just can't happen. I already have the CIA breathing down my neck because I was stupid enough to show off some of our tech when they were snooping on us."

"The CIA is investigating you; why?"

"Well, we stopped two nasty warring nations, built a tech mountain, and turned around two nations' economies in 18 months. They think that's suspicious, go figure." Art let out a little chuckle, and Mike saw the humour.

"So, what did you do that freaked them out?"

"WELL... I made the ARK disappear... from their spy satellite."

"Jesus Christ, Art, didn't you think that would raise some red flags? And they still let the President come here."

"Well, he was the one really pushing to come and wouldn't let them say no. He told them to make it happen."

"And you know this how???" Art gave a wry smile and shrugged his shoulders.

"Oh my God, you're in the White House! You're playing with fire, you know that?"

"I will not confirm or deny that report," Art replied.

"So where do we come into it?"

"Well, knowledge is power, and I only use my power to make our company's lives easier. You guys are the pinnacle of information gathering, So I have a President here, and the Rolling Stones of information gathering, plus I thought it might give me a chance to help upgrade your gear," Art added.

"And, I know there's more you're holding back, you're tippy-toeing around something. What is it?" Mike wanted to know it all; the story isn't complete, not yet.

"Well, you see the importance of what I'm trying to do for the world here, don't you, Mike?"

"Yes, I do," Mike said patiently, waiting for the BOOM! to drop.

"Mike, they are going to try to take it away from me. I can do a lot, but I can't do or think of everything. I want your team to join my team here defending the ARK and what it stands for."

'BOOM! Actually, BOOM BOOM!' Mike thought, "Woo, seriously! Wow, like no, we couldn't become mercenaries. I can't speak for the team anyway, but to leave the service to become a merc wouldn't suit me."

"NO, not a merc, but private security to defend a chance for humanity. You're not hitmen, I know that, but a chance to help defend a project worth your efforts. I thought it might appeal to your sense of worth to fight for something worth fighting for." Art was not desperate; Mike could sense it in his voice. It was like he knew it was the right thing for him, and he was just trying to get him to see it.

"You realise the team could not just get up and say 'We quit' to the Australian defence force? We are contracted up to certain periods?"

"Yes, I know when your next sign-ups are coming up, and I also know of the ways to leave immediately."

Mike laughs. "Of course you do!" There was another silence between the two men; Mike spoke up first. "Yes, it is a worthy cause, but I can't speak for the rest of the team. You would have to approach them individually, and I don't know how they will respond. For myself, I would have to speak to my family to see what they think."

"Of course. I would think nothing less, and I suppose you would have to speak to your CO Colonel Briggs. I believe he is a close confidante."

"I'm not going to even ask how you know all this," Mike added.

"Probably best not to," Art said with a laugh.

"Sorry to drop this all on you now. I was going to chat with you before you left, but it just seemed the right time when we started talking. Well, I will leave you to your thoughts, and I should go back to mingling and see if the USA and Somalia are at war yet. Thanks for the chat, Mike."

"Thanks for the offer," Mike replied.

"I wouldn't offer it if I didn't need you and your team; thanks for listening." At that, Art walked off back down the hallway towards the function room.

Mike was quiet. It didn't seem wise to talk to himself, with so many Secret Service guys around, 'Crazy guy level 5 approach with extreme prejudice, because he cheats!' Mike's mind seemed to be trying hard to avoid his honest thoughts. 'What if the world could see actual proof that a better life for all is possible? Art is sitting on top of a house of cards. So many who will want to pull him down'. Mike sighed! Was this even workable? I have another three years to go before I resign, and what would the team think? Would they join me? They have great careers ahead of them. There'll be time to think about this when I get home. For now, "I need another drink, a double."

Sherlock headed back to the function room, getting a wary eye from the agent on the door. Hobbs was on his name tag.

CHAPTER 23

A DOLLAR MADE IS A DOLLAR EARNED

A fresh, low, light mist covered the shrubs and plants after a new shower of rain through the night. The fog continued into the dark foreboding shadows of the dense forest cluster, giving it an eerily evil presence. Then, finally, the plants and shrubs moved back into place, and the mist evened itself out again as if nobody had ever travelled through there. Sherlock looked back at the path he had just run. 'If I fell over, would I just be swallowed up and never be seen again?' he thought; that gave him a shiver. Maybe run somewhere else tomorrow.

As Sherlock returned from his morning jog, he came across Steel outside, doing stretches, "Morning Steel."

"Morning boss, good run?"

"Yes, you can't beat the scenery; it changes on every corner. So, where are the troops?" Sherlock asked.

"Well, Kid is inside playing with his gizmos; the rest of the team went off to the troop barracks 'to get something' Steel gave Sherlock 'a boys will be boys look.'

"I better round them up; we don't have long before our demo this morning."

"Boss, I might suggest you change shirts; you're a bit on the nose... Old man sweat," Steel teased.

"Cheeky shit," Sherlock took a whiff of his armpits, "Yeah, a fresh shirt, then get the team."

"I'll go with you; I could use a stretch. I'll grab the Mad professor too before he blows up another toilet." They both had a laugh and walked off.

****

It was just over a 15-minute walk to the barracks. As Sherlock, Steel, and Kid came into the clearing and onto the service road, they saw the African Security force gathered in a circle, looking into the centre. As Sherlock got closer, he saw that 2 Planks, Quassy and Smith, were in the centre of the ring. Across from 2 Planks, in the centre of the ring, was Major Tamoa Acondia, commander of the AZTECK Security guard. Mike knew what was happening or about to happen, a local bare-knuckle fight; 2 Planks didn't have time for this.

Sherlock pushed his way through the crowd of soldiers to the group's centre.

"Morning 2 Planks, you don't have time for this; we have a demo this morning. Sorry Major, I need my troops," Sherlock said.

"Aw, afraid I might break one of your toy soldiers? Sherlock turned and looked the Major up and down and then looked at 2 Planks.

"Yes! Come on, Sergeant, we have work to do," Sherlock gave a hand signal to move on.

"Maybe, commander on commander then, Captain, or are you afraid too?"

"Oh, shit!" Steel said, standing at the back of the soldiers next to Kid.

"What! What's the matter???"

"He called Sherlock chicken! You can call Sherlock lots of things, but not chicken," Steel said worriedly.

"Be prepared to run or fight," Steel said to Kid.

"What! Which is it?"

"Just watch and see," Steel added.

Sherlock let out a large sigh and turned to face the Major. "You know your team is supposed to be at this demo too," Sherlock told Major Acondia.

"Well, we just have to make it quick, won't we, Captain," Sherlock looked at the size of his opponent and thought, 'yep, this is going to hurt.'

"Standard bare-knuckle, knockdown or knockout or submission, no time limit, no rounds?" Sherlock asked the Major, "Knockdown or submission is fine, Captain, though I usually knock out my opponents quickly."

The Major started laughing heartily, showing off a perfect set of teeth and lots of them; he had a grin like the Cheshire Cat from Alice in Wonderland.

Mike was feeling limber after his run and stretch this morning, so he was ready to fight.

"When you're ready, Major!" Sherlock offered.

"Ding-Ding," Major Acondia said as he pretended to ring a bell. The two fighters circled around each other, trying to understand how their opponent would strike. Sherlock decided to be patient and see what Acondia would do first. He saw the Major move his feet, signifying he was about to attack. The Major moved in and threw two quick jabs with his left and swung a round arm with his right, which would have taken his head off if Sherlock hadn't had ducked quickly.

'Moves pretty fast for a big man,' Sherlock thought. No sooner did the thought end when the Major charged like a wounded bull, swinging left to right, trying to take Sherlock's head off again. As the last arm shot past Sherlock's face, he shoved the Major on the right elbow, making him turn faster and lose his balance. That move brought an Owww from the excited crowd. The African commander hadn't ever lost a fight. 'Poor balance,' Sherlock thought; I can use that.

Sherlock moved towards his opponent as he turned around to not let him set his feet again. As the Major turned, Sherlock threw an obvious right arm haymaker that Blind Freddy could have seen coming. The Major threw up his left arm to block Sherlock's right. Sherlock pulled the punch just enough to stop the Majors' left arm block, so it was open to Sherlock's left. Mike drove his knuckles hard into the Majors' left biceps, giving him a nasty stinger. The Major then swung his right fist around to counter-hit Sherlock in the back of the head. Sherlock, suspecting that this would be the Majors' next move, ducked in time and then came up with his own counter by driving a right-handed fist into his breadbasket, forcing the wind out of him. As the Major was still turning for his right punch, Sherlock hit him in his side with his left. The crowd was getting right into it now, booing Mike as if his shot on the side was a cheap shot. Steel was calm, watching every move between the two fighters. She was, without a doubt, the most skilled hand-to-hand fighter on the team. Sherlock often trains with her to keep a high level of skill needed for the field.

The Major stood up, stretching and sore from Sherlock's attack; he nodded a well-done gesture to Sherlock right before he charged him again. This time with more calculated punches and jabs that Sherlock only just moved out of the way of. He was obviously madder or a lot faster than he had made out to be.

Sherlock went into survival mode. He had no time to think, just react to what his opponent was throwing at him. Dodge left; dodge right; left-right; left, right. Sherlock was backing back, trying not to get hit by one of these straight jabs. The soldiers were cheering wildly as they believed their commander was moments away from victory. Then came the opportunity Sherlock was waiting for. The Major threw a right cross as Sherlock was hoping. He got under it and came up with another blow to his opponent's windbag, bringing a grunt from the Major. This time he stayed toe to toe with the Major and hit him with four fast blows to his stomach, causing him to buckle down on a knee to the ground.

A shocked "Aww" came from the African soldiers, watching as their commander went down. Still, in the blink of an eye, he threw himself at Sherlock with the speed of a leopard, grabbing Sherlock in a bear hug. 2 Planks turned his head sideways in an 'I can't watch this face' expecting to hear his Captain's spine snap. Instead, this move brought a rousing cheer from the African Security men, as they believed the fight was done and dusted. Their commander would squeeze the Australian commander until he passed out, or the Australian tap out.

"Ah, Captain, a gallant fight. You move beautifully and hit with some force, but my body is a mountain and can take a lot of punishment. You fell right into my trap, do you concede!" Major Acondia asked Sherlock with his Cheshire Cat grin.

"Major... You talk too much!" before the Major knew what was happening, Sherlock clapped his hands over the Majors' ears hard enough to sting and disorientate him. As he grabbed his ears, Sherlock pounded his stomach and solar plex area again, but didn't pull any punches like he had before. Fortunately, the Major was not the only one underplaying his hand. The men and women watching lost count of how many times the Major was hit before he went down. It was a bit of a blur, but eventually, the Major grabbed his stomach with both arms wrapped around it and fell to his knees. As Sherlock lined up to deliver a knockout blow, the Major put up his hand to tap out.

****

In the hub, almost 3 kilometres away, Art jumps up out of his seat.

"Yes! Haha, 20 dollars, my friend," Art yelled. The sudden commotion startled Doby and Lexi, perplexed by what Art and Ab were watching on the screen behind them. From what they were saying, it was like some kind of game or sport the way they were cheering. It was also clear that whomever Art was cheering for had won. The way Ab looked and the fact he had to open his wallet to give Art some money was evidence enough.

Everything calmed down; Lexi looked around and saw Doby working intently, checking and rechecking every system repeatedly, the last two days. He looked like he was looking for flaws where there were none.

****

The crowd was aghast at seeing their commander lose his first fight, but was marvelling at the skills of the Australian commander. Sherlock helped the Major to his feet.

As the Major composed himself, he stuck out his hand to Sherlock.

"My name is Tamoa; I'm very pleased to meet you."

"Mike." both men shook.

"Will you still be at the demo?"

"I might take, ah, what do you Australians call it, a sickie?" the men laughed together.

"Major, I don't think you've taken a day off your entire career," Sherlock patted Tamoa's shoulder.

"This is true, Mike," the Major stretched his back, "But there is always a first time," the Major laughed.

Sherlock joined 2 Planks and the rest of the team. "Well, how did we do?" Sherlock looked at 2 Planks, Smith and Quassy.

2 Planks spoke up, "Converting to Australian, just over 2 grand, these boys get paid well."

"What! You were betting on the fight?" Kid said, confused.

"Don't worry, Kid, they do this often," Steel said, patting him on the back.

"Put it in the kitty for Christmas," Sherlock said.

"This team's weird," Kid said, still confused.

"And don't we know it," Smith added as they turned to head to the lorry 2 Planks had used to bring them here.

****

LATER THAT MORNING...

It was a gathering of all. All the President's men. All of Tamoa's men and Sherlock's team plus Art and Ab. To demonstrate how the laser suits and weapons work. Art had sent down a suit earlier for Sherlock to get one of the team to wear for the demonstration; Sherlock chose Smith.

"Good to see you all well. Looking a little stiff there, Tamoa, are you alright?" Sherlock noticed the slight smirk on Art's face. 'he saw the fight. Of course, he did; he sees everything,' Sherlock thought.

"Now, to tell you about these fantastic gizmos. These are the first prototypes of weapons and suits for our hunting safaris. So, any input afterward would be much appreciated.

"The crotch is too tight," Smith calls out; everyone turns to look. Smith is standing there in a lycra suit that resembles something from the movie TRON.

"Maybe you're too well-hung, Mr. Smith?" Art offered.

"Well, there could be that too," Smith added immodestly.

"No, he's not," Steel calls out, which everyone laughs.

"Shut up, Steel," Smith throws back.

"Now, like other laser games, this works the same way. The weapons' lasers detect the suit's sensors." Art grabs a pistol off the table and points it at Smith.

"Bang!" he shouts, and a sensor light goes off on Smiths' right shoulder.

"Now, we have been working on different ways to make it more real. So, if you wish to grab some weapons from the bench, you will see they are exactly the same dimensions as the actual weapons, same weight, length, etc. Now, Ab, if you don't mind," Ab hits a few keys on his laptop.

"Bang!" Art said again as he reshot Smith.

"Hey," Smith calls out. "This time, you not only see the light go off, but Mr. Smith feels a small electric shock to know he's been shot, Ab please," Ab taps a key a few times. Art aims the pistol at Smith's knee.

"Bang!"

"Ahh fuck," Smith yells as he drops to one knee as if shot.

"You see, we can set the game to be very realistic, so if I go to shoot Mr. Smith in his nuts," Art goes to aim between Smith's legs.

"Hey, no, they get the point," says Smith as he wraps his hands around his genitals.

"You can wear normal clothing over the top of the suit. The sensors will still go through clothes and flesh. The same goes for you, Mr. President, and your party. The animals hunting you will automatically stop once they're in strike range. They don't need to actually make physical contact, and once again, you can set the modes from *PUSSY WILLOW* to *MAN LEGEND*, depending on how real you want it to be. If you hit an animal with a shot, the sensors will register it on the animal, and the animal will go lame in that area. Questions?"

"Art, I noticed a muzzle flash when you shot Smith?"

"Yes, Mike, good eye. We added a muzzle flash for realism; we just haven't perfected the sound yet and still keep within the weight range of the weapon. So yes, there will be muzzle flashes to help detect the enemy. Also, this is not Hollywood; you don't have endless bullets; you will need to reload by taking out the magazine and putting back in to reload. Ammunition will be set at the start of the game for how much ammo you can carry. Anyone else? Nobody, good."

"Art, one last thing. What would happen if someone went Rambo and unleashed a magazine onto someone?"

"The same, I suppose, as in real life," Art answered, puzzled. Sherlock made his way to the table and picked up an M16, hitting the switch for full auto. The penny had dropped for Smith.

"No, NO," Smith turned and started running; the surrounding people stepped aside so as not to get shot in the crossfire or give the captain a better shot.

"Ratta tat tat, Ratta tat tat," Sherlock yelled as he pulled the trigger while aiming at Smith. Smith let out a scream and then a yell as he fell to the ground.

"EEE AAA, AAGGHHHH, ahhhh Motha fucka," he groaned from the ground.

"Ab, we might have to turn the suit down a little on Mr. Smith," Sherlock said jokingly.

"Fuck you," came the defiant voice from the ground as Smith spat out dirt from his mouth. Everyone laughed; as they walked off, a voice came from behind Sherlock over his shoulder...

"And you expect people to follow you?" Chad Langdon said from behind.

"To the Death," Sherlock replied, "To the Death!"

CHAPTER 24

GAME ON

The first round of training was a capture-the-flag scenario. Sherlock chose a mountainous hillside covered in boulder outcrops and shale-covered dirt, making it easier to defend and a more complex attack site. Tamoa's team was defending the flag first. It was a hard-fought battle that lasted 3 hours in the sweltering African heat. In the end, Sherlock's team won, but three of the group got hit, two critically. As they got back to the barracks for the debriefing, Sherlock had his cranky face on, which meant they were in for a serve, and a serve they got.

"Pitiful! If this was an actual mission, I'd be sitting by Kid's hospital bed, writing letters of condolences to the parents of you two." Mike pointed to Steel and Smith. "If we are going to treat this training as a game, we might as well pack up and go back to base now."

"To review, our team goal is to get each other home first and then secure the mission. Smith, you left Steel pinned just so you could get the shooter and left yourself open to counterfire. Kid, make 100% sure of your cover before moving positions. If it looks tight, ask for cover fire. Since you treat this as a game, I will treat it as a game. First, the setting is going to be put on the highest level."

"Shit," Steel said.

Sherlock looked them right in the eye. "We'll play a bonus round; every time you get hit, it's $500 from your cut of the Xmas money and $1000 if you get killed. If two of you get killed, we pack up and head back to base for real training."

"Xmas fund?" asked Kid.

"We have a side fund from different adventures we partake in," 2 Planks said.

"Like the fighting?"

"Yeah, among other things. There's always something going on around the bases. We pool the money till Xmas and split a portion of it between our families and give the rest to a charity," Sherlock said.

"Ok, I see" Kid now grasped what was going on.

"Don't worry, Kid, we will spot you till you start putting into the pool," Mike assured him.

"Now, second round, we will be defending; get your head in the game. I've passed the changes on to the Major, who has agreed that he wasn't happy losing all his men. So now they have defended the area, so they know it better than us.

Sherlock laid out his plan with a step-by-step playbook approach so Kid could see how the team works together. Kid has been put on flag duty for his first defence and says he has some tricks he can use.

"Sherlock, can I ask one thing?" Kid asked.

"Sure, what's up?"

"Do I have to have Kid tag?"

"Tags come from something you do or the type of person you are; the right tag will come along in time; for now, just go with the flow and concentrate on your work," Sherlock assured him.

"Roger that," Kid agreed.

The second drill went better than the first. The Major started with ten men, and he was down to four, with no one injured or killed by Sherlock's team. The Major and another squad member were laying down suppressive fire to pin Sherlock's men down while two of his last men had been circling in for over two hours. Kid saw them making their way to the flag from fifty metres out and showed what he could do by letting them into the flag area.

The two soldiers scanned the area from twenty metres and saw no one defending the flag. Feeling that it could be a trap, they approached slowly, waiting, watching for any hidden movement. Not seeing any, the temptation of a victory got too great for them as they stood up six metres out from the flag.

Swinging side to side, expecting an ambush, the soldiers were only two metres from the flag when they tripped Kids' sensors, setting off an experimental mine Kid had been working on. It was a flash-bang grenade redesigned into a small, round canister. Apart from the difference in shape, this little mine had an extra nasty side effect. As the force of the mine goes off, it triggers a concentrated substance used in pepper sprays, an ear-piercing squeal that startled the soldiers; in an instant, they were deafened, blinded, and immobilised by the use of the new anti-personnel mine. Once the trap was triggered, Kid appeared from nowhere. He appeared out of the sand like a character from '*The Mummy*' movie quickly took the two soldiers out before they knew what had happened.

"What the???" the Major and the last soldier popped their heads up from behind their cover. A moment later, a figure appeared beside them, sitting up and going, "BOO! You're dead." Steel had been beside them for fifteen minutes without them knowing, choosing to lay there till the end of the game or till spotted.

"Aagh!" the soldier yelled as Steel sat up, startling him as he concentrated on where the explosion came from.

"Great work, young lady. Your skills of camouflage and stealth are a credit to your team," the Major praised Steel.

"What was the bang?" Steel asked.

"You don't know?" the Major queered.

"No."

"Well, maybe we should check since it seems this game is a bust," the Major said.

As both teams made their way to the top of the hill where the flag was, they came across Kid offering first aid to two soldiers sitting on a log.

"What happened?" Sherlock asked.

"I did," Kid answered.

"I set up a trap at the flag with an experimental mine I built. A cross between a flash-bang grenade and concentrated pepper spray. Seems the pepper spray side of it is very effective," Kid answered sheepishly.

"They will be fine in a few minutes. Well, within an hour anyway."

"Amazing, and you built this all yourself, you say," the Major queried.

"Yes, Major."

"You should show this to Mr. Damani to get it patented; I could use these around this park as we expand as a deterrent. Captain, you have an incredible team at your disposal," the Major praised Sherlock.

"Yes, I am proud of their skills, but some members need to know when and when not to use weapons without prior approval." Sherlock looked at Kid sternly.

"I think maybe a bottle of scotch each for these men would be an appropriate apology," Sherlock said. One man started coughing, and then the other, obviously putting on a show that Sherlock responded to.

"Maybe two bottles would be better," Sherlock added.

"Yes, Sir," Kid agreed.

"And I think two of those bottles should be donated to the rest of your team for you both failing to capture the flag, don't you agree, gentlemen?" the Major said sternly.

"Yes, Sir," the soldiers said, obviously not impressed.

A spy drone sails around above, unknown to all the combatants below. The drone was in the shape of an eagle. Sitting back at his desk, Art looks at his screen intently.

"Amazing. Mike's team is as good as their reputation." Art turns off the screen and sits back, thinking and thinking and hoping.

Later that evening, Mike's team sat around the campfire before hitting the bunks. Seb noticed Mike looked fidgety, which was a sign Mike had something big on his mind.

"What is it?" Seb asked Mike.

"What's what?" Mike replied.

"Whatever it is, you're trying to figure out how to tell us."

All eyes turned to Mike.

Mike lets out a sigh. "I had a conversation with Art at the ball, over many things actually, but mostly about us."

"Go on," Katelyn said.

"We weren't asked here by chance. Art came across our team awhile a go while tracking info in Somalia. He has been following us."

"How's that even possible?" Deen asked.

"I'll get to that bit," Mike replied.

"Basically, we were invited here to meet with us under the ruse of training and a goodwill mission. For job recruitment!"

"What? That's insane. We're not mercenaries," Smith bellows angrily.

"Yes, he knows that. He has looked into us leaving the service. His pitch was fighting for a better cause," Mike said.

"He's not wrong," Deen said.

"Yes, I agree. We would be fighting directly for a symbol of peace for the world. I'd consider it because I know you're considering it." Seb said, now looking at Mike.

"Yes, I am considering it. But it's not that easy; we all have a family to consider." Mike said.

Smith sat there with a stunned look, staring at his team. "Really, what about you, Katelyn? Are you buying this story?"

"Yes, I would too, but I want time to consider it all," Katelyn said.

"I don't believe you lot," Smith said, still amazed.

"Well, look at what he's done already. Stopped two countries from fighting and built an endangered wildlife park between them. This screams peace is possible. But there's more to it, isn't there, Mike," Deen said.

"Yes, that's right, Deen. Azteck has tech world powers would love to get their hands on. Outfits like the KGB and CIA."

Kid joined the conversation. "Yes, he's right. Ab told me of some of their capabilities. Some serious Sci-fi stuff. So, what else do they have that they haven't told us?"

"This place is a huge target; you all realise that, don't you?" Seb said.

"On that note, I want you all packed to rock and roll as if we're going on a mission in the morning," Mike said.

"You don't think they would attack now, do you?" Katelyn asked.

"Look who's here," Seb said.

"Shit, the President!" Smith got up from the log and turned, and walked away.

"Where are you off to?" Deen calls to Smith.

"I'm going to pack my kit," Smith calls back.

The rest of the team looked at each other, got up, and quickly made their way to the barracks.

CHAPTER 25

THE PLAN

The night was quiet, except for the sounds of barking camels and the wind rustling through roofing that was not appropriately secured during the hasty build of this transient town. A place to rest and wet your whistle. A place to seek work or news of work in neighbouring Somalia, or a place for some of the world's leading terrorists to meet and discuss a plan. Anything is possible in a town in the middle of nowhere...

Ji-tae Jin, Min-Ki Gwan, and Chao Zhang stood around the table, looking at the maps of the regions, which included the ARK. They had taken two tourist tours around the ARK to familiarise themselves with the terrain and the animals. Unfortunately, they had the Security forces to deal with, but they also had wild animals in each area quite capable of killing them too.

1st

"This is a 6-pronged attack. First, President Abdi was organising a march and riot on the newly reopened American Embassy, which will turn violent, causing local troops to be tied up, so no reinforcements come to help the ARK."

2nd, 6.00pm

A group of ten hired poachers from Kenya will attack the West fence. They will enter near the monkey sanctuary to hit the panda, tiger, and elephant areas. This will draw the Security guards on shift because the poachers believe the security fence will already be down, but they are our bait. Once the Security forces battle with the poachers, that will leave fewer soldiers for the actual mission to deal with.

3rd, 6.05pm

Doby Heinlinker will take down the security and communication for the ARK, leaving them blind.

4th, 6.10pm

Zhang's team will breach the fence near the airport and take on the American President's backup, two Apache helicopters, and two Delta teams. They will start with a rocket barrage on the helicopters and troops plus two rockets to take out communication on the President's plane.

5th, also at 6.10pm

The mercenary team will breach just below the barracks of the visiting Australian Special Forces team. Their job is to take out the Australians, which shouldn't be challenging as there are only 6, and then secure the post so no one comes through behind the primary team.

6th

The primary team breaches the perimeter at the end of the airfield and beside the security barracks. With communications down with the destruction of the EAGLE's plane, we will eliminate any security force left there at the barracks and offer assistance to Zhang's team if needed. After the initial breaches, the primary team will progress around the base of the ARK. They then proceed past the mercenary post and onto the President's area. We will engage the Secret Service with stealth, overpower them, kill the EAGLE and leave South West to the border, where we will break up the team, using our escape plans in different countries.

"While we are attacking the President, Zhang's team will move into the ARK after dealing with the Delta teams. They will make their way to the top level and take out the communications hub and personnel. If Art Damani is there and the opportunity arises, kill him. Then exit South using their exit plans. Are there questions?" Ji-tae Jin asked.

Zhang looked at the map. "My team is ready to execute the mission, but there are a lot of moving parts and variables."

"Very true, Zhang. There may be a need to reassess on the run, but so long as we remember, the primary mission is to eliminate the EAGLE; that comes first. If you get into the ARK with few men, burn it to the ground to ensure no communication gets out, is that clear?"

"Yes, that is clear," Zhang acknowledged.

"Once we execute this mission, we will not see each other again, as the world will be looking for us. It has been a pleasure working with you both," Jin said. Gwan and Zhang bowed, acknowledging the same. Zhang picked up his pistol off the table and made his way out the door. There was nothing left to do but wait.

CHAPTER 26

THE HUNT

The desert camouflage blended in with the sandy, dusty earth, a distinctive mix of browns and reds. Even the camo face mask was a nice touch to sneak around this desert zone... But you could hear the air being sucked into his lungs a mile away; the President was sucking in the big ones.

"Well, Chad, what did you think of that?" asked the President of his head of Secret Service as he was trying to catch his breath. The President just completed his first game on the Safari Hunt, while Chad Langdon stood there, hardly breaking a sweat after shadowing the President for the last two hours.

"Pussy level, Sir, my kids could have done that," Chad told the President.

"Man-up and do it on one of the real levels... Sir," he told the President.

"Well, Chad, why don't you tell me how you really feel," the President said jokingly.

At least the President made it to the end; his two companions on the trip got killed by animals. One, while he was taking a leak against a tree, the electric shock came as a big surprise when the panther got him from behind.

"Ok, we'll stop for lunch and then kick it up to Man level, and maybe we'll jump to Secret Service level! Yeah!!" The President said to his minder, imitating he was flexing his muscle.

"You'd be dead in five minutes," Chad Langdon said to the President. The American President watched Chad's face for a sign of humour after the remark... None.

"You know you should take your comedy act on the road; you're outstanding," the President said, eyeing up his face.

"I'd be no good, Sir; I can't stand humour," The Secret Service officer said.

"Yeah, I'd believe that. Let's go have lunch." As the President and the Secret Service Head walked off, the agent afforded himself a slight smirk. He liked this, President. He was about the people and the job, worked hard, but the position didn't go to his head. He remained humble, a natural leader; no wonder people tout him as the new JFK.

The next level was a treat, more complex. The animals were more intelligent, faster, and had more sensors switched on; they went on scent. The President got killed by a Tiger after a two-hour hunt. Finally, it ended in a scramble over rock faces, trying to elude the animal. His companions were done in half an hour. The shock of the Tiger biting him and then dealing the killer blow was actually a scary thing to go through. The suit shocked him so much his heart rate shot up from the adrenaline rush, and the President's medical minder contacted Chad Langdon to check on the President's health.

"The Eagle is fine; he just got his feathers ruffled," responded the Secret Service chief. Chad thought it was a unique and eerie thing to watch. The Tiger looked and acted so real, locked on the President's scent or person, and slowly cornered him. The President got a shot at the Tiger but only wounded it. The Tiger knew the terrain and stayed hidden and behind cover till he was close enough to strike. The eerie part was the Tiger walked straight past Chad several times as if he wasn't there, eerie.

As the hunting party all returned to the camp, everyone felt tired, but the President was exhausted.

"Ah, come on, doc, I'm fine. I just did a 2-hour workout with a tiger. That has a way of exhausting you."

"You're the President, but you know you can still have a heart attack. I've been told to keep you alive. The country needs you," The President's doctor said.

"A rest, some fresh night air here at the camp. A few shots of whisky and all will be great," The President said.

"NO alcohol while you're in this state."

"Gee, doc, you're as much fun as smiley over there," The President points to Chad, who stands there with an expressionless face.

Before hitting the tents for the night, he told Chad he would do that last level again, but he would beef it up this time. The President hit the bunk at the same time Mike's team checked their weapons, being ready for the coming morning.

CHAPTER 27

A DAY LIKE NO OTHER

The smell of fresh air, clean fresh air, was invigorating. The smog of major cities makes you forget what fresh air is really like. The smell of food cooking wasn't bad either. So, the President stuck up his nose and whiffed the air, bacon, hash browns, and pancakes.

'Yum,' he thought.

The President was up at 6 am, so used to the early starts. At the White House, there was so much happening worldwide as he slept. He was given a coffee by the chef they brought with them as he went through communiques from the Chief of Staff and the CIA chief. Nothing of significant consequence going on. Still, that chatter the CIA keeps bringing up about a possible something, somewhere... No details augh, what did they expect him to do with no authentic information, go DEFCON 1 and bomb everybody everywhere? He finished his emails and headed out to breakfast.

Chad was there to greet him as he came to the table, "Morning, Sir, the important news this morning is the Red Sox went down to the Yankees, 7 to 2."

"Well, that stinks; I suppose it could get worse. I'll probably get gouged to death by a rhino today, too," the President said jokingly. He looked up at his companions for today's hunt, and they looked white as ghosts and had stopped mid-chew while eating their breakfast. The President looked at Chad and shrugged his shoulders, silently asking, 'What's wrong with them?'

"I believe there is a rhino in the hunt today," Chad informed the President.

"Oh, my apologies. I was only joking." The President's companions for today were one from the African delegation and one from the American trade delegation, whose services were not required for today's talks.

****

While at the HUB

Lexi was up a little early this morning and, after grabbing her breakfast at the food mall, decided to just head to the office this morning instead of finding a quiet place to chow down. Upon entering the HUB, she discovered Doby beat her to the punch.

He greeted her with a good morning, but it looked like the opposite. She still had feelings for Doby. Doby hadn't ever said anything wrong to her, hadn't brought up her snooping on his computer again, but today, he looked like he was coming down with the illness that struck him just after they went out together, which saw him working from his room for weeks. They exchanged pleasantries for a few minutes before Art came in.

"Good morning. And how is Lexi this morning?"

On which Lexi gave her usual response, "Any better, and I'd be deadly."

As Art looked at Lexi, she nodded her head towards Doby to inform him to check on Doby; Art got the message.

"And how is the Dobster this morning? All is well in the kingdom, I hope?"

"Yep," Doby replied, "All systems running perfectly," he added.

"Doby, are you feeling 100% today? You're looking a little peaked."

"Didn't have a good night's sleep, I suppose, still getting over that bug."

"Ok, don't forget that we can manage if you're not feeling well."

"Thank you, but I will be fine," Doby replied. Art tilted his head towards Doby to tell Lexi to watch him; Lexi nodded she understood.

****

Back at the HUNT

The first hunt was a rousing success for the President; he shot the rhino before it killed the second delegate, the screams of the first still ringing in his ears and putting a chill up his spine. Unfortunately, the second delegate was killed by a rogue male Lion made to look like Scar from the Lion King movie. The President wounded the animal and then went on a 5 km hunt to track the injured animal down. It even impressed Chad Langdon as the President snapshot the charging lion on a high grassy plain as it was charged him. The President was settling in after his first days on the hunt. The doctor seemed happy with the president's recovery this time around. One of the president's companions asked for a more extended lunch to recover, while the other opted to stay at home base for the next hunt. Seems like getting gouged to death by a rhino upset his bowels.

****

Ab was happy to greet his new friend Thomas this morning. He enjoyed their time together since he had come to the ARK because Thomas spoke his language. Unfortunately, Ab didn't have anyone to share his passion for engineering things. He had Tyson Lumming to throw around ideas to, but Tyson was always too busy lately to spare much time for chatting. Thomas, on the other hand, got AB. He understood his line of thinking and could continue on and then add new processes to an idea on the run. His visit in the morning would be brief, as he knew Thomas had drills planned with Major Acondia's team.

"Good morning, my friend," Ab greeted Thomas.

"Good morning to you too, Ab; what brings you down from your ivory tower?"

"I have an invention I would like you to trial if you have the time." Thomas's ears pricked up. A new toy to play with. Ab handed Thomas the device. It looked to Thomas like Night vision goggles with some alterations. Lighter with a different vision plate.

"These are what I call spectral goggles. Small solar cells powered them on the side, so they don't run out of power as much. Instead of just your normal night vision heat sensor goggles, they go through dozens of visual sensors by turning the knob on the side. So, if you don't find what you're looking for in one array, keep scrolling till you find a spectrum that picks it up."

"Amazing, Ab! It's so light and would be easy to wear. What did you design them for?" Thomas said.

"They were for groundskeepers and security to tell the difference between live and animated animals, especially at night."

"Brilliant idea, Ab, I can't wait to test them, but we don't have any animated animals here," Thomas asked.

Ab laughed, "None that you know of. Anyway, let me know if you get time to test them, and I will send Loki and Thor down to play with you."

"Arts bodyguards, awesome!"

Ab placed his hand on Thomas's shoulder, "Thank you, my friend, and good luck in today's missions."

"Thanks, Ab," Thomas replied.

Ab turned and walked back to his lorry. As he sat down and called out to Thomas, "Oh, and congratulations on the successful test of your new mine yesterday."

"How did you know about that?" Thomas asked, puzzled.

"Remember, NONE that you know of," Ab laughed and drove off.

Thomas looked around at the birds flying around and wondered which ones were spying on him.

The Major and his team turned up at 9.30am as scheduled, eager to have a better crack at these Australians after the first rounds of games. He had never seen a team so efficient and with so many skills, all in one unit. They were ghosts in any terrain and as fierce as tigers when fighting toe to toe when they wanted to be. The Major and his men learned plenty of new skills for the fights ahead. The Major was no fool and had been in war mode ever since he was a teenager. Recruited into the Somalian armed forces, he knew war, and he knew this shining new citadel of hope to the world would attract certain people who would want to tear it down but, 'over my dead body,' he thought... 'over my dead body.'

Sherlock and the Major greeted each other warmly. Sherlock had a lot of respect for the Major after only a few encounters on the field. Each time, his team was learning and challenging his team. For soldiers, they called simple grunts; these men knew how to fight and were quick learners, a credit to the Major and his training. After yesterday's mine attack, Kid handed over the four scotch bottles as promised to the soldiers. Both the Major and Sherlock agreed. NO mines today, but the Major requested smoke grenades in today's drills, to which Sherlock agreed. The mission today, defend the barracks; the Major's team was defending first. Sherlock and his crew left to walk to the Major's team barracks, then turned around and headed back, giving the Major's team time to set up a defensive pattern.

****

Doby felt like he was walking in a dream. It all happens tonight; hopefully, my Mum is released, the President doesn't get assassinated, and I go to prison for the rest of my life. 'I should eat a hardy last meal,' he thought, but he couldn't stomach anything.

Doby wanted to tell someone to ask for help, but he couldn't risk his mother's life. The only glimmer of hope Doby had was that he had been working on a plan, but it all depended on his mother contacting him once they released her. Would she be able to? Would she be disorientated after weeks under lock and key? Would she even remember his mobile number? So many ifs.

Doby's plan is that the worm will take down the link for security and communication, the HUB will be in a panic, and he'd work on getting a mobile phone link up first. Then, his mother would get to a phone and call him. Art could call in

Somalian troops to help the President. Once his mother was safe, he could introduce the proper sequence again to bring the security and communications back online. He couldn't do that until the next rotation, which is 90 minutes. A lot can happen in 90 minutes, especially when you don't know what's happening outside. 'Surreal, everything seems surreal,' Doby thought.

****

Ji-tae Jin sits calmly at his table six hours before meeting his second Min-Ki Gwan and the team to prep before heading in. The phone rings, breaking him from his thoughts.

"Is all prepared?" the voice said.

"Yes, everything is in place. We are on final countdown," Jin says.

"Your predications?"

"Success, with 55% causalities."

"Why so high of casualties?"

"Because I didn't prepare this mission, the fact I am relying on so many new people," Jin informs the voice.

"We can't afford prisoners."

"It won't matter. Only myself and my seconds know any details."

"And what about Abdi?"

"He wants his country back; he will do as he is told or he will answer to me."

"So long as the Eagle is dead, that is all that matters."

"He will be. I will send confirmation. But why him and why now?"

"... You have never asked these questions before," the voice asked questioningly.

"I am about to become the next Osama Bin Laden. I will be hunted forever for killing this, President."

"We need him out of the way. He will impede our future plans. The same as Damani and AZTECK but he is more accessible, so he isn't a priority. I wish you success in your mission and enjoy your retirement."

"Thank you, but I will be looking over my shoulder for the rest of my life."

The phone went dead.

Jin could not help to worry about the unknowns in the missions. Two outside groups had to attack at precisely the right time. If one goes early, the entire plan could go crashing down or have to be rearranged on the run. He hated loose ends, but the orders were clear, and there was no time to train teams to handle all sections. He knew in a worst-case scenario, he could split his squad in two, and Gwan could execute a mission on his own. Now to wait... five and a half hours.

****

As they reached the Major's barracks, they turned and stopped.

"Well, is everybody set on their part of the mission?" Sherlock asked.

He got a 'roger' from all the team.

The Major's team didn't disappoint. They learned from competing against Sherlock's team. Their skills increased quickly, and the Major led them exceptionally well. The battle raged fiercely as the Major's team used a fluid defence. Moving around so as not to get outflanked. Sherlock's team meets the demand, adapting on the run. The training drill ran on for many hours. The Major's team tried to turn defence into attack, pushing Sherlock's team out of any set patterns. In the fight, Sherlock's team received several wounds, with Quassy being killed by an ambush. The squad had to use all their skills to finish the Major's team. Eventually, they rounded up the last three members of the Major's team in like an 'Alamo' situation. Kid had taken down the last of the men in the barracks. They tried to use smoke grenades to mask their positions. But Kid used Ab's new spectral glasses, and he found a spectrum that allowed him to see images in the smoke.

"Very impressive, Captain. Your entire team can readjust their battle plan on the run. They truly are a credit to your training," the Major complimented Sherlock as he came out of the clearing.

"Thank you, Major. Your men are learning and adapting each time we train together. Thank god we are only here for a week; otherwise, you'd be getting too good to deal with, and I do like to keep my winning streak intact." Sherlock and the Major started laughing. The laughter was interrupted by one of the Major's soldiers coming in from the road; it was a soldier. Steel scared out of the tree and unloaded a magazine of bullets on him on the ground.

"I ache all over," he said, looking at Steel. Steel walked over to him and put her arm around his shoulder.

"Would you like me to kiss it better?" she said aloud to the soldier.

"Yes, please," the soldier said with a smile.

"Not happening, buddy," she said aloud as she jostled his hair. That started a round of laughter from everyone.

"Well, I don't know about you, Captain, but I am starving; time to eat before I waste away," he said as he patted his stomach.

Mike went to see Thomas taking off his gear and putting it on his bunk.

"Thomas, great work today. How did you know where to shoot in the smoke?"

"These," he handed Mike the goggle.

"Ab gave them to me this morning to test. They're for trying to tell the difference between the animated animals and real ones."

"And they worked through the smoke?"

"Yeah, they're spectral googles. They have dozens of different visuals to look for anything. It was bloody handy Ab came this morning," Mike laughed.

"Yeah, it was. These would have a lot of useful purposes for the team," Mike added.

"I was thinking the same thing myself," Thomas agreed.

Mike cleaned up and went and sat down beside the Major. Once he sat, he looked around and saw that the team wasn't sitting together; they were seated among the ARK soldiers chatting, eating, laughing. The Major followed his gaze and realised what he was also seeing.

"Shame it's only a week, Captain; our people seem to get on well."

"Yes, but the fairy tale must end one day." The Major nodded and continued speaking.

"I must ask, 2 Planks? What does that tag mean?" the Major asked.

Mike smiled, "In Australia, there is a saying that says 'you're as thick as two planks of wood', meaning you're not real smart."

The Major looked at Seb, confused.

"He doesn't look dumb to me; on the contrary, he comes across as very capable and intelligent," the Major praised Seb.

"He is actually he has just short of a genius IQ, way higher than anyone in the team."

"Then why have the dumb tag?" the Major asked.

"Well, Seb doesn't like to show off his IQ or knowledge; he hides it until he needs it. He believes that when he shows his IQ, people act differently around him. Seb's an easy-going type of guy. The beach, surfing, and eating are all that interest him," Mike said with a laugh.

"You Australians are complicated; you call yourself dumb when you're not and hide your intelligence. In Africa, things are simpler. You see that one," The Major points to one of his men.

"Yes," Mike replies.

"He's dumb, so I call him DUMB. That one," he points to another soldier.

"He is even dumber than him, so I call him REALLY DUMB, and him," the Major points to a third soldier, "He is not as dumb as he was last week, so I might actually give him a tag this week," the Major informed Mike.

Mike looked at the Major's men, "Don't they ever complain?"

"No, they must be delighted. I have a complaints box outside my office for anyone to complain," the Major said.

"Who handles the complaints?" Mike queried.

"I do, and no one ever complains!" He looked at Mike with a straight face, then bursts into laughter, slapping Mike on the back and nearly breaking two ribs. Mike thought, 'I wouldn't complain either.'

"Let's mix it up a little for the next mission?" the Major asked.

"What did you have in mind?" Mike asked.

"Let's break till tonight and have a night mission and try our hand at stealth!"

"Sounds like a great idea. We can start at, say, 6 when it's just getting dark."

"Excellent, maybe the night might favour my team more... if they can stay awake," the Major paused, then burst out laughing again.

They sat around eating lunch and relaxing. Mike noticed the troops had broken off into two groups. Seb, Deen, and Smith were off to one side, teaching some soldiers how to play two up. Thomas was sitting with Katelyn as she demonstrated her knife skills, which the soldiers were enthralled with, trying to see if they could copy what she did.

The Major spoke again, "I don't like to stick my nose into your teams' training and ways of doing things, but I wish to ask something of you if I may?"

"Please go ahead," Mike assured him. "I noticed during the training match while we were in the barracks that all your team had their battle gear fully loaded and weapons locked and loaded. Is it the American President?" Mike paused a moment and wondered whether he should tell the truth.

"Yes, he is a huge target, and so is the ARK," Mike answered.

"I totally agree; we only have thirty soldiers and twenty on-site at any time... and our truck is loaded with our gear as well."

CHAPTER 28

EVERYTHING HAS A PLACE & EVERYTHING IN ITS PLACE

Trundling along this deserted dark road, the canopy was so thick it gave a night-time appearance. The headlights on this Mitsubishi glowed a dull orange in the darkness ahead. His was the only light in all the darkness around for miles. Suddenly, as he rounded a corner, a glowing ember of civilisation beamed ahead, a light for hope, a light for the end to capitalism, the first step anyway.

The Water-Tiger showed up at their appointed meeting place at 3pm; it was an old abandoned farm twenty kms from the ARK. His second Min-ki Gwam had the team show up an hour early to go over their gear to make sure nothing was out of order before the mission. Gwam acknowledged the appearance of the team leader, as did the rest of the team. Then they all turned immediately to their duties to make sure everything was as it should be because failure is not an option in this team, and incompetence comes with a high penalty. Still, there was a buzz around the camp, a more heightened sense of purpose. The team was excited to be back together. However, they kept their adrenaline in check by concentrating on their jobs.

The Water-Tiger made his way to the command room, waiting on Min-ki Gwam to finish his inspections. During this time, he went over new plans in his head, new alternatives to produce the same end result; this was not how he usually worked his missions. Precision, planning, and training got him the reputation of No.1 on the world's most-wanted terrorist list. Now he looked at the maps and plans and wondered. This wonder had kept him up at night the last week. So many moving parts he didn't have his fingers on. Relying on others wasn't his style. If things went south, he was always prepared to take the blame.

Gwam came up after his inspections and walked into a brooding commander. This was not a sight he was used to; the commander was usually every team member's strength and assurance. His attention to detail always kept casualties to a minimum.

"What has happened to give you such a worried look, my friend? Has one of the teams called with difficulties?"

"No, no calls, everything is as planned... yet!" Water Tiger replied.

"Yet?" asked Gwam.

"So much we aren't controlling, so much reliance on strangers."

"There are five fronts to fight on in the Water Tigers' plan, and he controls only two."

"You have hired the right people, as you always do. President Abdi will cause riots in town because he wants his country back. The poachers will stop at nothing to reach the animals they require and have the firepower to stop the ARK Security."

"The mercenaries, what if they fail in destroying the Australians?" Water-Tiger asked his second.

"We will already be past that area when they know what is happening. We would have killed the EAGLE and be gone," Gwam reassured the commander.

"Exactly as I assessed it also, my friend. There is only one major goal; the others are merely distractions. Our men, are they ready?"

"Yes, commander, all ordinance is stored away; the men await your word."

"Excellent, we shall be away shortly," Water-Tiger informed Gwam.

The team had been promised three times their regular fee, and secrecy has been vital to stop any leaks. So first, the men were told the area and the type of resistance. The goal was a single person, but no prisoners was the scenario, which the soldiers found more straightforward. Kill everybody, then leave, use your appointed exit plan, then stay hidden for twelve months or longer if you think necessary. This part the soldiers found surprising. At worst, they were told to stay low for a month, so they believed the target was important, but they didn't care; the money made up for it, and they knew their commander left nothing to chance... Nothing.

The men gathered in formation, awaiting words of confidence and a rallying cry to stir the hearts of all who listened. Water Tiger stood on the balcony outside the command room, looking over his men. He was always proud to lead them. Some had been with him for several years and had performed their duties exceptionally.

"Men, we embark again on a mission of great importance of which there has been no greater target worthy of annihilation. At the moment, at the ARK is the President of the United States, who snuck in, scared of telling anyone he was here. This coward has been chosen by the world to be destroyed. And the honour has befallen upon our team to rid the world of this western disease. Stick to the plan that has been afforded you, and victory will be ours. Once he has been destroyed, it would be best to never speak of this night again. The world will be looking for us for a long time. Your payments will go through the usual procedures. Bask in private glory, knowing you have rid the world of this menace. VICTORY!" Water Tiger raised his fist in the air, which brought a thundering VICTORY scream from the men; the atmosphere was electrifying.

"Load up and let's go to our destiny!" another round of yells as the men loaded quickly onto the trucks. They loaded two old African troop carriers with men and ordinance. Twenty hardened mercenaries with nothing but destruction on their mind.

CHAPTER 29

THE NIGHT COMETH

"One leopard left. Are you going to help me find it?" The President asked his head of security.

"No... Sir," Chad responded, straight-faced and devoid of emotion.

"WHY not?" the President asked, huffing and puffing after chasing down an injured lion for five km.

"Because I want to see you electrified again... It's very amusing," Chad said again with no emotion. The President looked over at his head of security, noticing NO expression, NO humour on his face.

"Hmm, you should really take your show on the road; you're terrific," the President said. Langdon's head turned ever so slightly; his sensors alerted he was hearing something.

"I like you, Mr. President... So could I offer some advice for you?" The President intently searched the bushes ahead where he thought the leopard would be.

"Advice... Yeah, sure," the President responded.

In a hushed voice, Chad said, "Don't turn around."

The shocked look on his face came first, then the muscle reaction 2nd, then the look of abject horror as he saw the leopard he was hunting racing out of the bushes behind him. He swung his rifle around to get a shot off, but his speed was no match for the female leopard. It pounced and raised its paw to strike; when it came within the range of a kill, the animal automatically shut down, but not before the crippling electroshock on the suit of the President. The President was wriggling on the ground, yelling "Fuck, fuck!" between each shock.

Suddenly, the head of the Security's face appeared in front of him while he was lying convulsing on the ground.

"See, now this is funny, Sir," he said to the President with a smile.

"Fu fuc fuck yo you!" the President returned between shocks.

"Is the EAGLE alright?" came the doctor over the headset.

"Yes, Doc, he's fine, but you might want to get his valet to put a clean set of underwear out for him," Chad said with a straight face.

"What?" the doctor replied.

"Nothing, the EAGLE, is fine; we are heading back to camp," Chad responded.

The President was getting up off the ground as the head of Security offered him a hand; the President hesitated briefly before taking Chad's hand.

"I don't have a valet; I'm quite capable of changing my own underwear, thank you," the President joked. Then, the leopard that killed the American President got up off the ground and started running back to wherever he went to charge.

"Sneaky bastard," the President said to the leopard, disappearing into the brush.

"It's getting close to dark; did you want to walk back or drive, Sir?"

"Let's walk; I have a few aches I need to walk off," the President responded. It would take ½ hour to walk back to camp, but it was a beautiful dusk. Oranges and reds lined the horizon. What else would you want to do on an evening such as this?

****

Lexi noticed Doby looked better than he did this morning, but seemed fidgety, always moving and continuously checking everything twice. She hoped he wasn't coming down with something again; he had had such a hard run of things the last month.

'Everything is in place,' Doby kept telling himself. Now I can't be here as it all goes down; I can't be connected to it. Who am I kidding? I am going to jail no matter how this plays out! So long as Mum is safe, that is all I care about. 20 minutes left; I must get out of here; his heart rate raced.

"Lexi, I'm heading down for a coffee; can I get you something while I'm there?" Lexi was taken aback for a moment; Doby hadn't been this forthcoming for a while.

"Yes, that would be wonderful; Doby, could you see if the bakery has any custard pastries I like, please?"

"Yeah, sure, I might be a few minutes; I might pop in to see the nurse while I'm there," Doby replied.

"Are you alright?" Lexi queried, worried about her friend.

"Yes, just a headache I can't get rid of, that's all; I'll be back shortly." Doby left the room. 'I will go see the nurse; my head is killing me,' he thought.

****

Everything seemed normal in the ARK. Art and Tyson were in Tyson's lab checking the results of tests for the Monster squad to see how their development was going.

The Wolfman's muscle reaction was still a work in progress; they both surmised that getting them to behave like human muscles may be a long way off.

Ab was tinkering in the experimental lab, working on ideas Thomas had given him for updates on his new mines. Fascinating how Thomas got all this into such a compact system. They didn't have the range of the usual mines, but you could carry 7-1 against a standard mine, and they could program these to be set off in multiple different ways.

Last, Dan Hooper was driving past the baboon sanctuary for the 6th time today. If he sees just one trying to escape; it's on. There will be no planet of the Apes in his lifetime!

CHAPTER 30

HEAVENS ON FIRE

The shadows were growing, but there was a golden colour to everything. Ahead there was a vast glowing ember, the ARK, lit up like one of those grotesque shopping malls in America. The Water-Tiger knew that all the teams in his plan were working on time for his schedule. It was 5.55pm, and the group of poachers from Kenya were 200 metres out from the fence line, engines running, lights out on their two trucks. Without detection, the drivers used night vision goggles to approach the ARK'S fence line. There were two trucks and ten experienced men in their crew. The information they were given was that the security for the ARK'S defences would be down at 6.00pm. So, they could enter without detection, grabbing as much as possible, and be gone before the security knew they were there. Little did they know they had been set up to draw the guards, making an easier path for the real offensive to begin. Maybe they might have opted out had they known of the bloodbath they were facing in only a few minutes.

****

President Abdi was sitting at his desk when his 2nd in command came racing in.

"Sir, I have just received word that a truckload of protesters has arrived at the American Embassy, and streets are being blocked to prohibit entry to the areas."

"We cannot have this while the American President is here; it will make us look weak if we can't control our own streets! Call in all the reservists and police. I want control of those streets; do you hear me! Do whatever is necessary to protect the embassy and control the crowds; the protesters bring shame onto our country."

"Yes, Sir, I will have it controlled immediately," the second quickly turned and was out the door. The President sat back in his luxurious throne chair.

"Soon, it will be all mine again," he said to the empty room, grinning like a cat that had just swallowed the canary.

****

It was a balmy night with a lot of cloud cover, not that anyone was really noticing. The Water Tiger and Chao Zhang had their teams ready to strike. The mercenaries taking out the Australian team had to make a last-minute change as three of their team didn't show up at the meeting place. This still left them with thirteen men, ample fighters to take out six soldiers. The mercs were ready to strike. Four men were on the perimeter breach, each with a miniature oxy torch to cut through the fence quickly. They would come up from the South of the Australian barracks and hitting them with a surprise attack. Zhang's men were encroaching on foot with rocket launchers to shoot the American Special Forces helicopters and the President's plane.

****

Lexi was sitting at her desk waiting for Doby to come back with the coffee and tarts; she has had a severe case of the munchies lately. Suddenly, an alarm went off, and the screens automatically switched on to the area in question. It took a second for her brain to register what she was seeing, two trucks with chains pulling down the fence in sector 11. She immediately hit the alarm button that sent a signal through the ARK and the Security barracks.

"Breach in sector 11, two trucks, multiple armed men," Lexi yelled through the mic.

The alarm was enough to get everybody moving; Lexi yelling into the PA system had everybody running; the ARK had drilled for such an occasion. Staff shut down stores and moved to the accommodation level. In-house security locked down the delivery docks and outer doors and waited for the staff member on-duty in the Security room to bring extra weapons and tactical gear down to the food mall to reinforce the men.

Art, Ab, and Tyson were running to the HUB, and Macca led a group from the delegation into a safe room at the end of the conference centre, acting calmly, telling the members that everything was under control and that they were just following safety procedures.

Ab crashed in through the door of the HUB, nearly tripping over and taking Art down with him, who was right behind him.

"Holy shit!" Lexi yelled.

"Now what?" Art asked with a frantic look on his face.

"Well, we just had a breach in sector 11 with what looks like poachers, and now the systems crashed, and I can't get ANYTHING!"

Ab took Doby's seat and started hitting the controls, trying to bring something up, ANYTHING, but with no luck. Art tried his mobile phone as he moved over to the communications area.

"No cell reception," he turned on the radio and other devices.

"Nothing, it's all down!" Just then, Doby and Tyson made their way through the door.

"What's happening?" Doby asked.

"Everything's down," Lexi said frantically.

"That's not possible," Doby said as he jumped into the spare console seat.

****

Zhang's team moved in slowly and silently, keeping to the time schedule. The eerie sounds of the night are a stark contrast to the noise that was about to fall on the airfield. "Zirrff, Zirrff" as two rockets left their casings, heading towards the helicopters.

The attack on the American soldiers couldn't have worked out better for Zhang's team, who worried all week that he would be lucky to survive the initial attack against two Delta Force teams. It was certainly in his favour tonight if there was such a thing as luck.

As Zhang's team fired at the two helicopters, they were lucky that one group of Delta force were at the helicopters checking their gear as the rockets hit simultaneously. Explosions and fireballs lit the air with the sound of screaming men. The double explosion, plus the ignition of ammunition on the helicopters, blew the two copters across the tarmac, killing four of the Delta team and critically wounding the other two. Delta Force training is precise, effective, and reactive; within seconds, the men in the back of the President's plane had grabbed weapons and were heading out to assist the other Delta team.

As fate or Zhang's luck on the night had ordained, Zhang had ordered the second wave of rockets to be fired on the President's plane. One hit the radar antennae dish with an explosive ball of sparks on top of the aircraft, causing a blackout of the plane's communication and starting an internal fire. The second rocket was dead on target as it flew through the air, weaving its trail of smoke behind it and hit the second Delta team as they were exiting the plane's rear. The explosion blew four of the soldiers onto the tarmac and two back into the end of the burning plane. Seconds later, two men jumped out through the flames onto the rear ramp and started running for cover as a hail of bullets from Zhang's men started showering the Delta Force men on the tarmac.

Smoke was billowing everywhere, and the intense heat from the burning copters and plane covered the runway. Two of the Delta Force men had made it to cover with only minor injuries. In contrast, two others were severely injured by the rocket blast.

One injured Delta member made his way to the plane's rear ramp for cover, bleeding profusely from his wound. Locked and loaded with some cover, he murmured, 'Till the end.'

The other wounded Delta member was hit by the fire laid down by Zhang's men while crawling for cover. The encroaching mercs laid down more fire to get a bearing on how many of the Delta team were left. It was an obvious manoeuvre but nonetheless effective, as the remaining Americans returned fire as they were trying to control their space, trying not to get flanked by this unknown enemy.

The wind was blowing from east to west. Zhang knew he couldn't afford to get pinned down by a few men. So, he ordered five men to head upwind, using the smoke as cover and make their way across the ramp at the back of the President's plane as the fire inside burned ever brighter. 'How long before she blows? We need to be out of this area quickly,' Zhang thought.

As one team kept two of the Delta forces pinned behind a piece of the attack helicopter's fuselage, the other team made its way around the back of the plane. The smoke was a lot clearer here because of the aircraft's height. The merc team had a lead man followed by a standard 2 x 2 formation and, behind them, another five-man formation. The men hurried across the ramp, rifles moving sharply as they trained on all shapes in the smoke.

Corporal Lance Dinkley, the Delta member injured and using the ramp as cover, saw the team heading to move across the ramp. He wiggled himself into a firing position to attack. Not trusting his accuracy with his rifle because of his injuries, he opted for his browning pistol for better control. Cpl Dinkley counted the footsteps as they came across the ramp; he was right five members in the team. He waited until he saw the shoulder of the second merc before he made his move; opening fire at the head of the second merc. He took him down with one shot. Then, he turned his attention to the first merc in formation and fired three rounds into his back. Dinkley knew this was a no-win manoeuvre. He couldn't outgun all five mercs, but he intended to take as many out as possible with him. Dinkley grabbed a frag grenade off his vest and tossed it toward the remaining soldiers. As Dinkley watched what seemed like ultra-slow-motion, the grenade twirling through the air, one of the merc soldiers popped his head around the ramp and fired a burst into the Corporal. If there was a God of War, he would have given the Corporal the satisfaction of seeing the look on the soldier's face as he realised what was in the air in front of him and then kept him alive long enough to see the soldier's head explode like a smashed watermelon.

The grenade had done its trick, with the remaining mercs in the team dead or bleeding out quickly. The unexpected gunfire and explosion took the two men that jumped from the burning plane by surprise, one a Secret Service officer and the other a pilot. The Secret Service officer opened fire on the explosion area, hoping to kill any advancing enemy. Instead, the shots inadvertently tipped off the second team of mercs, heading up behind. As the mercs rounded the end of the ramp through the blood and guts of their compatriots, the Secret Service officer opened fire, hitting the first merc in the shoulder and spinning him off to the left quickly. The following two soldiers rounded the corner firing, pinning the Secret Service officer behind cover.

"Go, go, get out of here!" the officer yelled at the pilot, holding a weapon he barely knew how to use. The pilot, looking to run, couldn't see shit in front of him. The smoke here was so thick, but running was his only option. The Secret Service officer opened fire with controlled bursts through the smoke but eventually was overcome by superior numbers and fell fighting a gallant battle, giving the pilot time to escape.

Gripping a Secret Service light machine pistol, the pilot ran until he nearly ran straight into the muzzle of a Delta Force rifle.

"What the fuck? I could have shot you," the Delta soldier yelled at him.

"Well, if you don't, they will!" the pilot yelled frantically.

"They're coming from that way?"

"I knew they'd try to flank us."

"Kurt, we can't stay here; we need to get to the ARK and defend there."

"Yeah, but there's a lot of open space across this runway," the other Delta team man said.

"You, if you come with us, you're dead; they're looking for us. First, get that fucking white shirt off. If you can run, I would follow the smoke for cover and get into the jungle and wait till later when more troops arrive. Got it!"

"Got it," the pilot said. "Kurt, we have one chance; look to see any muzzle flash and keep their heads down and be ready to run."

"Roger," Kurt said. Kurt and his Delta Teammate steadied themselves on the helicopter fuselage.

"Ok, run!" The pilot ran like a man possessed, looking ahead, not slowing down, running for his life, which was precisely what he was doing. The mercs were waiting for the other teams to circle around. Then, in the light from the flames across the runway, they saw a pair of legs. Unwilling to miss the chance to kill another Delta member, some mercenaries opened fire on the legs. After a few warm-up shots, the mercs were zeroing in on the target. Just as the soldier was about to fire, his head snapped back, and part of his helmet and head disappeared; then, a few bursts of fire had the mercs ducking for cover themselves.

"Ok, it's now or never, man," Kurt said to his teammate, slapping him on the back.

"Fuck this, let's go!" Both Delta men turned and ran towards the man-made mountain. It was 100 metres to the first cover, but it seemed like they were running a marathon. Heart's racing and adrenaline pumping through their veins. The smoke was getting thicker from the plane, and minor explosions started popping off, which covered the escape of the two remaining Delta team members. They hit the dirt and rolled off in two different directions to avoid last-minute fire, but none came. They rallied together and made their way to the ARK, over four hundred metres away.

CHAPTER 31

AS LUCK WOULD HAVE IT

The night was falling, and the ghostly dark made the dense trees Mike jogs past in the morning even more ominous. The golden orange and reds of the sunset seemed to be absorbed into this void, never to be seen again.

Looking out from the front of the barracks, there is a clearing of twenty metres, around which the AZTECK Security and Sherlocks team gathered and ate around a campfire. Then there were fifty metres of low shrubs and bushes, and amid that low shrub was a large baobab tree with an enormous twisted three-metre diameter base.

Productive chatter filled the barracks as Mike's team went over their gear when the Majors team arrived. 'A lot of cloud cover should provide an interesting setting for a night mission,' Thomas thought to himself as he was packing the rest of his new mines into his battle pack. He lifted his pack and felt it was a lot lighter than expected. That was good news because he was working on the next project as of tomorrow. Updating the sound and vision of the team. He picked up the special vision goggles that Ab had given him; Thomas was tempted to take them for tonight's mission, but he had promised Mike no unfair advantages this time, so he threw them on top of his pack.

Thomas made his way outside to greet the African soldiers he had made friends with. He literally bumped into the Major in the doorway, and the Major's large girth, made of pure muscle, threw Thomas back like a rag doll being chewed by a dog. The Major, with lightning reflexes, pulled his machete halfway out of its sheath; its gleaming blade could show your reflection on it.

"Look where I'm going, boy," the Major said in a very menacing voice, staring down at Thomas for what seemed like an eternity; just as quickly, the Major broke into a large toothy grin?

"Just messin' with you, Thomas. Is the Captain in?"

"Yes, he's in the command, Major," Thomas said, still trying to get over the gleam on the Major's machete and the chips in the blade he noticed.

'I'm not asking him where he got those dents from,' he thought.

Night had come; the Major and Mike had gone over the rules of engagement and were coming out of the room.

"Sergeant, you and the lovely lady with the killer knives are on my team tonight," the Major said as he addressed 2 Planks and Steel. The pair were bewildered and looked around the great hulking African to confirm this. Mike shook his head.

"No, you're not," He assured them.

"The captain refused to fight me again for you both, something about he couldn't afford to lose either of you," the Major joked.

"I didn't say that either," Mike protested.

"Well, there you go. If you were in my crew, I would fight to keep you and tell you I couldn't afford to lose you!" the Major continued his joke.

"Well, I don't know about you, Smith, but I'm feeling left out and insecure," Quassy said, joking.

"Welcome to my world. I can't fly anymore cause I'm afraid of being shot down…" the room turned into spontaneous laughter, trust Smiths' dark humour to crack up the crowd.

"Well, Major, I suppose we sho… GET DOWN!" Mike shoved the Major as hard as he could before a barrage of bullets came flying through the windows, shattering glass and sending chips of timber and wall all around the room.

Reflexes. Constantly aware of your surroundings. Being ready to react in a second. This is the training that Sherlock has drilled into his team for seven years. Now was the second it either worked, or it was a wasted seven years. Sherlock had seen something out of his peripheral vision; it wasn't there, and then it was. When he first caught sight of numerous red lights in his vision. The alarm bells sounded, and when his brain acknowledged, it was laser lights. The sirens rang. "Get down!" was all he had time to say, but it was enough. Sherlock's speed and strength were enough to push his hulking counterpart off balance and send him to the floor. Sherlock and the Major rolled on the floor and came to a stop up against the far wall. The Major's training had him rolling and coming up ready for action, just like Sherlock. Sherlock's first initial action is always the team. He looked over and saw the last seven years were not a waste.

Reacting to "get down" in a second, hitting the floor, and automatically grabbing their kit off the bunks in one movement made him proud. Now, if we live through whatever this is, I'll remember to praise them for it. Now react, "OUT OUT OUT!" Sherlock ordered.

"Go, Major, get to your truck!" Sherlock yelled as another wave of bullets riddled the room. Sherlock's team was already heading out the door and crouched down, hidden from the incoming fire. As Steel was about to make her run for the door, she noticed Kids pack on his bunk; she grabbed it and hurled it through one of the broken windows. Next, she grabbed his rifle and made her way out the door.

Kid was making his way back into the barracks to grab the goggles to show his African friends. As he approached the barracks, Sherlock yelled, "GET DOWN!" The intensity of his voice made Kid react as he did. He immediately threw himself to the ground as the barracks exploded with gunfire, sending glass and timber over him through the decimated window frames and walls. Although only new to Special Forces, Kid's training was just as well drilled. He hit the dirt and immediately recovered to react. His kit it was inside the barracks.

Everything was happening around him, and he had sensory overload from combat. One of his African friends was in line with the windows as the hail of bullets came flying through, and he caught two rounds in his left arm and was screaming with pain as he hit the ground. The screams, a voice yelling "OUT OUT OUT!" and another hail of gunfire all ringing through his head together.

Kid had been in heavy combat before, but they were controlled actions; the enemy was there; you are here. Shoot and kill the enemy, but he had never been in an ambush before. The fog cleared within a few seconds, but it seemed like he had time to make a coffee and debate with himself all the possible actions. His kit, he was in the fight, like a miracle, a sign from the heavens. His kit came flying through the window, landing beside him. HALLILEUA! As Kid pushed his arm through one sling. The rest of the team flew through the door, including the Major. Sherlock had made his way to the command room to grab his kit.

"Kid, you're with me," Quassy yelled to him as he came through the door. What in later years would come to be Kid's version of Sherlock's famous instinctive decisions under fire, he yelled. "The goggles, I need the goggles." Never doubting a teammate, Quassy yells back, "Kids goggles" to Sherlock.

Once again, not doubting a team member, Sherlock made his way through the barracks as he saw above him that the laser targeting lights were getting close to the side of the barracks. He scuttles fast past the bunks, sees the goggles on the ground, picks them up, and makes his way out.

2 Planks had been guarding the side of the barracks in case the unknown assailants appeared before Sherlock was out. He heard Sherlock come through the door behind him and turned to see the instructions. All the team had eyes on Sherlock to see how he wanted to respond. Sherlock made several hand signals, and the team members nodded. He had told them, 'Go under, back 50 metres and go silent', meaning working with silenced weapons or knives.

When the last round of fire finished, the Major's men made their way quickly to their truck to grab their weapons; two soldiers jumped on the back of the truck. The first soldier jumped up onto the back deck, grabbed his rifle, and ran to the front of the truck. He watched and gave cover to his fellow team members while the other soldier grabbed weapons and ammunition to hand out to the rest of the team. The first soldier's adrenaline was racing, and his reactions were too quick; his lack of combat training made him open fire at the first sign of the laser lights coming through the darkness. He never knew if he had hit any of the enemies, as a concentrated fire response tore up the truck's cabin and riddled the young soldier with bullets.

As an added response to the firing from the truck, a trail of smoke shot through the air as one soldier yelled, "RPG!" as he dived to the ground. The RPG hit the side of the truck, causing it to tip on its side as the petrol tank exploded in a vast mushroom ball of flames.

The Major was heading to the truck as the RPG was fired. He was thrown to the ground for the second time during this encounter. With all the commotion of bullets flying past his ears, explosions, and thick smoke billowing everywhere, he still rolled to his feet and ran into the flames. With no self-regard, he dragged his men away from the burning truck. Three of his men's lives were taken in one horrible move, and now they would pay with theirs.

Keeping a cool head, the Major saw that some weapons and ammunition were thrown away from the truck in the explosion, so he grabbed rifles and ammunition belts and threw them to his men. The training missions with Sherlock and his men instilled some of the same processes into his own team. "Go under, wait for my signal," and his men disappeared into the surrounding bushland.

Kid received his goggles from Sherlock and then automatically followed orders and went to join Quassy. He had scrambled 30 metres out from the barracks, staying low in the underbrush, when Quassy called to him, "Here, Kid."

Quassy asked, "How strong are those goggles of yours?"

"Not sure 100-150 metres max," Kid replied.

"Ok, head back another fifty. Get yourself a clear line of sight to the barracks. See if there's a tree worth shooting from and call them out to us. Got it?"

"Roger," Kid replied and was gone in a second. Quassy got on the comms, "Kid is spotting for us." A call of Roger came back in reply. Kid made his way to a grove of trees and found one which gave him a perch to see and shoot from, 'bring on the wrath,' he said to himself.

All was quiet, except for the crackling of the burning truck. It was now a deadly game of skill and cat and mouse. The AZTECK soldier hit in the arm was clenching his wounded arm tightly. Biting his lip to stop himself from screaming and giving away his position as he crawled to the tree line where Kid was. He applied a field bandage to his arm. He had two wounds on his left arm. One was a flesh wound that was easily treated, but the other must have shattered a bone as it went straight through his arm. It was like a searing hot knife stuck in his arm. He applied the field bandage to one wound and made up another out of rifle straps and a face mask to stem blood flow from the gaping hole. He looked up and saw Kid in the tree beside him; Kid nodded to him, and he nodded back. He was going to live through this night; he hoped.

Sherlock and the Major's team now had to turn the defence into offence. They had been attacked by surprise, and with the flurry of rounds shot into the barracks, they meant business and weren't taking prisoners. On the left, facing the barracks, was an AZTECK burning troop truck and the two of the four men remaining in the Major's squad, the third injured and back in the tree line with Kid. The Major had blended with the gigantic tree in the centre. But, with his height and bulky body, hiding in small underbrush didn't suit, so he blended in with the roots and trunk of the massive tree. One of his men watched and was amazed at how his enormous leader seemed to hug the tree... and then disappear. Quassy hung back twenty metres behind the Major's men for support on that side.

Sherlock and Steel had taken a stance in the underbrush beside the tree on the left, facing the barracks, ten metres apart. They were close enough to support each other when they lured the enemy in, and it became a hand-to-hand fight. 2 Planks and Smith took a stance off to the left of the barracks to stop anyone from trying to flank them. All this was done, and the teams were ready in less than a minute. Years of training had them prepared for such an occasion.

The teams waited and watched as the laser lights bounced around behind the barracks, getting closer and closer... then nothing. Obviously, the enemy isn't as stupid as he thought, 2 Planks surmised. Let's play in the dark, he said to himself.

"Incoming, two barracks left, two truck right, four holding beside the barracks on the left." Came the call from Kid over the comms. Quassy moved across and taped one of the AZTECK soldiers on the shoulder, making him jump. Quassy signalled for him to follow. He led the soldier to a spot ten metres past the burning truck. He tapped the mic on his headset and then signalled that two of the enemy were making their way past the burning truck. The soldier nodded. He understood what was happening. Quassy then showed him where he wanted him to hide and wait. The soldier nodded again in recognition of what was going to happen.

Then Quassy quickly pulled out his knife and held it up in front of his face and the soldier then promptly did the same, except the look in the soldiers' eyes was menacing, as if he was going to enjoy this. Quassy thought maybe he lost one of his friends in the explosion. It's hard to hide payback from one's face. Two mercenaries made their way to the service road beside the burning truck. The lead soldier turned on his night vision goggles to get a reading of where the enemy had gone into hiding, but all the small fires around the area made it impossible to distinguish anything around them.

Time was running out, so the lead soldier chose a spot to cover the advancing team. The two mercs made their way quickly past the burning trucks. Unfortunately, the smell of burning fuel was the last thing their senses would have picked up as a dark figure came with speed from a bush to the left. Before he could react, the first merc had a blade thrust up into his throat as the weight of his assailant knocked him to the ground. The second soldier, five metres behind, had turned to see what was happening to his squad member. Then a hand went across his mouth as a knife was forced into the side of his neck. Quassy laid on top of his prey until he was sure he was dead. As he was getting up, he looked over to his partner and saw the soldier was covered in blood as he repeatedly stabbed his victim. He approached the soldier and put his hand on his shoulder; as the soldier turned and he saw on his face that look of revenge was replaced with anguish for a lost comrade, Quassy squeezed his shoulder to tell him he understood and indicated it was time to join the fight.

2 Planks and Smith were listening to Kid. Through the goggles, Kid has spotted two enemy heat signatures were moving around behind about thirty metres from their

position. They're trying to flank us. 'Fuck that,' he thought. He signalled silently for Smith to handle the two mercs beside the barracks, and he would turn back and take on whoever was behind them. Smith smiled wickedly as he pulled out his combat knife. 2 Planks shook his head and showed him his silenced pistol. Smiths' shoulders dropped, and he put on a sulky face as if to say, 'you spoil all my fun.' 2 Planks shook his head, wondering how Smith had lived so long in this business with his thirst for action, and then he turned to go after his prey.

It didn't take long for 2 Planks to track down the rear soldier. The other soldier was 10 metres in front, which was a concern. 2 Planks had to take the rear soldier down silently to get the jump on the lead man. Moving like a panther stalking a wounded prey, he moved silently but quickly on the soldier so as not to lose his advantage. He grabbed the merc from behind, clasping a hand over his mouth and thrusting his blade up into the base of his enemy's skull, using all his strength to hold the man upright, so the noise of him hitting the ground didn't alert the other soldier. Success. The other soldier was not alerted as he placed the merc on the ground. Now to do the same again, he thought.

One branch was all it took to change this cat-and-mouse game. As the lead soldier turned to tell his teammate to keep the noise down, 2 Plank's mind swept through the possibilities. His best bet was to make a lunging dive at the soldier using the knife and his body size to overpower his enemy. As 2 Planks pounced like a giant cat, he held the knife ready to strike, and he should have hit him before he could pull his rifle up to shoot… if only that's what the enemy did… but he didn't. Knowing that he didn't have time to get his weapon up to shoot, he used it to block 2 Planks' knife attack. Action, reaction, muscle memory, and training. Lots of training. As 2 Planks' knife struck the enemy's rifle, he countered by rolling off to one side and snatching the weapon from his enemy's hands. The soldier, feeling he was being disarmed, countered by releasing the grip on his weapon.

Reaction… The next phase in this dance of death was a secondary weapon. Who could draw the fastest? 2 Plank's mind told him his enemy had the advantage as he had to release the grip on his enemy's weapon. Both men positioned and drew their weapons; 2 Planks' mind slowed and turned over in microseconds, judging whose weapon would win the race. Halfway through the draw 2, Plank's mind gave it up as a lost cause; they had lost. Now who was going to come to his funeral? Would his family be surprised it happened? Oh my God, is there surfing in heaven? The GODS of WAR dice have many sides, and as it rolls on, the fate of this soldier. It changed all with one word… Mate!

"Drop the weapon, mate!" the merc shouted. 2 Planks stopped the rise of his weapon. His mind couldn't comprehend what he heard, but his mouth reacted to help delay the inevitable.

"Mate, are you an Aussie?" 2 Planks said back.

"Fuckin Hell, you're Australian. What the hell are you doing here?" the merc asked.

"Well, you're trying to kill me, so you might want to tell me what's happening here."

"Nothing personal, mate. They hired us to take out six AZTECK Security guards and then piss off home," the merc told 2 Planks.

"Well, someone has set you up well and truly. We're Australian SAS recon' and ten ARK Security."

"Fuck that, I didn't come here to kill Australians" the merc lowered his weapon, and 2 Planks couldn't believe he wasn't about to die.

The merc spoke, "if you don't mind, I would like to turn around and leave. I would be very appreciative if you wouldn't shoot me in the back," he said, laughing.

"Not my style," 2 Planks joked.

"You have skills; you've obviously been trained?" 2 Planks asked.

"2nd battalion out of Kalgooli. Just needed some extra cash. Kind of like betting on the ponies too much, if you know what I mean," the merc turned to leave and then suddenly turned around, "a piece of advice! Someone has paid a lot of money to get you guys out of the way; something else big is going down," the merc turned and left.

Apart from what they saw and heard when Smith took out the two mercs beside the barracks, Steel and Sherlock didn't know what was going down; their focus was here and now, but they didn't have long to wait. Four soldiers moved out from beside the barracks on the Major's side, coming out fast, hoping the enemy would be stupid enough to poke their heads up and be cut down by their flanking troops… which would have been perfect if they were still alive. They split up into 2 x 2, and each team moved to each side of the large tree in the middle of the clearing. The enemy moved slowly, going over every inch in front of them, but not beside them.

If the merc beside the tree had lived, he would have had a tale to tell. It would go something like, "I was moving forward, sweeping side to side to clear this area of the enemy. The night seemed still, except for the local birds and animals calling out. I was moving past this large tree when suddenly, the tree came to life and smiled at me. Then, it brought forward this large machete and slammed it down into my neck, ending my life…" and that's precisely what happened.

The next few seconds were anyone's guess as bullets flew in all directions. As the Major came to life from the tree and slammed the machete into the mercenary's neck, the soldier beside him swung towards the Major to return fire. Sherlock came from his cover and took down the other merc to cover the Major. Now Sherlock was in the open with two mercenaries getting a bead on him. Steel sprung from her cover, pistol raised, to take down one merc. Then, suddenly, a volley of shots came from nowhere, taking down the last merc in the open. Kid had been watching and had his sights on the last man standing.

Before anyone could breathe a sigh of relief, Kid yelled through the comm system, "Movement in the barracks!"

As they watched and took down the enemy in the open, the last three mercenaries had been moving into the barracks in shadow, ready to offer any assistance. Now it was a turkey shoot as they peered out the front windows. Four soldiers Steel, Sherlock, The Major, and one of the Major's men, were standing right in front, in the open. As the mercs opened fire, Steel and the Major were hit. Steel took two rounds on her vest, and the Major took a round high on his arm just below the shoulder joint.

The enemy's ambush was short-lived as the cover support came firing in, lighting up the barracks. Once the firing had opened up, 2 Planks, Quassy, and the other AZTECK soldiers came in on flanking positions and set the barracks alight, ending the mercenaries' fight back. As they came around to check on Steel and the Major, Sherlock issued new orders.

"Smith, check for any stragglers." 2 Planks moved in beside Sherlock while checking Steel's vest.

"Lucky lady looks like you'll get away with just a couple of broken ribs," Sherlock tells Steel.

"Sherlock, we may have more to worry about," 2 Planks tells him.

"I bumped into an Aussie, conscientious objector, who saw the light on his wicked ways. He told me they never told these guys who we were. He thinks someone paid them a lot of money to get us out of the way for something else."

The obvious hit Sherlock like a hammer. "Shit, the President, someone's going after the President."

"What is your plan, Captain? We will need transport to get to where the President is camped. I suggest we go to my barracks and use our jeeps and trucks."

"A good course of action, Major. Grab all you need now because we don't know what we are walking into," Sherlock ordered. Everyone scurried around, checking the dead mercs for equipment they could use. 'Keep moving,' Sherlock thought, think on the run. All the troops headed off on the run to the ARK Security barracks at the end of the runway.

****

The noise from the attack on the president's protection was constant. There was an endless barrage of rocket and rifle fire until it slowly petered down to spasmodic bursts of semi-auto rifle fire. The Water Tiger looked at his watch. "Time," he yelled as the two 4x4 troop carriers pulled panels of the security fence down with chains and grapples. Then, as the men jumped back on the vehicles, they headed into the Ark's Park, only fifty metres from the ARK Security barracks. Only one young officer operating the now non-functional radio system guarded the barracks. He had sent all the on-duty security detail to a poacher's break-in and was now the only man left to protect the radio station. The panic in him was rising by the second as he stood in the doorway with his rifle, watching the President's detail going up in flames.

The roar of engines behind the barracks caught his attention. 'The Somalian army backup has arrived' was the thought going through his mind as he ran to the edge of the barracks. As he turned the corner of the building, gunfire cut him down as groups of heavily armed men exited the trucks swarming through the barracks.

"It is clear, commander," one soldier addressed Water-Tiger.

"Excellent." He grabbed his hand radio.

"Team 2 report." A crackling came across the handset.

"All clear, no support needed. "Continue with phase 2 of your mission."

"Roger," came the reply from Chao Zhang. Everything is as planned. The President's guard is destroyed now; all that is left is to finish this mission. Water Tiger gave himself a rare moment to smile.

"Nobody can stop me now; he is mine," he said to no one around him. Then, he motioned for everyone to get on the trucks and continue with the mission. The trucks rolled off just as Sherlock and his team were finishing off the last mercs.

CHAPTER 32

ROUND & ROUND & ROUND

The flames soared high into the night and glowed like the burning walls of Hades. Smoke, thick and black, blew across the tarmac like a scene from a Dante play.

Nero stood there watching his empire burn, but this Nero had no fiddle to play, nor did he want to. The first few minutes for Art were abject horror, the next few abject revenge! The look of horror on their faces as they stood at the guardrail on the landing pad. It resembled a scene from a Hollywood disaster movie. The President's plane was entombed in flames, and smaller fires littered all over the runway. Art could hear gunfire coming from the area.

"They're after the President; we need help. Let's get back to the comms to see if we can get a call out," Tyson said to a dazed Art.

Art felt like Nero standing here watching Rome burn. Tyson put his hand on Art's shoulder, knowing that watching his dreams burn around him must be soul-destroying. Then to their left, a small explosion was heard with a heavier sound of gunfire also, 'the poachers' Tyson thought, but why would they be after the President, and why hadn't the CIA warned him?

"Come on, let's get back in," Tyson said to Art, but the Art Damani that turned wasn't the destroyed Nero that Tyson thought he'd see but a fierce, angry and determined look of a man with a laser focus.

"Let's go," Art said as he turned to run inside.

As Doby, Lexi, and Ab fought with the computer to get it to respond, all they could do was to report on what was happening, not what they wanted to happen.

"The President is under attack; that is what has happened. Tyson head to the armoury and tell security to arm up, as we are under attack by trained soldiers. Ab, get on the comms and try to get some kind of communication up and running; I don't care what." Everybody ran to their new duties. When Art's mind is ticking, there's no time to waste.

"Doby, what are the most secure areas in the ARK?"

"The HUB and the conference room, why?"

"If we still have control of the doors, lock down the conference room to keep the delegation safe."

"You don't think they'd come in the ARK?" Lexi asked, concerned.

"I would," Art said gravely.

Minutes were ticking over. When Doby told Ab to try getting a cell line working through the old internet cable, they used at the start of the build but later changed to a more hi-tech system, this had been the first stage of Doby's fightback plan.

"Yes, got a line; great work, Doby!" Ab yelled. As Art started dialling, a sense of relief opened the door to hope, only to have it slammed in his face.

"Hello, President Abdi, this is Art Damani. I need your reserve troops to the ARK. We are under attack, and the American President is in danger."

"Mr. Damani, I cannot send any troops to you. The streets of the capital are in chaos, with marches and street battles all over the city, and the American Embassy is under siege. However, I will send support as soon as possible; Abdi out," the line went dead.

Art stood there a moment; this was bigger than he imagined. "The Australians, where are they? Didn't they have drills tonight with the Major?" he asked everyone.

"Yes, but how do we contact them?" Ab asked.

"We have to find them first. Lexi, bring up the gaming scheme and see if it's running."

"Yes, it is. They're heading towards the Security barracks. The Major and some of his men, but some men are offline." A sinking feeling hit Art's stomach. In the back of his mind, he wondered who would have the capability to do this. Who?

"Doby, what can you tell me?"

"We've been hacked, but the Ark's systems still seem intact. No security and no communication. We have two choices. Stay put till help arrives or turn off all the systems and reboot with a new Sphere system."

"How long will that take?" Art asked.

"Not sure. 10-15 minutes with nothing working, including outer door security."

"Shit shit shit," Art cursed."

"That's an enormous risk," Lexi said.

"Especially if you think they're coming here," Doby added.

CHAPTER 33

HI MUM

Art could hear the seconds tick by on a digital clock, or was it his own biological clock…both sounded like a countdown.

Minutes were ticking by, and every second without an answer or response meant that lives could be lost. The life of the President of the United States, no less, and the chance to prove that peace can prevail.

The air was electric in the HUB. Art was trying to develop anything he could do to help the President and the ARK itself. He was confident that it was a matter of time before the ARK was attacked directly. No, that's not what was bothering him. He failed! Failed miserably, and people's lives were in jeopardy because he was too arrogant to listen. If only he had talked his plans over with Ab, he would have seen the ARK wasn't ready for such an important visitor. But that's then; this is now. Who could have done this? He had the best security on the planet? That gnawing doubt kept jumping in his mind, and he fought to keep it in check. Someone inside! But not his team; why would they? They are just as protective of the ARK as he.

Art got on his phone and called for backup.

"Tyson Art here; get the boys online and the monsters too."

"Seriously, why?"

"I believe we will be attacked too; it stands to reason, and I would rather have the robots destroyed than lose human life," Art said.

"OK, will do Art… online. Art, you're brilliant!"

"I used to think so, but how does that help us now?" Art said, confused.

"I just had an idea that might get us some visuals outside. I'll meet you in the HUB in 5," Tyson said excitedly.

"Make it 3; I don't know if we have 5," Art replied.

Tyson ran into the HUB puffing.

"Lexi downloaded this as a separate system with no protection; that should keep it off your grid and whoever has hacked it." Lexi snatched it out of his hand, having no idea what it was.

"What is it?" Ab asked.

"My Bats!" Tyson said this as if that would clear everything up, but it didn't. Tyson looked around and saw nobody understood what was going on.

"My new bats for the bat cave have Abs optic patterns built-in; they can fly and see anything even in the dark!"

"Brilliant!" Art said.

"We can fly them outside and see what's happening." The optimism in the room picked up.

"Lexi, if you go into the program, I have them numbered individually. Number them in two groups, then we can split them." Lexi punched away on the controls, fingers moving in a blur of speed very few can simulate.

"Done! They're up and flying. Tyson, take the other console, and we can run them separately on the screens." The security team looked in amazement as they watched two groups of bats fly from Tyson Lumley's office, make a couple of loops in the air and head up towards the HUB. Art and Ab watched as the bats flew out the Hubs exit and off into the night.

Arts watch beeped, and a smile came on his face. He hit a button on his watch, "Come to daddy," he said. The Security guards watched as Loki and Thor came thundering out the door of Tyson Lumley's lab. Two of the guards looked at each other.

"This place is a madhouse," one security said to the other. "The pays good though," the other responded; they both nodded and agreed.

They all gathered as the screens came online with the views from optics on the bats.

Holy shit, Tyson, these optics are brilliant for night flying; we'll have no trouble finding the President with these. However, it seems they can have another purpose. Saving a President.

"Lexi, you head off to Captain Madden's team," Art said.

Lexi was enthralled with her job of flying the bats, "Ok, woohoo, here comes batgirl."

"Lexi, we're in the middle of a major disaster; try not to enjoy it too much," Art said.

"Sorry, Art, but these guys are way cool. I gotta get me some of these," Lexi said as she was dodging and weaving to the views of the bats.

On the other hand, Tyson set a straight course for the President's camp. Zeroing on the homing beacon of the President's base camp, the bats flew over an outcrop of trees and dived in to get a closer visual.

"Oh God, no!" The room was silent as the camp came into closer view. The base was a disaster. Bullet riddled bodies lay strewn everywhere, tents ripped apart, paper and bags emptied all over the ground. Art and his team were in shock, a horrible scene that all realised could potentially start another war similar to that after the 9/11 attacks.

Art was the first to snap out of visual horror.

"Tyson, can the bats make a visual of the dead?"

"Not sure, maybe if they are facing directly up."

"Wait a moment, how many people were at the camp?" Art asked anyone who could answer; he knew he just wanted it confirmed.

"Sixteen" Lexi yelled.

"There's not sixteen there!" Art yelled.

"Doby, bring the President's hunting suits up." Doby's fingers started punching keys as nine beacon lights, including the Presidents, came upon the screen.

"YES!" Art screamed as he jumped, punching the air.

"He's alive, thank fucking god for that… excuse me, Lexi" they all laughed at Art's moment of manners in a crisis.

"Yes, but we can't help him," Ab pointed out.

"No, but they can." They all turned to Lexi's screen as they watched Sherlock and his crew, plus the Major and two men, load onto two lorries.

Doby's phone ringing made everyone in the room jump except Doby.

Grabbing the phone from his pocket, he answers it, "Mum is that you! Thank God. Yes, I know you were being held. Did they hurt you? Thank God for that. No, get the police to hold you. No, it's for your own safety; those men may come back. No, I haven't rung up gambling debts. No, Mum, Mr. Damani isn't smuggling drugs. Mum! Please put the policeman on the phone… Hello officer, my name is Doby Heinlinker; I work for AZTECK industries. Those men who kidnapped my mother may come back, so please don't let her leave. I will ring back shortly and explain what's going on. Thank you! I will ring back shortly; bye."

Doby hung up the phone and looked around. Everyone was staring at him, some with anger, some with shame, some with pity. The person he thought would be angry was Art; he had potentially destroyed his dream, and he looked at him with kindness.

Doby looked at them and looked for the words to explain what had happened, but all he could do was cry. A month of living on the edge. Living in fear for himself and his mother, betraying his friends, and spending the rest of his life in prison had taken their toll. Here didn't sit a traitor, here sat a man teetering on the edge of insanity, one push was all he needed to go off the deep end, but a hand of a friend pulled him back.

"I know you. How did you plan to fight back? Remember, there's always a back door, you told me."

The words and the hug from Lexi were what a destroyed man needed to hear, to turn sorrow into hope.

CHAPTER 34

THE HUNT - PART II

"Come on, Mr. President, we need to put distance between them and us before they pick up your scent," Chad said.

"What about our Delta backup?" The President says between puffing breaths.

"We must assume that they have been compromised. Until help shows up, save your breath, you'll need it."

****

The sudden eruption of gunfire was like cannon fire in this peaceful forest setting. The bright muzzle flashes lit up the dusk skyline like a miniature firework display. The fight was short but extremely fierce as the Secret Service men on duty tried in vain to fight back.

****

As the President's team was approaching their camp, the sudden eruption of gunfire made the President's detail hit the ground hard. Automatically, the head of security pushed the President to the ground, watching in horror as his camp and teammates were gunned down. The way they executed it and the number of enemies they were facing all summed up in seconds; as the head of the Secret Service analysed the situation, he came up with a plan... RUN!

'We're outgunned, outmanoeuvred. Get the hell out of there and keep the President alive till backup comes' was the thought crashing through his mind.

"On me," Chad said into his service mic; within seconds, seven team members appeared.

"It's us; we have the ball. You three spread fifteen, you two with me on the President, to the caves" In his briefings with his men, the alternative was always to hold up in the bat caves and mount a defence.

"Ok, let's move; it won't take them long to track us." So, all nine men took off at a sprint, heading towards the ARK's bat caves, which weren't functional yet.

****

The attack on the President's camp went off perfectly. The defences were unprepared for the Water Tigers' teams, sweeping through quickly and only losing one man. Now, as his men were checking the faces of the dead for the American President, Water Tiger sensed something was wrong. It was the number of dead. There wasn't enough! The President would have had more people around him, "He is not here; span out and find tracks." As the mercenaries started searching for tracks, another group went through the gear in the camp.

"Commander, I found this with the camp medic. I believe it is the President." As the Water Tiger read the laptop's screen, it showed the vital signs of the EAGLE; his heart rate was up, he was running. But running where? Water Tiger turns around, looking at the natural landscape. His gaze fell upon the rocky hills that he remembered from the tours, the cave for bats. Assured of his assessment, the men gathered around him as he issued his commands.

"Our Rabbit is on the run. Team 1 spread out in a line; we are heading to that hill of caves, Team 2 in two groups behind. We do not know how many men he has with him, but they have limited ammunition and provisions. So let us get this done and return home to a better world."

The President and his men were entering the cave's main entrance. Using the personal torches they had on their weapons, trying to get an accurate assessment of the entrance to make a stand. Chad sent two men deeper into the caves to see what lay ahead. They needed fallback positions, last stands, and possible exits. The entrance was a suitable spot to defend. Luckily, it only had enough room for two people to come through at a time, with great sandstone boulders blocking the way in. The initial cave was around fifty metres deep before it wound on a path to another set of two caves. Either was as good as any other for the last stand, but they found no exit.

The Water Tiger's teams approached the caves carefully and spread out around fifty metres from the exit, moving in, making sure they herd their prey into the caves with no way out.

CHAPTER 35

JOHN WAYNE NEVER FACED THIS

"Keystone cops! That's what we look like, Keystone fucking cops." Smith made his thoughts known as the two teams puttered down the access road of the training area part of the sanctuary. Like large electric golf carts, the vehicles weren't designed to carry this many people and gear. Hanging out the sides to make room, they resembled the infamous Keystone Kops from the silent movies of 1912.

As the lorries took off toward the President's camp, the anger in the Major was growing. 'They killed another fine soldier defending his post; heads will roll, literally!'

"Is this as fast as these crates will go? Sherlock, we might as well walk," Quassy said in disgust.

"Yes, but we won't be in any condition to mount an attack by the time we run there," Sherlock answered. The night had cleared up with more visibility. Smith was driving the first lorry with Sherlock in the front and Kid, 2 Planks, and Quassy in the back. The second had one of the Major's men driving with the Major in the front passenger seat hanging half in and half out. The weight distribution was so lousy that Steel and the other ARK soldier had to sit behind the driver to keep the lorry from tipping.

They passed through each fenced area and closed the open gates behind them. The enemy must have hoped that the animals roaming may cause extra havoc, but none had been seen so far. Kid was standing up with Ab's goggles and going through the different visual cycles to find the best vision available when he turned and yelled, "Incoming!" The rest of the team went on instinct, looking in all directions for rocket or RPG fire, but nothing in all of his years had Kid ever learned a call for "Rhino on the right!"

Thundering through the brush came an 800 kg female rhino, affectionately known as Buttercup. Buttercup was so named for her placid ways with the rangers, but like some women, there were times she just wanted 'Her space!' and unfortunately for the team, they stumbled right into the middle of it. Smith hit the accelerator, nearly pushing the pedal through the floor, but at a top speed of 35kms an hour, Buttercup was doing 55kms and closing fast.

Smith could see that there would be a collision. "Get ready to jump," Smith yelled as he tried to lure Buttercup away from the other lorry. Buttercup was livid as she tried to catch this different beast that dared encroach in her area.

Smith could see Buttercup in his rear-view mirror, nostrils flaring, ready to rip the team apart, "Ready... Jump!!" As Smith saw his team jump from the other side of the lorry, he swung the wheel around and turned the lorry side onto Buttercup's attack. Bang! There was a metal and timber ripping and splitting sound as Buttercup slammed into the driver's door; the force of the impact sheared open the outer and inner parts of the door, impaling part of Buttercup's horn into the side of Smith. As the gentle giant bucked and kicked to free herself, she moved the embedded horn in Smiths' side up and down, bringing screams of pain from the wounded soldier.

Sherlock and Quassy jumped in the lorry to pull Smith out as Buttercup tossed the lorry around like a carnival ride. Freeing him and dragging him to a safe area, Steel worked on him to stem the bleeding.

"I think you'll be alright. I don't think it has hit any vital organs. I need to get you patched up or you'll bleed out."

"That was some brave shit Smith, crazy, but brave." Steel told him.

Buttercup had tired from all her struggles and was panting heavily. The Major asked for help to pull the lorry off her horn. He had one of his men ready to put her down if she charged again. As the teams yanked the lorry off of Buttercup's horn, she seemed to realise that they had helped free her... Or she had just enough of this game, so she snorted, flared her nostrils, and ran off in a huff.

Smith was pulling himself to his feet when Sherlock turned around. "I'm right; let's get going," Smith said.

"Not a chance, buddy; you can't go on with a rip like that," Smith's complaints and arguments fell on deaf ears.

"Major, how far is it to the ARK?"

"About 5klm straight in that direction, it is three times that, by road." The Major informed him.

"Right, Steel, you take Smith and head to the ARK, get patched up, find transport and join us at the President's camp. Find out what the hell is going on, and is there any more support coming?" After seeing the carnage on the airfield, Sherlock doubted there was any, but where were President Abdi's troops? When are they coming? Steel started complaining, but Sherlock's quick glance told her to soldier up and get the job done.

Fortunately, Buttercup hadn't done any significant damage to the lorry, except for the driver's door, which the Major quickly ripped off with his bare hands and threw it aside, the act reminding everyone of Buttercup, but everyone kept that to themselves.

CHAPTER 36

QUEEN OF THE MOUNTAIN

"Come here."

"I'm ok. I'm patched up enough," Smith said to Steel insistently. "Have a look at where we have to go. Up over the rocky cliff and up that hill just to get to the base of the ARK. The first rock you climb will rip that wound apart again."

"Geez, not so tight. I can hardly breathe."

"Good, you might stop whining, then."

"Yeah, well, your bedside manner sucks," Smith said.

The banter helped. Steel knew their task would be as arduous as the rest of the teams. She was having trouble breathing, and she knew Smith was in a lot more pain than he was letting on.

Neither could afford to take pain relief if they expected to make it... Five kilometres.

The pair set off, one badly wounded, one with two broken ribs, a sad sight, but both were pissed off that they had been taken out of the fight. They both agreed to get patched up and get their arses back to the battle as quickly as possible. As they approached the rocky climb, it looked more challenging than from a couple of kilometres away. With their injuries, they had to move slowly as the boulders were large and difficult to transverse.

"What is that STINK!" Smith yelled.

"I hope we don't find out who made that Stink." The place reeked of piss and shit everywhere. Steel was leaning over an edge to give Smith a hand up. There looked to be smaller boulders ahead, working up to a clearing.

Suddenly, there was a blood-curdling animal scream that came from just ahead.

Smith and Steel froze in their tracks.

"What the fuck!" Smith yelled.

This scream was primal and furious. A mini avalanche of small rocks came tumbling down towards them. As they looked up, they saw the most enormous baboon either of them had ever seen. There was another scream. This one was different in tone, but just as forceful. He was summonsing the family. As the last cry was still echoing in Steel and Smith's ears, twenty baboons came out of nowhere and started surrounding Steel and Smith. Jumping up and down while screeching like plebs at a Roman Gladiatorial event. They jumped in excitement at the ALFA's challenge to Steel and Smith.

"Fuck, this isn't good; they have us cornered," Steel said, thinking of an exit plan.

"We'll just have to shoot our way out; Damani can bill me," Smith replied.

As if understanding every word they said. The Alpha let out another scream, and another thirty baboons appeared from nowhere. 'The reserves' no doubt, Steel thought.

"These apes can think," she said to Smith.

"Let's see who's the boss here, monkey face," she yelled at the Alpha. Steel stood tall, showing she wasn't afraid, and pulled out her pistol. The Alpha started bouncing around, getting agitated. 'Did he know what a pistol was? Had he seen them before? Hopefully, he's afraid of them,' Steel thought. Steel let off three rounds, and the gunshots seemed to reverberate around the rocks, making the echoes seem louder and longer. The baboons screamed and squealed in fear as they kicked up a mountain of dirt and small stones as they ran for cover, but there stood the Alpha; he didn't leave. Screaming and hitting the ground, he challenged Steel, bouncing and spinning. 'Come and fight, come and fight me!' The family returned slowly as Steel fired another three shots in the air, but this time the family stuck by their King, feeding on his strength.

"Great work, Steel; all you've done is piss them off," Smith griped. One baboon threw some dung and hit Smith on the leg.

"Oh, you just didn't throw shit at me, you filthy ape!" he grabbed his rifle and shot the ape dead. This show of force started an avalanche of rocks and dung hurling down on the two Special Forces members. The second wave of the baboon attack, all orchestrated by the Alpha, involved rocks, manure, and physical aggression by random apes from different directions. The apes didn't stand a chance, being shot down before they could lay a hand on the soldiers.

"The Alpha is just checking our firing power; we will not last long, pinned here."

"What else can we fucking do? We can't go backward. They'd be all over us in a second," Smith said.

"I'll have to go forward and take on the Alpha. You wedge yourself between those boulders that should give you some cover. Here, take my pistol and mags and give me your rifle; I'll see if I can shoot a path through; Damani can bill me."

"Crazy bitch," Smith joked as they laughed and swapped weapons. Once again, as if able to understand English, the Alpha disappeared back beyond the ledge. So did his forward troops, but the apes beside and behind stayed in position. Steel looked up. "Well, that's not good." Unable to see what's over the ledge and climb over the last small boulders to the clearing gave King Loui and his troops the advantage. Just as Steel made it to the clearing, she had the boulders behind her, which she couldn't get over quickly. And with the Ape army in front of her, she had NO options but to fight. The worst part was that she didn't consider that she had isolated Smith now, too. She couldn't come to his defence.

She didn't have to wait as the Alpha screamed to attack as a massive, overwhelming wave of apes came charging at her.

CHAPTER 37

THE CAVALRY

Riveted to the screens, with nothing to do but watch and hope…

"Something is happening! It's Thomas's suit."

"Is it malfunctioning?"

"No, Father, I don't think so; it was fine and then this. Could it be a signal?"

Doby came running over and listened to the scratching sound. "It's repeating; I think it's morse code."

"Do you know what it's saying, Doby?" Art asked frantically. As Doby grabbed a pad and pen from the desk, he waited for the start of the message again, 'SOS STEEL SMITH INJURED COMING ARK,' Doby listened again and checked his translation. "Yes, it says that Steel and Smith are injured and heading here."

"Doby, get back on the screen and find out where they are."

"Lexi, get your bats and try to signal them," Art barked the commands.

"Signal them with what? The bats don't speak!"

"Oh, I don't know. We need them to understand the bats are with us. Ah, fly the bats overhead in a circle; that should do it." Tyson had been quiet as he tried to get his bats to the cave to find the President.

"Caves up ahead," Tyson yelled.

"Great, find the President and signal him somehow."

"Ok, will do." Tyson flew his cauldron of bats into the cave, immediately seeing the Secret Service Team and the American President, but how to get their attention. Tyson flew around the first cave to see a way to make the bats behave in a way that would tell the Presidents' men that they were from the ARK. He saw the enormous boulders that blocked the front entrance, so he flew the bats and landed them on top of the largest boulder, then he moved them to the next smallest, then the next. Soon he could see the looks of confusion on the men's faces as he kept jumping from one rock to the next. Then the penny dropped for the President, and he gave a thumbs-up; Tyson flew the bats to the top of the cave, where they hung upside down, awaiting their following command.

"I found Steel and Smith; they're… Oh shit!"

"What! Where are they" Art yelled frantically.

"They're on Baboon Rocks!" The look of horror swept the room; everyone at the ARK knew you never go through the baboon sanctuary. It's as deadly as a tiger's cage with blood on your shirt. Art instinctively started running towards the exit door, calling Loki and Thor by voice command to life. Art did not know what his plan was; he just started running as if the plan would just unravel as he ran… and so it did.

"What the hell are you doing!" Ab yelled as Art ran through the exit. Before him lay his Chariot, a lorry, one of the groundskeepers' vehicles. Art jumped aboard and commanded his feline friends to jump in the back as they mounted a heroic rescue. The Moon was high, stars were shining, determination was in the air, the super cat's artificial fur was blowing in the wind… and Art didn't know how to drive the lorry.

To be fair, Art Damani was a billionaire. He didn't need to drive, though he had a licence in India and the United States for a brief time. After several accidents in both countries, his board of directors never lets him drive again. A driver and personal bodyguard were employed to keep him from doing so, as if he died, stocks would plummet and the shareholders couldn't have that.

As he started the lorry, it all came back to him: the clutch, the gears, the brake. As the Chariot leaped forward, hopping like a gazelle with a broken leg, Art was determined he would get there in time. The lorry flew down the hill with no care, travelling at forty km an hour, swerving from one side of the road to the other but managing to stay on track. Art Damani was coming; he was the cavalry. As the lorry rounded a sharp bend on two wheels, Loki did something he wasn't supposed to be able to do; he NOTICED. Looking over the rail of the lorry and then over at Thor, he had the look of an animal with concerns.

CHAPTER 38

KNIGHT IN SHINING ARMOUR

Steel raised the rifles, one in each hand. The weight of the rifles pulled hard on her broken ribs, sucking in hard to block the pain. She pulled them tight into her body for better control and dropped to one knee to get a better height perspective on the charging horde. The baboons looked like a tidal wave of claws and barred teeth. As she opened fire, she had picked the proper stance and twisted at the waist to get a protective ring of fire. The scream of injured and dying baboons filled the air with a blood-curdling effect. She was trying to stay alive, but Steel still felt a hollow shame at having to kill the apes.

The scream of the dying started another attack, but this time at Smith, picking off the apes one by one; kept himself safe… for now, but he didn't have an endless supply of ammo. Steel used the break in the attack to reload her rifle. 'I can't hold off too many attacks,' she thought. Then, the screams came again from the Alpha as small groups of baboons started jumping all over the place but heading in Steel's direction. "Moving targets, sneaky bastard," she yelled. Steel tried to stay calm and control her shooting, working on the closest apes to give herself the most time; they were getting closer and closer. She knew her magazine was low, but she wouldn't have time to reload before they got to her. Then, the gut-wrenching sound, click click of an empty magazine, hit her just as the baboons hit her as well.

Knocking her to the ground, they started snapping at her but not biting. They were constantly hitting her, which felt like being hit with a baseball bat. Suddenly, a roar bellowed out, and the baboons stopped beating her and moved back; Steel realised the attack was just to soften her up till the King arrived. The King moved in over her and started sniffing and snorting, emitting a guttural growl that had Steel waiting for his attack, but it didn't come. As she turned her head slowly, she could see the King had moved back and was shuffling side to side. A chance was what the King was offering, an opportunity for a fair fight. Get to your feet and face me.

As Steel rose, she stretched out her back after the pummelling she took from the rest of the family.

"So, you're offering me a fair fight, that's a lot more than any human would do, but I bet you're in a higher league than me," she said to the King.

Steel looked around, trying to formulate a plan.

"How you going down there, Zikmund?" Steel yelled.

"Holy shit! Are we that screwed that you're using my Christian name?" Smith called back with a laugh.

"Well, it's not looking good; I don't have my rifle, and King Loui is offering a one-on-one challenge."

"You gave it a fucking name! Cut its nuts off and let's get out of here," Smith yelled.

"Roger that," Steel replied. Steel straightened up and banged herself on the chest, letting her broken ribs remind her she was still alive. The adrenaline started rising through her as she pulled her two favourite knives from their sheaves.

She had a plan; all she had to do was stay alive long enough to try it.

Her actions summoned King Loui that the fight was on. She moved around in a circle as the King did the same, each fighter looking for an opening. Steel thought she saw that her angry opponent favoured his right side, so she moved in to launch an attack; the King recognised she was moving forward to strike and charged at Steel, only to hit the brakes at the last metre in front of her.

Steel swung a roundhouse swipe with her left knife to get the King to move to his right into her attack, which he did, but it didn't have the effect she was hoping for. Her attack with the right should have hit her opponent in the chest or shoulder. The King dodged backward as Steel struck, and the knife missed him by 6 inches. She had been faked out. King Loui had set her up to let her strike to see how fast her reactions were. Now he knew, and so did she. As old as he looked, this primate still had speed and flexibility far more than Steel.

The King moved in for his attack, waving his arms together, swaying side to side like two giant sledgehammers, knowing contact with his enemy would force her to the ground. As he moved in, Steel held her ground, waiting for her moment. Then, as the King was confident, this fight was over. He raised his arms to bring the final blow of this fight down on her. At the last moment, Steel brought up her arms in defence of her chest with both knives in hand; as the blow hit, she let her body go with the force, sending her flying back, but not before she brought both knives down, slicing to the bone on the arm of the King of Baboons.

Steel went flying across the dirt. King Loui let out a scream, but it was a scream of pain as blood flooded down his arm this time. He waved his arm around, licking the wound, but that was not his only problem. There is a reason humans are on top of the food chain. King Loui's blow had sent Steel flying across the dirt right beside her rifle. She grabbed a magazine from her vest, rolled over, changing the empty magazine, and even though she was in great pain from her beatings, jumped to her feet, ready to fight. Realising the advantage was hers, the King moved to charge but was cut short as Steel fired a round in the dirt between them. Steel could have ended the fight there and then; she could have shot the baboon down but didn't. The King of Baboons was still a primal animal; he could hear the yells and screams of his family around him, waiting for the command from their King to attack.

As the thought went through his mind, he reverted to his primal instincts and roared to order the charge; Steel lifted her rifle, ready to repel the attack as long as possible. But before the baboons could launch, a new command came forth. A roar so loud, Steel had never heard anything like it in her life. Then, as they all turned, baboons and humans alike, they saw two figures in the opening, Thor the Bengal Tiger and Art Damani, holding a garden rake. The pair marched in with the air of command, the dare challenge me look, as they walked in and stood beside Steel.

"Are you ok, Miss Katelyn?" Art asked.

"Better now, but you realise we're still outnumbered," Steel replied.

"Maybe not, Miss Katelyn, maybe not. Thor DEFEND!" Thor moved forward, letting out a roar to challenge anyone, even the King. The move spooked the family of baboons, but they still hadn't fled, waiting on a response from their King.

"Loki, APPEAR!" Art yelled; Steel couldn't believe her eyes as Loki, Art Damani's Black Panther, appeared out of nowhere on a ledge above the family of baboons. Appearing from nowhere, set in a position ready to pounce, Loki let out his own roar. The positioning of the great cats, the black one, appearing from nowhere. The majestic presence of this giant Bengal Tiger was enough to scare anyone, especially this family of baboons, as they scattered in all directions. Finally, the King saw that the family had run off, and the fight was over. The King huffed and snorted at them, then turned and walked off with what dignity he had left.

Smith saw the baboons retreating and called, "What's happening?"

Steel looked at Art and called back, "A Knight in shining armour."

"Come and get me out of here; I smell of ape shit."

Steel looked at the garden rake in Art's hand, "What were you going to do with that?" pointing at the rake.

"Anything I had to do to save you, Miss Katelyn." Steel was as hard as any SAS there is, a great warrior, to be feared for her fierceness and courage, but at that comment, she felt like a schoolgirl with a huge crush and thought it was the most romantic words anyone had ever said to her.

Breaking the thought, Smith called, "I'm still here if anyone's interested." At that, Art helped Smith up to the clearing.

"Your animals need anger management programs." Art couldn't help but laugh and admire the man; after all they had been through, they still could see the humour in the situation… Australians go figure.

As they walked up the service road, they passed a lorry that looked like it had rolled off the road and smashed into a tree. The side of the lorry was crushed in from the impact; Steel looked at Art, "What's that?", "That, Miss Katelyn, is why I don't have a driver's licence."

CHAPTER 39

THE HUNT - PART III

No one was happier than the Major to ditch the lorry for travelling on foot; he was losing feeling in his legs all cramped up.

"What's with these bats circling us?" The AZTECK guard asked.

"If one turns into Art's robot, I'm shooting it," Quassy added.

As the teams came to grips with the fact the bats overhead were from the ARK, they hopped out of the lorries not far now from the Presidents' camp. They moved in closer on foot to avoid detection by the enemy. As they headed off, the bats started acting out, "Wait! I think the ARK is trying to tell us something," Kid called out.

Lexi was confused about getting the teams to follow her to the President. So, she got the bats to fly towards the bat enclosure and then turn around and fly back to the groups, repeating the process until they got the meaning.

"Well, Kid, you're the Wizz; what is it doing?" Sherlock asked.

"I think they want us to follow the bats," Kid answered. Sherlock pointed his rifle towards the hill where the bat enclosure was. The bats started doing loop the loops as a signal, yes!

"I guess you're right, Kid." Sherlock looked out towards the direction the bats wanted them to go, "Major, what is that hilly area ahead?"

"That's the bat caves; it's not functional yet, an enclosure for breeding and studying bats." Sherlock looked at where the President's camp was and where the caves were.

"I think that's where the Secret Service has taken him; that's where I'd hold out." So, the Major and 2 Planks agreed, and they headed off on a course for the caves.

****

Water Tiger knew the advantage was with his prey. They knew the inside of the cave, and he didn't. He knew the Secret Service would mount an ambush with the men they had left. He didn't want this to get drawn out before anything changed the course of his already successful plan. In a battle of attrition, I have more men than they do. So, he commanded his second to begin a frontal assault to gauge the enemy's strength.

The commotion would give his sharpshooters time to mount an attack from the top of the boulders.

The team of four slowly started their way into the cave entrance, covering each other. The Secret Service men had the entrance covered, waiting till the mercs were inside enough to get trapped by crossfire. Then, unleashing on the enemy with controlled bursts to conserve ammunition, they cut two soldiers down quickly as the other two dived for cover. One merc made a break to one side to get in a better position to cover fire for the other member of his team. Unfortunately, the Secret Service had positioned perfectly, killing the soldier before he could reach cover. The last member kept poking out now and then to engage the enemy.

The sound of gunfire from the direction of the caves told the teams they were heading in the right direction. Sherlock signalled for the teams to stop and circle him. "We are getting close now; watch where you step; we don't know how many there are. Plan, we get to the President and get him back to the ARK to mount a stronger defence. Quassy and Kid, find your spot and cover the cave entrance. 2 Planks, you're with me. Major, take your men fifteen metres apart; we'll work from this direction, giving us an exit area." The teams split up; Quassy already had a spot in mind as he searched as he came in to be ready.

"With me, Kid, keep your eyes open." The pair headed off to a rock ledge about two hundred metres from the entrance. Close enough for a 'no miss' vantage spot. The merc sharpshooters were in place to attack from an elevated position once the next attack started. The Water Tiger had sent in a soldier crawling undercover to make eye contact with the soldier pinned by the Secret Service. In hand signals, he told the messenger the positions of the Secret Service and approximate numbers guarding the entrance.

****

"Mr. President, move back under cover; the next attack will be more calculated. The first was to see how many men we have. Be ready, men, protect the EAGLE."

The men lined up for the next attack, sharpshooters ready to cover; the signal to start the next attack came from the soldier pinned behind the rock in the entrance. Grabbing a frag grenade from his vest, he tosses the grenade toward one of the Secret Service men firing at him. The explosion echoes through the caves loudly, signalling the start of the next phase of the attack, as six mercenaries' storm through the entrance firing in the positions of the men covering the entrance.

Two extra Secret Service agents opened fire to support the forward positions like a deadly chess game. Simultaneously, the sharpshooters moved into place on top of the boulders. A rain of accurate gunfire shot down one officer and wounded another. A shot rings out, echoing through the cave, as one sharpshooter falls from the boulder, dead. Within seconds, a second shot rings out, and the other sharpshooter falls, hitting the ground.

While this was going on, the second wave had shot its way into the front entrance. In a blaze of fire, with bullets ricocheting the cave walls, the Secret Service lost one officer and a foothold at the entrance. Chad Langdon ordered his men to fall back to a stronger position.

The shots that rang out that took down the sharpshooters caught the attention of the Water Tiger and Chad Langdon. Langdon heard the shot; who is that, Madden? As much as he despises the man, he is grateful for the help to get the President out, but he knows these people would not walk away. The Water Tiger also had noticed the shots. His anger grew as his sharpshooters were gunned down by an invisible enemy, but as his head turned to the sound of the first shot, he caught the muzzle flash of the second shot. Leaving his second in command, he picks up his rifle to hunt this new prey.

****

"Lexi, these bats won't last much longer and there's no recharging station for them yet. So, get as much use out of them as you can," Tyson said.

"Ok, I'll see if I can help the guys spot these mongrels."

Not wanting to lose an opportunity to help, Lexi flew the bats over the area in front of the cave, searching for the enemy. Spotting a reflection of something metallic, she flew the bats down for a closer look and found a mercenary guarding the front of the cave. Spinning the bats above the hidden man, Kid caught sight of the bats and relayed it to Quassy. Within seconds, Quassy had picked the enemy up through his scope and ended his chance of a successful mission. Suddenly, the bats started shaking and losing altitude, dropping to the ground from the loss of power.

Quassy was concentrating, picking out other enemies in the thick shrubs. Kid was searching intently with Ab's special goggles when his hearing picked up some noises beside him that alerted him to a coming danger. He saw the Water Tiger emerging from the brush, rifle raised, preparing to fire as he turned. Instincts told Kid that he didn't have time to turn and raise his weapon. So, his training with the team, all four days of it, told him to protect each other. Not bothering to call out to Quassy, he used all available strength to grab Quassy and shove him over the edge of the rock cliff. Kid mustered all he had available in strength to get Quassy over the edge, but the Water Tiger had the jump on them, and shots rang out in the night as Kid and Quassy were hit with automatic fire.

CHAPTER 40

WHERE THE MEAT MEETS THE MONSTERS

The highs and lows of Steel and Smith's arrival were bitter-sweet news. The chance they could rescue the President from the enemy soldiers was lost already, and people were injured. But unfortunately, the HUB update wasn't any better. Failed communication, lost security, no reinforcements.

Steel and Smith had made their way to the infirmary. Steel was halfway through stitching up Smith, when an explosion rang through the inside of the ARK.

"Looks like the fight has come to us," Steel says to Smith.

While Smith had the look of 'What the fuck now!'

"Quick, cut the cord and wrap me up again; I think we're needed. Does this mean we're employed by Damani now?" Smith jests.

"You wish, matey, you wish." Smith and Steel made their way to the Security office they saw on the way to the infirmary. Best to load up as much as possible; we don't know if we will be able to come back.

As the explosion rang through the ARK, rattling windows and echoing like the Grand Canyon, everyone inside was startled but not surprised, trying to help the President and now defend the ARK with only a couple of Security guards and some injured Aussie troops.

"Got it! I can re-establish our network in five minutes, but it will take another ten to load," Doby informed the group; it hadn't been as easy as he had thought. The system Lexi and he had built was fighting back the whole time.

"I don't think we have that kind of time, my friend, but let me know when it's ready," Art informed him.

"Tyson, get to the monsters; we need to place them so they look like statues if they will be of any use. Take one of the Australians with you for cover." Tyson didn't question, he just got up and ran, he knew what Art had in mind but didn't really think it would have any effect, but they had nothing to lose.

****

The mercenary team that conquered the Delta backup placed explosives on a side door to enter the ARK. Seconds after the controlled explosion, they filed through quickly as their paramilitary training had taught them. Sweeping corner to corner, everything seemed perfect, with the hallway empty. But the end of the hallway emptied into the food mall, which was a different scenario altogether. Art Damani was good at many things but brilliant at others, and his choice of staff was one of his finest attributes. Even though a little long in the tooth, the ARK Security were all ex-military. They had positioned and armed themselves appropriately for this encounter and had set up firing lines to cover the entrances. Once the enemy breached through one door, the other security came running with support.

"Booom!" The explosion rocked the Ark. Sending an echo through the halls like the Grand Canyon.

The mercenaries stormed through the door immediately after the explosion, guns blazing. They overwhelmed the officer guarding the door, forcing him further into the ARK. Luckily his support had got there quickly with the necessary firepower to halt the advancing mercs. An ensuing gun battle raged before a standstill was established. One side defending the other stuck in their tracks.

****

Tyson met Smith and Steel, as he was running to his lab.

"Hey, I will need someone to help cover me in the lab," Tyson said.

"This is no time to be doing experiments, Doc," Steel answered.

"I'm not; Art has a plan to use the monsters to help fight the attack."

"Seriously! Count me in, fight with robot monsters; I have to see this," Smith said excitedly.

"I'll head up to the HUB and see what other measures Art wants," Steel said.

They headed to their posts; Tyson had the monsters awake in seconds, all charged for whatever they could do with them.

"Art thought we could set them up like statues and use a surprise attack."

"Great idea, like a Scooby-Doo cartoon, brilliant. How strong are these things, doc?" Tyson turned and looked at Smith with a sneaky evil look.

"Inhuman."

"Ahh, sweet!" that was it; Smith wanted one for Christmas. Smith ran out the door and looked over the balcony making sure he didn't stick his head out too far to become a target. He quickly assessed the area and made some judgement calls, then went running back into the lab.

"Ok, I gather they are like, what their characters are like?" Smith asked.

"Yes, exactly."

"Ok, get the Creature from the Black Lagoon into your swimming pool, but you will need to keep him low; otherwise, he will get his head shot off. Send Drac to that little corridor to the right."

"That's the maintenance area."

"Ok great. Put Frankenstein at the top of the second floor like a statue and keep Wolfman and The Mummy with us here as the last line of defence before the HUB."

Like Art, he respected the Special Force's combat knowledge and got straight on the job. Tyson set up control of the animations with a gaming control for easier usage. Within a few minutes, the robots were in position.

Chao Zhang knew he didn't have the time to be pinned in this position, the security could have access to more ammunition, and his was limited, as all reserves were left at the vehicles. Zhang envisioned a new plan. Confident in the outcome, he relayed his plan through his comm set. Soldiers started dispersing to his commands. As the mercs all checked that they were in position, the order was given, "Go!"

The area erupted in explosions as flash-bang grenades ignited. Simultaneously half of Chao Zhang's force moved forward in one place while the other half pinned down the Security guards. It was a practical move; the ARK Security had lost their positions as two of the men were gunned down, while the other two guards moved back to hold up at the base of the steps, which go up to the first level.

Holding their new position, half of Zhang's team split off and headed back out of the destroyed ARK door they had entered. It wasn't long until the Security guards were in an untenable position. Unfortunately, making a break for the first floor, the ARK steps' decorative design had the siding under the rails made of glass, which left the guards wide open to a barrage of fire. Running up the steps as his fellow officer fell to fire, he could swear he saw in his peripheral vision Art's Dracula statue. Diving for cover in the last couple of metres, he slid along the polished floors into cover before the steps were blasted around him.

Zhang ordered four of his team to sweep the area they had just taken over to not leave any surprises. Moving quickly and efficiently, the soldiers spread out and then returned to Zhang's position at the steps. The last of Zhang's men finished clearing the pool area and locker rooms. As he passed the pool, a giant bubble came to the surface. Curious, he leaned over to look in the pool and froze as a figure came flying up out of the pool like a dolphin. His mind still not comprehending what he was seeing, reacting too late, the creature grabbed him with both arms and dragged him into the pool. Tyson Lumming hit the button to turn off the robot creature, as the last vision processed through the mercenaries' brain was the vision of the Creature of the Black Lagoon staring at him.

"That's just wrong, but effective," Smith said as he watched the man drowning in the pool. "I'm going outside to help the Security guard; stay in the lab, don't move!" Smith commanded as he ran out the door. Smith checked on the Security officer, sending him to reload on the next floor at the security office. Smith watched as the mercs set themselves to continue up the floors, two men left to defend and two floors to hold them, before the HUB, 'Oh! And three monsters, don't forget the monsters Smith', he thought to himself. Timing. I need to time this perfectly.

Smith checked his weapon and placed his back against the wall. Chao Zhang's men moved up the steps checking all corners. Zhang pointed to a corridor ahead and told one of the men to cover that area and check the door. One of the mercs turned the corner and came towards the maintenance door before he noticed the robot of Count Dracula in the shadows beside him. He jumped back and laughed at himself until the statue moved towards him. Tyson moved Dracs forward, grabbed the soldier, and tried to get Dracs to bite the soldier's neck. Hoping to rip a jugular but the soldier, even though screaming, managed to move his head forward using his helmet to block the robot from biting him. Zhang moved quickly around the corner, not believing what he saw, fired his pistol, and struck the robot in the head, sending him back to the floor. Hydraulic fluid and sparks flew from the creatures' forehead. The two soldiers gave each other a look of disbelief.

Smith swung around the corner at the top of the steps and opened fire on the distracted soldiers. Even in body armour, one mercenary took a round to the neck, throwing him to the floor, as the other spun and returned fire at Smith, but the SAS member was already moving back into cover.

'Two down,' Smith thought. All of a sudden, the floor behind him started to vibrate heavily. As he turned around, Frankenstein's Monster came thundering past. Obviously, Tyson could see something he couldn't and moved his last chess piece into the game. Frankenstein turned the corner and started down the steps with his booming presence. Zhang's men were charging up the steps as Franky turned the corner, another disbelieving look took over the mercenaries, but their reactions were quicker. They opened fire on the robot.

'Well, that would have shredded him!' Smith thought. Not knowing that Tyson had built the Monster with Kevlar and Titanium parts. Zhang was the first to realise their body shots weren't slowing him down and turned his fire to its head. Even though the shots did the trick by destroying the computer mechanisms, Franky had grabbed the first soldier, and as his mechanisms failed, he toppled to the rails and smashed through with his massive weight taking the merc to his death smashing into a table in the food mall.

Smith used the commotion to open fire on the mercs on the steps. Zhang quickly returned fire as Smith thought about an exit to the next level. Suddenly another burst of fire joined from above. The Security officer had returned fully loaded and opened fire on the mercenaries. The Ark crew had enough firepower and a height advantage. Zhang, not willing to fight to the last man, issued a retreat, losing one man on the steps on the way down.

Chasing Zhang and his last man down the levels, they made their way through the food mall, passing the surreal image of one of his team lying dead next to Frankenstein's Monster. 'A MADHOUSE,' he thought to himself as they raced through the exit they came in through.

As Smith saw them charging through the door, he was startled by a burst of fire ringing out and saw Zhang and his man fall to the ground. Moments later, two Delta soldiers walked through the door.

As the soldiers introduced themselves, they explained how they were heading to the President's camp when they heard the attack on the HUB. Deciding to try and protect the undefended, they turned around and headed back in. Smith informed them of what he knew. They asked the Security officer where they could find a ride. Pointing to the loading docks and explaining how to open the door, the Delta men went on their way.

CHAPTER 41

WHAT'S IN A NAME

There were only seconds from when Kid grabbed Quassy and shoved him off the cliff edge, to when he heard the gunshots. Quassy felt he was free-falling for minutes, but it was only seconds before the rude awakening of the thud as he hit the jagged shale ground. He couldn't control himself on his way down the rocky slope, bouncing, rolling, and sliding. He caught glimpses of Kid, who wasn't faring any better at slowing his descent. Quassy felt he had the grace of an Olympic ice skater… whose blade had snapped; then face planted on the ice and could only watch as he slid into the sidewall while all the world watched.

There was an unceremonious thud as Quassy came to a stop on his stomach.

"Ouch." Quassy looked over and saw Kid wasn't moving and jumped to his feet; a searing pain in his side made him buckle over and drop to one knee; he'd been hit. Grabbing his side, he shuffled over to Kid. As he approached, he saw two bullet holes on his back but no blood. Quassy knelt down beside him, grabbed his vest, and rolled him over. He was still breathing but was unresponsive. Shaking him and slapping his face, Kid sat up startled.

"Wha…" Quassy started laughing; Kid was alive. A wave of relief hit Quassy, but he knew they weren't out of the woods yet. The person who had shot them knew where they fell, and more troops could be on them in seconds.

The Water Tiger looked over the cliff face where the soldiers had jumped and could see a dust trail down the cliff. He knew he had hit at least one of them, sending a message on his comms for his team to check them out as he made his way down the hillside. Kid was lucky. As he was pushing Quassy off the cliff, the angle the bullets hit his vest in the back prevented them from penetrating.

"I've lost my rifle, and we need to find the others quickly." Quassy's wheezed. As the soldiers headed off, Quassy fell to one knee.

"Shit, matey, you've been hit; give me a look." As Kid checked his teammate, he realised the injury was severe, the blood really started to flow, and he was sure one of his lungs had collapsed.

"I'll patch it, but you need to rest," Kid said.

"We can't stop here; we're too open. We need to keep moving and find the others." Kid helped his friend up, and they started towards the area Sherlock wanted to clear. They had only walked 10 metres when Quassy hit the ground again.

"Come on, buddy, let's find a spot to put you down, so you don't bleed out on me," Kid insisted.

"No, you go," Quassy said between whistles.

"We're both dead if you stay with me, now GO!" Quassy insisted.

"No fucking way, we don't leave each other." Before either could say anymore, they heard rustling in the bushes. Too late, someone had found them. Kid had propped Quassy up against a rock and took a stance on one knee, ready to fire if it wasn't his team.

Quassy tried to suck in as much air as possible and was trying hard not to blackout as the pain increased. He watched Kid's back as he prepared to face whatever was coming toward them. A figure emerged from the thicket behind Kid, ready to take out his enemy. Quassy realised the merc hadn't noticed him. Summoning all the strength he had left; he calls to the mercenary to distract him.

"Hey fucker." As the heavily armed soldier spun, Quassy opened fire with his pistol catching the merc in his throat. A muscle reaction from being shot made the merc squeeze on his trigger, letting loose a burst of semi-automatic fire, which caught Quassy on his shoulder. Kid had spun around on Quassy's call. Seeing the merc fall, instincts and training told Kid to circle back around again.

Quassy felt everything slow. Like a slow-motion scene from the Matrix movie, it felt surreal. A mercenary started exiting a bush in front of Kid. Kid went to open fire with his rifle, but it jammed, most likely damaged from the fall off the cliff, but Kid didn't flinch. Instead, he automatically drops the rifle and pulls out his pistol. Kid still had time to pull off two rounds to the enemy's head before turning to another bush to his right. Quassy didn't even see the merc in the bush; as Kid charged, firing his pistol. The merc reeled back from shots falling to the ground dead. Then suddenly, Kid charged down the path, seeing everything in his mind before it happened; another mercenary rose from the bushes, but Kid was already heading towards him as if it was a shooting range, which he had done hundreds of times before. Kid was enraged, clinical, and deadly as he fired the last shots from his pistol and he then crash-tackled the dazed merc. Finally, he grabbed his knife and ended the fight for good. Quassy might have been bleeding out and his time short, but he had just witnessed one of the bravest things he had ever seen or the craziest.

Kid reloaded his pistol and grabbed his damaged rifle as he headed back to Quassy, but the fight didn't seem to want to end. The GODS of WAR wanted an end to this battle but not one Kid had planned. Min-Ki Gwan, the Water Tiger's second in command, stepped up to fire. Kid had no time to turn, and he knew it. His only concern was to protect Quassy.

Fuck the GODS of WAR, as Sherlock came from nowhere and crash-tackled Gwan. Gwan lost his rifle as he rolled off to the side but instinctively pulled his pistol as Sherlock made a dive for him. Kid saw the shot go off, but Sherlock was already in flight, and he didn't know if he'd been hit. Kid drew his pistol but couldn't fire as Sherlock and Gwan were wrestling on the ground, trading blows. Kid put away his gun and came up with another plan. Sherlock will be pissed at him, but at least he will be alive. Just then, Gwan kicked and pushed off Sherlock. As they both rolled apart from each other and jumped to their feet. Sherlock immediately grabbed his arm; he had been wounded from the shot.

A small silver canister flew through the air; the size and the shape distracted Gwan for a second, as he had no idea what it was. This gave Kid the seconds he needed to yell, "Get down!" Sherlock grabbed his ears and turned his back as one of Kid's unique mines exploded in front of the merc commander. Gwan had no defence as the mine disabled him completely. Kid took advantage of the situation, drew his pistol, and finished him off with one round.

The Water Tiger saw the whole thing as he came down the hill, enraged at the loss of his long-time friend but professional enough to go join his men at the cave entrance. He made his vow of revenge, and it has NO time limit.

Sherlock joined Quassy and Kid, "How you doing, buddy" Sherlock asked Quassy.

"Been better, Mike; let's get the hell out of here," Quassy replied. The use of Sherlock's Christian name told him Quassy knew he was hurt, fatally.

"Kid, we'll take him over to the trees there till we can get him out; scout ahead for us, will you" and with that, Kid was off, adrenaline still pumping from all that had happened in the last few minutes. Sherlock went to lift Quassy up, but he stopped him. Quassy pulled him in close; his breath was low and seriously laboured.

"Kid saved me twice...so I...get to name him...Jedi...he is a Jedi...he is another...you," and with that, the GODS of WAR got their pound of flesh. Sherlock lifted Deen on his back and carried him to a clump of trees for protection till this was over. He was heading to Kid when they crossed paths.

"How's Quassy?" Kid asked. The look on Sherlock's face told him the answer. Kid went to run to Quassy, but Sherlock put out his arm to stop him.

"Let's get this finished for him. Quassy knew that protecting the ARK and the President was worth our sacrifice." At that moment, Sherlock saw an enthusiastic young man turn into a hardened warrior; the painful loss of a family member bitters the blood and hardens the heart.

CHAPTER 42

HOLD THE FORT

"Got it; we're up and running again." The views started coming up on the giant screen. Doby's hands flew over the keys on the console as he commanded the closest active aerial surveillance over the bat cave to see what was happening. Lexi was going through the security footage to see what else was happening around the park when the camera showed six of Zhang's men heading around the base of the ARK. You didn't need a college degree to know where they're heading.

"Shit, they're coming around the service road." Steel came to look at the screen.

"I'll head out and hold them back as long as I can; someone has to get weapons for the rest of you; they won't care who they shoot," then Steel headed out the door.

"Lexi, come with me; we'll grab some," Ab said.

"I have an idea; I'll be back shortly," Art said as he left, running through the door and heading back into the ARK. Ab and Lexi looked at each other, shrugged, and then left the room running.

Steel picked a spot further down the track to mount an ambush. As the mercs realised they were getting closer to their target; they slowed and moved strategically. Steel swore under her breath; she hoped they'd be dumb arses and come running up the road in the open. Taking aim, she brings the lead soldier down and loses any hope of surprise she has. As both sides swapped fire, she saw some mercs were moving to flank her. 'Time to move your arse, Katelyn,' she says to herself. Running back to her fall-back position near the entrance.

Art came running through the door and ran to her; she had to pull him down behind the cover as bullets flew.

"What are you doing here?"

"I came to give you this." Art shows her what he had brought; she grabbed it. It was shaped like a mini-gun but was as light as a water pistol and had a belt-fed ammunition feed, but with a bullet she had never seen before, it looked like a big Toy gun.

"What's this?" Steel asked.

"It's an experimental weapon," Art replied. Another volley of shots sprayed around their defensive spot to remind them they weren't alone.

"How experimental, and when did you go into weapon manufacturing?"

"I'll get you to write the first review, Miss Katelyn. I'm a realist; I knew I'd have to fight for peace. But I didn't think it would happen this soon." Steel looked at him; well, why not? Steel flipped off the safety and moved up to fire at the closest mercenary. The Toy whined and started firing; Steel was shocked. The Toy had very little kickback, and the experimental ammunition was ripping big chunks of rock off the hiding place of the merc. Steel ducked back down.

"Wow! Ok great. Now get your arse inside before you get shot. Get ready to run." Steel moved and started firing again.

"Run!" prepared for the non-kickback; she was a lot more accurate and took out the lead merc as Art ran back inside. The Toy was effective. She could hold the mercs at bay, but she knew they wouldn't sit there long before they tried to flank her or resort to explosives.

A little rock slide alerted her to someone climbing above her. As the merc came into view, rifle raised to fire, shots from behind her rang out and tore into the merc, killing him instantly. The dead merc fell down the rocky slope. Steel spun around to see who had saved her bacon. Standing there with a 45 magnum was Art Damani. To her utmost frustration, Art was back, and he grabbed a box and ran to her.

"Are you trying to get killed? What are you doing here?" Katelyn said, frustrated because she was concerned for his safety.

"Bullets, Miss Katelyn, you'll need more bullets," Steel shook her head.

"Thank you for the save too, Art."

"You're welcome. I said I would do anything to protect you, Miss Katelyn." Steel looked at him, 'My God, he's serious,' she thought. At that moment, the mercs made another push, moving forward up the service lane and coming over the top. Steel opened up with the Toy and virtually tore one merc in half; Art opened fire on the mercs up top, and a bullet grazed his shoulder. Behind him, his companions, Thor and Loki, were linked to him. The injury registered with their programming. They were to protect their friend at all costs, and the pair sprang into action.

Art was firing to keep the mercs back behind cover as Loki leaped onto rocks to get on top, to stop the assailants. Reaching the top, he automatically went into cloaking mode to confuse his enemy... the response was on his own. Reappearing before, he grabbed one of the mercs by the throat. Then, he swung around to face the other merc, staring in frozen horror as this invisible Panther had his teammate in his mouth. The strength of the merc was futile as he kicked and swung his arms around. Staring intently at the second merc, Loki squeezed his jaws together, the gushing blood and the sound of bones being crushed, a show of pure horror and strength.

Then Loki leaped at the frozen soldier and knocked him down. Blood-curdling screams start as Loki is on his back, ripping through his bullet-proof vest like tissue paper. The screams hit a new level as Loki rips through the flesh and bone until the mercenary becomes quiet.

Steel decided to end this by counter-attacking, moving forward with the Toy. The sheer volume of shots from the experimental weapon had the mercs moving back.

"Thor, protect her!" Art yelled. Thor leaped into action, running past Steel and pouncing on the pinned soldiers. The ensuing fight between man and beast was one-sided, as Thor tore through the men with ease. Finally, the last man-made the best decision he had ever made. He ran! He would not be torn apart by any animal. Running for his life down the service road, he glanced over his shoulder and saw the panther was following him along the top of the cliff. He stopped and opened fire on the black cat, hitting Loki with several shots; Loki fell, hitting the ground hard. Loki couldn't move; his AI automated software was overridden by the AI sense of the moment: self-awareness. As Loki felt the power drain from himself, he felt something new.... fear. Like the flashback humans have when they die, Loki accessed his memories. Fun times with Thor and Art. Loki stared off, scared, helpless, unable to move; as his eyes faded, the last thing he saw was his brother Thor.

Thor was standing beside Steel when he sensed his partner's injuries. He let out a roar and started jumping up the cliff, running at speeds Art didn't think possible. He reached his partner as his lights extinguished. Thor let loose a roar that shook the mountainside. He took off after the animal that killed his brother.

Bouncing from boulder to boulder with ease, he made it to the road in seconds, sniffing the path where the soldier had been. Then, he switched on his unique detection skills on his own and ran after his prey.

Art and Steel made their way up the hillside of the ARK to find Loki, their friend and protector. Moving along the stone ledge, they came across him lying on his side, sparks flying and fluid oozing from his side. Steel and Art knelt down beside him. Art grabbed some wires and stopped the sparks. Steel placed her hand on Loki's side to show affection for the valiant warrior.

"Miss Katelyn, may I ask you something?" Art said.

"Yeah, sure."

"Would you marry me?"

"WHAT! Are you mad? Did you take a shot to the head? We nearly got overrun by terrorists, and you want to marry me?" Katelyn said, amazed.

"I'm not hearing a no, Miss Katelyn."

"You're serious, aren't you? You must be mad."

"I built a giant zoo in the middle of a hostile country and then painted a giant worldwide target on it... I think the MAD boat has already sailed."

Steel couldn't help but giggle. Thor walked up beside Steel and dropped the arm of the last merc that killed Loki beside her.

Art looked at Thor with a mixture of horror and amazement. Then he turns and looks at Katelyn. "Full stop!"

"Are they supposed to..." Steel said, not finishing the question. Art just shook his head and mouthed the word 'nooo.'

Thor lay down beside Loki and stayed there until they collected him several hours later.

Steel and Art made their way back to the HUB, quietly walking up the path together.

"I still haven't heard a NO yet, Miss Katelyn."

"Remember, I'm armed, buddy," Steel replied.

"That's still not a no."

"Ahhh," Steel screamed.

CHAPTER 43

THE HUNT -

*Conclusion: 'Forget all the reasons it won't work
and believe in the one reason it will.'*

2 Planks joined Sherlock and Kid just as the Major and his men showed up.

"There're fourteen attacking the front of the cave," the Major said.

"There's three patrolling the cave's perimeters also," 2 Planks added.

"Hitting them in the front may be the only way," the Major said.

"We don't know how much longer they can hold out inside," 2 Planks added.

"Kid, if you were building a man-made zoo, wouldn't you build exit tunnels into it?" Sherlock asked.

"I would. It's basically a big theme park. Are you thinking of sneaking him out?" Kid asked.

"Our goal should be the President's safety, and we can't do that if we are in a running gun battle. So, we need to find and secure the exit and then cause a distraction so we can get him out." The idea was sound as they all headed out. Finding it first might be the problem, though.

Fanning out across the outside of the cave, the rescue team had a stroke of luck. They found the roaming patrol, and the roaming patrol had found the exit. Well hidden in a grove of trees, it was not visible at first glance. Sherlock and 2 Planks moved in quickly. The Water Tiger's men were still patting themselves on the back for finding the exit. Expecting huge praise for their efforts from their leader, they weren't expecting trouble but trouble they found. Sherlock and 2 Planks dispatched the enemy before they had time to turn, while Kid swept the area for sentries.

The Major and his men joined 2 Planks and formed a perimeter around the entrance as Sherlock and Kid went inside to retrieve the President.

Inside, Chad Langdon was doing a running battle in his head, trying to figure out the enemy's next move and how they could counteract it without losing any more men. Holding his ground with the last of his men, conserving ammunition, waiting till the Delta's or Madden's men arrive. He could tell the mercs were getting ready for another push, and Chad had to push back if he was going to hold this spot.

"Grab all the flashbangs we have," Chad asked one of his men. Moments later, he returned with four grenades, placing them beside a rock wall, hidden as you came up the path.

"Ok, they're about to move again. When they do, fire a few shots and then fall back. They will think we have retreated further into the cave. Then we ignite the grenades and counter. Make your shots count." They suddenly heard footsteps coming from inside the cave. Madden and one of his men rounded the corner right into their barrels.

"Whoa, we come in peace," Sherlock said. Chad does not want to waste any time on chit-chat.

"Are you locked and loaded?"

"Yes," Sherlock responded.

"Ok, get ready to counter-attack."

As the Secret Service officers got in position for their ruse, Sherlock spoke to the President, "Hell of a night, Mr. President."

"Yes. I thought being killed by a jaguar was the most dangerous thing I'd do tonight," the president said in a half-dejected laugh. Kid stood there emotionless; he was still processing Quassy's death.

'I will have to keep an eye on him so he doesn't get reckless,' Sherlock thought.

The enemy made their move, a significant push from all angles trying to overpower their enemy; they had no plans to be overwhelmed. The Secret Service returned short bursts of fire, falling back one by one like they would in a controlled retreat. The mercs bought the ruse and pushed forward up the path where the Secret Service had been.

"Ready?" Chad said before he spun around low and shot the stun grenades; it had the exact result that Chad wanted. As the sound echoed through the caves, the stunned mercs were trying to fall back, knowing they had walked into a trap. Bouncing off walls and tripping over rocks, they had no defences as Chad and Sherlock's team joined in a joint offensive. Charging down the path, they gunned down the blinded mercs and rushed forward with concentrated fire as the other mercenaries who were caught in the open. Sherlock and Kid flanked the enemy and made short work of their resistance.

Racing forward to the entrance, Sherlock called out, "Kid, go with Chad and get the President through the exit. We will hold the entrance. Go!" Kid spun on the orders and ran towards the President. As he was passing Chad Langdon, he stopped, "Let's get him to safety." So, the pair made their way to the next cave where the President was standing.

"Come on, Sir," Chad said.

"But the other men," the President protested.

"Move when I tell you to move… Sir!" Chad snapped. The President realised his life was in the hands of this man. Each was prepared to put their life on the line for him.

"Yes," the President said as he assured Chad, he was on the right page now. Kid took off, and the President followed with Chad Langdon close behind.

Sherlock knew if he was the commander outside, he would still plan to attack again and counter with explosives. So, Sherlock spun and started running back to the path.

"With me!" he called. So, they got themselves into defensive positions and waited.

The Water Tigers team in the cave was unresponsive, and so was the patrol on top. They found an exit! Realising his men could be ambushed coming out of an exit, he placed three men at the entrance, split the rest into two teams of five, and had them circle around the cave to the top.

Sherlock had expected a counter by now. "He knows about the exit!" he yelled.

"Let's go, get to the President" the men rushed through the caves and headed up the exit. At the top, as the President and his protectors came through the emergency exit, all members emerged around the President. Immediately 2 Planks took control.

"On me, to the ARK!". They formed a perimeter around the President, with 2 Planks leading the way and Chad right on the President's hip. Two kilometres to the ARK, a brisk jog, or a highway to hell.

Sherlock and the others came through the exit; no President, good. 2 Planks got him on the move straight away. Taking off quickly, He knew they wouldn't be able to travel as quickly and hoped to catch up reasonably soon. Kid turned back to look towards the exit and saw Sherlock and the rest of the men heading down the hill.

"Sherlock and the others are out," he yells. 2 Planks afforded himself a slight grin. The grin was short-lived as shots came from their left. Chad shoved the President to the ground and jumped on top of him to cover him.

As the team returned fire, one of the Major's men was caught out in the open, and was killed instantly. The other soldier moved to a better position to cover the

President and was hit in the leg, sending him to the ground. Suddenly, the Major raced forward, shooting one-handed like Rambo, using his free hand to pull his man behind some rocks for cover.

"Enjoying yourself yet corporal?" the Major asked.

"You think this is fun?" the soldier said, amazed.

"Well, we're still alive, that's a bonus."

"Well, there is that Major, but I'm getting low on ammo."

Chad grabbed the President by his vest, pulled him to his feet, and started running to a grove of trees ahead, where he could protect him better. 2 Planks knew they had to keep moving forward but trying to move from cover to cover would leave them targets to be picked off. A shot whizzed past 2 Planks head as the bullet grazed his cheek, drawing blood. As 2 Planks fell to the ground as Kid returned fire.

"Another team," he yelled to Kid. They were trapped between two teams.

"This guy is pissing me off!" 2 Planks said.

'Sherlock would know they were pinned' he thought. 'How will he respond?'

"Hold your positions!" 2 Planks yelled. He was relying on Sherlock to break the deadlock. Sherlock and the other members came through the middle, driving a wedge between the two enemy teams, making them take cover, and slowing their advancement. They were still outnumbered and outflanked, but the extra numbers would help them hold a position while moving the President forward. Chad saw where Sherlock was positioned, and years of military training told him what was happening.

"Get up; we're moving! This is Secret Service level. Stick with me, or you're dead in five minutes." Chad pulled the President to his feet and started moving forward.

As the intense battle raged on, the calls started coming.

"Low on ammunition!"

"Me too."

"Also me."

There was still a kilometre to go.

"Kid, do you have any of those Party Favours left?" Kid knew he meant the mines but loved the idea of marketing them as Party Favours.

"Yeah, two."

"We need to slow them down to move on."

"Roger," Kid answered. Then, Kid dropped to his knees and started punching buttons on what looked like a TV control.

"Major, you and your man move back first." Just then, as the Major was bending over to grab his injured team member, a mercenary charged him, hitting him in the arm and causing him to drop his rifle. Riled and fed up with being on the defensive, the Major charged his attacker with his machete. The law of averages would say that the bullets being fired at the Major by his attacker and the closeness that these men meet, would suggest the Major should have been hit several times. But even the GODS of WAR know not to stick their noses in the Major's personal battles. As the men got within spitting range of each other, the mercenary realised this was a stupid idea and paid the price. Like his own God of War, the Major brought a blow down with his machete on the merc with two hands and lifted the head off of his adversary; walking back past his last surviving team member, he bent and grabbed him, lifting him to his feet. Later on, the man would tell the new troops of the Major running through the enemy chopping off heads as bullets bounced off him. This was how a Legend was born.

Kid called for everyone to move back, which they did promptly. They knew what Kid's devices were like and didn't want to be caught anywhere near one. The ARK entrance was in view, but they still had the enemy slowly circling in, ammo low, walking wounded. Sherlock and Chad knew they would make a charge before they got close to the ARK. Kid's devices slowed some down, but there were at least ten coming in. Coming in fast.

The Water Tiger decided to end this charade. "Close in, grenades if you have any, NO survivors! ATTACK!" The mercenaries came in two lines, firing at once so there could be no return fire, shredding trees and bushes, everything in their path towards the President. Chad had the President on the ground and was laying over him, pistol out and prepared to give his life to defend him.

Suddenly, a new hell opened up. Screams from enemy soldiers filled the air with rocks and trees flying everywhere. Confused Sherlock and his team couldn't see who was shooting or what that high-pitched whining noise was. Then, suddenly, Steel and Smith came out through the bushes. Steel was firing with what looked like a toy gun as they flanked one of the enemy teams. Smith picked off anyone who tried to run. No sooner had Sherlock put his head up to see what was going on, than the Major wondered about the extra fire coming from the other side. Different weapons and the fact that he was not being fired at for a change. He was surprised and happy to see two Delta Force soldiers flanking the other side, taking down the enemy.

"Who else is shooting?" The ARK security soldier asked.

"More friends, I believe, Sergeant," the Major replies.

"Major, I'm only a Corporal?"

The Major let out a hearty laugh, "Well, you're getting a promotion if you actually survive this."

Without bothering to reply, the Corporal, come, Sargant, started opening fire on anywhere he thought the enemy was to secure his promotion.

The Water Tiger hadn't got his reputation and lived as long as he has for not being able to judge a battle. The battle was lost once he saw the enemy had flanked them with new troops. He moved forward while some of his forces were still fighting, grabbed a knapsack from one of his fallen soldiers, and turned and left the scene. When the firing had stopped, he was back with the three soldiers he left guarding the cave entrance.

"All is lost; it is time to leave." Water Tiger pulled a device from the ruck pack; it looked like a shiny camping stove. As he fiddled with buttons and knobs, he started jogging off into the night, two hours till sunup.

The device had a thirty-second countdown. As the seconds began counting down, the machine whined, which got higher pitched as the seconds counted down. 3... 2... 1... A shrill and a thump sound comes from the machine as the Water Tiger tells his men to change direction.

****

"What the hell is this?" Doby yells.

"Yeah, I've lost my screens."

"All the security is down too." Art stood by Doby's side as he checked everything on the screens.

"An EMP," Art said.

"No, it couldn't be, not that small, and wouldn't it take us down too?"

"No, a localised blast and the ARKS built against that," Art said.

"Seems like our friends were well prepared and well-financed. I just got word; the cavalry will be here in 20 minutes."

CHAPTER 44

THE ONLY THING NECESSARY FOR THE TRIUMPH OF EVIL IS FOR GOOD MEN TO DO NOTHING

As two teams of marines and a Delta Force team from the 5th fleet patrolling in the Indian Ocean secured the ARK. Sherlock's team had come back after they had lost track of the Water Tiger. Placing Quassy in the infirmary with the other soldiers lost in this battle, Sherlock left Kid there, sitting in the corner on the floor staring at Deen; he needed his time to process it all.

Mike entered the HUB and went to the conference room; he was asked to give feedback on the unknown enemies' getaway. Mike walked past Chad, standing behind the President like a faithful junkyard dog.

"What took you so long?" Chad said, straight-faced.

"I was still hurt that you called me a cheat," Mike replied with the same straight face.

Chad smirked, "You did."

Mike smiled and walked over beside Art. Just then, Tyson leaned over and showed Art some video footage of Thor lying beside Loki in the lab; they both looked at each other confused.

"Bring him back," Art said.

"Is that wise, after what you said happened out there?" Tyson replied.

"You tell Thor you're not going to."

"Good point." With that, Tyson turned and was gone.

Brnng! Brnng!

"Ahh!" Art squealed, startled by the mobile phone ringing.

"Hello."

"Art, is that you? Did you know your communications are down?"

"Dan, yes, I do."

"What's going on?"

"Well, multiple groups of terrorists attacked the ARK to get to the President. Many people have died, animals killed, Loki has been killed, and Thor brought me the arm of his killer. So, how's your night been?"

"…. You're not kidding, are you?" Dan said.

"No, not in the least."

"Ok, I'll grab the team and head in to help!"

"NO! Dan, gather your team and any extras you can. The animals will need care. Some may not be in the right areas. Oh, also Dan, I have bad news…."

"What Art???" Dan asked.

"There was a fight in the baboon's enclosure…. Many were killed," Art said.

A grin grew across Dan's face. "Oooh, Art, that's terrible."

"Your sincerity voice needs work, Dan."

"Shoot some more baboons, and I'll work on it."

"Ok, you gather the troops and wait for my call," Art said.

"Will do, matey."

Mike gave the President and Art a brief report on what they found and didn't find while tracking the perpetrators.

"I will find who's behind this, Mr. President."

"I have no doubt, Mr. Damani," the President returned.

Mike spoke, "Not being disrespectful to you two, but you both made some horrible judgement calls, which got many good men killed and some injured. I know that you, Art, will make the required changes here, but you, Mr. President, have to make up for this; my friend and teammate died not to just save you but because he believed in this." Mike lifted his hands and circled around.

"It is now the biggest call for peace and saving the planet, and possibly the start of a new generation of change. But it is also the biggest threat to many in the world, and it needs heavyweights to protect it, NOT just a few good men." Mike looks over the President's shoulder and sees Chad smiling and standing proud.

"I have to bunk the team down, so please excuse me."

"Certainly, Mike, and thank you and your team for what you did for myself and Mr. Damani's dream."

"Mr. President, I think you'll find it's a lot of people's dream… it's just Art's money". Art and the President had a laugh as Mike left the room. As he left, Chad Langdon saluted, and Mike returned the salute.

The Major, soon to be 'THE TERROR OF THE ARK, LEGEND', was waiting outside.

"How's the arm?" The Major asked.

"I would ask you the same thing," Mike replied.

"Straight through."

"Yeah, mine too," Mike said.

"I'll catch up with you and the team before you go," The Major said.

"Looking forward to it, just leave the machete at home." The Major let out his huge laugh, and his Cheshire Cat grin shone again.

After checking the infirmary and seeing Kid wasn't there, he headed to the rooms where they were bunked as Katelyn came around the corner.

"Hey, Mike!"

"Hi, Katelyn, heading to the rooms?"

"Yeah, hey, can I ask you a question?"

"Always," Mike replied.

"Do you think your boys would like to be page boys?" Katelyn asked.

"Page boys? A wedding, who is getting married??" Katelyn looked shy and smiled.

"Nooo, who?" A voice came across the PA system.

"Is that a YES, Ms. Katelyn?" Katelyn looked shocked as she looked around the area for cameras and then yelled at the ceiling.

"That's just creepy, Art... and yes!"

Mike was laughing, "Ok, well, congratulations, I guess."

The team met in the conference room with Ab and his laptop. They had a two-hour debrief going over everything they had seen during the fight to get to the President, details about the enemy's weapons, facial recognition, languages, every little detail. In minutes, Ab had come up with the face and names of Ji-tae Gin (the Water Tiger), Min-Ki Gwan, and Chao Zhang. They handed over the details for Ab to process. Mike knew Art would use every resource to track down who ordered this attack. Gin was a terrorist, but he was a gun for hire. Somebody paid a lot of money for these dead bodies. The night was uneventful as the adrenaline wore off, and all the aches and injuries took effect.

"Don't worry Lexi. He'll have the best lawyers to get him out quickly." Art and Lexi stood there watching as military police marched Doby out the Ark door. The President said he would consider the position he was in and the fact his skills helped the effort to save him. Doby knew all along this would happen. He had his mother to think about.

****

Doby's mother was picked up by an AZTECK Security detail and taken to an undisclosed address under the care of a 24-hr nurse and her own security detail, which she liked because it gave her a reason to cook for "all those nice men."

****

The following day, Mike's team had their gear transported to the airfield, waiting for their transport back to the base in Afghanistan. They were down in the food mall grabbing a bite, and Mike noticed Kid wasn't there with them.

"Where's Thomas?" Mike asked.

"Haven't seen him all morning," Seb answered.

"He went out this morning at first light," Katelyn added. After they finished, they headed to the HUB to say their goodbyes and look for Thomas.

At the HUB, congratulations were given to Katelyn, as Art had told them all about the wedding. Lexi turned to Katelyn.

"You know I had first dibs on you, then you go and marry the boss." Katelyn laughed and gave Lexi a present she had held behind her back.

"What for me? Oh, it's not," Lexi asked.

"Yep, I thought it would remind you of me since I went off and married the boss." Lexi tore off the wrapping paper like a child at Christmas and held up the dress against herself, moving around like a model on a catwalk.

"I have one more favour to ask," Katelyn said.

"Anything," Lexi replied,

"Would you be my Matron WITHOUT Honour for the wedding?" Lexi let out a squeal only women can do when excited, bouncing around as she hugged Katelyn. Katelyn wasn't used to this girly behaviour, but she liked it.

Quietly, Thomas walked in through the entrance of the HUB, dusty and dirty from his mission this morning. He was carrying Deen's sniper rifle. Silently, he raises it and hands it to Mike. Mike accepted the weapon. The room is quiet as the pain in Thomas's face is still raw.

As Thomas went to walk off, Mike said, "Quassy would want you to have this, Jedi… He told me before he passed that you saved him twice, so he gets the right to name you, and Quassy chose Jedi by the way you fight … so here, he would want you to have it," Jedi walked over and took the rifle.

"I'm not trained for this weapon."

Seb laughed, "Then you do what Quassy always said. Practice, practice, practice, then fake it till you make it."

Everyone laughed, even Thomas.

"Lexi, is there a tattoo parlour around here?" Thomas asked.

"Yeah, there's a good one, but it's like an hour away."

"What are you getting done?" Katelyn asked.

"I was going to get Quassy's flag off his rifle and service number," Thomas said.

"I'll tell you what, Thomas. We'll all get it done when we get back to base, and I'll pay; Art owes me a pay rise anyway." They all laughed, except Mike.

"Where's Art?" Mike asked,

"He went up topside," Ab said.

****

Mike walked up the ramp and saw Art leaning on the rail, looking towards the airfield.

"So much death," Art said solemnly.

"The world's full of it; trust me on that," Mike replied.

"But I caused this."

"Everyone who died knew what they were doing. Even Deen knew what he was fighting for. Now you know how important this site is. But, Art, this isn't the last. You and the ARK are a target."

"There's a lot more behind this attack; I've already started looking at everything that happened here. There will be retribution... So, my friend, don't be a stranger and bring the family next time."

"I definitely will." The two men grabbed arms, and Mike turned and walked away.

****

The team headed out towards the airfield. As they made their way to the air transport, Mike wondered what happened to the Major; he said he wanted to catch up before they left.

"Get a load of this," Seb said, as they walked through the door. Standing there in their dress uniforms. The Major and the last of his team were lined up in a guard of honour. The team lined up for the effort and respect the Major and his men had shown, and Mike returned the salute. Mike and the Major shook hands. As they were crossing the tarmac, Seb said, "Hey Jedi, do you surf?"

"All the cool kids do."

And with that, Mike and the team were off onto the transport.

****

As Art walked into the HUB, Tyson saw him enter and walked over. "Hi Art, I thought I'd start with a scan of what's working and not working. Then start on high-priority areas first. Does that sound good to you?"

"Yes, Tyson, a splendid plan. We will meet tomorrow and see what needs to be done around the park. I suppose you will have a huge report to write?" Art asked.

Tyson looked confused. "Report? Which report?"

"The one for blood and guts Spelling, Director Damien Spelling of the CIA." Tyson put on a blank face and pretended he didn't understand, while feeling his stomach was about to give way. "Why would I have to do a report for the CIA?"

"It's alright, Tyson, I already know. I've known from the start," Art said.

Tyson dropped his head. "Why did you hire me then?"

Art laughed. "Because you're the best bio-engineer on the planet. Plus, I got bored not hiring all the others he tried to get in here. Don't worry, Tyson, stop kicking yourself. You wouldn't be here if I didn't trust you. Don't upset blood and guts too much; we might need him one day."

"Thank you, Art; I really appreciate it. I'll get to work. I'll give Director Spelling your best. I know you are one of his favourite people." The pair laughed heartily.

"Yes, especially since he doesn't have Osama Bin Laden to chase anymore," Art said.

CHAPTER 45

COUNT MARSHALL

The air transport rattled, clanged, and roared over the Atlantic, heading back to their Allied base in Afghanistan. Not that anyone noticed, which was nothing new for the team. Seb was asleep, as always. Katelyn and Smith were disagreeing over something. Thomas was watching over Deen's coffin and seemed in reflection of all that had happened. 'He is me!' Mike thought. Did Deen mean he thinks like me, fights like me? It was a long and tiring trip back to base, and when they grabbed their gear off the tarmac and headed back to their barracks, they looked like they had been to war, which they had.

Passing the basketball courts, a familiar and irritating voice sounds out.

"Looks like you've had some trouble," Capt. Sipple yelled.

"Did your woman burn your breakfast, Madden?"

Even if Mike wanted to stop Katelyn from doing something stupid, she was way too fast for him on this occasion. Not too many saw the blade; not too many saw its flight. But everyone saw and heard it as it was embedded in a post inches from Capt. Sipple's head. The shock of the near-miss was over shone by the laughter. Men in his own team were hysterical as Sipple struggled to get a word out.

"Wha… Ya. Bitch! You're gone. That's it! Attempted murder of an officer. You're gone. You'll do 20 years!" Mike had switched off after Wha and Ya as he walked over and grabbed the knife from the post.

"If she wanted you dead, you'd be dead. Stop being a bitch and go play with your balls," Mike said calmly as Capt. Sipple stormed off. Mike walks over to Katelyn and hands her the knife.

"You missed," Mike says to her.

"I should have hit him if I'm going to do twenty."

"Yeah, never leave a body," Mike said, and patted Katelyn on the shoulder as they walked off. By the end of the day, Katelyn was marched off peacefully by the MP's and ordered to stand trial for a court Marshall in one week.

****

Mike and Colonel Briggs had a two-hour meeting going over the entire episode. The loss of Deen. Who had attacked? The importance of the ARK as a symbol of a better world. Briggs reminded him that in their line of work, the politicians tell us what makes a better world.

Mike gave the team a lazy week instead of standard training; Colonel Briggs had arranged for the team to go on leave after the hearing at the end of the week. However, Mike was summoned to a special pre-hearing the day before. Mike, as Katelyn's team leader, was requested to attend.

At the meeting in General Thomas Blaine's office was Katelyn, two MPS, Colonel Briggs, Mike, and Capt. Sipple. "What are we waiting on, Briggs? You called this meeting," the General bellowed in an 'I haven't had my coffee,' voice.

"Actually, I didn't call this meeting; the officer who did is on his way here." Moments later, a very shiny officer with a well-pressed uniform walks in; he wore the rank of Major but was better known as PITBULL KELLY. Major Mike Kelly, JAGS number two officer and chief of prosecution. Mike's stomach sank at seeing him here, but the man who came in behind him lent hope that something good was about to happen. Striding in behind Major Kelly was Art Damani.

"General, I have requested this meeting to let you know of a problem arising in the case of the court-martial of Corporal Gouws. It seems there's more to the case than it appears."

"She threw a knife at me and nearly killed me," Sipple whined.

The Major threw Sipple a look of, 'Let the big boys talk.'

"It has come to my attention that Capt. Sipple has been harassing Corporal Gouw with sexist remarks for over 18 months."

"Bullshit!" Sipple proclaimed. "I have four affidavits from members of his own team claiming they witnessed it frequently… with the delicate nature of the defence forces image, General Slater does not want to proceed with the court Marshall. If Capt. Sipple does not wish to drop the charges, I will defend Corporal Gouws and then charge Capt. Sipple with sexual harassment, and the base will go under review."

General Blaine knew what 'GOING UNDER REVIEW' meant and didn't want anything tarnishing his career in its twilight.

"What do you propose, Major?" The General asked.

"This is bullshit; this bitch shouldn't be in this man's army!" Sipple yelled.

The General shook his head.

"Son, you don't know when to keep your mouth shut."

"Major, continue."

"We propose a sporting exhibition between Capt. Sipple and Corporal Gouw," Capt. Sipple butted in again. "I'm not fighting her," he protested.

"COWARD!" Katelyn yelled.

"Oh, you're on bitch!" Sipple returned.

"Gee, that was easy," Mike said, grinning at the ease Katelyn sucked Sipple into a fight.

"Fine, Major, you have your fight a week from now, and who are you?" The General said, pointing at Art, "I'm her fiancée," Art said calmly.

"Her Fiancée... Wha" before the General could continue, the Major interceded and spoke.

"He is with me as my guest; he has clearance."

And your name would be?" the General persisted.

"Art Damani, General," Art answered.

"Art Damani, Damani. I know that name... you're the guy who nearly got my team killed."

"No, your team saved the President of the United States and a hope for the future of mankind," Art said proudly.

"Well, that's debatable... and that's what we train them for, I suppose. You people are giving me a headache. Is that all, Major?"

"Yes, General," Major Kelly said.

"Young lady, you're free to go. No more knife throwing on my base," the General turns to Sipple, "And you, keep your mouth shut, dismiss."

Katelyn gave Art a big hug and kiss; she turned to the Major and thanked him for helping.

"I would have missed our wedding if you hadn't stepped in," Katelyn said.

"Don't thank me, Miss Katelyn; I just provided the transport; it was Mike who made the call and got the affidavits to the Major," Katelyn turned to Mike and offered him a salute; Mike smiled and returned the salute.

"Well, I suppose we should get you into training for the fight," Mike said.

Katelyn turned to look at him, "Seriously!"

CHAPTER 46

EPILOGUE

Not since Bob Hope visited the troops during the Vietnam conflict in the 1960s was there so much excitement around a US Army base. This joint US/Allied base in Afghanistan was used as a forward base of command for six countries, including Australia.

It was all anyone talked about all week, 'The Fight'.

The entertainment on the bases doesn't get any better than this. The brass made it a charity fight, and a billionaire covered all bets for the night.

The crowd was abuzz with excitement as the countdown for the fight rolled in. Betting was frantic as money was being poured into Capt. Sipple's side to start with. However, Katelyn took Mike's advice and did some training, only because she wanted to look her best for the crowd, plus she had respect for Sipple. He was a captain in the SAS and had to be worthy of the spot to hold it.

Fight Night, they had it all, a famous announcer from the UFC, the supermodel card girls with barely anything on, and mountains of popcorn and beer.

"Ladies and Gentlemen. Welcome to the fight of the CENTURY! Man V Women, Officer V Enlisted, It's a personal grudge match of the ages. Your fighters tonight in the red corner, a captain from the Australian SAS, CAPTAIN LORRY SIPPLE!"

The crowd let out an excited cheer as Captain Sipple entered the hall. Sipple looked pumped with a focused look on his face. He has been waiting for his chance to put this woman in her place.

The announcer went into overdrive in the blue corner, "Wearing all black for this fight. Also, a member of the Australian SAS, CORPORAL KATELYN GOUW." As he announced Katelyn to the ring. The crowd went 'WILD.' Easily the crowd favourite, with people yelling to kill him, wolf whistles, and two enlisted men from the kitchen at her base holding up a sign 'MARRY ONE OF US PLEASE.' Katelyn was dressed in all black, with blood-red stripes of makeup down one side of her face, like the war paint of an American Indian.

"That's my fiancée," Art tells Smith as he jabs him in the ribs with his elbow.

"Yeah, I know; stop rubbing it in," Smith grumbles.

Because men were still on duty, they telecast the fight around the base, like a Melbourne Cup, but NO Melbourne Cup had this much interest.

Ding-Ding Fight!

It was a cautious start to the fight as both moved around, working only with their hands in a boxing style. Sipple had seen a gap and moved in with a flurry of head punches with impressive hand speed. Katelyn made a mental note of it to avoid getting caught out later. She had a plan, a vision of how the fight would end, and she had no intentions of not following through. She backpedalled to get out of Sipple's reach, and as he overstretched, trying to continue his head barrage. Katelyn stepped slightly to one side and pounded Sipple dead centre in the midriff, buckling him over. The crowd let out a huge "OOOOW" and then started cheering. Instead of pushing her advantage, she hesitated and gave him a second to recover and gave the audience what they came for, CARNAGE. She returned fire with an onslaught of head punches like Sipple's attack, but she landed more, making Sipple cover up to stop a knockout.

Ding! The end of the round one saved Sipple. As they walked to their corners, a crowd of about thirty enlisted women started screaming at Katelyn. They had a new champion. Katelyn put her gloves on her lips and blew them a kiss for their support; the women went, Wild!

The second round went much the same. Katelyn let Sipple make the first attack and then finished with a pounding on Sipple; the only difference was that they started using their legs in powerful attacks. Again, Sipple was strong, but Katelyn had him beat for speed. Then Ding! Sipple hobbled back to his corner as Katelyn jogged back briskly. Mike hopped out of his chair and went to Katelyn's corner.

"What are you doing? You could have won this in the first round." Mike said to her.

"Just giving the crowd a fight… I'm doing it for them." Katelyn pointed to her female fan club.

"There's Sipples everywhere in the force; this is just as much their fight… But, don't worry, Mike, this is the last round." She turned and gave Mike a smile, which made him worried that he might have to contact the JAG lawyer again.

ROUND 3, Katelyn thought Sipple would be angry by now. He would use his size to overpower her. Getting her to the ground, trying to punch a submission out of her. She nailed it! Captain Sipple did precisely that, charging Katelyn to knock her to the ground, but Katelyn charged, too. Like two wounded rhinos fighting for the herd, they charged. Katelyn jumped with perfect timing and landed a knee right on Sipple's nose; not being content with that, she locked her legs around his throat, and her body weight and the force of the blow sent Sipple backward, crashing to the canvas with a sickening thud.

"Ooow!" The crowd pulled back in horror at the blow to the face and the force of Sipple hitting the canvas. Blood was streaming from Sipple's nose, and his eyes were closing up, but to his credit, he kept fighting. Thrashing around with his arms and legs, Sipple hit Katelyn's face so hard it would give her a black eye in the morning. Sipple kept thrashing, so Katelyn grabbed an arm and started twisting the wrist; she kept the pressure on his throat, slowly choking off the air. He would pass out soon, and the fight would be won, but that was not her plan. She didn't want to win the contest; she wanted...; Sipple raised his other hand and tapped three times on the canvas; Sipple had had enough. He showed everyone that he was giving up to her. She quickly let go of him and checked him like an excellent medic to ensure he was ok. He'd live. Katelyn stood, and the announcer went through his rhetoric again and announced Katelyn, the winner, holding up her arm. She got the victory she wanted, a win for many. Her smile beamed with the thunderous applause from the crowd.

****

3 WEEKS LATER

As Katelyn and Lexi were at the ARK planning her wedding, Ab and Art used all their contacts and lawyers to get Doby released. The ARK was being rebuilt with unique fortifications designed by Thomas and Ab. Thomas was invited to the ARK to work in their labs on projects unspecified. Tyson rebuilt Loki, but with the strange behaviours of both cats during the siege, where they both showed signs of individual thought patterns, Art added some new protocols. Not that they didn't trust the boys, but they saw firsthand that they were capable of more thought patterns than what was expected.

****

Seb and Smith exited the beach, just a hundred metres away from Mike's house at Byron Bay in Australia.

"That was intense. No wonder you're so fit doing this all the time," Smith said to Seb.

The beauty of everything hadn't been lost on them. The warmth of the sun as it peters away to dusk. The golden glow of the sand. The roar of the waves crashing on the beach behind them and the female surfers smiling at them as they walk past.

"It was nice of Mike to let us crash at his place while the waves were huge here," Seb said.

Aidan and Ollie loved having them there; it was like having two big brothers who loved to play on the PlayStation as much as them.

****

Later that night

Ab came rushing in as Art was sitting in his office back at the ARK, going over a promising letter from one of Doby's lawyers.

"I think we had some hits." Ab showed him some photos.

"Yep, definitely him; where were these taken?" Art said. Ab showed him the map.

"Oh, no!" Art yelled. He picked up the phone and started dialling.

On the other side of the world, a phone was ringing silently on a table, a request from Sam to turn it off while they were watching tv before bed.

"No answer!" Art started typing on his keyboard, and a conference line came up, and he hit send. Phones began ringing through the house at once. Seb, Smith, Sam, and Mike's work phone direct from the base, the house was alive with ringing. Seb answered the call.

"Hello?"

"SEB, IT'S ART. GET OUT OF THE HOUSE. I THINK THE WATER TIGER'S COMING. HE COULD BE THERE NOW!"

Always ready at a moment's notice is their training. Seb swung his legs out of bed, and Smith jumped out of his bunk, only catching part of the conversation.

"Water Tiger could be here; you take the perimeter, and I'll clear the house," Seb ordered. They both grabbed pistols from their bags; Smith, not wanting to use the doors as exits, used the bedroom window in case they were already there.

Mike heard the conversation as Sam answered her phone. He was already up and heading to the door; the boys were all that was on his mind. Get to the boys! "Stay here," he said in a hushed but firm voice as he snuck out the door to the boy's room.

Opening the door carefully, he checked the room; the boys were sleeping peacefully, and there was no one else there. Next, he checked the window and made sure it was locked.

He headed to the door. Next, get his pistol from the safe and get Sam and Kid to safety. With his hand on the bedroom knob, Mike heard a board creak in the hallway outside and knew someone was there. Just then, shots rang out from outside, and he hoped it was Seb and Smith clearing the area. Taking advantage of the distraction of the gunshot, Mike charged out into the hallway and came face-to-face with Ji-tae Jin, the Water Tiger. He continued his charge, not wanting to lose momentum and not being armed. Mike hit the Water Tiger with the full force of his weight, knocking him off guard and into a wall. Grabbing his battle vest and using his momentum, he spun, throwing the mercenary through the balcony's railing onto the floor on the level below.

Seb was coming down the hallway on the bottom level as another mercenary went through the kitchen door into the hallway. The thundering crash of the Water Tiger hitting the floor startled both of them, but Seb still had the advantage. Ramming the mercs rifle and arm into the door frame, Seb broke the mercs arm; he brought up the handle of his pistol and smashed it into his nose, sending the man flying backward. Finally, two shots to the head ended the fight.

Once again, furious that they had known he was coming but still knowing when a battle can't be won, the Water Tiger got up, turned, and ran out the front door. Seb was too late to get any shots off at him, and Smith was on the other side of the house and didn't see him leave. Mike bolted down the stairs for the front door, and Seb went to follow.

"No, stay here and protect the family," Mike said.

A shout came from the top of the balcony. "Mike!" Sam was standing there. He only paused for a second, but it was long enough to say, I love you, and I have to do this. Mike disappeared out the door.

Jin was heading up a path that led to the beach. He had lost his pistol in the fall from the landing but didn't care; it was time to leave. Running through the sand, Jin heard a squeak from the sand behind him. He couldn't believe his luck when he saw the Australian running to catch up with him. The Water Tiger led Mike onto the sand, where it was firmer.

He noticed Mike's injured arm, "Extremely brave or extremely stupid to follow me."

"You came to my house, and you didn't stop to say hi," Mike jibbed.

"Aw, that great Australian humour, laughing in the face of danger," Jin taunted.

"Why are you even here? We are no threat to you," Mike asked.

"You killed my friend!"

"You killed one of mine, but I don't go running to your house and try killing people in their sleep, Like a Coward!" Mike said angrily.

"No need to try to rile me; you are not leaving alive." Jin attacked with a flurry of punches and kicks that reminded him of Steel's skill level. He was fast, very fast, and hit with a powerful strike. Jin attacked again, trying to… "Ahhh," Mike was hit on his wound, and immediately blood started soaking into the bandage. Jin pushed his advantage, and only the training with Steel helped him read his attack. Mike's arm was throbbing, so he used Steel's training and tried to throw him off balance with an unorthodox move, but Jin's fighting level was too high, and he kicked Mike in the stomach, sending him to the sand. Jin pulled out his knife.

"This has been fun, but I have a boat to catch," Jin joked. As he raised his knife to end this fight with this annoying Australian. A shot rang out, and Jin could hear it zing past like an angry bee. Turning his head, he looks and sees Samantha on the grass at the edge of the sand.

"Well, this looks like more fun; I will kill you and then her. Your poor children, what will they do? Maybe you should have trained her on how to shoot straight."

"Be careful what you wish for," Mike said confidentially. Jin quickly turned and saw Samantha in a squat military stance to give herself more control of the pistol. The first shot hit centre mass, and so did the second, sending Jin reeling back on the sand. The 3rd hit him in the shoulder, sending him flying into the water; he lay there lifeless as the surf crashed over him.

Mike made his way to Samantha, blood running freely down his arm; she helped him up the bank when torch lights shone in their eyes and a local police officer told Sam to drop her weapon. After explaining that the perpetrator was on the beach, the Sergeant sent two officers to check the body as the rest of them made it to the house. Mike explained who he, Seb, and Smith were, explained who Jin was, and about as much info as Mike was allowed to tell her. Then he said to her that men would be here shortly and requested that she forget everything she'd heard. The Sergeant said no one would believe her, anyway.

Sam patched Mike up for the night so he wouldn't bleed through the house. She made Seb stand guard on the kitchen door till the dead body was removed. Mike decided to tell Sam the entire story about what happened at the ARK. He was going to tell her he was just waiting for the right time. She sat there with her jaw dropped. Invisible panthers fighting to save the American President, futuristic guns, and robot monsters fighting on the side of good. Sam sat there staring at him with a disbelieving look.

"I swear it's all true. Art has invited us all back."

"We're not going if the President is there; it all sounds like some Mike Hooper novel."

"Yeah, that's what I thought," Mike added.

The Sergeant of the investigating police spoke to Mike and Sam.

"Excuse me, Mr. Madden, we checked the area where you said this dead terrorist was. Well, we found some scuff marks in the sand and some blood. It headed up the beach a bit, then disappeared into the water. Unfortunately, we have lost the trail."

CHAPTER 47

THE HUNT CONTINUES

"It is with deep regret that we hear of the death of President Abdi of Somalia. His positive action in working with AZTECK to build the ARK in Somalia and Ethiopia has worked towards peace and achieved it; he worked towards a better living in Somalia. Many will miss him. On that note, the United States has decided to help advance the ARK. For what it stands for, a possibility of peace for all." Art and Ab stood there in front of the tv screen, pondering the sympathy words of the American President on the national news.

Ab spoke, "Was it necessary?"

"You saw the photos of who he meets with. He made his choice… I warned him," Art responded.

****

In a town on the back end of nowhere.

"That's two failures we've paid for."

"That's what happens when you rush a mission; you should have given me all the information, and I would have planned it better instead of relying on others. If I meet the Australian again, I won't miss." The Water Tiger responded.

"Forget the Australian; we have work to continue. You will probably never see him again. We need to burn Damani and his ARK to the ground; he is bad for business. There are bigger plans in play. We will have to continue with the American President still in play. Also, congratulations on President Abdi. He was a loose cannon that couldn't be left alive.".

"I agree… but I didn't silence him. They ruled his death an accident, but my sources say otherwise," Jin informed him.

"Who then?"

"My guess, Damani."

Then, maybe he is a bigger threat to our future plans than expected. I will pass the information to the top. Stay in contact range; you will have plenty more to do." The caller hung up.

****

Mike was back at the ARK, packing his kit.

"Art, thank you for this. The family wouldn't be able to sleep at night knowing he was out there, and could come back."

"No problem, Mike, he has a lot to answer for. I have made all the arrangements and have all your passports and papers for you to move around. Oh, and I have also put together some of the best hi-tech gear for your mission," Art said.

"Thanks, but no thanks, Art. I'm old school, remember."

"Ok, but at least come and have a look at it and see what you think."

As Art led him through the door, here standing before him was his team, all geared up for a mission.

Katelyn smiled, "You'd be lost in 10 minutes without us."

****

While at the same time.

Lexi sat in the visitor's room of a prison in southern Texas. As Doby walks in with a guard, Lexi thinks that he isn't too bad for his 4 months in prison.

"Hey Asslicker."

"How did you get into here? Aren't you still in hiding?"

"New papers from Art. Here these are for you." Lexi slides a manilla envelope across the table.

"What's this?" Doby asks.

"Your papers. Ready to come home?"

"Fantastic. Now I can be there for Art and Katelyn's wedding."

"Yeah, if Katelyn comes back alive."

THE END

The ARK: World of Greed
Coming Soon

ACKNOWLEDGEMENTS

I would like to thank the *World Wildlife Fund* and *World Animal Protection* for information from their websites. Plus, also thank all the staff and volunteers for their tireless work around the world protection our Earth's animal species.

Many thanks to the members of the *Australian Defence Force* for their courage and dedication to protecting Australia and other countries around the world.

Wildlife Rescue Queensland (WRQ) is a non-profit organisation specialising in the rescue, rehabilitation and release of native Australian wildlife.

As wildlife ambassadors, WRQ strives to further foster public awareness via social media campaigns, educational workshops and community engagement.

To report sick or injured wildlife,
please call our 24 hour emergency hotline for assistance:
0478 901 801

Please visit WRQ website for more information:
https://wrq.org.au/

www.ingramcontent.com/pod-product-compliance
Lightning Source LLC
Chambersburg PA
CBHW070005120726
47909CB00003B/807